Fire and Flood

FIRE& FLOOD

A Novel

DAWN MORRIS

NEW YORK

LONDON • NASHVILLE • MELBOURNE • VANCOUVER

Fire and Flood

A Novel

Scriptures are taken from the NEW AMERICAN STANDARD BIBLE® (NASB), copyright© 1960, 1962, 1963,1968, 1971, 1972, 1973, 1975, 1977, 1995 by The Lockman Foundation. Used by permission.

Published in New York, New York, by Morgan James Publishing. Morgan James is a trademark of Morgan James, LLC. www.MorganJamesPublishing.com

ISBN 9781631954740 paperback
ISBN 9781631954757 ebook
Library of Congress Control Number: 2020952598

Cover Design by:
Rachel Lopez
www.r2cdesign.com

Interior Design by:
Chris Treccani
www.3dogcreative.net

Morgan James PUBLISHING Builds with... Habitat for Humanity® Peninsula and Greater Williamsburg

Morgan James is a proud partner of Habitat for Humanity Peninsula and Greater Williamsburg. Partners in building since 2006.

Get involved today! Visit
MorganJamesPublishing.com/giving-back

When you pass through the waters, I will be with you;
And through the rivers, they will not overflow you;
When you walk through the fire, you will not be scorched,
Nor will the flame burn you.
Isaiah 43:2

For my favorite child!
(*Inside joke*, I have **five** favorite children!)

Acknowledgments

First, I want to thank my husband, Dennis. He's a natural editor and has lovingly and humorously encouraged and challenged me through the writing process. His notes written in the margins spurred me to dig deep and made me laugh!

Next, I honestly have two of the most gifted editors on my team, Arlyn Lawrence and Kerry Wade with Inspira Literary Solutions. Each of them has helped me become a better writer, teaching me the importance of clearly showing the reader the world and characters in my story. *Fire and Flood* is an epic novel, and they truly helped me do some heavy lifting in bringing the story to life!

I can't express how excited I am to be working with Morgan James Publishing on this novel! They have been so encouraging and helpful. Bonnie Rauch, thank you for guiding me through this process! David Hancock, thank you for the opportunity and your positive comments about Fire and Flood. Cortney Donelson, having someone who edits books for a living say that Fire and Flood was "soo good" is a great compliment! And thank you for catching some key storyline snafus. It takes a village to bring a book to market!

I want to also thank my family and friends who've been so supportive and encouraging to me! A special thank you to my prayer partner, Rachel Braaten. Thank you for always pointing my attention back to truth and making me laugh! Julie Kott, who always encourages and celebrates with me! Jeannette Hand, a true and faithful friend who loves me just as I am!

To everyone at Adorned in Grace Tacoma, and my long-time friend, Christine Gilge! You women and men serve our community in so many life-changing ways. Thank you all for letting me join you!

Finally, to the lovely women I got to lead through a study of Revelation as I was editing this novel. Their support in the process was greatly appreciated, and their questions and comments helped me in aspects of writing this story.

FIRE

Chapter 1

Many false prophets will arise and will mislead many.
Because lawlessness is increased, most people's
love will grow cold.
Matthew 24:11–12

I was born after the Vanishing.

As American cities, along with cities around the world, were disintegrating into violence and war, my parents aligned themselves with a group of religious zealots hidden away in the wilderness of western Montana. Like many, they were stunned to find themselves left behind on the earth after the Vanishing. In this landscape of chaos and confusion, my parents—Jack and Karen—came under the leadership of Dominic Webb, a charismatic religious leader.

Webb stepped into the devastation and disorientation and provided direction and leadership to the chaos. And so, just days after millions of people vanished in an instant, two hundred lost souls gathered around their new prophet of God and followed him across the country to his father's extensive ranch in Montana. He named the ranch "the Compound" and called his followers "the Chosen." Dominic Webb preached with relish about the evils of mankind, detailing the atrocities of the outside world.

1

No one was allowed to leave, but we were so well indoctrinated that no one dared venture outside the Compound.

It was evening and I'd just finished putting my younger siblings to bed. I was cleaning the bathroom, the last thing on my endless chore list. When I bent over to scrub the bathtub, pain exploded in my left side, and I fell to the ground.

"You idiot! What are you doing in here?" My father yanked me to my feet and slapped me across the face.

"Please, Dad, please stop!" I screamed. I could feel the all too familiar warmth of blood pouring out of my nose.

"Don't you call me 'Dad,' you skinny, ugly freak," he slurred. His face moved so close to mine that I could smell the whiskey on his breath.

"What is going on in here?" My mother stood in the doorway, hands on her hips, a sneer on her face. "You're going to wake the children, Jack. What'd she do now?"

He dropped me. "Sorry," he muttered. His tone turned pleading, as if he feared her wrath, like the rest of us. "I was just talking with Dominic, and we had a couple of drinks. I came back here to use the bathroom, and this lazy cow was in the way."

"There's blood all over the floor, Jack! Have her clean it up." At this directive, Mother turned on her heel and marched back to their bedroom.

Jack moved back into the bathroom and kicked me in the stomach. Still on my knees in front of the bathtub, I was an easy target.

"Clean it up, then get out," he muttered, "You aren't welcome under this roof. Move into the shed with Daphne." He left me in the bathroom—hands to my stomach, curled in a ball on the floor. Silently, holding back the tears that stung my eyes, I sat up, picked up the rag, spat on it, and cleaned up the blood.

It was dark in the room I shared with my little sisters, but I easily found the few things that were mine, put them in my pillowcase, and made my way out of the house to the shed. There was a light on in the window, and

I could see Daphne's grey head bent over her book. I knocked on the door gently.

She opened the door right away. "Child, come in."

Bursting into tears, I threw myself into her arms.

Daphne was my only comfort on the Compound. She'd been here when the Chosen arrived, so Dominic let her stay on and work the ranch. She was hard but fair, and she treated me well. I think I liked the fact that she wasn't really one of us. She hadn't moved here enamored by Dominic's leadership. She loved the ranch and wasn't going to leave it just because Dominic had returned with a group of ragtag fanatics. I think she was the only one on the Compound who didn't revere him as the Prophet of God.

After I was kicked out of my parents' house, I lived with Daphne in the shed and found a place of refuge from my family; for the first time, I felt like I had a home with someone I loved. Daphne kindly picked up the broken pieces of my heart, taking care of me as if I were her own daughter.

As I entered my early teens, I had noticed Dominic's eyes on me during the mandatory community meetings. Just before my eighteenth birthday, my mother and father called me into their living room, something they rarely did. Daphne and I had just finished cleaning up their dinner dishes. I walked in, alarmed, wondering what I'd done wrong. Making sure to keep my eyes down, I murmured a faint, respectful greeting and waited.

"I don't know what he sees in her," my mother sneered. "Surely Jacqueline is a better choice?"

Jacqueline was my fifteen-year-old sister and the beauty of the family, according to my parents.

"I told you already, he was emphatic. He wants her."

My stomach turned. I didn't dare raise my eyes to face them, but I knew now what they were talking about . . . and who. It wasn't unusual for Dominic to take an "interest" in the young teenage women in our community. Many children of the Chosen had a distinct resemblance to the Prophet.

"Look at me," my father commanded. I looked up at him, careful to keep my face expressionless and my eyes dull.

"Dominic has decided that you will be the recipient of his blessing. Tomorrow morning, you will report to the main house. You will be married at sunset.

"This is a huge honor for our family, as you know. I expect you to behave. If you do not, I will kill you myself. Do you understand me?"

My heart began to race in fear. This wasn't an idle warning. More than once, his regular punishments of the household help had gone too far. I had been forced to help carry limp bodies to shallow graves dug along the back fence. It was always their weakness that was blamed, or God's divine wisdom—never alcohol or my father's overuse of the stick.

"Yes, sir," I answered, bobbing my head up and down.

"Leave us."

I ran to Daphne's shack. Flinging myself on the cot, I shook in dread. I don't know how long I lay there in fear before drifting off to sleep. I woke up in the early morning, stiff with cold and alone.

Where was Daphne? I got out of bed, still dressed from the night before, and went to the small window that looked out to the back of the house. All was still. Filled with foreboding, I staggered through the yard to the back door, which led to the kitchen. There, Daphne, my only ally, my only friend, lay on the kitchen table—dead.

I retched uncontrollably. It took some time for the dry heaving to stop. Standing up, I approached the kitchen table and her body, and gently pushed Daphne's silver hair away from her face. Her eyes stared unseeingly at me. Gently, I closed them.

Oh, God, oh God, I called out to Him in my mind, over and over, desperate and horrified. I began shivering uncontrollably. I wrapped my arms around myself, wishing desperately it could be Daphne hugging me. Silently, I begged God to make it not real. I knelt on the floor by the table, moaning silently. There was no doubt in my mind that my father had killed her in a fit of rage for her challenging him.

I pulled myself together. I had to get out of here. No matter how bad the world was outside of the Compound, it couldn't be worse than this. I put some food into a cloth towel and wrapped it up. I snatched a canteen from the pantry, checking to make sure it had some water in it before heading quietly out the door, tears silently streaming down my cheeks.

I raced across the dusty yard to the shack. Once inside, I reached under Daphne's bed and pulled out the small Bible hidden there, Daphne's secret treasure. I put it carefully in my makeshift bag before stuffing the few clothes I had on top of it.

Then I planned my escape. It was still early and most people were sleeping, including my family. I thought I might be able sneak to the creek, cross it, and go west, following the sun. Gathering my courage, I slowly opened the shack door.

My mother stood there smirking and looking murderously angry. Three men, dressed in suits, stood just behind her. She pushed me inside the shed and told the men to wait. Closing the door, she turned on me.

"Where do you think you're going?" she demanded in a low, frigid tone. Grabbing the bag out of my hand, she threw it to the floor.

"All you've done from the day you were born is cause me grief. Do you know that? I'm so sick of having to look at you. If it weren't for you, I wouldn't be stuck with Jack, that sadistic monster."

Something inside me snapped. "How is that my fault?" I snarled back at her.

Karen cackled, shaking her head. "Are you really so blind?" she asked. "Did you never once wonder how it is that your father and I both have brown hair and brown eyes and your brothers and sisters *all* have the same brown hair and brown eyes, but you . . . you have blonde hair and green eyes? Are you telling me that you've never once questioned it?" She laughed in disgust.

Stunned into silence, I glanced at the wall to my right where a chipped mirror hung and saw my image reflected back. My blonde hair was still braided; wild hairs escaped, creating a halo.

"Dominic?" I whispered aloud. His eyes were the same shade of green as the ones staring back at me in the mirror.

"Yes, he stopped wanting me once my belly swelled up with *you*. Then he passed me on to Jack as a reward. If it weren't for you, I'd still be his favorite. There's no way I'm letting you anywhere near him." She spit each word out of her mouth like a curse as she scuttled over to me and grappled my chin between her fingers, her sharp nails digging into my flesh.

She shoved me backward, gouging my chin with her nail as she did so, and ordered me to get the bag she'd thrown on the floor. Grabbing my arm, she marched me out of the door and pushed me again—this time into one of the three men.

"You can take her now. Head out on that dirt track I showed you earlier." She stretched out her hand. "I'll take that fee we negotiated."

One of the men picked up a wooden crate filled with bottles that was sitting on the ground and handed it to my mother, while another pulled me along to a black car waiting behind the shed, out of sight of the house.

I turned back to see my mother staring hard at me, the crate perched on her hip. "You go on now, Dani, and have a real good life. I'm sure you're going to enjoy what's ahead for you." Her sarcastic laughter shot across the yard at me.

One of the men pushed me into the back seat of the car, and the same man sat in the back with me, warning me to keep quiet and not cause any trouble. The other two got into the car, and we drove down the dirt track and away from the Compound. The makeshift bag sat in my lap, and I was thankful to still have it. As we drove away, my fingers fumbled through it for the small Bible that had belonged to Daphne. I held it like a good luck charm against the onslaught of fear and confusion that swirled in my mind. I had been betrayed by family, and, for the first time in my life, I was leaving the Compound and the Chosen behind.

FLOOD

Chapter 2

Now it came about, when men began to multiply on the face of the land . . . the sons of God saw that the daughters of men were beautiful; and they took wives for themselves . . . The Nephilim were on the earth in those days, and also afterward, when the sons of God came in to the daughters of men, and they bore children to them. Those were the mighty men of old, men of renown.

Genesis 6:1–2, 4

While my father, as the director of the Games, spent most of his time traveling back and forth from our estate in the country to the great city of Sumeria, it was my first time in the city and attending the festival.

On our way to the stadium, we passed glittering white homes surrounded by greenery. Flowers and sparkling fountains lined either side of the street before giving way to stores filled with all sorts of goods and food. Vendors hawked their wares to the citizens winding their way past them. My mouth watered as I smelled roasted meat spiced with cinnamon and ginger. I was enthralled, but my mother sat stone-faced beside me.

Mother followed the Old Ways and wanted to keep me from the moral pollution of the city where the Magistrate ruled. But my father, who was in charge of the Games, said the Magistrate had requested our whole family be present at the festival.

"We're almost there." My father patted my mother reassuringly. "Really, dear, you don't have to worry. The Magistrate isn't a monster."

Mother pursed her lips tightly. My father didn't follow the Old Ways—doing so was forbidden by the Magistrate—and this caused tension between them.

I saw the stadium ahead. It was the biggest building I'd ever seen, constructed of glittering white stone with rising tiers of seats that could be seen through its arched openings. Crowds thronged outside. I'd never seen so many people at once.

"Mother!" I whispered, "Those men are Nephilim!"

The two guards towered over us as we sat in the cart; both had massive frames and a shock of red hair. Bowing to my father, they greeted him respectfully. "Director, sir, the Magistrate is waiting. Come, we will escort you to your seats."

The stadium was crowded, but the people parted quickly for the giant Nephilim who led us. I trembled. Mother noticed and wrapped an arm around me.

"Remember, the Nephilim are only part human, Ariana," mother whispered as we followed. All of the Magistrate's guards were Nephilim, the offspring of the Fallen Ones and human women. My mother had taught me about the Fallen Ones, those angels who had rebelled against the Creator and followed their leader down from the heavens to roam on the earth. The Nephilim had some of the powers of the Fallen Ones . . . and all of their darkness. Some, like these guards, were giants. As we followed them, I was simultaneously terrified and curious. I had never been this close to Nephilim.

Finally, we came to the great podium where all the dignitaries sat. Still following the Nephilim, we were shown to our seats, to the right of the Magistrate.

I stared at the wild mass of people around me. The heat and smell of the crowds were overwhelming. Women and men openly fondled each other; many were already drunk. Music, played by the orchestra sitting on the center stage, mingled with the shouts of the multitude as the Magistrate entered into the stadium on a chariot. The racetrack wound around the stadium in an oblong circle, with the rectangular stage in the middle.

Father stood up and applauded enthusiastically along with the crowd. He pulled Mother up to her feet. "Both of you, show respect!"

Clapping obediently, I strained to see the most powerful man in the world. The crowd roared in approval as the Magistrate neared the great podium. To my left was his massive throne under a golden awning. A table piled high with delicious-looking food had been placed within reach on the right side of the chair. I turned back to the spectacle before me just as the Magistrate's chariot stopped at the bottom of the stairs.

Women, naked from the waist up, stood at the bottom of the stairs, tossing blood-red flower petals as he walked up the stairs, shouting, "Our king!"

"He's not a man but a god!" the crowd yelled in reply.

The Magistrate was a Nephilim, hundreds of years old. As he strode by us proudly, dressed in golden robes and wearing a jeweled crown, it was difficult to believe how ancient he was. I'd imagined him wrinkled and white-haired, but he looked like a man in his prime.

After seating himself on his throne, the Magistrate nodded to us, his eyes narrowing a bit as he looked at my mother. "Smile and bow," my father hissed, while bowing. Mother and I bowed. Trumpets blared, and the crowd took their seats.

The crowd shouted with glee as the dust swirled on the track. The participants entered, each contestant on a vehicle he had built himself; the only parameter was that it had to be pulled by four horses. Everyone in the audience had a favorite challenger, and many wore the colors of their chosen heroes to show support during the festival. The race was the main event, the finale of the festival.

That was when I noticed him. He was taller than the other young men, well-built and strong. Even though it was my first time in the city, I knew most of the challengers. Since my father was the director, many of the competitors trained on our estate. But the handsome blonde-haired man in front of me now—he was new.

As the men circuited the arena, I turned to my father, "Who is the young man in white?"

"That's Japheth. He comes from a reputable family outside of the valley. His family owns a large farm somewhere, has orchards, sheep, cattle . . . they're quite wealthy."

Japheth stood apart from the other contestants, checking on his horses. Methodically, he stroked each one along its well-arched neck before checking all their harnesses and mouth bits. His arm muscles rippled as he went from horse to horse, checking their gear. They were the color of cream—powerful beasts, broad chested with flowing manes and tails, perfectly matched. I stared, mesmerized by their impressive beauty—and his.

"What does the winner of the race receive as his prize?" I asked my father. Surely those powerful horses would give this Japheth an excellent chance of winning.

Father peered at me bemusedly. "The custom is for the winner to claim whatever reward he desires, my dear. Often, it involves a great deal of gold and silver." Mother asked him a question, and he turned back to answer her.

Japheth jumped onto the back of his chariot-style vehicle and moved the horses to the starting line in preparation for the opening ceremony. Stunningly handsome, Japheth embodied masculine virility. The crowd, hazy with lust and liquor, responded wildly.

My mother shook her head in disgust at the leering crowd, and I saw my father place one of his hands over hers in a silent warning. Displaying any sign of judgment or disapproval was suspect. Only those sympathetic to the Old Ways found anything wrong with expressions of strong desires.

Since my childhood, my mother had taught me about the Old Ways. Before the Magistrate's rule, hundreds of years ago, there had been respect for the Creator and His ways. Now, anyone who spoke up about immoral behavior, who disliked the Nephilim, or who questioned the Magistrate or his men in any way, would find themselves before the court and sentenced to death. That is, if they even lived that long.

Carefully, I kept my expression enthusiastic and clapped wildly, hoping to draw attention away from my mother's obvious disapproval. I wore reams of silver bangles that tinkled and glittered in the sunlight as I clapped. The crowd roared in anticipation of the race beginning; the competitors were lined up on the starting line. Excitement was building.

I was startled by a tap on my shoulder. One of the Magistrate's Nephilim guards stood behind me and indicated he wanted me to follow him. Mother grabbed at my dress, but Father pulled her hand away.

"The Magistrate would like to see you as well, Director, and your wife." The guard's tone was ominous. Since the Magistrate was only a few feet away, we arrived before him quickly—too quickly.

"Turn your face to me, girl," he commanded. His voice was entrancingly melodious, beautiful, and compelling. I lifted my eyes and stared into his and was caught in the flinty depths of dark obsidian. Beauty and evil melded together in an expression of great intelligence and cunning. My heart froze in terror, and I tried to keep myself from trembling.

My father bowed lowly before the Magistrate on his hands and knees. "Your Excellency."

"You've kept your wife and daughter away from the Capitol until now. I can appreciate your reasons, Director. Your daughter—what is her name?"

"Ariana," my father stuttered.

"She's magnificent. I find her enticing." The Magistrate continued to stare into my eyes, and despite my fear, I found myself drawn to him.

He turned his gaze from me and looked with frank interest at my mother. She was not bowed before him but was looking at me. Mother smiled at me reassuringly before turning her attention to the Magistrate.

"I presume by your manner that you disapprove of me." He smiled cruelly and hissed, "If you renounce the Old Ways, I may take pity on you and show you mercy."

Silent, she stared at him unflinchingly.

"I denounce her, my Lord!" My father sat back on his knees and pointed at my mother. *How could he so easily betray her?*

The Magistrate looked bored. "And yet, you allowed this to go on in your own home, Director. Take them both." One of the Nephilim guards yanked my father to his feet and led him off, while another pulled my mother away. I knew I'd never see them again. I swayed as I watched them disappear from my sight.

"Look at me," the Magistrate commanded. The shouts of the crowd applauding the entertainment going on behind me sounded surreal. I steadied myself and turned. Caught again in his dark regard, I found myself wanting desperately to escape. Then his voice spoke into my mind. I knew this was possible; Nephilim had the powers of the Fallen Ones, but I was shocked and horrified by his lurid words in my mind.

The words he spoke aloud were much more pragmatic. "You will stay with me now, Ariana. Sit here by my side."

Silently, I obeyed. A cup of wine was thrust into my hands by one of the serving women. "This will help," she whispered. I gulped the wine. The taste was strange. *She must have drugged the wine,* I thought briefly before I lost consciousness.

I am not sure how long I was unconscious; the roar of the crowd woke me. It couldn't have been long. Struggling to order my thoughts, I opened my eyes and saw the final race was about to begin.

"Welcome back," the Magistrate whispered seductively in my ear. Startled, I realized I was leaning against his shoulder. I sat up quickly and moved away from him, which made him laugh. Revulsion and longing warred inside me as we watched the race. Closing my eyes, I silently begged the God of my mother to help me.

The roar of the crowd interrupted my plea as the whole amphitheater reverberated with their shouts. I opened my eyes and saw that Japheth led the pack. Watching him round the curve of the dirt track, I sensed that somehow this was more than just a race. Four powerful grey dappled horses surged just behind him, driven by one of the massive Nephilim. As the track straightened out, the Nephilim closed in on Japheth until they were side by side.

The race continued. I saw the seventh marker as Japheth pulled into the lead on the last lap of the race, holding my breath as he crossed the black line in the sand. Japheth had won! He was escorted from the track and brought before the Magistrate, and me beside him, to claim his prize.

Japheth stood in front of us, the sweat glistening on his face, his eyes defiantly flashing.

"I'm surprised you dare come here," the Magistrate jeered viciously at the young man.

"I thought nothing could surprise you," Japheth responded quietly, firmly. "I am here to claim my prize." He turned his gaze from the Magistrate to me. "I've come for her."

The people around us gasped. Who was this man to claim what the Magistrate clearly desired?

"The Father has sent me for you," he said kindly to me with a smile, holding out his hand to me.

"She is mine!" The Magistrate screamed for his men to take Japheth.

"You forget yourself, Magistrate! The victor of the race has the right to choose his prize. You can't violate your own law!" Japheth shouted back. There was a strong authority about him, even as a young man. Incredibly, the Nephilim guard staggered back from him, compelled by some unseen force.

"Ariana," he said, "You must choose now."

I wish I could say that I went with him wholeheartedly. Surprisingly, the dark beauty and power of the Nephilim was strong, and it was a great struggle to speak the words that freed me. "I . . ." Closing my eyes, I pushed the words out with effort, ". . . choose to go with you." Immediately, the darkness lost its grip on me.

Japheth caught me up in his arms and carried me out of the amphitheater in his chariot, away from the Magistrate. No one challenged him. Once outside, he smiled down at me. "We have a long ride west."

"Where are we going?" I asked.

"We're going to my family home. Just east of Eden."

Chapter 3

Can a mother forget the baby at her breast and have no compassion on the child she has born?
Isaiah 49:15

I'm not sure how long I was in the car with the men in suits as we drove away from the Compound. No one said a word. I looked out the window, frantically trying to figure out where we were. I thought of the map of the area from before the Vanishing, hanging in Jack's office. It was all marked up with areas where other people had been seen or the location of small settlements with which to trade for food or supplies. I'd studied it, trying to memorize the marks in case Daphne and I finally had a chance to escape. Now, I was leaving, and she had been left behind. I wondered if someone had already buried her by the back fence with the others.

I also wondered where these men were taking me. Recalling the look in my mother's eyes, I was sure it wasn't anywhere good. One by one, I thought of different scenarios, my speculations fueled by the deviant stories the Prophet loved to tell of the post-Vanishing world outside the Compound.

The morning sunshine streamed along the base of the mountains we were passing. Covered by massive evergreens, the mountains stretched up, their summits still shrouded in darkness. There was a lake next to the road we sped along. Sunlight dappled its smooth surface.

With a start, I realized that most of the trees growing along the banks of the lake were ashy grey or brown. As the sunlight increased, it revealed the red, sludgy-looking water of the lake, with hundreds of dead fish and trash floating on its surface. The smell of death wafted into the car, and I covered my nose. None of the men responded to the smell or the sight of death as we rolled alongside the lake.

As we drove on, there were more signs of devastation. The entire sides of the hills and mountains looked as if they'd melted, like wax running down a candle. Trees and dirt were heaped up in piles, and there were places in the road blocked with rocks, fallen trees, and dirt. The driver seemed familiar with the obstructions as he skillfully turned the wheel, navigating around the obstacles. Finally, we came out of the maze, and the road wove through a valley with fields fenced in with wire.

I was anxious, certain somehow that we were nearing our destination. The driver barked at the man sitting next to me to wake up. He sat up quickly and glanced over at me. I didn't like the look on his face.

The car sped up a small hill. As we crested it, I saw a town ahead—large vehicles and piles of debris blocked the entrance. About twenty men guarded the perimeter, all armed with rifles.

"Let us pass; we've got a volunteer for His Excellency," the driver ordered through the open window. Too soon, we pulled up to our destination.

"Get out," the man in the front seat ordered, as his partner opened my door. Clasping my bag to my chest, I climbed stiffly out of the car.

The guy grabbed my arm and pulled me in front of the car toward the building's entrance. No sooner had we reached the door than the car squealed away.

"What'cha got there, Stan?" A uniformed man stood next to the door, holding an automatic rifle like the ones our scouts carried back at the Compound.

"A volunteer," the guard smirked. He smiled weirdly and looked at my body with a look I knew to be lust. I felt sick to my stomach.

We entered a sunny room. I was stunned by how beautiful it was. Big windows framed the mountains in the distance along each wall, except one. That one had a massive fireplace constructed of large, smooth rocks. In front of the fireplace was an old woman sitting at a desk. Stan ordered me to sit in one of the chairs and stood behind me with his arms crossed, glaring down at me.

"Well, Stan," the old woman crowed up at him. "I haven't seen you in ages."

"Yeah, it's getting harder to find premium stock," he muttered. "Took us quite some time to get this one. We expect a lot for her."

The old woman ordered me to stand up and turn around for her. "If she is pure, you will get your pay. His Excellency needs his volunteers. Take her to a room and have her clean up. She stinks." She waved her hand in the air dismiss us.

The guard grabbed my arm and pulled me along a hallway. "You'll be here for a few days," he muttered grimly, opening a door to a small room and pushing me in. "We're waiting on a couple of others to send along. The sooner you realize that no one here cares, the better. Behave and you won't get hurt. Cause any trouble, and you will."

The guard left the room, locking the door behind him.

The room was furnished as a bedroom, and I fell onto the bed. Curling back into a ball, I hugged my legs tightly and sobbed. I cried for Daphne, the only real mother I'd known, while my "real" mother's mocking voice played over and over in my mind. Surely my mother knew what she was sending me into—no, *selling* me into.

Shrill shrieks interrupted my thoughts. A woman was screaming for someone to stop. I put my hands over my ears to shut out the sound. Looking out of the window, I could see it was still dark outside.

I thought of all the things Daphne had taught me, then noticed my bag on the floor by the bed. The little Bible she loved was in there. We had not been allowed to read the Bible at the Compound; Dominic was the only one with that privilege. But Daphne had hidden this small copy in her shed.

"How can any of it be true? She loved You, God, and look where it got her! She always told me to trust You, and this is where I am!" I muttered, sniffing back my tears.

I put my head in the pillow on the bed and screamed into it in rage and fear. I was unloved, alone, and at the mercy of evil people who wanted to use me. I screamed until I had nothing left in me.

Finally, I got up and went to the bathroom. It was beautiful, with brown and cream-colored tiles lining a massive shower. I wondered for a second what kind of place this had been before the world went crazy. Daphne had told me stories about what life was like before the Vanishing. There were stores you could drive to and buy all kinds of food or clothes. She and her husband would go to restaurants for dates or to theaters to watch movies where they ate popcorn and drank sodas. She would have been able to tell me what this place had been. Now, it was just a prison.

After my shower, I sat in the deep leather chair that faced the cold, dark fireplace. I had no idea where they were going to take me. I didn't know a lot about the outside world. Information was closely restricted at the Compound. Without being told, I knew that my father and Dominic Webb parceled out only what they wanted us to know. Knowledge was power.

According to Dominic, he was a prophet sent by God to rescue the faithful remnant. The Compound was our refuge from the coming Apocalypse. *What if he was right?* I recalled Dominic's railing condemnation.

"America was never great!" he'd yelled, eyes blazing with righteous indignation. "America only had a veneer of greatness. Under its fake surface, it was full of sewage, its soul diseased. Its government was totally corrupt; its churches filled with evil men peddling false religion."

Jack had shouted loudly, "Amen, preach it, brother! Only the Chosen are safe from that evil because of godly men like you!"

I pulled the small book out of my bag, rubbing the old brown leather. Many sweet memories were tied to it. Daphne had taught me to read using this Bible. Nothing my father or Dominic ever said or did fit with what I'd read in its pages. But Daphne did. Everything Daphne said and did fit with what was written in this book, almost perfectly.

"Daphne fit," I whispered.

"Wake up! Wake up!" Someone was shaking me hard. Opening my eyes, I looked around, confused. I was alone in the room, still sitting in the chair, holding the leather book, and everything around me was pulsating.

Before I could move, the entire building shuddered around me and dropped. The chair I was in fell over less than a second later, and I was tossed onto the floor. I screamed as the shaking continued, putting my arms over my head as bits of debris crumbled around me. It seemed like it went on forever, but eventually the building stopped moving and everything was still.

Keeping my arms over my head just in case, I peered around the room. Shocked, I realized an entire wall was gone. I sat up carefully. My bag and the book were on the floor next to me. Without thinking, I pushed the book into the bag and stood up, slinging it on to my shoulder. Maybe I could escape.

Another wave of shaking caused the floor to roll under my feet, and I struggled to stand. It didn't last long, but I knew I had to get out of what was left of the building. I looked at where the doorway had been, but it had collapsed, so I moved to the open wall. It was still dark outside, but the moon was full, illuminating the destruction.

I'd fallen asleep in a chair on the fourth floor of the building and was now only a few feet from the ground. In a daze, I clambered out and away from the collapsed building. Another tremor caused the ground below me to roll, and I dropped down unable to stand.

I screamed as the rest of the building disintegrated into pieces, debris flying all around me as the earth violently shook. I must have been knocked out.

I'm not sure how long I lay there before I felt a hand on my back.

"Are you okay?" It was a man's voice. He felt for my pulse on my neck.

Terrified, I held my breath, pretending to be unconscious. *Please leave me alone, please,* I silently pleaded, but he scooped me up and carried me over his shoulder like a rag doll. Opening my eyes, I saw we were heading away from the collapsed building.

He stopped, shifted his balance, and opened a car door. I quickly closed my eyes again, willing myself to stay limp as he put me down on the back seat and belted me in.

"Can't have you flying around," he whispered.

He got in the driver's seat and started the car. As he sped away from the town, I decided to "come to," figuring it was better to know who and what I was dealing with. I moaned and opened my eyes.

"Are you hurt? Anything broken?" he said, his eyes meeting mine in the mirror. He didn't look much older than me.

"I don't know." I sat up a bit straighter, feeling around the floor with my feet for something I could use as a weapon. "Where are we going?"

"I have a place just up the road. You'll be safe there," he spoke reassuringly, smiling.

Sure enough, we turned down a road a few minutes later and pulled into a large paved lot filled with cars. A flickering big light on the building to our right spelled M-O-T-E-L. Although there was debris everywhere, the building was still standing.

The boy got out of the car and opened the door for me.

"Follow me," he whispered, "and don't draw any attention to yourself; it isn't safe."

FLOOD

Chapter 4

...in the day of trouble he will keep me safe in his dwelling.
Psalm 27:5

Japheth and I rode side by side on two of his majestic horses; the other two followed behind. We left the cart by the track. The sky was azure, and the sun was warm as we rode through the fields surrounding the city of Sumeria.

Japheth turned to me and said, "Ariana, the Creator told my father about you. That's why I joined in the race today, to find you. We've been getting ready for your arrival for over a year."

I was so overwhelmed and confused that I did not know what to say, but I was startled at his mention of the Creator. "So you follow the Old Ways?" I asked hesitantly, thinking of my parents and their unknown fate.

"My mother and father both follow the Old Ways, worshipping the Creator." Japheth's voice warmed when he spoke about his parents, but his face grew serious as he turned toward me again. He said earnestly, "I know you are worried about your parents. We will find out what has happened and help them if we can."

I smiled at him, feeling grateful and shy at the same time. "Thank you, Japheth." I tried to keep my thoughts from worrying. We rode on for a long while in silence.

Hours passed, and as we drew farther away from the city of Sumeria, the fields gave way to wooded hills. The tall, ancient trees offered a pleasant relief from the sun's heat. As we rode through the dappled wood, Japheth told me stories of his family's life, obviously trying to draw me out.

"We only have a short way to go once we're out of the woods," he told me. "My family will be glad to meet you."

"Do you have brothers and sisters?" I asked.

"Two brothers, Shem and Ham. Both of them are married."

"What are they like?"

He took a deep breath. Shem is a craftsman like our father—and an inventor! Truly a problem solver and a peacemaker. Ham is, well, Ham."

"Does your family keep to the old traditions, or do they have their own homes?" I was curious. So many younger people shunned the Old Ways and moved away from their families to their own homes.

"We all live together in the old tradition. Each of my brothers has added on to the family home a place for their wives. Truly, they did a fine job, but wait until you see what I've prepared for you, Ariana." His eyes twinkled with excitement and pride.

"I can't wait to see it," I said, trying to keep the anxiety out of my voice. *For me? He's been planning for me?* The nearer we got to his home, the more apprehensive I felt. Absently, I chewed my thumbnail for a moment until I saw that Japheth was looking at me. Quickly pulling my thumb out of my mouth, I asked him how he had prepared for the race.

Japheth went on to describe in detail how he had readied himself for the competition—choosing the horses and building the cart to the specifications his father drew. His brothers had helped him practice for the event, pushing him to improve his cart and his racing skills, so he would be ready.

We rode for about an hour longer before arriving at Japheth's home. The sun was setting in the deep blue sky, which was brushed with wispy rose and purple clouds. Flowering trees lined the packed-dirt road leading up to the house. The horses, sensing an end to their toil, picked up the pace, kicking up dust.

The wooden house ahead of us sprawled against the horizon. Almost the entire building was encircled with porches; even the second story rooms led out to adjoining decks. Charming arrangements of chairs and tables and flowering plants abounded.

I felt a strange mixture of emotions. Nothing seemed real. Twenty-four hours earlier, I was at home with my mother preparing to go to Sumeria for the first time. Now, my parents were most likely dead. I did not know how to prepare to meet my rescuer's family, who apparently would soon become my own. I was tired and overwhelmed.

Reaching the front of the house, we pulled the horses to a stop. Japheth leapt off his horse and quickly helped me down from mine. I was glad for his help. My legs were so unsteady, I feared I would fall.

Loud, excited shouts welcomed us as the family spilled out of the carved double doors onto the wide front porch. Although they weren't as tall as many of the city dwellers, whose ancestors included Nephilim, they were healthy, strong-looking people. I was immediately enveloped in embraces, and my cheeks were kissed enthusiastically. Although I was overwhelmed, I felt welcomed and wanted. Japheth's mother, whom he introduced as Laelah, wrapped an arm around my waist and led me inside.

We walked straight into a great hall. Along the wall opposite the entrance was a long table, set with plates of bread, cheese, a variety of fruits, dried meats, and cups of water, wine, and beer. Despite my feelings, my mouth watered at the sight. I'd been too excited about the festival to eat breakfast.

Laelah guided me through the hall room and asked if I wanted to freshen up before dinner. That sounded lovely. "Certainly, you want to have some time to rest up and change after the long ride here," she said understandingly.

We left the rest of the family in the great hall, and Laelah led me down a hallway to the right. "This is the wing Japheth added onto the house for you, Ariana." We walked into a room similar to the great hall but on a much smaller scale and with an intricately carved stone fireplace.

I walked toward the mantel, entranced by the detail of the workmanship. On the top of the mantel, a scene was carved into the stone. Centered in the picture was a lush tree, abundantly covered in fruit. In its branches, a serpent was barely discernable. Its long tale wrapped around the trunk of the tree, as if choking out its life force.

"I know this story!" I exclaimed.

"Yes, Eden is close to here," Laelah told me.

"It's the most beautiful place on the earth, or at least, that's what my mother always said." My voice broke as I remembered the Magistrate's guards dragging her off.

Laelah placed a hand on my shoulder. "Has something happened to your mother?"

I began to sob and didn't resist when she pulled me into an embrace.

After a while, I pulled away and wiped my eyes with the sleeve of my dress. "It was so awful. My father betrayed my mother to the Magistrate. She believes in the Creator, the Old Ways. I'm afraid they've already been executed, and I'll never see them again." My words came out in gasps between ragged breaths.

Laelah shook her head from side to side sadly and grimaced. "We live in a time where it's hard for many to resist the strong power of the enemy. He dominates either through fear or allurement. Surely, your father panicked and gave into fear of the evil one."

"The Magistrate?" I'd felt the pull of his attraction myself, despite the obvious evil intent revealed in his cunning expression. I shuddered at the memory.

"No, there's a worse enemy than the Magistrate." She hugged me fiercely as she spoke. "But that can wait for later. You're tired and hungry. The bedroom is over here."

I followed her into a spacious, airy room to the right. The plastered ceiling was high and rounded, with a night sky painted on its surface. Wood-paneled walls beamed a golden hue on the room, with tones of red streaked in their polished surfaces. The large bed was carved from a darker wood. I'd never seen anything so beautiful.

Each of the four posters had been whittled into the form of a slender tree, bending toward the one opposite, their branches reaching out in an embrace. The branches were woven together at each end, forming an arch. Intricately carved leaves sprouted from the branches, each painted in lifelike detail.

"Did Japheth make this?" I gasped.

Laelah nodded with a smile.

"I still don't understand all of this. How did he know to expect me? How did he know about me at all? Why did he do all of this for a girl he doesn't know?"

"But he did know. The Creator told him to prepare a place for his bride, just as his brothers prepared a place for their wives."

My thoughts raced. None of this made sense. I did believe in the Creator my mother had taught me about, but I had never heard of Him talking to people.

"Why don't you bathe, my dear?" Laelah asked. "Everything you need is in here." She indicated a door to her right. "We even have some fresh clothing ready for you. Take your time. Everyone's waiting for you in the Great Hall when you are ready."

She hugged me and left the room.

It was all too much. I fell to my knees by the stone tub and sobbed. I cried for my mother and father and the life that was now over. I cried until I had no more tears.

I gazed at my reflection. The blue dress set out for me fit perfectly. The steamy air from my hot bath had turned my curly hair into a dark halo. I leaned into the mirror and noted the greenish brown of my eyes contrasted with the rims, red from my tears. It would have to do. I could not keep everyone waiting.

Making my way out of my room and the part of the house Japheth had built for us—*for us*, how odd was that thought!—I found my way back to the front hall.

Japheth crossed the room to meet me. I was worn out from the day and my tears, but I managed to smile up at him. Those brown eyes of his were so warm and tender. He understood.

Putting his left arm around me, he led me to the group waiting by the table. In addition to his family, there was someone already seated at the head of the table. I tried not to look shocked. He was clearly one of the ancients. Never had I seen someone so old.

"Ariana, this is my father's great-father, Methuselah."

Sitting in front of me was a legend. Mother had told me about Methuselah many times. It was prophesied that he would live until the end of the world. His father was the famous prophet, Enoch—the one who walked with God and then was taken from the world without dying.

Methuselah smiled at me, his deeply lined face crinkling up around eyes the same shade as Japheth's. He was the oldest person in the world. I felt humbled meeting this legendary man.

"I have been waiting to meet you, young lady. I am so sorry to hear about your mother and father."

Japheth pulled the chair out next to Methuselah, and I sank down onto it. "Thank you." Methuselah took my hand between both of his and welcomed me with a short bow.

No sooner had we exchanged greetings than another man strode into the room. He was strongly built, and though his hair and beard were as white as Methuselah's, his swarthy complexion retained a youthful appearance. Everyone except Methuselah stood up, so I pushed my chair back as well.

"Father," Japheth bowed his head in respect, "may I introduce Ariana to you?"

Noah turned toward me with a welcoming smile, and his dark brown eyes twinkled with affection. "Welcome, dear one! All of us have eagerly waited to meet you—though none as eagerly as my son!"

Noah embraced me, kissing me on each cheek. Pulling back, he bowed his head a moment before looking at me. "How we have prayed for this moment! Welcome, welcome!"

Then he turned and took a place at the head of the table next to Laelah. Everyone settled back down in their chairs.

"I apologize for not being here to greet you, Ariana. I was concerned about a small settlement of believers to the south of us. They didn't show up at our last gathering, so I rode out early this morning to check on them. A mob had attacked their settlement. Their barns were burned, and their cattle slaughtered in the fields." He shook his head in disgust. "Thankfully, no one was killed. The Magistrate has had many followers of the Old Ways murdered in the past few years. He grows bolder and bolder," Noah said grimly.

"Still, he is restrained, Father," Japheth said. "He couldn't do a thing to stop me from saving Ariana."

"Yes, but evil is growing strong," Noah insisted.

"Now is not the time for that," Laelah interjected. She turned to Methuselah, respectfully nodding her head to honor him, as was proper. "Would you like to offer a blessing over the food?"

The ancient man lifted his large hands upward in a receiving posture and murmured words of thanksgiving to the Creator. As he prayed, I looked around at the others gathered around the table—strangers, who it seemed, were meant to be my new family.

FIRE

Chapter 5

He rescued me from my strong enemy, from those who hated me, for they were too mighty for me.
Psalm 18: 16–17

We entered the small motel room, and the boy who had claimed me from the earthquake's rubble closed and locked the door behind us. A bed and dresser were pushed against one wall. The opposite wall had a counter with open shelves below it and a small sink with dishes neatly stacked to the side. The boy walked to the refrigerator and pulled a pitcher from it. After carefully pouring water into two glasses, he nodded for me to take a seat at the small table next to the room's only window. The shades were drawn.

I sat down and sipped the water. Dark hair tumbled over his broad forehead. He looked like he was just a few years older than me—young to be on his own. His blue eyes were carefully scanning my face. He looked troubled by what he saw.

"You're not from around here, are you?"

I swallowed the water. "No."

"Why were you in that building?"

I decided to tell him the truth, with some revisions. I didn't want to reveal too much. "I'm from a community not too far from here, a religious community. But it's not a safe place. The leader is ruthless, violent—evil. My mom and dad refused to let him, well . . . " I couldn't finish. It was a lie, but the lump forming in my throat wouldn't let me speak.

"I get it."

Feeling a little safer with his understanding response, I brushed the hair out of my face and, tucking it behind my ears, looked into his eyes. I couldn't tell what he was thinking.

"I ran," I made up quickly, as I continued lying. "I'm not sure how long I ran, but I finally came to a clearing by a dirt road. Some men drove by, and I thought they would help me, but they took me to that place."

"What's your name?" he asked.

"Dani," I said, quickly choosing a new name. "What's yours?"

"Tomas." He sighed. "I shouldn't have helped you, but you were all alone. I couldn't let the Global Union soldiers pick you up."

"Who are they?" I asked.

"You really must be from the middle of nowhere! The Global Union controls the cities and towns; those outside are considered lawless, fringe groups."

Obviously, there was a lot about the world I didn't know. Old movies and Daphne's stories about the past hadn't prepared me for the reality of life outside the Compound. Apparently, we were part of the wild, lawless fringe groups.

"But who are they?"

"They're the part of the Global Union government; they've been around since the riots. You know about those, right?"

I shook my head, "No."

Tomas ran a hand through his dark hair. "The riots came after the Vanishing. We lost so many people, and the ones left behind wanted answers." He sighed. "My mom disappeared. I don't remember her, though. I was just a toddler. My dad told me only the Christians disappeared. He became one right after she vanished."

"I didn't know people disappeared." I didn't know why I kept lying to him, but I wanted information.

"Yeah, well, they did. Suddenly a big part of the population and economy was gone. People like my dad became Christians and expected some day of reckoning to happen. Many of those folks left the cities and went out to unpopulated areas like your parents did, waiting for the end of the world to come."

I thought about Dominic.

"After the riots came the War."

I tried to piece together a timeline in my head.

"After the Christians disappeared and the riots were raging across the United States, war broke out. Canada and South American countries attacked."

"But why would they attack when the world was already in chaos?" I asked.

"The real reason? Because we once were a wealthy, nationalistic country that refused to join the globalist movement, and we had military technology they wanted to control. Violence and chaos reigned for almost five years. Money was worthless. Food was scarce. Family turned on family."

Tomas drew a breath before continuing with his mini-history lesson. I think he realized it was a lot for anyone to absorb. He continued explaining, "Finally, in an effort to establish peace and stability, the United States, Canada, Mexico, and Greenland—what was formerly known as simply "North America" joined together as the "United North America" and joined the Global Union as one of the ten regions. We lost our freedoms, and I my father, but at least we have security."

"What happened to your father?"

"He was beheaded," said Tomas quietly. "The Global Union brought peace and stability to the world, which is what people were looking for after the Vanishing. They outlawed Old Christianity. Those who wouldn't denounce their faith were killed."

"How old were you?"

"Twelve. In order to live in the city, I had to swear allegiance to the Global Union, or they would have killed me, too." Tomas looked away from me, his eyes searching the floor as he spoke. My heart warmed a little as I realized he, too, was probably feeling vulnerable.

"What's "old" Christianity?" I asked, hoping to distract him from obviously painful memories.

"The kind that is exclusive and judgmental. The kind that believes there's only one way. Just as the countries and governments came together under the Global Union, His Excellency was able to persuade the Global Union to supervise uniting all the major world religions."

"Who's His Excellency?" I asked.

Tomas shook his head in amazement. "You really don't know much, do you? When the disappearances happened, there were a lot of people left behind in various Christian churches. They had different groups and denominations. There was one denomination that was larger than the rest, and its leader spent a lot of time working to unify all the world religions into one."

"And that's His Excellency?'"

"Yes, his name is Angelo Cain. He's worked hard to build unity among the different religious sects, bringing them together. He was able to bridge the gulf between the different religions by showing us that we all have some light. The Vanishing was a warning to the world to unite together. The Global Union made him the religious leader, His Excellency."

I tried to work out what Tomas was saying. It seemed to me like the world was a larger version of the Compound. At least I knew the rules back there.

"So, we are in United North America?"

"Yes, the cities and towns are closed off and controlled by the Global Union. For the most part, fringe groups, like the religious compound you escaped from, are left to themselves unless they cause trouble."

"Okay, so we are in United North America, which is a part of the Global Union. Who is in charge, Angelo Cain?" I tried to sort out what he was telling me.

Tomas laughed, running his hand through his hair. "No, no. Angelo Cain is the religious leader. President Emanuel Bellomo is the leader of the Global Union; Angelo Cain works with him. When the Global Union formed, the leaders of the ten regions, called regents, vied to take control. There was a power struggle, and it seemed the pockets of localized violence would erupt into another world war—especially in the Middle East. One man did something no one else ever did in the middle of that chaos."

"What did he do?"

"He got Israel to sign a peace treaty with the Palestinians. There's been violence between them for . . . like forever, and he was able to get them both to sign a ceasefire agreement for seven years—to give real peace a chance."

"So by doing something that seemed impossible, he got to become the world leader?" I guessed.

"It was more complicated than that, but I guess you could say that was the thing that got him such worldwide approval. He's done wonders for the entire globe—an incredible man."

Tomas picked up his glass and took it to the sink. "Listen, it's late. I need time to think about what to do with you." He looked down at me, his eyes troubled. "I'm going to take a walk and think."

Fear made my stomach roil. I'm sure he could see it on my face.

"Don't worry, I'm not going to turn you in. I just have to figure out how to help you." He nodded at me, trying to be reassuring. "I'll be back in a little while."

He walked to the door, opened it, and left.

I stayed in the chair by the table for a bit after Tomas left and stared at the door. There was so much I didn't know. The United North America was one of ten regions controlled by the Global Union led by President Emmanuel Bellomo and his religious counterpart, Angelo Cain. I recited it all in my head, trying to memorize it.

I saw a tablet on the dresser and grabbed it. Dominic had one of these in his house. I'd seen it in his study one of the times I'd been sent over to clean.

There was a button at the bottom. I pressed it and was surprised when it lit up with a picture. A smiling woman and man held a baby between them, Tomas surely. I touched an icon and a video began playing. An attractive, nicely dressed woman was talking.

There were reports of earthquakes and flooding in areas of the world I'd never heard of, along with stories about famine and battles. The screen shifted and images of starving people flitted across the small screen. I stared in horror. Was this real? Or a movie, like the ones we'd watched at the Compound?

Then the screen shifted to an ancient-looking city; the words on the bottom of the screen said "Jerusalem." The woman's voice spoke about two men who were terrorizing the whole country.

"As you know, it has not rained in the entire region for almost eight months, all because of these two men—the Witnesses—and their curse on the land." The picture showed two men next to an ancient wall, speaking to a crowd. "For three and a half years they've been able to torment us, disturbing our peace. You've seen what happens to anyone who tries to approach them." The screen changed back to the woman. "The Witnesses, as they call themselves, have supernatural powers. They aren't just a menace to Israel. You know they have caused disasters and famine all over the Global Union. Each of the ten regions has also been tormented by these men. The Israeli Defense Force has attempted to arrest the two Witnesses . . ."

I heard Tomas at the door and turned off the device. Tomas entered and closed the door softly, locking it. "It's almost curfew, so we have to stay in here for the night." Walking over, he took a seat again at the table and ran a hand through his dark hair. "I know someone who can help us, though."

"Us?"

"I'm leaving too. I was planning on leaving anyway. I have a friend who can get us out of town safely."

I felt nauseous. Something seemed off with Tomas, but I didn't know him well enough to be sure.

"Where would we go?" I asked.

"My friend can get us to Spokane. This is my chance. I talked it over with Frank. He has a good plan. I have to do what's best for me."

Something was odd. It seemed like Tomas wasn't talking to me anymore, but himself.

"What will we do once we get there?" I asked.

"Frank has a place there where we can stay. He's got it all figured out. There's no need to worry. There's work in Spokane for both of us." Tomas managed a half-smile. "I know you've gone through a lot, Dani. This is the best I could come up with. I'll make us a cup of tea."

FLOOD

Chapter 6

A spirit glided past my face, and the hair
on my body stood on end.

Job 4:15

My first night in Japheth's home I slept for fifteen hours. I woke very early in the morning while it was still dark outside. Everything was strange and so different from my home. As I lay in bed, I kept thinking about my parents. The pain in my chest was so intense, I could hardly breathe. I rolled into a ball and sobbed until I fell back asleep.

Later in the morning, I awakened to sunlight streaming through the window. I wandered into the kitchen and found Laelah washing dishes. She handed me a cup of tea already prepared. I took the tea from her hands and smiled gratefully. I was touched by her kindness.

"Where is everyone?" I asked as Laelah turned back to her dishes.

Laelah told me Japheth and his brothers went out early in the morning to build the wedding chamber, a tradition of the Old Ways. I had never heard of the tradition and had to ask Laelah to explain.

"The groom and his friends and family will find a suitable, private place, and build a bridal bower. Tree boughs and flowering vines are woven together to make a lovely shelter for the wedding night."

35

Setting down my tea, I took a plate from her and dried it. "I'm very grateful, but . . . " Unexpectedly, tears began to pour down my face again.

Laelah pulled her hands out of the water, gently took the towel from my hands, and dried them. "I'm sure this is hard for you, Ariana. The other wives knew Ham and Shem from childhood. Taina and Nua were familiar with my sons and with us. Everyone, everything is new here for you, and you're far from your home."

I wondered something. "Laelah, is it possible to talk to the Creator?"

"Well, yes! I speak to Him all the time. Men have called to Him since the days of old. Fewer speak to Him now."

"But does He talk back to you?"

"Yes, in different ways—sometimes through a thought or in a circumstance. Often Noah speaks with the Creator; he and his great-father, Methuselah, both hear from the Creator directly."

"Would it be right if I spoke to Him?" I asked.

"Of course! Would you like me to help you?"

"No, thank you, I just wondered if it was okay to do. Is there somewhere I should go to speak to Him?"

Laelah smiled up at me and patted my shoulder. "You can speak to Him anywhere, anytime. It doesn't even have to be out loud. He can hear your thoughts. The Creator is a kind Father, who longs to hear from His children."

I had learned a lot from my mother but not enough. My father disliked her teaching me about the Old Ways, so there were gaps in my understanding. I needed fresh air and time to myself, so I decided to take the path that led to the forest.

I walked along the broad, even path. The further along into the forest I went, the larger the trees grew. As I ambled along, I noticed colorful birds flitting about. I stopped walking to watch a particularly striking one. It was a larger bird, pure white with a long, curling, yellow tail. Perched on a tree ahead of me, it stretched out its large wings in a gallant display, which made me smile. It seemed to be showing off.

Slowly folding its wings back, the bird turned its head and caught my eye. Winking, it flitted down and landed on the path in front of me. It was so beautiful; I wanted to touch its shimmering feathers, so I tiptoed slowly toward it. As I got nearer, I realized the bird was larger than I'd thought. I was almost close enough to touch it when its body began to morph and take the form of a giant man. The Magistrate!

Instead of the lovely white bird, there stood the Nephilim in all his dark and evil splendor. His obsidian eyes glinted with pleasure and desire.

"I found you alone. What luck!"

I gasped in horror and turned to run, but he grabbed my arm in a vice-like grip. "Let me go!" I screamed.

"I don't think so," he whispered softly into my ear, his breath warmly disturbing. "That son of Noah should have taken more precautions for your safety. These are perilous times, my dear. I promised your mother I would make sure you were safe."

I froze.

He relaxed his hold on my arm and began to caress me with his other hand, stroking my check before tracing my lips with his finger. Fear began to turn into something else, and I pulled in a shallow breath before asking him what he'd done with my mother.

"Oh, nothing at all! She is a most welcome guest in my palace. Your father, unfortunately, met with a serious accident." He leaned his head down and brushed my neck with his lips. "He lost his head!" I struggled against him in horror, unable to break his hold on me.

I opened my mouth to scream for help, but he began to sing. They say that many human women have been won by the Nephilim's music—deceived by the power of their siren song. Bewitched, I stayed even when he let go of me.

Visions of us living together appeared all around me, laughing and loving, with children roaming in and out of the picture. I was enchanted. I stood before him in a hazy stupor, filled with longing for all he showed me.

"You only have to choose, Ariana." He breathed my name out, annunciating the last syllable of my name oddly as he bent his mouth to kiss me.

Something inside me screamed to resist.

"God. Help. Me." I struggled to get the words out before his lips touched mine.

The Magistrate vanished.

But I was not alone. A man stood in his place, unlike any other man I'd seen. He radiated with kindly goodness and kingly majesty. He did not reproach me, yet I felt within myself such vileness that I fell to my knees before Him in shame.

"I am unworthy," I sobbed. I wanted to pour out all my fearful failings along with my heart-wrenching tears. In the light of His presence, I saw myself clearly for the first time in my life, and I felt undone.

Then I felt His hand on my head. "Do not be afraid," He reassured me.

Comforting love enveloped me from the inside out. I felt the burden of my failures and misplaced desires fall away like the chaff does when we winnow the wheat. I felt peace.

"I am with you always."

I looked up, but He was gone. I stood and looked around. The forest birds still flitted about, undisturbed by all that had occurred.

"Ariana!"

I smiled as I caught sight of Japheth at the end of the path and quickly walked toward him. His blonde hair was damp. "Have you been swimming?" I asked.

His eyes crinkled as he smiled down at me, and I wondered how it was that in so short a time he meant so much to me.

"Yes, it was hot working. I'm just heading back to the house. May I walk with you, or did you want to be alone? I know there's always someone at home."

"That's thoughtful, but I'd like to walk together." As we walked along the dusty path, I told Japheth what I'd experienced in the woods, stumbling a bit when I spoke of the Magistrate.

"I don't want there to be any secrets between us," I assured him.

Japheth's eyebrows drew together and shook his head. "Of course, no secrets. But you didn't ask for him to appear like that, Ariana."

"I know, but in my indecision I think I left a way for him to . . . if that makes sense? I've always had misgivings about my mother's faith. She was so judgmental and critical of others that I felt a bit repelled by it. But in just a short time, your family has shown me another side."

"Father says that some who follow the Creator are the enemy's best argument against putting faith in Him, not to disrespect your mother in any way." Japheth softly beat his fist against his chest. "I myself fall short in so many ways."

Thinking about the man I saw after the Magistrate vanished, I nodded my head in agreement. "I, too, fall short. I feel that I judged my mother too harshly. I hope I get the chance to apologize to her and tell her I love her. If the Magistrate was telling me the truth, she is still alive. But not my father . . . " my voice trailed off. I could not bring myself to voice what the Magistrate had told me.

Japheth took my hand in his and squeezed it, and we walked along in silence. I felt better just being with him. Words were not necessary.

The next day, Noah returned to Sumeria to find out about my parents and gather supplies. I waited impatiently for his return, anxious for any news of my mother. On the evening of the third day, Japheth and I were sitting on the porch when I saw Noah riding up the road. I let go of Japheth's hand and ran to meet him, hoping that by some miracle my parents still lived.

He was dismounting the horse when I reached him. Japheth was just behind me. "Did you find out anything?"

The expression on his face was somber. "Yes, I did. I am sorry, Ariana. Both of your parents were executed the day of the race."

"But the Magistrate, he said my mother was still alive! He said she was a welcome guest in his palace!"

Noah grimaced. His lips drew into a thin line of disgust. "Indeed, I am so sorry, Ariana. He had her body hung over the entrance to his palace as a warning to any who would follow the Old Ways of worshipping the Creator."

I fell into Japheth's arms and wept bitterly for my mother and father, even more devastated now that I knew for certain they were both gone. Japheth wrapped his arms around me and waited quietly as I mourned.

"When will the Creator save us from this evil?" I cried. "I know He has the power. Why did my parents have to die?"

"I am sorry for your loss, my dear, truly." Tears filled Noah's eyes. "The world has become increasingly violent and wicked. The Magistrate is no longer content to rule Sumeria. His soldiers have been hunting in the countryside. I passed by a few settlements where whole families hung dead from trees. It was horrific. The persecution has begun, but do not fear; God spoke to me long ago about this. He has a plan. We've been preparing." He patted my shoulder.

"I am very sorry," Noah said gently. "I'll go in and tell Laelah what's happened."

I followed Noah into the house and made my way to my room. Pulling a pillow to my face, I screamed into it over and over as I imagined my mother's body hanging over the evil Magistrate's palace.

How did she feel? What did she suffer? Over and over, images of my mother dying played in my imagination. I felt hatred for my father. *How could he betray her?*

My grief lingered into the next day and the next. I kept to myself, only wanting solitude with my haunted thoughts and tears. I went back to the forest and cursed the Magistrate. *I will kill him!* I vowed. But he never appeared.

A few days later, as I walked in the forest, I came upon a mother deer with a speckled fawn at her side.

"Where were you?" I screamed. "She believed in you and you left her alone!"

She was never alone.

The thought calmly spoken in my mind quieted my heart. I knew that thought was not mine. I looked around. No one was there.

"Are you here, Lord?" I whispered. Again, I pictured the moment of her death, trying to see Him by her side, but I couldn't.

You must stop thinking about her last moments there.

Immediately, I felt warmth fill my sorely blistered heart. I tried again to picture my mother's death, but I stopped myself, knowing that she would want me to obey the voice. I don't know how long I walked in the forest, but I do know one thing: I didn't walk alone.

FIRE

Chapter 7

The shape of the locusts was like horses prepared for battle.
On their heads were crowns of something like gold, and
their faces were like the faces of men. They had hair like
women's hair and their teeth were like lion's teeth ... They
could torment men without the seal of God on their fore-
heads for five months. And the agony they suffered was like
the sting of the scorpion when it strikes.
Revelation 9:4–8

I struggled to open my eyes. I felt like I was drowning and couldn't pull myself to the surface. Finally, I pushed myself up on the bed, and a wave of nausea washed over me. Everything was spinning. My mouth was tacky. I clutched the sheets in my fists and took deep breaths, slowly in and out the way Daphne had taught me when I would begin to panic after a bad day back on the Compound. I knew that panic only made a bad situation worse. *Where was I?*

After a few moments, I was able to open my eyes. I was alone. A fire cheerfully burned in a large, stone-framed fireplace. I was in a large bed with pristine white bedding. With difficulty, I staggered out of bed and found a bathroom behind a door to the right of the fireplace.

I caught a glimpse of myself in the floor-to-ceiling mirror on my right and turned, startled. I was dressed in a simple white gown that gathered in just above my waist. My green eyes were accentuated by an outline of some kind, and my cheeks were an unnatural shade of pink.

Oh God. Where was I?

The last thing I remembered was Tomas. He came back to the motel room, and we drank a cup of tea. *It must have been drugged! Someone must have brought me here. Changed my clothes. Painted my face. What else had they done?*

I slid open a glass door leading out to a balcony. I was on the second floor of a tall city building. It was close to sunset. *Sunset? How long had I been here?* Looking over the railing, I gazed in horror at the devastation below me. Buildings lay in heaps around a river. What was once a bridge was now twisted sculptures on either side of the water. Fires burned here and there across the city. As far as I could see, only a few buildings still stood. The discrepancy between the luxury inside and the devastation outside this building frightened me.

I saw soldiers and military vehicles in front of the building. They had a large bonfire built in the middle of the street, and closer to the building, a chain across the road. I had to figure out what was going on.

I staggered back into the room and tried to open the other door. Surprisingly, it wasn't locked. I walked out of the room onto another kind of balcony. Dozens of rooms like mine encircled the hollow middle center of the building.

Music and the sound of people drifted up, and I peered down over the railing. Tables, covered in white linen, lined one wall of the huge open area below, laden with food. Men were dressed in clothes I'd only seen in movies, shiny black suits and crisp white shirts. The women wore long gowns that sparkled with color.

Suddenly, I heard shouts and sounds of chaos. I ran back into the room and shut the door, bolting all three locks. Making my way out to the balcony, I heard more shouting and petrified screaming. Then the hammering began. It sounded like the rhythmic pounding of horses' hooves, only a hundred times louder.

What was going on? The sound was growing louder. My heart beat wildly.

Then I saw them. A wave of dark creatures scaled over the fallen buildings. They moved forward like a terrifying mass of insects, some pouring through doors and windows.

As they got closer, I could see them more clearly. They were men, but not men—long tails, flared like those of scorpions, flicked behind them as they scaled the buildings. They were dressed in black armor. It felt as if I was in a nightmare, but I couldn't wake up. Dark clouds filled the sky, but as the creatures got closer in the fading light, I could see crowns glittering on their heads, holding their long dark hair away from their faces. I have never seen such terrible, hideous beauty. I couldn't tear my eyes away.

The soldiers below me shot at the monsters, but their bullets had no effect on the approaching army. The creatures didn't slow. They didn't break rank. None fell.

As they got closer, I heard piercing screams. I watched in horror as one of the creatures lifted a helpless soldier up off the ground. The dark attacker laughed mockingly, revealing long, razor-sharp teeth. As the man struggled, a tail slithered over the right shoulder of the man-like creature. It rose above the creature's head before plunging into the soldier's chest.

I screamed and turned back toward the room, desperate to escape, but it was too late. A shadow flew over me and one of the terrifying monsters landed right in front of me on the balcony, blocking my getaway. My knees buckled as I stared up at the massive beast. Its muscles were larger and more defined than any man I'd ever seen. Lustrous, long hair curled around its enticingly beautiful face. I was terrified and mesmerized at the same time. It smiled at me, revealing pointed teeth, and took a step toward me, its tail waving menacingly behind its body. It was the very personification of wickedness and evil.

Panicked, I tried to lunge away, but the creature grabbed me around the waist with one of its hands and pulled me closer, its sharp talons pricking into my skin. I screamed and struggled, kicking as hard as I could. The smell of its breath was like sulfur, and I turned my face away, terrified. Suddenly, the creature hissed in my ear, "Sealed!" and let go of me, dropping me onto the ground and knocking the breath out of me.

I watched in relieved disbelief as the creature jumped off the balcony and disappeared. Scrambling on all fours, I crawled inside the room and slid the glass door shut, turning the latch.

I'm not sure how long I stayed in the room as howls of terror from the creatures and their victims combined in a dreadful symphony. I tried covering my ears, but I couldn't block out the sounds. At some point, I think I passed out. When I awoke, it was dark outside. My dress was soaked with sweat.

Lying still, I listened cautiously. It was quiet and dark in my room. Staying on all fours, I crawled to the bathroom and drank some water from the sink. Shivering uncontrollably, I looked around and noticed a white robe hanging on a peg on the bathroom wall. Pulling it on, I cinched the cloth belt on my waist and made my way to the door that lead to the inside balcony. Cautiously, I opened the door. Crying and moans of pain filled my ears, and I tiptoed to the railing to look down below.

It was a disaster. People lay in broken heaps everywhere. The luscious tables of food were smashed and tossed about the place. Furniture was overturned and there were holes in the walls where the creatures had burst through. I watched for a full minute before backing into my room. Closing and locking the door behind me, I ransacked the drawers and closet looking for clothes. There was no way I could travel dressed the way I was. Finally, I found my clothes and shoes in a bin in the bathroom.

Dressing quickly, I left the room and walked along the hallway, scanning ahead and behind for anyone—or anything. I heard some scrambling noises below, and I dropped to the floor, carefully maneuvering to the railing to get a look. I saw one of the monsters skittering through an opened door.

I made my way down the stairs to the main floor. People were everywhere, lying on the ground, screaming in pain. It didn't look like anyone was dead. I crossed over to the water fountain in the middle of the room and was surprised to see Tomas slumped next to it. He was barely conscious when I bent over and shook him.

"Tomas! Wake up!"

He stirred and woke with a shuddering wail. I jumped back away from him, not sure what he would do. I watched as he rolled back and forth on the floor, crying in pain. There was a rip in his shirt and I could see a bloody gash where one of the creatures had stung him in the gut.

His eyes opened. "It's you!" He grabbed my arm. "Dani, you have to help me! Get me some help. Please, I'm going to die!"

I yanked my arm back and slapped his face as hard as I could.

"Shut up!"

He did, staring up at me with a blank expression.

"How did we get here?" I hissed. "What is this place? What the heck are those things?" He began whimpering in pain again, wrapping his arms around the wound in his stomach. I kicked at him with my foot. I was angry. "Answer me!"

"I'm so sorry," he cried. "I shouldn't have done it, but it was so much money . . . and a chance to live here."

"Where's here?"

"Spokane, Washington. Bringing . . . you . . . meant . . . I got to . . . join . . . the operation here." He spoke in bursts before screaming in pain. "Make it stop! God, make it stop!"

"I don't think God's going to make it stop any time soon," a gravelly voice offered.

Startled, I turned to see who had spoken. An older man stood with his arm wrapped around a young woman—neither of them looked like they had been stung. Looking around, I noticed we were the only people standing.

"I'm Mitch. This is my daughter, Sierra. What's your name?"

"Dani," I answered simply, not wanting to give too much information but recognizing I might need this man's help.

"We need to get out of here now," he told me urgently. "Do you want to come with us?" He spoke directly without further explanation, clearly eager to get away.

Tomas started screaming again. I looked around and realized my options weren't any better if I stayed.

"Okay, I guess so." Turning my back on Tomas, I followed them warily out of the building to the street. The soldiers I'd seen from the balcony lay on the ground writhing in agony like the others inside. I picked my way through the fallen men, following closely behind Mitch and Sierra and listening intently.

"What were those creatures?" Sierra sobbed, clutching at her dad as he helped her hobble along.

"It's one of the judgments—those monsters are demons that have been let out of the abyss," Mitch told her.

"Wait, wait!" I spoke loudly. "What judgments? And what the heck is 'the abyss?' What's happening?"

Mitch stopped walking and turned around. I moved closer, my breathing ragged. "I've been a prisoner all of my life and managed to escape only to end up here. I woke up to a living nightmare. What's going on?"

He sighed, rolled his tongue around in his cheek, and shook his head. "I'm sorry, kid, but we've got to get out of here. No time to talk. The long and short of it is that we're living in a world under God's judgment. Those demons are part of that judgment."

"Why didn't they sting us?" Sierra asked.

"Honestly, I don't know. If your mom were here, she'd know."

Sierra looked at him in horror. "Didn't you find her? You didn't rescue her?"

"Sierra, if this hadn't happened, I don't think I'd have even been able to rescue you." Mitch spoke patiently to his daughter, despite his obvious desire to hurry them all along. "The place was too well guarded." He looked down on her, a pained expression on his face. "I had to choose who to follow."

"What happened to Mom?" Sierra's voice crackled. She bit her lower lip as she looked up at her father. "After they split us up, I didn't see her again. Do you know where she is?"

I stood awkwardly by, watching as Mitch explained that the older women were put on a train while the younger women were taken to Spokane. Mitch had chosen Spokane.

"But I know where they sent your mom; I overheard some of the men talking. So, I came here to rescue you first. And right now, we need to get out of here."

"We need to find Mom," Sierra answered forcefully.

I followed them in silence, peering nervously into the darkness in case more of the creatures were around. Sweat trickled under my arms, and I started shivering. I had been betrayed by my mother, betrayed by Tomas, and attacked by monsters, and now I was forced to trust two strangers. I breathed slowly in through my nose and out of my mouth. I refused to panic.

FLOOD

Chapter 8

*So the Lord God said to the serpent, "Because you have
done this, cursed are you above all livestock and all wild
animals! . . . And I will put enmity between you and the woman, and between your offspring and hers; he will crush your
head, and you will strike his heel."*

Genesis 3 : 13–15

I didn't get to see my future husband much in the days before my wedding.
Besides constructing the wedding bower, Japheth and his brothers were
busy helping their father with his building project, and the women were
taking up the slack in the fields. Noah's project was all-consuming and
absolutely crazy. On his land, nowhere near water, he was building a huge
boat, an ark. He'd been working on it for the past seventy years.

Life was busy but good. I enjoyed spending time with my new family,
especially Methuselah. Since everyone was so busy, he and I spent much
of our free time together. Despite his advanced age, he was quite spry and
quick-minded. We ambled together on long walks and talked about many
things.

One day, when everyone was busy, I asked Methuselah if we could ride
out to the forest in one of the wagons.

"I don't think Laelah needs any extra help, and I have some questions I've been wanting to ask you."

He smiled. "Of course, I'd enjoy that," he said.

Eager to get my questions answered, I ran to the barn and took two of my favorite horses out of the stall and hitched them to one of the family wagons. They pulled the cart to the front of the house, where Methuselah sat waiting in the shade of the porch.

It only took us a few minutes to pull into the cool forest. We got down from the wagon and made our way to one of our favorite spots. As soon as we sat down, I blurted out my most pressing question.

"So, you believe the Creator actually told Noah to build this boat—the ark?" I asked. I wanted reassurance that the family I was marrying into was not deranged.

"Yes, I do," the elderly man answered.

"But why? Why has the whole family spent so many years building it? Noah says the Creator is going to flood the whole earth. I don't understand why. It doesn't make sense to destroy every living thing."

Methuselah's voice was deep and soft. "Not every living thing. Later today, at the community gathering, you will meet the other people who will join us on the ark. Not every human has been tainted. The Creator will save us all through the Flood."

"What do you mean by 'tainted?'"

"Let me explain. My father was a great prophet. You've heard of Enoch?"

"Yes, of course! Everyone has heard of him. He is the only man who never died but left the earth to be with the Creator."

"It's been over six hundred years since I saw my father. I was there when the Creator took him." Methuselah stood up and plucked a few of the lush yellow fruits for us both. We ate in silence for a few minutes, enjoying the juicy sweetness of the yellow fruit.

Methuselah wiped his mouth with the back of his hand and began to pray. "I thank you, Creator, for the fruit of Your creation." Methuselah lifted up his arms and spoke with his eyes wide open. "Long have I lived on the earth, and never have You failed to provide for me in any way."

He pulled a flask of water from his bag and offered me a drink. "My father, Enoch, walked with the Creator daily. He loved my mother, brothers, sisters, and me, of course, but the Creator was his first love. The Creator would often speak to my father and reveal things yet to come. My father would warn others, but still, evil continued to grow. Enoch prophesied about the rise of the Nephilim long ago, and so far, all that he foretold has been fulfilled."

I shuddered, thinking of the Magistrate and the evil of the city. "How are they able to do the things they do?" I asked, a grimace on my face.

"The fallen Mal'akh, an angel known as Satan, knows the prophecy that there will be a savior child born from a woman. In order to stop this, he had the Fallen Ones that he controls take human wives to pollute humanity with the half-breed Nephilim. That contamination has spread so far and wide that most of humanity has some measure of Nephilim in their ancestry. That's why evil has grown so strong and why the Creator must flood the earth, so that we who follow the Old Ways, who have no Nephilim in our ancestry, can repopulate the earth and a full human savior can be born."

I looked down the pathway into the ancient forest. Lined on either side of the pathway were gigantic, towering trees. Eden was at the end of that path. Japheth had sternly warned me it was forbidden to go there.

"Methuselah, is the Garden still down the pathway there?" I asked, changing the subject for a moment. It intrigued me.

He sighed and shook his head at me. "It is forbidden to try and enter Eden, Ariana. The taste for the forbidden is one we must resist. Too many of my own children chased after the forbidden and joined the ranks of the Nephilim." The older man's eyes filled with tears.

We sat in silence for a while before Methuselah leaned back against the rough trunk of the fruit tree and closed his eyes for a moment. "The world was much different when my first son was born. Lamech was Noah's father. In those days, Adam still walked the earth, and death was unfamiliar to us."

Although my mother had taught me the Old Ways, she had many gaps in her knowledge. I wondered if what she'd told me was accurate.

"Once people began dying, they began to curse the Creator. Despite the fact that the first father, Adam, still walked the earth, many turned away from worshipping the Creator. Instead, they began following the desires of their own hearts. People began gathering together in cities and encouraged each other to follow evil desires. They gave a place in their hearts over to the enemy, and so the Nephilim came into existence. Part human and part Mal'akh, they are relentlessly evil and incredibly strong."

His expression hardened as he continued. "Lamech refused to follow the Creator and went down a dark and evil path. He tried to get into Eden one day and met one of the fallen Mal'akh—a demon—along the way. That evil one deceived my son with visions of greatness and pleasures beyond human knowledge."

"When did that happen?"

"Shortly after Noah's birth. Lamech left one day in a fit of rage. Despite our many attempts to help him, to change his mind, he left his wife and Noah here."

"You and your wife must have been devastated!"

"We were, but his wife more so. She died of grief months later. We were left with Noah and raised him ourselves, grateful to have the comfort of our grandchild."

"Did you ever see Lamech again?" I asked.

"Yes, many decades later I heard that he had built a city, Sumeria, the one you visited. The city was much as it is now; you have seen it for yourself. He became its king. His arrogance knew no limits." Methuselah shifted uneasily; the memory was obviously distressing for him.

"I made my way to his palace and asked to see my son. When I reached the throne room, I was led before my son and told to bow before his majesty. Of course, I refused." Methuselah stood up and began pacing back and forth as he related his story.

"Lamech looked much different than the last time I had seen him. He sat on a golden throne, and the room was filled with people . . . and Nephilim."

"When I refused to bow, the crowd exploded with mocking laughter. I could feel the presence of great evil in the room. It threatened to overwhelm me, but I stood fast, for I am a son of the Creator.

"Lamech stood up and walked over to where I stood. His countenance was more beautiful than before, but evil now twisted his expression. He boasted of his power and his god, Malumek, who fathered many of Lamech's children."

"Is Malumek one of the Fallen Ones?" I asked.

"Yes. The Nephilim are the offspring of human women who give themselves to the Fallen Ones; Malumek was one. Many women don't survive the birth of the half human, half fallen angel. The children, the Nephilim, are often giants. Because they are the children of the Fallen Ones, they live very long lives."

I slowly nodded my head. "So, what happened next?"

"Lamech paraded his children before me, boasting how each one of them had united with one of the evil spirits to make them even more fearsome. My stomach felt sick, and incredible sorrow welled up within me as my son bragged that all his human children were given to Malumek as blood sacrifice to assure his continued power and wealth.

"I began to call out aloud to the Creator and the room erupted in chaos. The guards tried to grab at me, but the Creator would not allow them to lay hands on me. I prayed boldly, calling for judgment upon them all. Then I left."

I realized I'd been holding my breath and let out a long sigh. "Did you ever see him again?

"No."

I thought about Methuselah's story and looked at the path toward Eden again, thinking of how Lamech had been tempted.

"Is the Magistrate Lamech's son?"

"In name only. He is one of the accursed Nephilim."

The Magistrate, almost six hundred years old, appeared to be around the same age as Japheth. So, along with great strength and size, the Nephilim obviously did not grow older at the same rate as human men.

"No wonder so many gave themselves over to the evil ones," I said, voicing my thoughts out loud. "Since death was uncommon for so long, many must have thought the curse was a lie. They probably thought Malumek could save them from death."

Methuselah was watching me thoughtfully. "Yes, that is exactly what happened. The Nephilim grow in power and many are joining their ranks. Although my grandson, Noah, has preached righteously for many, many years, the depths of evil grow and the Nephilim's boundaries expand."

"How much longer do we have?" I exclaimed.

"Noah was told a hundred and twenty years, We're almost to that mark. So the men must work to finish the ark."

"Then what will happen?" I asked.

"The world will be covered with water. A great flood will come over the land, but those who take refuge in the ark will pass through the waters without harm."

At that moment, the deer and fawn I had seen earlier emerged from the woods and crossed the path that led to Eden.

"What about the animals?"

"The Creator will bring them to the ark. Hopefully, there will be many people not tainted by the Nephilim bloodlines who will choose to enter as well. There is room for many, many people." Methuselah said. "Noah has managed to win some others to faith in the Creator."

I looked up at the sky. The sun was almost overhead. It was getting late.

"I think we should probably go now; we must join the others tonight for the community celebration. I am excited for you to meet more people who follow the Old Ways." Methuselah stood up and gave me his hand. My earlier questions had been answered, but there was clearly more to discover.

FIRE

Chapter 9

*God sent me before you to preserve for you a remnant in
the earth, and to keep you alive by a great deliverance.*
Genesis 45:7

I followed Mitch and Sierra through the destroyed city for about a mile. It
was slow going navigating the ruble of destroyed buildings and fires that
still dotted the city. We stayed low, avoiding people, most of whom were
still writhing in pain from the stings of the creatures. The invaders seemed
to have swept through the city and kept moving, but we stayed as hidden
as possible, just in case.

After a while, we came across an empty army truck idling in the middle of the street. It was huge with six large wheels, making it even taller.
There were narrow rectangular windows along the sides of the truck, with
locked boxes under them on the sides.

We didn't see the soldiers who'd been traveling in it anywhere, so
Mitch bundled Sierra into one of the jump seats in the back; she was
asleep within minutes. I climbed into the passenger seat where I had more
options to escape, just in case.

We drove out of the city, wanting to get away from the smoke and
the screaming. The roads were empty, except for the occasional crashed

or burning car. Mitch looked grim as he drove, his knuckles white as he gripped the wheel. I noticed a bottle of water shoved into the space between my seat and the boxy barrier that separated the driver's space from mine. Pulling it out, I saw it was unopened and offered it to Mitch.

"No, I'm fine," he muttered, his voice tight.

I opened the bottle and sipped on the water as we drove onto a highway and headed east.

"Ah, no," Mitch muttered. He slowed the truck to a stop. The road ahead was filled with abandoned vehicles. Turning the truck to the left side of the road, he drove on the grassy area that separated the two sides of the highway.

"You seem familiar with driving this thing," I remarked, glancing sideways at him.

"Two tours in Iraq when I was younger," he answered. "I drove an MRAP much like this one. You can drive through any danger in one of these bad boys." His voice dropped as he whispered, "Just another coincidence."

I had no idea what MRAP meant; I guessed it was some kind of army truck, or whatever he was talking about. Reluctant to expose my ignorance, I latched onto his whispered comment.

"What coincidences do you mean?"

Mitch was silent for a moment.

"When the Global Union soldiers came to our town, they rounded up all of the women."

"Yes, you said the younger ones were taken to Spokane."

"There was nothing I could do to protect my wife or Sierra. It all happened so fast—they came in the middle of the night—broke down the front door. Before I knew what was happening, they took them away. We live in town, and I was able to make my way to the main street where they had gathered the women and were loading them onto trucks."

He stopped talking to maneuver the truck off to the side of the highway to get around a snarl of abandoned cars. I scanned the area, fearful of an ambush from the creatures or the Global Union soldiers, but we drove on unchecked.

Mitch continued. "I overheard some of the soldiers talking about where the women were being taken. I guess that's the first coincidence, that I would hear that conversation and know where they were going. Not really a coincidence, though." He shook his head and laughed. "No, not really a coincidence. Cheryl has believed for a longer time than me. She kept telling me that He's in control of it all."

"Cheryl? Is that your wife?" I asked.

"Yeah. I'm stubborn. When all those people disappeared back fifteen years ago, I wouldn't believe, but she did. She's been a real believer ever since then."

I wondered if he was talking about the Christians. According to Tomas, they were all killed . . . beheaded.

"I thought that was outlawed. Are you a 'real believer,' too?" I blurted out.

Mitch nodded. "It was . . . it is. I know it's all true, but I'm not as into it as my wife. Cheryl showed me that the Bible has answers that will keep us safe. For me, it's all about my family, really. We managed for the last decade to keep our heads down and stay off the radar, but that's ended. The real bad judgments have begun."

What did he mean? I was about to ask, but he kept talking. "Cheryl knows more about what's supposed to happen than I do—she warned me about the demon army. That's the next coincidence."

Bile rose in my throat as I remembered the terror of last night. "Was that what those things were? Demons?"

"Yes, it's one of the judgments," Mitch asserted. "It couldn't have happened at a better time. That's another 'coincidence.' There's no way I could have rescued Sierra without their help."

"Help?" I shuddered remembering the reeking smell of death as I was gripped by one of the fearsome creatures.

"Yeah, they only sting those who aren't sealed. Everyone who's stung is going to suffer for the next few months. I didn't know how much I really believed until the past few days. I guess I really am one of the sealed, a believer. Hard to see those things and not believe there is a God."

Mitch stopped talking suddenly, awkwardly, then he spoke again in a strangled whisper, "Those demons attacking now is gonna give me the chance to rescue my whole family and find a good place to hunker down." Mitch grimaced. "I had no hope or idea of how I was going to get them back, but now I do!"

My mind raced as the truck rumbled down the highway. I glanced out of the passenger window and saw nothing but devastation. "What do you mean that the people who got stung are going to suffer for the next few months?" I asked numbly.

"This is one of God's judgments," Mitch replied. "These demons are going to be around tormenting people."

I replayed the attack of the demon horde from last night in my mind. "That can happen again?" I knew panic only makes a bad situation worse, but I couldn't help myself. My heart started racing, my head felt like it was going to explode, and I started hyperventilating.

"Hey, calm down! Listen, I know they're terrifying!" Mitch spoke loudly but confidently. "But you don't have to be afraid of them. Think about it! Did you get stung?"

I felt his hand on my shoulder, patting it in an attempt to comfort.

"Listen, you're going to be okay. If they didn't sting you, it means they can't sting you." He kept repeating that over and over, almost like he was talking to himself. "You must be sealed."

"One of them grabbed me but flung me aside and muttered that word: 'Sealed.' What does it mean?"

Mitch looked over at me before turning his attention back to the highway. "All I know is what the Book says. The demons have the power to torment people for five months, but they're not allowed to touch those who have the seal of God on their foreheads."

"What does that even mean? I don't have anything on my forehead."

Mitch shook his head. "I'm really not sure. Do you believe?"

"Believe in what?" I asked.

"Do you know, like trust in Jesus?"

Jesus. It had been so long since I'd heard that Name. I closed my eyes wearily and saw Daphne's smiling face as she taught me to read from her Bible. Thankfully, I'd found it with my clothes in the trash can back in Spokane. Now, it was tucked into the inner pocket of my jacket. For the first time in days, I knew what someone was talking about, sort of.

"I know about Him. Is that what you mean?"

Mitch laughed. "Not quite. I've known about Him for my whole life. My dad was a preacher. I rejected all of that stuff when I joined the Army. I never thought about it seriously again until after the disappearances. My parents, my brothers, and my sister all disappeared. Cheryl and I had gone home to visit with Sierra. She was just a toddler, so she doesn't remember. We were eating dinner, and they all just vanished. Cheryl was hysterical for days. I had to take care of Sierra. The world fell apart."

I thought about Dominic and what he had taught the Chosen at the Compound. "I thought the only ones who vanished were the ones who were deficient in some way."

"No, the only ones who vanished were the Christians. There were many left behind who said they were Christians, but the ones who really believed in Jesus, like my family, those were the ones who vanished."

I thought about that for a few minutes. "And those creatures, demons, are going to keep attacking people for five months?"

"I think so."

We crossed the river, and Mitch drove the military truck around abandoned cars, up a ramp, and then to the right. I kept a lookout for the demon army. Mitch thought the Guard might be around.

"They like to ambush the unwary," he said in a clipped, tone. "Hopefully the whole stinkin' lot of them are rolling around in terrible pain from those demonic creatures."

Mitch turned the MRAP down a residential street.

What are we doing?" I asked.

"Making a pit stop." He drove slowly, looking around carefully before making a choice. Putting the vehicle into reverse, Mitch backed up into the driveway of a house and crashed the truck right through the garage doors. I screamed in surprise more than terror. I was beginning to trust this man.

"Give me a few minutes to make sure the house is clear. Lock the door, Dani." Mitch pulled a gun out from the belt at the small of his back and got out of the truck.

Two minutes later, he reappeared. "All clear. Let's go!" he ordered. I scrambled out of the truck, holding the door open as Mitch tenderly helped Sierra out.

"There's a bathroom inside to the left. I'll stay here with the truck while you girls do what you need to do. Then we'll hit the road again."

I went into the house, helping Sierra. She was feeling nauseous and groggy. She told me they had given her drugs to keep her in line. She didn't look very good. I got her to the bathroom and left her there alone, while I explored the rest of the house.

The kitchen was easy to find. It was a mess. Someone had already been here scavenging, and stuff was piled up all over the floor and the counters. I turned on the tap at the sink. Unbelievably, there was water! Looking around, I found a big plastic bottle on one of the counters. I grabbed it and filled it with water.

"Hey, I'm done!" I heard Sierra call. Quickly, I made my way back to the bathroom. When I was done, I hurried back to the shattered garage, fearful they had left me behind, but they were still there waiting by the vehicle.

Sierra returned to her place in the back, and I pulled myself up into the passenger seat again, buckling the seatbelt just as Mitch pulled back out onto the street.

"Let's go get Cheryl," he said.

FLOOD

Chapter 10

And about these also Enoch, in the seventh generation from Adam, prophesied, saying, "Behold, the Lord came with many thousands of his holy ones, to execute judgment upon all" . . . So Enoch the prophet named his son, Methuselah, which means, "When he dies, it shall be sent."

Jude 1:14–15, Genesis 5:21

When I arrived at the gathering, Japheth tenderly helped me out of the cart. He set me on the ground but kept his hands on my waist. I stared up at him.

"I've never seen such beautiful brown eyes, Ariana. They have just a hint of green."

I felt warm, despite the breeze blowing my hair in my face. He brushed it aside.

"Japheth, we could use your help if you can tear yourself away from Ariana," his mother called, grinning widely and shaking her head.

"Of course, Mother," Japheth said. As he took my hand in his, we walked over to his parents' cart. Each of us took something, and we made our way to an area where tables had been set up under a group of trees.

I stuck close to Japheth, who seemed to know everyone in the crowd that surrounded the family. He proudly introduced me to each of them before leading me toward the shade of the trees.

"Ariana! Ariana! Come sit with us!" Taina yelled, waving at Japheth and me. Over the past few weeks, I had gotten to know Taina and Nua, the wives of Japheth's brothers. Nua sat with Taina on a yellow- and white-spotted blanket. Nua waved, too. Their eagerness put me at ease. Shem sat next to Nua. It was hard to believe he was Japheth's brother; they looked so different. His black hair and deep brown skin contrasted with his brother's light features.

"Sit next to us," Nua ordered, telling Taina and Ham to move over.

"You need to keep your wife in line," Ham teased Shem. "She's so bossy!"

Nua pushed a wooden cup into my hands as I sat down. "Here's some wine Noah made. It's one of his special wines. It's very light."

I took a sip. It was excellent. Noah took great pride in his vineyard. Nua poured another wooden cup and offered it to Taina.

"No," Ham said, pushing the cup back. "Taina and I won't be drinking any of Father's special *vintages*. Actually, I think we're going to join one of the other groups."

Abruptly, Ham stood up and told his wife to follow him. Taina's eyebrows were drawn together, but she got up and followed him, turning to shake her head at us and shrug her shoulders.

"What just happened?" I wondered. "Did I do something to offend him?"

"It's not you," Japheth responded. "Ham gets into strange moods. He'll get over it and be fine."

"Until the next time," Shem laughed.

We sipped our wine and chatted as we waited for Noah to speak. Finally, he and Laelah made their way to the front of the crowd.

Noah welcomed everyone and started talking about the ark and the plans God had given him for preparing for the coming judgment. "There is plenty of room in the ark for all of us!" Noah assured us. "And we will have plenty of work to do as we care for the animals the Creator will send. There will be two of each kind, male and female, of the land animals but seven pairs of the clean animals and birds, so we may have some for sacrifices to the Creator, while leaving the others to multiply and fill the earth."

Looking over at Japheth, I felt an earnest sense of gratitude. Without knowing me, he had rescued me from the hands of the Magistrate. He saved me from death, or worse. I shivered and scooted closer to him, so our shoulders touched. I was safe with him. More than safe.

Dappled light played on his tanned face as I peeked over at him. I noticed the highlights in his hair, bleached white in the sun's light. He was gazing across the small meadow at his father, and a smile creased his face.

"You're proud of him, aren't you?" I asked.

"Yes, my father is a man his sons can look up to," he stated. His smile faded just then as Ham cackled with laughter, his wife Taina joining in.

Just then Noah began speaking. Japheth looked up, took my hand in his and kissed it, as his father's voice boomed across the field. Noah said a few more words to the crowd, and the meeting ended.

Men and boys began setting up long tables. Baskets of food and casks of beer and wine were pulled from the wagons that brought the families to the celebration. We had come in two wagons, both filled with good things from Laelah's storage room. Everyone brought something to share. I watched, smiling, as Laelah directed people. Soon everything was ready and people sat down at the tables to eat and drink.

After the meal, people started playing music, and the dancing began. I was unfamiliar with the particular dances, so I stood by and watched. A young woman about my age joined me.

"Have you enjoyed the celebration so far?" she asked.

She was a bit taller than me, so I had to look up. Bright, yellow hair framed her beautiful face and cascaded down her back in waves. She was smiling broadly, making her blue eyes crease with humor.

"I am, thank you! I am Ariana."

"I am Nua's sister, Eritza."

"Oh, I should have known! You have the same lovely hair color!"

"Yes, there are seven daughters in our family. My younger sisters are over there by the water." Eritza pointed to the water's edge. Many of the younger children were wading in the creek while the older people danced or mingled. Although there were quite a few children there, her sisters were easily identified. They had the same cascading yellow hair.

"I have no sisters or brothers. It must be wonderful to always have someone around. Do you live far from here?"

She shook her head negatively. "We live in the village over the hill there. Most of us do, actually. Well, at least for the time being." Her smile faded a bit.

Methuselah had told me the entire group here in the meadow would be going into the ark when it was time. "Are you worried about going?" I asked. "Methuselah has reassured me many times, but I must admit, I'm anxious about it."

"Have you seen it yet?"

"Yes, of course. Its size is incredible!"

She laughed. "Yes, there is plenty of room for all of us, and the animals! It has taken many years to build. Of course, there are many who do not believe Noah, but these do." She gestured to the people around us.

"I like to think about the animals," Eritza went on. "Noah said the Creator will call them all to board the ark. My sisters and I love to imagine what that will be like! Lions and lambs together on the same boat? Will we have to keep the peace?" She chuckled.

We chatted for a while before Japheth came to get me. "Mother's not feeling well, Ariana. Would you like to stay for a while longer, or go back with the rest of the family?"

"Oh, I am sorry to hear that! I'll go back now!" I hugged my new friend before following Japheth back to the others. I noticed Noah and Laelah were already in their wagon, headed down the path with Shem and Nua. Waiting for us in the second wagon were Ham and Taina, already seated.

The journey home was quiet. Ham slept, leaning against his wife. It felt strange after the liveliness of the gathering we had just left.

When we arrived home, Noah was pulling his wagon back out onto the road.

"Father, what's wrong?" Japheth asked.

"Your mother is in a lot of pain. I'm going back to the Celebration to fetch the healer."

Ham stirred awake and spoke up. "You go with Father, Japheth. I'll take the horses and put them in their stalls. Taina can help Nua tend to mother while you're gone."

The trip back to the meadow was jolting as Noah lengthened the reigns, allowing the horses to gallop. Noah's face was stiff with concern, and he did not speak much, even in response to Japheth's questions.

Bodies. The meadow was filled with bodies. We had not been gone more than an hour, but everything had changed.

Bodies lay in heaps across the field. Noah and Japheth jumped down from the wagon. Japheth helped me down and held me close. "Stay next to me," he ordered in a harsh whisper. We turned to follow Noah.

"This is the Nephilim's work," Noah said flatly as he bent to check a man on the ground in front of him. His throat had been sliced open. Women and children lay alongside the men. No pity. No mercy.

I saw the lovely yellow hair of my new friend floating in the creek. Without thinking, I raced over and tried to pull her out. She had one of her sisters clutched in her arms.

Screaming for Japheth to come and help, I yanked both of the girls toward the bank. Noah and Japheth ran to help me. Her sister was dead, but Eritza was still breathing.

"She's been stabbed," Japheth said. I could see the bloody gash across her stomach.

Her eyes fluttered open and she moaned. "Eritza, who did this?" I asked, cradling her in my arms. Her blue eyes fixed on mine, and then the life left them.

"She's dead!" I wailed, clutching her.

Japheth and Noah were searching the meadow for Methuselah.

"He is not here," Noah said. Turning to Japheth, he said tersely, "We don't have time to go back and get your brothers. "They slaughtered the healer, and they have taken Methuselah. I must go to the city."

Noah was a gentle man, but his face shone with ominous wrath. Japheth silently wrapped an arm around me and pulled me close. I'd never seen him look so fierce. "What about Ariana? We can't leave her here, and I don't want to take her into the city."

"There's no hope for it," Noah was already pulling on the reigns. "Laelah is in pain, and we must get to Methuselah in time. You remember the prophecy: when Methuselah dies, the end comes! The Magistrate doesn't believe the Creator will flood the whole earth. He plans to kill Methuselah and boast when nothing happens. Then he will rid his kingdom of the knowledge of the Creator by destroying everyone who knows him."

We reached Sumeria hours later. Noah raced our horses toward the stadium, where not long ago Japheth had raced in the Festival. The bellows of a great crowd roaring with cursing and cheers.

As soon as Noah pulled up the horses, he threw the reigns aside and leaped from the wagon, running to the stadium. Japheth jumped down and pulled me after him.

What met our eyes was as terrible a sight as the massacre in the field. In the center of the arena was a giant golden statue. At its feet were the bloody pieces of Methuselah's body.

"They've killed him!" I screamed.

At the foot of the statue stood the Magistrate, hovering gleefully over the gruesome scene, his mouth opened in mocking blasphemy against the Creator and praising the name of Malumek, his god. His voice carried out to the raucous crowd. "Me-thu-se-lah." He mockingly saluted the body parts with each syllable. "It was foretold that he would die in the year of judgment. If there is a Creator, let Him show Himself. I dare Him to bring His judgment on us!"

Raising his bloodied fist to the darkened skies, the Magistrate laughed victoriously. Noah pushed through the crowd with ease, making his way to the center of the arena, where he confronted the wicked ruler.

"Mock away! Call out to your worthless god, Malumek, when the waters overflow the earth. Scream for his help when the flood overtakes you, and you drown in its depths. Who will help you? You will cry out to the Creator, but it will be too late!"

The crowd roared with jeering laughter as Noah left the arena. Their screams of victory followed us as we left the city.

FIRE

Chapter 11

*I looked, and there before me was a pale horse! Its rider was
named Death, and Hades was following close behind him.
They were given power over a fourth of the earth to kill by
sword, famine and plague, and by the wild beasts of the earth.*
Revelation 7:8

It took us a day to get near the place where Mitch thought Cheryl was
being held, a former military base east of Spokane. Major sections of the
highway were almost impassable. Either snarls of abandoned vehicles
blocked our way, or the road was too heavily damaged to pass. Mitch had
to take side roads around those points. We saw no one as we drove.

"Why are there no people? So many buildings and houses but not a
single person." I was puzzled.

"Between the war and the Tribulation, this area has been devastated,"
Mitch replied.

"I've heard that word before, I think."

"The Tribulation?" Sierra piped up. "It's the Bible's description of the
time between the Vanishings and when Jesus returns for those who follow
Him. My mom told me all about it. We are in the "time of Tribulation,"
of God's judgment. God's wrath is finally being poured out on the world

for rejecting Him and His ways. It's a major wake-up call. It's time for everyone to turn back to God."

I had heard bits and pieces of this from Daphne and her book, but it had seemed like a story then. Now, looking out the truck window at the piles of debris around us, it all seemed too real.

"Yeah, Cheryl had us go to a Bible study about it. The Tribulation includes the judgments described in the Book of Revelation, natural disasters, war, and those creatures. In this area," his hand swept over the view through the windshield, "it began with an earthquake then Mt. Rainier—that mountain you see over there. It's a volcano. It erupted; thousands of people died. The people who were left had to fend for themselves because the government was busy fighting the war."

As Mitch continued describing the terrifying events of the previous few years, I sat in the passenger seat, stunned. Back at the Compound, I'd been sheltered from much of what he detailed. I could hardly comprehend what had been happening in the past few years.

"Horrible stuff has been going on all over the world. Devastation. Over a fourth of the world's population died, mostly as a result of the famine of the last two years," he concluded.

"And you're saying all of this is God's judgment on the world?" I asked.

"Yes," Mitch replied thoughtfully. An odd look passed over his face and then quickly disappeared. I wondered what he was thinking.

"I know it sounds bad, Dani," Sierra answered. "But all of this was foretold a long time ago. God is patient, and He's given humanity a long time to turn to Him, but we only moved farther and farther away. Things got bad after the Vanishing when all the Christians disappeared, but they got *really* bad when President Bellomo's peace deal was signed between Israel and the Global Union. Mom said that was the thing that started all of this stuff, and it was all predicted in the Bible."

I stared at her as she spoke and noticed she was shivering. What she was saying sounded a lot like one of Dominic's rants. "Mom said God is punishing the world for rejecting Him and His ways.

"Are you sick?" I asked. Mitch glanced over at me and then back over his shoulder at Sierra. She nodded her head and leaned it against the door.

Mitch swore under his breath. I thought he was upset Sierra was sick, until I turned back and looked at the road ahead of us. The bridge crossing the river was gone.

"What do we do now?" I asked.

"There's a road that runs along the river. I'm going to take that and hopefully, find somewhere we can stop." He turned the truck around expertly and took the next exit off of the highway.

It was getting dark when Mitch turned the truck into a long drive and pulled to a stop in front of a large brick building. "Stay here," he commanded as he got out of the truck. I watched him in silence. Sierra was asleep or unconscious. I wasn't sure which. He disappeared around the back of the building and came back a few minutes later.

"Let's go." He pulled the seat back and shook Sierra. "You have to get up, sweetie. We need to find Mom, but you need some medicine and rest first." With some difficulty, he got her up. I grabbed the empty bottles in case there was running water inside of the building.

"This was some kind of medical building. It's been ransacked, but it's vacant." Mitch said. As soon as we got in the front door, I could see the place had been looted. It was a mess. Mitch led the way up a flight of stairs. We entered a long corridor and came to the end where it opened up into a large sitting room. One of the walls was a series of windows overlooking the river. I could just make out a park across from us on the other side.

Mitch tenderly led Sierra to a couch. "Lie here. I'm going to go through the building and see if there's anything useful left. Dani will stay with you."

He motioned me to follow him, and we left the waiting room and went into the corridor. "Can I have those bottles?" he asked. "I'm going to see if I can get some water. I doubt there's much left here, but this was a pretty desolate area to begin with, so maybe I'll be able to find something."

Silently, I handed him the empty bottles and went back in the room.

Sierra was curled up on the couch, her body shaking with fever. We'd had some medicine back at the Compound for fevers, but Dominic only allowed the doctor to give medication with his approval. I wondered what was happening back at the Compound now.

For the first time, I allowed myself to think about Daphne's cold body laid out on our kitchen table. I clenched my eyes closed as I remembered gently turning her over. Both her eyes had been swollen dark purple from Jack's ready fists. One of her arms was clearly broken, likely trying to defend herself from vicious hits with the bloody bat tossed on the floor next to her body.

You'll never find me, Jack, I thought bitterly. Jack had never been my real father. I had been lied to my whole life about my father, about Dominic, and about life outside the compound. It had all been false. But now that I was in the real world, everything felt so unbelievable and strange. I looked out the window, but it was completely dark now. Not even any stars or moonlight.

I tried to make sense of all that I had learned since I had left the Compound, from the devastated landscape and cities controlled by the Global Union, to the information I had gleamed from Tomas and Mitch and Sierra. Sweat broke out on the back of my neck and armpits as I recalled the demon creatures. They were still out there somewhere, tormenting humanity . . . or what was left of it.

I hadn't asked for any of this. I felt anger building inside me against a god who would allow such evil to torment people. It felt good to be angry.

"I found some stuff," Mitch said as he came back into the room with a box. He set it down on the floor by us and reached into his pocket. Lighting a match, he pulled a fat candle out of the box and lit it.

"Let there be light!" he joked. I didn't smile.

"What else did you find?" I asked.

"There was one room in the basement that was intact. I think it might have belonged to the janitor. He had a locker full of stuff."

Miraculously, Mitch pulled some chocolate bars out of the box and handed me one. I'd only had chocolate once in my life. Slowly, I peeled back the wrapper and took a small bite. Some kind of nut was wedged in its creamy goodness. I closed my eyes as I savored it.

"I also found some aspirin for Sierra and some water." I watched in silence as he woke his daughter and tenderly cared for her. My anger toward God twisted into something else as I watched the two of them. Here there was real love. *Maybe there was something good that would come out of all this?*

"Will that help her?" I asked.

"It should." He pulled a jacket out of the box and covered her with it before turning back to me.

"Dani, I want to ask you something. The military base isn't too far from here, but I don't want to risk your safety. Would you stay here with Sierra while I go try to rescue Cheryl?"

Panicked thoughts bombarded my mind, and I considered the very real possibility that he might not come back. One thing I knew was that no one could be trusted. I racked my mind for a way to convince him to let us go with him. "But have you considered the possibility that we've been seen?"

"What do you mean?"

"I mean that there's likely to be *some* people around here. It's not as bad as what we've seen traveling. We might have been spotted. What if someone sees the truck and comes here to investigate? I have no way of protecting your daughter. I would run." I spoke in a high-pitched, childish tone, hoping he would realize what he was asking of a teenage girl and change his mind.

He pursed his lips together as he listened to me. "I hadn't thought of that. I just wanted to give her time to rest, but you're right."

He moved away from the couch and pulled a couple of chairs close to the candle. "Let's get some rest for a few hours. Then we'll all go together and find Cheryl."

He put the chairs together and motioned for me to lie down on the make-shift bed. "I found a couple of jackets in the locker. Here's another one." Mitch bent over and pulled another jacket from the box. "It's not a blanket, but it'll help."

He tucked it around my shoulders and said goodnight. Tears welled up in my eyes and ran down my face, so I turned my head into the jacket to hide. I fell asleep right away.

"Time to get up," Mitch said quietly before moving over to wake Sierra. Wearily we made our way out and got into the truck. Mitch started the engine and pulled back out onto the road. It was still pitch black outside.

"What time is it?" I asked.

"3:00 a.m."

We drove for a while before Mitch came to a stop. It was so dark; I couldn't see a thing.

"Stay here while I take a look," Mitch ordered before opening his door and getting out of the truck. He flipped on a flashlight, and I watched it flitter back and forth. A roaring sound came through the slightly opened window.

"Sounds like water," Sierra whispered. I looked back at her. She had been groggy when we got up, but she seemed to be doing better. About twenty minutes later, I saw the light headed back our way.

Mitch pulled open his door and leaned in. "Get out. We're going to have to walk from here." He pulled back his seat so Sierra could exit. I pushed open my door and stepped out of the truck. It was so dark, I couldn't see much at all.

"Where're we going?" Sierra asked.

"We're going to cross the river. All of the other bridges we've passed were down. This one's intact."

"Why are we getting out of the truck?" I asked.

"It's a railway bridge for trains and some numb nut barricaded the head of the bridge on this side. We can't drive across, but we can walk. Hopefully we can find another vehicle on the other side of the river," Mitch explained.

"If they keep prisoners here, aren't there guards?" Sierra hung back against the truck.

"I checked; there are none from what I can tell."

As we neared the bridge, the roar of the water intensified. The light from Mitch's flashlight shone on the dark metal trusses of the bridge.

It took us a long time to get across, but we finally made it to the other side.

"There's light up ahead there!" Sierra whispered. In the distance, we could see electric lights piercing through in the dark.

"I think that's the military base," Mitch said.

As we walked in silence toward the light, I fell behind Mitch and Sierra, afraid of what was waiting for us up ahead.

FLOOD

Chapter 12

My beloved is mine, and I am his.

Song of Songs 2:16

The massacre at the gathering, the journey to the city, Methuselah's murder—it all felt like a nightmare.

When we finally returned home, we sighed with relief to find Laelah had recovered from her illness with Nua's help, although she could hardly lift her head

"I am feeling so much better. It must have been something I ate." Laelah leaned against the headboard of her bed. "Where is the healer?" She looked around the family to the empty doorway. "Why have you been gone so long"

Embracing her, Noah broke down. With difficulty, Japheth told the other family members what had happened, and everyone joined Noah in grieving. The days that followed were heavy and sorrowful.

Noah called the family together for a meeting about a week later. Ham and Taina straggled in late and sat together on the empty bench next to us.

"Oh, Ariana," she leaned over and hugged me. "You're taking this so hard."

My eyes felt hot and tired. I couldn't even respond; I just shook my head and struggled to listen to Noah, vainly trying not to replay the horrific images of Methuselah's body chopped up in that wicked place.

Noah sat in his favorite chair. He looked terrible. Dark shadows underlined his bloodshot eyes.

"We all are heartbroken for our people and for Methuselah. You know the prophecy his father Enoch made: 'When he dies, judgment comes.' The Creator wants us to pack and get ready to enter the ark tomorrow."

We had been prepared to go for some time, but no one had expected it to be so soon.

Noah instructed us to get some sleep before we headed to the ark. As we walked back into the house, Japheth lamented that we would not be able to spend one night in our wedding bower.

"Oh, I didn't think of that! What a shame!" I exclaimed, thinking of how devotedly Japheth had labored to finish the bower for our wedding night.

Laelah, following closely behind us, overheard. "Oh, surely husband, we can give them a proper wedding? Before we go to the ark?"

Noah stood on the porch leading to the entrance of the family home. He looked haggard and worn. Closing his eyes a moment, he lifted his face up to the sky, drew in a deep, ragged breath before turning to look at Japheth and me. "Of course, you must take advantage of our last night here." For the first time in a week, Noah's eyes sparkled again, briefly.

"Ariana, go change your clothing. I believe you have something special you wanted to wear? Laelah, you and the other women can prepare something simple, some cheese and bread and wine. Yes, some wine will be good. The Creator has given it to gladden our hearts. Tonight, we celebrate your love and marriage."

I went to my room and looked at the clothes I'd packed in a carved wooden box. Nothing seemed right to me. I heard a knock on the door.

"Come in," I called. Nua came in with something white in her hands.

"I wondered if you might like to wear this," she said softly. "I made it for my sister."

"Oh, Nua, it's beautiful."

It was a simple white dress made of the softest material I'd ever felt. Silently, I hugged her and whispered my thanks. Nua's sweet sister would never have her wedding night.

I put the dress on, my hands shaking.

"Are you nervous?" Nua joked.

"Honestly, I am feeling so many different things right now."

"I know. There's never been a night like this in the world before. The night before it all ends." She sat on the bed and patted the spot next to her. I sank down next to her, and she put her arm around me. "But it's also the night where everything begins for you and Japheth!"

We sat together for a few minutes in silence.

"Ariana, Nua!" Laelah called from the other room. "We're ready!"

I got up, pulling Nua up with me, and we joined the others outside in the small orchard. The trees were covered with pinkish-white blossoms.

Japheth and I faced each other, our hands joined together as pink and white petals fluttered in the soft breeze around us. Dappled sunlight shone through the leaves with a special glow. I looked into Japheth's dark brown eyes and squeezed his hands.

Noah asked the traditional questions, and we responded with the traditional answers, sealing our promises with joyous kisses and laughter. We shared a bit of food and a glass of wine with the family before going to our wedding bower.

That night, I began to learn about marriage and love. That night, in the midst of terrible sorrow and fearful anticipation of what was coming upon the world, Japheth and I discovered joy and pleasure in married life.

I woke the next morning in the arms of my husband, and despite all the horror of the past few months, felt peace. *We are together.* I gazed at Japheth's profile in the early morning light and smiled sleepily as his dark brown eyes opened, and he turned his face toward mine.

"Good morning," he whispered, lightly kissing my mouth. A horn blew in the distance, and he pulled away with a sigh.

"Is it time to go already?" I asked, desperately wanting to stay where we were and never leave.

"Yes, I'm afraid it is." The next kiss was filled with passion and promise, and then we reluctantly left our wedding bower for the house.

Laelah prepared a simple meal for us, and we all ate gratefully. Instead of the heavy silence of the last week, Japheth's brothers gently teased him about the previous night, which made everyone smile and my face turn hot.

After we finished eating, Noah asked to pray. "This is our last time around this table, where Laelah and I raised our sons. This is our last time in the home where each of them brought their wives and added to our family number."

His eyes filled with tears as he raised his hands up to heaven. He spoke of those who were to have entered the ark with us, thanking the Creator for the comfort of knowing they were with Him.

When Noah finished speaking, we left the table for the last time, bundled up with extra blankets against the chilly morning, and climbed into the wagons for the ride to the nearby valley where the ark waited. As Japheth drove our wagon, he talked about all of his friends who had helped the family build the large boat over the years. Tears ran down his face as he mourned their deaths. No one had ever expected it would only be eight of us entering the huge boat.

Japheth worried about the Nephilim. "Father is not worried," he told me. "But the Magistrate knows what is to happen. I can't help but think he will try to stop us somehow."

I agreed and shuddered. As our wagon lumbered along the track made over the many years the family had traveled to the valley, I kept watch for any sign of trouble. The horses were pulling the wagon up the last hillock when I spotted movement in the woods to our left and alerted Japheth. "There! Look!"

But to our relieved amazement, there were no soldiers marching toward us but hundreds of animals. All the wagons pulled to a stop at the top of the hill as we sat and took in the incredible scene below us in the valley. The ark towered over the west side of the valley; the east side was filled with creatures advancing toward it. The noise was deafening. We sat watching the scene unfold before us, marveling over the approaching creatures.

"Look!" I pointed to the lumbering yellow-spotted giants that appeared right beside our wagon.

"Those are young giraffes," Japheth observed. We enjoyed watching the diversity of creatures, many strange and unknown, for awhile before continuing to the ark. The men had brought the clean animals to the valley a few days before. I saw them in an enclosure in the field next to the huge boat. God had instructed Noah to take more of the clean animals than the unclean because we would need some of them for sacrifice.

Japheth nudged me. "Look at the lambs." There were a few of them on top of a pile of hay. I laughed watching their antics for a few moments in the bright sun before we headed into the ark. Japheth led me around, showing me what the men had added in the last month.

"Methuselah had a brilliant idea for piping water into the troughs in the section over here. We have one central tub we fill with water, and these bronze pipes carry the water to all of the animals in this section."

He took my hand and led me up the ramp to the top floor of the ark. Each of the three levels of the boat was the same height. The family quarters were at the top. As we walked up the ramp, I wondered what it would be like once the animals were on board and the door was shut. We passed shelves of provisions neatly stacked in specially made racks designed by Noah. There were rows of jars: wine, oil, and honey, even *shekhar* made from various grains. Dates and other fruits had been dried and put into clay pots.

As we entered the family quarters, I noticed the area for preparing food. I walked over and ran my hand on the wooden surfaces where we would cook, spotting the ingenious oven designed by Shem. It had taken him quite a while to figure out a way for us to heat food and water, but he drew on his skill working with pottery.

"This is amazing!" I exclaimed. Three vases acted as chimneys, which directed hot air from the brazier below.

"Ariana, look here!" Japheth walked across to the doorway of our compartment just off of the family living space. Each of the brothers had designed his own living space, and each reflected his individual character. The youngest, Ham, was inclined to do only what was necessary. Taina followed his lead; their apartment was functional and tidy. Shem, I was learning, was especially devoted to the Creator. He and Nua had decorated their living quarters with a large painting of life as they imagined it in Eden before the fall.

As I entered our compartment, I marveled again at its warmth and beauty. Japheth was a fine craftsman. Across from the entrance was an alcove. Vines bursting with flowers were carved on the frame. Within the alcove was a plush couch, piled with colorful pillows. My favorite blanket was draped on the right side. A table in front of the couch held a tray with the most exquisite goblets I have ever seen. I picked one up to admire the dark veins that ran through the golden wood.

"They're made from a small tree that grows in clusters. Do you remember the family box, that holds the treasures from the First Ones? It's made of the same kind of wood. When I saw Shem and Ham bringing it onto the ark, it occurred to me I could make a beautiful gift for my bride using the same idea."

"It is lovely." Japheth moved closer and I leaned up to thank him with a soft kiss.

"I have some other gifts for you," he whispered, pulling back from our embrace.

"I only need the giver." I smiled, pulling him back into my arms for another kiss.

"I love you," he whispered into my ear, brushing my cheek with his lips before moving away. "Let me show you the other gifts," Japheth said. He loved to give gifts to others and was always eager to see how they would be received.

He pulled a basket from under the table, which stood in front of the couch. It was filled with small pots of paint and brushes. "I deliberately left the alcove and other carvings unpainted, so you could finish them. I thought that would help pass the time."

He showed me around the rest of our small home, pointing out the carvings he had left undone. Even as I was thanking him, he bent down and pulled another box from under the bed.

"Inside here are slices of wood that I've smoothed out, so you can paint or draw on them. You draw so well; I thought you might even do a likeness of each of the family. Mother and Father would treasure such a thing."

There were dozens of small wooden panels inside the box. In whatever free time we would have, I knew I would enjoy using the creative gift.

"These gifts, and the way you have thought of every comfort and need I might have speaks deeply to my heart." Tears filled my eyes as I looked up at my husband. Incredibly, despite the terrible events we'd gone through and the unknown future ahead of us, I was completely happy in that moment.

FIRE

Chapter 13

*And I saw the souls of those who had been beheaded because
of their testimony of Jesus and because of the word of God, and
those who had not worshiped the beast or his image, and had
not received the mark on their forehead and on their hand.*

Revelation 20:4b

As we neared the military base, we could see light coming from a large
building near the main gate. Everything else was pitch black.

Mitch signaled for us to hide behind a bush while he went ahead to
check things out. We crouched close together, huddled in the dark, alone.
Sierra started to whisper something, but I elbowed her in the ribs. "Shh!"

It seemed like forever before Mitch came back. I could just make out
the dim glow of his flashlight as he crept back toward us.

"The building is a barracks, but I don't think anyone is there," he whispered. "We might as well go in and rest until daybreak. I'm not sure what
else we can do tonight."

Sierra and I followed him without a word. We passed unchallenged
through the gate shrouded by vines.

There didn't seem to be signs of anyone around, just the eerie light of
the barracks building amidst the dark and empty shadows. It seemed like

every light was on in the building, while every other building was dark. I felt the hairs stand up on the back of my neck.

Mitch led us through an open door to the right and we followed. I went in reluctantly. It was strange that the lights were on and the door opened. I was reminded of something Daphne used to mutter when my father called me. "'Step into my parlor,' said the spider to the fly."

Mitch locked the door behind us. The echo of our footsteps sounded like an erratic heartbeat. I wanted to turn and run, but Mitch and Sierra walked down the long hall and into a room. We were all on edge. *Where was everyone? It didn't look like there were any prisoners here, so where was Cheryl? Had we come all this way for nothing?*

"There's a room on either side of that bathroom. You two girls take this room. I'll take the other one. Once it's light outside, we'll take a look around and figure out what to do next."

With that, he said goodnight and left. Sierra looked sickly again, so I let her have the bed to herself and stretched out on the floor with a pillow, my back against the wall facing the door. We left the light on.

I woke up feeling cold and stiff. Sitting up, I could see daylight outside and decided to leave Sierra sleeping. I wanted to take a look around on my own. Mitch wasn't my father, so I didn't feel like I needed to say anything to him. I just left.

It was still eerie outside, even in the early daylight. The buildings were broken down, many slathered with vines so thick the architecture was indiscernible. I saw an airplane sitting on a kind of spike, pointed at the sky. I gazed past it to the clear blue sky and wondered what it was like to fly over the earth.

Turning, I noticed some planes sitting in a field to my right and decided to explore in that direction. There was a large, silver hangar next to the field; its massive door was slightly opened, and refrigerated air curled out of the opening like tendrils of fog.

I crept along the side of the building, looking for a window to peer into, but there was none. I moved carefully to the door and squatted down low, a trick I'd learned at the Compound. Moving at eye level might catch the attention of someone inside the building. Reaching forward, low to the ground, I peered around the edge of the door. I took a quick glance and pulled back, terrified. My stomach roiled. Inside the hangar were rows of stainless steel tables, holding bodies. Beheaded bodies.

I stood up, shaking, and hesitantly stepped into the hellish scene with my hand over my mouth and nose. The smell of decay mixed with disinfectant was sickening.

In the middle of the vast space was a platform, holding the tall frame of what I recognized, to my horror, was a guillotine. I moved toward it, stifling a scream. I stumbled to regain my bearings and ran out of the building.

Terrified, I tore back to the barracks and into the room where Sierra still slept. Gasping for breath, I shook her. "Wake up! Wake up now!" Then I rushed through the bathroom and banged on the adjoining door, screaming for Mitch. Panic overwhelmed me. I vomited on the tile floor, shrieking, "No! God, no!"

Mitch came into the bathroom and said something, but I couldn't hear him over my retching. He pulled me over to the toilet and held my hair back until I finished getting sick.

I pushed away from the toilet and lay in an exhausted heap on the cold tile floor. Some time passed before I felt a cold cloth gently wiping my face. It was Mitch. Opening my eyes, I saw his brown eyes dark with concern. Sierra stood shaking in the doorway, hair askew in all directions and eyes wide with feverish fear.

Mitch helped me stand, and I moved to the sink and washed the sour taste of bile from my mouth.

He handed me a small towel.

"We've got to get out of here right now." I had to push the words out one at a time.

"What is it?" Sierra whimpered, wrapping her arms around her body.

I shook my head at Mitch. He got it and bundled his daughter out into the other room. I could hear him murmur soothingly but could not make out the words. I closed the toilet lid and sat down waiting. My legs were shaking and my head felt strange, disconnected. My heart was racing, and I tried to breath slow, deep breaths. Mitch came in and gently closed the bathroom door behind him.

"Okay, she's resting now. What happened?"

Mechanically, I recited the events of my morning exploration. My voice broke when I described the bloody scene I'd witnessed.

Mitch pulled me up by the hand and led me into the room he'd been sleeping in. He sat me on the bed before turning to pick up his backpack. He rummaged through it and pulled out a metal flask.

"Drink some of this," he insisted.

I reached up and took a sip, choking and coughing as its fiery heat slashed at my sore throat. He told me to take another drink, and I did so grudgingly.

"You're in shock. You need to rest." He said.

I just handed him the flask and rolled myself in a ball on the bed. Mitch covered me with a blanket, whispering to rest and giving my shoulder a quick squeeze. "I'll be back soon."

I'm not sure how long it was before I passed out. I only know I slept because of the nightmares. In them, I walked into that deathly tomb. Headless bodies chased me through long hallways with no escape. I couldn't run fast enough as they grabbed at me with their pale hands. I woke up with a start, sitting straight up. The room was empty.

I got out of bed and went through the bathroom to the other room. Sierra was asleep again. Her face was flushed. I touched her forehead. She was burning up.

"Where is Mitch?" I whispered as I looked out the window. But I already knew.

🔥

My back slid down the side of the hangar as I sat down next to Mitch. I waited for him to speak. He didn't. Instead, he reached out his hand toward me and opened it. A yellow-gold band lay in the palm of his hand. It had a dark, swirling pattern on the outside and words engraved on the inside. I could only make out, "Never apart." My throat tightened.

"You found her?"

Mitch nodded, putting the ring between his fingers and rolling it. I saw his own ring, still on his left hand, had the same kind of swirling pattern, and I gently asked him about it.

"We thought it would be romantic to have part of the other's fingerprint on the bands—kind of like we were laying claim to each other. Her fingerprint is on my ring, and mine is on hers." He broke down sobbing.

So many questions raced through my mind as I thought of him going down the rows of bodies, looking for his wife. I pursed my lips together and just sat with him. I didn't know what to say.

I'm not sure how long we sat there, Mitch alternately sobbed and stared blindly ahead. Eventually, he wiped his eyes and said Sierra's name. "I need to get her," he said.

Alarm blasted intensely in my head. "You're not going to make her go in there?"

"What?" he looked dazed. "No, of course not. But I need to tell her that her mom is . . . " He stood up and wobbled for a few feet before his pace steadied. We made our way back to the barracks silently.

Before we got to the room, we could hear Sierra shrieking. Mitch ran to the door and smashed it open. She was curled up in the fetal position on the bed, her hands pressed against her abdomen.

"What's going on?" Mitch demanded.

"Dad, it hurts so bad! It hurts so bad!"

Mitch looked up at me questioningly. I shrugged my shoulders. "She was feverish before I went to find you."

He cursed and stooped to pick her up. "Let's go. We need to find some help."

I ran to the other room and grabbed his backpack then joined them, grabbing my own on the way out the door.

It was hard for me to keep up with Mitch, despite the fact he was carrying Sierra. Instead of heading to the gate, he headed in the opposite direction. Behind the building next to the barracks was a lot filled with cars. Mitch headed right for an old blue truck with a covered bed. I'd never seen a truck with a canopy before; all the ones at the Compound had been open. I hurried ahead to open the door for Mitch, who carefully helped Sierra into the back. She was still screaming.

As I moved around the truck to the passenger side, I scanned the area. Nothing.

"Get inside, quick," Mitch ordered. I obeyed. Neither of us spoke; it was pointless anyway, with Sierra screaming.

"I can't take much more," Mitch muttered as he backed out of the lot and drove out of the base. I wasn't sure if he was talking to me or not, so I just kept my mouth shut.

We drove down the mountain, and I watched the trees toss shadows on the road. After about an hour, Sierra finally stopped screaming and passed out. I could feel Mitch tense in the silence. I didn't know where we were going or what would happen next.

FLOOD

Chapter 14

Those that entered, male and female of all flesh,
entered as God had commanded him; and the LORD
closed it behind him.

Genesis 7:16

Early on the last morning, Laelah, Nua, Taina, and I went out to bathe in the stream not too far from the ark. The sky was tinged with pink as we dipped into the cool water. The air was oppressively hot, even though it was still early morning, making the water particularly refreshing. I scooped it up and slathered my face and arms as the others chattered together.

Wanting to be alone, I took a deep breath and dove under the water, swimming underneath the surface away from the others. I wondered what it would be like for all of the other people who refused to join us.

My underwater thoughts were interrupted by muffled shouts, which became piercing shrieks of terror as I came up out of the water.

"The Nephilim!" Nua was shouting over and over, pointing to the other side of the valley. Fear buffeted my mind in raging waves, and my chest constricted, forcing the air from my lungs. I gasped to get a breath. A terrified Taina was already out of the water, her robe clutched around her as she raced back toward the ark, her jet black hair swinging like a dark flag. Laelah got to shore next; she began running, yelling for help.

"Hurry, Ariana," Nua cried. I moved clumsily through the water. Images of the dead, slaughtered by the Nephilim, filled my mind. Despair enveloped me. I looked at Nua, her beautiful yellow hair piled in heavy wet heaps tumbling around her shoulders, and my mind flashed with images of her dead sister. I could not move.

"Come on, come on!" Nua screamed. Grabbing my hand, she yanked me along behind her to the shoreline and pulled me along toward the ark. I looked back at the hills behind us and saw Nephilim armies coming toward us.

"Don't look at them—run!" she ordered fiercely. I obeyed and ran along with her, desperately clutching her hand, my eyes focused on the boat ahead of us.

Nua and I got to the ramp just as horns blasted in the distance. Turning, I saw the massive army tearing toward us on their warhorses. Nua dropped my hand and ran up the ramp to her husband's side. I froze, looking back at the sight of the dark forces still approaching.

As I stood trembling at the base of the ramp, the ground beneath my bare feet rumbled. At first, I thought it was a vibration from the approaching army, but the shaking grew stronger and the ground between us began to tear. Huge gaps of raw, red dirt swallowed up the grassy surface between the ark and the army.

Just then, Japheth appeared by my side, scooped me up into his arms, and moved quickly back up the ramp. I huddled in his embrace, trembling with fear. It did not take long to reach the others, and they surrounded me, murmuring soothing words. Laelah, mother to us all, rubbed my shoulder comfortingly.

"Look!" Shem exclaimed. We all turned. The large rift in the ground on the valley floor between us and the Nephilim army was spreading wider. Japheth put me down, and I could feel the wooden ramp vibrating beneath my bare feet. Dust began to billow from the large hole forming in the valley, like a dense curtain, hiding the attackers from our view. Thunder rumbled, and the temperature dropped suddenly as a cold wind swirled around us.

"It is time for us to go into the ark." Noah shouted to be heard above the tumult. We hurried inside, and I didn't look back.

We made our way to the family living quarters where Japheth grabbed a fur robe and wrapped it around me. I sat down on one of the stools, shaking with cold and fear, my wet hair dripping.

"What about the door?" I stuttered. Once the Nephilim figured out how to cross the crater in the valley floor, what would keep them from entering the ark? There was only one way into the large boat, but the door was so large and heavy, it was impossible for even the eight of us working together to pull it shut.

"We have done our part, Ariana," Noah answered, "The Lord will do His. The day has come." He raised his hands up and began to pray. I leaned forward, resting my arms and head on my legs, huddling on the stool with the blanket over my head like one of the tortoises pulling into its shell for protection. Japheth sat next to me, his hand on my shoulder.

No one spoke after Noah finished praying. The floor and walls around us started rumbling. Stumbling to our feet, we all raced toward the balcony overlooking the interior of the ark.

Noah had planned this place, close to the family quarters, where we could look over the interior levels below, making it easier to check on the animals without having to run down the ramps. Across from us, on the second level, was the massive door to the ark. Through its opening, all I could see was brown swirling dust. I wondered how close the Nephilim were to us.

"It's moving!" Taina cried, pointing to the door. I grasped the railing as the ark lurched, and the imposing door, moved by an unseen force, slid closed, shutting out most of the light in the ark's interior.

We noticed that Noah had left, and we all moved to join him at the top of the boat. A narrow bridge followed the circumference of the boat, so that one could walk along the windows that ran under the parapet roofing that topped the ark. Each window could be shut up, if needed, by wooden hatches. They were now open, and we stared at the scene far below us. The Nephilim had already erected some sort of bridge across the crater. We watched in shock as men on horses began crossing over in large numbers.

As the first giant reached the other side of their makeshift bridge, the wind picked up. Dust swirled furiously, rushing around the bridge in strange billowy shapes, like flames leaping up in a fire. The shapes rolled together, forming a thick barrier and settling on the bridge. Howls of rage exploded from the Nephilim army, and they beat their shields with their swords in frustration. It did no good.

As we watched, the ominous cloud covered the entire valley floor, filling it up to the midpoint of the ark. For a moment, all was completely silent.

Suddenly, loud booms rolled across the sky above us, exploding into bolts of light that hit the ground. I had never seen such a phenomenon. Taina shrieked in fear, throwing her arms over her head, and falling to the wooden floor in a heap. I grabbed Japheth and the others also huddled together. But Noah stood at the window unshaken, tears running down his face.

"How long did I warn you, but you would not listen! Now your judgment has come. Who will save you now from the wrath of God?" He called out in anguished tones, his voice echoing across the valley.

Ham laughed scornfully, and I turned to look at him. My husband's brother stood to the left of Noah, gripping the window frame with both hands. Tauntingly, he yelled curses upon the army covered by the thick clouds, but his reedy thin voice failed to carry. A cacophony of roaring booms shattered above us, keeping his jeering words from being heard below.

"Enough." Noah put a hand on his son's shoulder. Ham turned. I'm not sure if anyone but Noah and I saw the fleeting expression on Ham's face. Perhaps I imagined it, but I thought I saw a resemblance to the Magistrate.

Ham's expression shifted, and his face became impassive. "It seems that only your words are meant to be heard, Father." His voice was flat, with no inflection of emotion. "Your predictions have come to pass. Let us hope we actually survive this flood of yours." He turned and pulled Taina up to her feet, whispering something in her ear. Shaking, she followed her husband back down the ladder to the living quarters below.

Noah caught my gaze and read my fears. He smiled at me reassuringly before addressing his other sons. "Japheth and Shem, it is time to close the hatches."

༄

The rain began that day—a loud, heavy rain that drummed on the roof of the ark. I had never heard anything like it.

"What's happening?" Nua shouted, clutching the stall door. We'd been feeding the large cats. The majestic creatures had stiffened, too, bracing themselves against the movement of the ark.

I had thrown my arms around the neck of the female tiger. I took a deep breath against its fur and tried to get to my feet. The sudden movement took me by surprise, too. "Remember Noah said that the water underground would be released, too." The sudden release of water must have filled the valley and begun to lift the ark. The boat lurched violently.

"Let's go to the family quarters," she said, "It's getting worse!"

Waves crashed into the boat, making it hard to walk. Nua and I staggered like drunkards after a long night, but we finally got back to our rooms. The rest of the family was already there. The violent movement lasted almost all night.

The next morning, I woke to the strange sensation of floating. Japheth was gone, so I got dressed quickly to go find him. He was up on the top floor, next to an open window, looking out into the dim light. It was still raining, but not as heavy now, just a steady pour.

"Can you see anything?" I asked.

Japheth turned and grimaced, "No, but I heard people screaming as we passed that mountain back there." He pointed to a mountain not too far off in the distance. Although it was morning, the thick dark clouds and rain made it difficult to see much.

"That's awful." I listened but heard nothing. "I didn't think about what it would be like. That people wouldn't all die right away."

"I didn't either. It's terrible." Japheth's voice broke. Wrapping my arms around him, we held each other tightly.

"How do we live through this?" I asked. "How do we live through the end of the world?" My heart beat so strongly in my chest that I was sure Japheth felt it; I trembled in his arms.

"We have to trust the Creator."

After dinner that night, Taina picked up her harp and sang for us. Her voice was so beautifully pure in tone that I felt myself relax for the first time since it had begun raining. I picked up my cup of wine and sipped it, enjoying the music and this moment of tranquility. Taina finished the song and made her way across the room to sit next to me and picked up the wineskin on the small table in front of the cushioned bench on which we sat.

"Would you like some more wine?" Before I could answer, she was already pouring more into my cup. "I think after the last few days, we all could use a few cups of wine." She drained her cup quickly and filled it again before settling back against the cushions.

"Are you all right?" I inquired politely.

"Not really. Everything is destroyed. Life as we know it is over." She looked into her cup. She lowered her voice so that only I could hear her words: "Noah and Laelah are confidant, but to be honest, I am not. I know the Creator exists—certainly we saw His power and destruction today—but can He be trusted?"

Shifting on the bench to face her, I answered, "How can He not? We are here safely, aren't we?"

"But my question is, why did He have to destroy the whole world? Surely the children could all have been spared, couldn't they? All day I have imagined them drowning. Even now, their small bodies float dead on the water's surface." Her hand holding her glass of wine shook. "Why did He destroy the innocent along with the guilty?" Taina's eyes flashed with emotion.

"Japheth says that much of humanity was corrupted with the blood-line of the Nephilim and so would never choose the Creator. God gave the others, who weren't corrupted, time to change their minds. They could have come on the ark, as well, but they didn't believe all the warnings."

"Ham keeps reminding me of that, but all of my family and friends are dead." With that, she drained her wine and poured another cup full.

FIRE

Chapter 15

My friends have abandoned me.

Job 19:13

We headed north in the old blue truck. Mitch said he had heard a while back that there was a hospital over the border, in Canada, that was still open in a place called Creston, a city controlled by the Global Union. As we drove through forest covered roads toward another town, I wondered if I should stay with Mitch and Sierra. *Would it be better to hunker down out here in the wild?* But I knew deep down, I didn't want to be alone, and Mitch and Sierra were all I had.

The military base had been east of Spokane, and so we made our way back and followed signs for the US-95N freeway. Most of time, the freeway was blocked with cars, but we kept near it, using signs for guidance, when we found them. Before all the devastation, it must have been an easy drive, just a few hours up the highway, but it took us most of the day to maneuver through old towns and beat-up roads.

Sierra was passed out in the back seat. Mitch hadn't told her about her mother. Maybe it was nice to have something else to focus on and give Sierra a few more hours before telling her something that would change her life forever.

We drove most of the day, only stopping to find fuel. Mitch was good at extracting gas out of abandoned vehicles, many conveniently left on the road. There was no one around. I wondered if people were still debilitated with stings from those creatures. I didn't know what I feared more, the large, inhuman creatures that were somewhere out there, or the people who had beheaded an airplane hangar full of people. Mitch was pretty sure it had been the Global Union soldiers, and we were heading right back into an area of their control.

The trip was long and, except when Sierra woke up, quiet. We crossed an abandoned border station into Canada, no longer relevant under the United North American government.

The sun was beginning to set when we pulled up to the town entrance in a broad valley surrounded by mountains. "Welcome to Creston" was painted in bright colors on a wooden sign, but the road was blocked. Old shipping containers were stacked across the road, leaving only a narrow gap to pass through. Armed Global Union soldiers and a large truck blocked the entrance. I wondered why they weren't suffering from the monsters' vicious stings.

Mitch muttered something but continued to drive forward carefully. Sierra was screaming again. My heart skipped a beat as one of the men approached us while the others aimed their guns at us, ready to fire.

"What's wrong with her?" the guard asked as he peered at Sierra. "Was she stung? Everyone in the area of the United North America and the Global Union were not hurt. President Bellomo's power is great. Even those demons obey him." He sounded like he was spewing memorized rhetoric. It reminded me of the Compound. I didn't like the feel of this town already.

"No, she wasn't stung. I don't know what's wrong. I am hoping the hospital is still open and we can get some help for my daughter. I'll do anything. You've got to help me . . . please." Mitch's voice broke.

The guard stared at Mitch for about thirty seconds, looked at Sierra in the back of the truck, and then motioned us through after giving Mitch directions to the hospital.

We pulled into the parking lot of an old school. A large, white banner hung over the entrance with "Creston Hospital" written in dark blue letters. "Stay here," Mitch ordered tersely and got out. Thankfully, Sierra had passed out again. I turned around to look at her. Sweat beaded on her face, and she was clearly flushed. I wondered if they could help her.

I kept my eyes fixed on the entrance and was surprised to see Mitch stomping out.

He got into the truck, slammed the door and hit the steering wheel with his fists. "Why does this have to be so hard?!"

I kept my mouth shut and moved slightly toward my door, hand near the handle just in case, but he broke down in tears. He started babbling, talking to his dead wife and apologizing over and over.

"What's wrong," I asked, confused. *What on earth had they said to him in there?*

"They say they won't help us if we don't have 'the Mark,'" he hissed, clearly shaken.

The Mark? What? I had no idea what he was talking about.

Sierra stirred in the back seat. "Dad, what's wrong?" she cried. I turned and saw that she was propped up on her left elbow, her right hand pressed against her stomach.

Mitch shook his head and turned around to face her. "Nothing's wrong, sweetie. We just have to do one thing before the doctor can see you."

He started the truck and pulled out of the parking lot and turned right. We drove for a short distance before stopping in front of one of the few two-story buildings I'd seen in the town. A large billboard sign in front of the building read, "Citizen Regulatory Board: Allegiance Center." Without a word, Mitch got out of the truck and stomped into the building.

I rolled down the front windows and sat waiting with Sierra. Something was very wrong. I wanted to leave, but Sierra was moaning again, about to pass out. I couldn't leave her alone and helpless without Mitch. So, I waited. That was my mistake.

When Mitch came out of the building, he wasn't alone; two armed, uniformed men were with him. He came over to my side of the truck and opened the door, pausing to wipe a tear from his cheek.

"You need to get out, Dani," he said. His voice cracked. *Was that shame I saw in his eyes?* "You're going with these men."

"What?" I fumbled as he pulled me out of the car. I saw a strange emblem, red and inflamed, newly imprinted on the back of his right hand.

I pushed away from him, protesting, but one of the men grabbed my arm and yanked me hard. Mitch just got into the truck and drove away without another word. I had been betrayed. Again.

"Come with us," the man holding me commanded. I obeyed and held back bitter tears.

No one spoke to me as I was hustled into the building. The first thing I noticed was the cold air. It was muggy and hot outside, but the air here was colder. We walked down a short corridor and into a large office.

There were desks throughout the room and people busy working at them. I noticed marks on many of their foreheads and realized it was the same emblem Mitch had had on his hand when he came out of the building. I wondered what it was and why no one here seemed to be suffering from the locust creature stings. *What had the guard said about a treaty?*

I was pulled past the busy scene and into another, smaller office. Sitting behind a desk was a beautiful woman.

"So, this is the girl?" She stood up and came around the desk. Dressed in a form-fitting black dress, a string of pearls around her neck and her blonde hair bundled up tightly on top of her head, she looked completely out of place in this austere environment.

Cold blue eyes lined in black stared into mine. "Well, if that guy was right, we won't have to run the lottery after all. She can be our volunteer!" The guards laughed. I'd heard that phrase before, in the first town, after I left the Compound.

"What's your name, girl?"

I looked down, away from her eyes, and saw the same emblem on her right hand. *What was going on?* One of the guards pushed me, and I answered, "Dani."

"Dani, what a charming name! I want to welcome you to Creston! I'm sure you've noticed that our community was not attacked by the creatures?"

I nodded my head.

"We enjoy a special relationship with President Bellomo." I wracked my brain to remember what Tomas had told me. President Bellomo was the leader of the Global Union, which controlled the world. "You know Dani, this world is full of uncertainty and harshness, but here in Creston, we're protected from much of it. The United North American government has designated Creston as an area of natural resources. The food grown here is shipped all over the world, even to the great city of New Babylon itself."

Babylon. I'd read that name before in the book Daphne had used to teach me to read. There was a story about a city where the people built a tower to heaven, but God confused their languages. I couldn't recall the details. I realized with a start that my bag was in the truck with Mitch and Sierra. I had nothing left.

I swayed and the woman grabbed my shoulder and led me to a chair, telling one of the men to get me some water. She sat in the seat next to me, patting my hand with false concern.

I was ushered out of the room, back through the bustling office with the screens, to a silver door. There were glowing buttons on the right. One of the guards tapped the top one, and the door opened up in the middle. I tried to turn away, but they dragged me inside and pushed another glowing button. The silver doors shut, and the box began to move.

The box stopped moving, and the door opened again to a different place. We walked down a long corridor of doors with numbers on them. One of the guards stopped at a door numbered 320, waved a plastic card in front of a metal plate, then opened the door.

"Take a shower," one of the men ordered. "Everything you need is in there. One of the women will be by with some food. Don't try to leave. One of us will be outside the door."

They left me alone. Mechanically, I went into the bathroom and did what I was told. Despite my fears, I stood under the clean warm water with relish. This morning I had seen a room full of bodies, but I was free; now, I was clean and wrapped in a fluffy bathrobe, but I was a prisoner yet again. And this time, I didn't think an earthquake or the creatures were going to help me escape.

There was a large television sitting on the dresser across from the bed. I looked around the room and saw a remote by the bedside.

At the Compound, sometimes as a treat, the children were invited in to watch a movie. I was never among them, but I would catch glimpses as I hustled in and out of the room, filling orders from my father for food or drink.

I clicked a button. A man sitting behind a table appeared on the screen. I turned up the volume a bit—not too loud, as I was unsure if I was allowed to watch. A man was speaking. Smaller screens would pop up around the man as he spoke, showing pictures or videos. I stifled a scream as one of the video clips showed one of the creatures stinging a woman.

"While most of the world was attacked by creatures," the man said, "the cities with special treaties with President Bellomo have been spared, once again proving his power. His Excellency, Angelo Cain, the religious leader of the Global Union, addressed the assembly today."

A man dressed in white and gold flowing robes stood on a stage in a large building. Other men and women filled hundreds of seats and clapped with fervor. Their faces looked at him with wonder and adulation.

I shuddered when the camera moved in closer to focus on "His Excellency." As he began to speak, I realized the words he spoke were right from Daphne's book! He talked about the "Savior of the world" and the great feast they would celebrate soon in Jerusalem.

Music swelled in the background and the man's voice rose in a fevered pitch as he detailed the many wondrous acts of this Savior. Apparently, it was his power that protected the faithful from the creature's stings.

The camera switched back to the first announcer. He continued to relate stories of earthquakes, droughts, and floods.

I turned off the television. I couldn't take any more. Curling up on the bed, I pulled one of the pillows under my head and began to cry softly so the guard wouldn't hear me. I was alone. The creatures were out there. I was a volunteer for some unknown horror. I didn't know what was going to happen to me, and somehow, this place felt scarier than the creatures. As I had many nights before, I cried myself to sleep.

FLOOD

Chapter 16

The flood continued for forty days on the earth ... And the waters prevailed so mightily on the earth that all the high mountains under the whole heaven were covered ... and all flesh died that moved on the earth, birds, livestock, beasts, all swarming creatures ... and all mankind.

Genesis 7: 17,19,20−21

Day after day, Japheth and I climbed the ladder to the bridge and looked out from under the hatch, but it was impossible to see anything through the relentless rain.

The ark rocked in the heavy waves. The motion made Taina utterly sick. I don't think she left her bed for weeks. I worried about her because she had difficulty keeping anything down. Laelah—a skilled healer— nursed her constantly, trying different remedies, but she had never seen a condition like Taina's before.

With Taina sick and Laelah busy caring for her, Nua and I took on the bulk of feeding chores with the animals. Tending them took a great deal of effort. The men shoveled the stalls while Nua and I did the feeding and watering. Fresh water, kept in large barrels, had to be hauled up by one of the men to fill the trough system.

Meals were prepared early in the morning for the day. We ate when we were hungry and only gathered for a family meal in the evening because there was just too much to be done to take the time for regular mid-day meals.

I found Nua hard at work shoveling feed from the storage bin into a bucket. "Here, I have one filled for you, too." She handed me a bucket we used to feed the animals.

"It's really amazing that we can be so close to creatures who usually will run away." I remarked. "Do you have a favorite?"

Nua's face scrunched up as she thought about it. "Not really. I kind of like the birds the best. There are so many different kinds and colors! How about you?"

"I think they're all interesting, but if I had to choose, it would be the elephants," I said, breaking off a banana and holding it out to one in the stall directly in front of me. The elephant grabbed it out of my hand with its trunk. That's when I saw the movement in her belly. The female elephant was pregnant.

"Nua, look!" I gasped, "She's pregnant!" I ran my hand lightly over the elephant's flank and gasped as her side rolled again, like a soft wave under my palm. "Wow!"

ᦉ

It was better to be busy than to have time to sit and wonder about the lost world submerged below us. I found it difficult to keep my thoughts from imagining the panic and terror all of those people had faced and wondering how the Flood would end.

One early morning, as Japheth and I gazed out of the hatch, I confided in him all my worries. "When will the rain end? How long will we be in this ark?" I twisted my hands together, an unconscious express of my inner turmoil. "I just want to get off of this boat."

"I think we all have had those same thoughts. I really do not know, love. The Lord tells my father what we need to know. He has brought us this far—and protected us from the Nephilim army. I remind myself of that when I become anxious."

"Have you wondered what the world will be like once the waters recede? Won't it all be mud? Deep mud?"

Japheth wrapped his arms around me. "When I was a boy, I spent a few weeks making a dam on the small brook that flowed through the south pastures. I wanted to make a pool to swim in. I only got to enjoy it for a few days before our neighbor came to investigate why the brook stopped flowing."

I rested against his chest, reassured by his warm embrace. "Did you get in trouble?"

"Oh, he was annoyed all right, but Father assured him that we would make it right. We went to the pasture and dismantled all my hard work. When the pool I had made drained, there was a huge pile of mud and rocks. Father helped me remove the larger rocks and instructed me to rake up the mud. I remember it surprised me how fast the grass grew once again."

I shook my head, "But this flood, it's so big. Surely this will be much more devastating? What will grow when the waters recede when it has all been covered for so long?"

"Truly, I have no answer, Ariana. All I can do is trust the Creator. Would He tell us to build an ark and save us through this flood, only to have us starve?"

"When you put it that way, I suppose it is wrong to worry. He saved us from the Nephilim; He closed the great door to the ark. I just wonder how long we'll have to stay in this boat?"

Turning to look down at me, Japheth smiled, his brown eyes crinkling at the corners. "I only wonder how many years we will have together." He bent his head to kiss me. We savored a few moments together before heading down to tend to the animals again.

◟

"Time to feed the bears!" I ran eagerly ahead of Japheth down to the level where the furry beasts were kept. Boldly, I entered their stall.

"Come here, Lazy Bones," I called to the male bear. He lumbered over to me and pushed me with his massive head.

"He acts just like a dog!" Japheth chuckled. "Look at how he pushes against your hand for you to pet him!"

Laughing, I grabbed the bear's fuzzy head and scratched under his ears. His eyes closed.

"Too bad his wife is so shy!" The female bear sat in a corner of the stall, not quite so sure of me as the male.

"She'll be confident enough when she has cubs," Japheth lobbed back, "Every female creature is as bold as a lion when they have young ones."

Japheth left for the storeroom to get a rake and new bedding. We worked together cleaning the stall and playing with the bears.

The foxes were next. The cuddly orange couple lay curled up in a corner with their luxurious tails wrapped around their feet and head. I sat down, and they both stretched and came to me, rubbing against me like cats before bounding off to play fight. I looked over just in time to see them stalking a mouse.

"Oh, no you don't!" Getting up quickly, I shooed the mouse away just in time. To Japheth, I said, "We need to fix the mouse cage again. They keep escaping!"

Japheth chuckled at my efforts to rescue the mice. "There are so many of those now, it wouldn't hurt to lose a few." I pulled a face at him. He pointed to the foxes, who were staring at us, panting. "You haven't drawn the foxes yet, why don't you sketch some pictures of them? I'll go finish the rest of the animals."

"Oh, I'd love that, Japheth! Maybe just a little while sketching alone? I don't want to play while everyone works, but by the end of the day, I'm so tired that it's hard to feel creative." Throwing my arms around him, I kissed him before running to our room to get my drawing supplies.

After forty days, the rain stopped falling. We all climbed up to the bridge to gaze at the sunny sky, even Taina. I was shocked when I saw her in the light of day, leaning weakly against her husband. Dark shadows smudged her eyes, and her face was tightly drawn. Laelah caught my eye and shook her head at me in a silent warning to not mention it. I turned my eyes to look out of the hatches. Shem and Japheth had opened them all. The fresh air was invigorating. Thankfully, the water was not so rough, and I hoped that would make Taina feel better. Noah prayed for the family, and for Taina's healing, then we all went to work, leaving Laelah and Taina to enjoy the fresh air and sunlight on the narrow bridge.

I don't know what caused the argument to start that day between Ham and Shem. I was on the second level with Japheth, holding one of the baby rabbits, when we heard the commotion. Shouts were coming from the living quarters. Running up into the family area, we found Ham and Shem throwing blows.

Ham was shouting curses at Shem. Blood dripped down Shem's face from his nose. I was shocked at the violence and the language. Noah and Japheth pulled them apart just as Laelah came out of Taina's room in alarm.

"What is going on?" Noah demanded. He was a kind man but absolutely the firm patriarch of the family. There was no tolerance for any dissensions or outbursts of anger among his family members.

Shem glared at Ham, wiping blood from his nose. "He attacked me."

"You were trying to steal the skins!" Ham shook his index finger at Shem, spitting out his words bitterly. "You know Japheth is the first born, but you want the skins God made for the First Ones for yourself."

"You're a fool, Ham." Again, I noticed that look pass across Ham's face. This time, I was sure I hadn't imagined it. There was *no* way Shem was trying to steal anything.

Noah placed a hand on Shem's shoulder. "Stop this. What were you doing, Shem?"

I noticed then the ancient, amber-colored box open on the floor, its contents spilled about the floor. That box held the family's treasures. The histories written on scrolls by the forefathers were preserved in the box, along with the garments fashioned by the Creator for the First Ones. A creamy white leather tunic was carefully placed next to the box. I recognized it as Eve's garment; Laelah had showed it to me when she was repacking the box to go onto the ark. Adam's was lying next to it.

"I remembered from the writings of Enoch there was a story about a woman who had the same symptoms as Taina. I was merely getting the scroll out to find out what treatment Enoch's wife gave her."

Shem bent over and picked up a scroll from the mess on the floor. He handed the scroll to Noah. I looked at the floor, embarrassed for Ham. Surely his anger was due to fear for Taina.

"I think I remember that tale," Noah said. He strode over to the table, and, pulling out a chair, sat down. Laelah went and stood behind him, reading along silently.

"Here it is. This was written by my grandmother; she was a great healer." He read us the short excerpt describing treatment for a sickness that sounded a great deal like Taina's.

"Ah!" Laelah exclaimed. "I think I understand how that would work! Ariana, get a small basket and come with me to the storage room."

Grabbing a basket, I gladly left the men and hurried after her. When I got to the storage room, Laelah was already rummaging through some jars, pulling the covers off and sniffing the contents.

"Here it is!" She pulled a strangely shaped root out of the jar. "Now, we need a few more things: some malt sweetener and some of the sour fruits from the preserves I put up there." She nodded toward the jars in the corner of the storage room. I moved over and pulled out some sweetener, carefully using the scoop to measure out the required amount into a small bowl.

When we returned to the family quarters, Ham was nowhere to be seen, and the contents of the box had been placed back inside. Now, it sat on the small table by the chairs where Noah sat with Shem. Japheth was heating water in the kitchen to make the healing brew.

Laelah began her preparation, and soon, a pungent, sharp aroma filled the room. Taking the pot off of the heat source, she added the sour fruit mixture before transferring the contents of the cooking pot into one of the heavy, clay bowls.

"It is going to have to sit here, covered, for a few days. I am hopeful it will help Taina," she said.

"Thank you, son," I heard Noah say to Shem. "I'm sorry your brother attacked you that way. Surely, he regrets it as well."

"I doubt it. Ham rarely feels regret or admits he was wrong. But I do hope this helps Taina." Shem smiled briefly at his father before leaving the room with Nua to tend to the animals.

As I returned to the animals, as well, I kept thinking about what had happened. We were all feeling anxious and cooped up in the ark, but to yell and fight, that was something more. Ham's reaction to the supposed theft of the animal skins seemed extremely odd and suspicious to me. Although I tried to like all my new family, there was something not right with Ham. I didn't understand it, but Ham's anger ran deep, and it scared me sometimes. Japheth had a very strict rule about talking to, not about others, so I never shared my concerns about Ham with him—something I would deeply regret later.

FIRE

Chapter 17

They sacrificed their sons and their daughters
to the demons . . .

Psalm 106:37

I woke with a start. An alarm was going off in the building, reverberating off the walls. My heart thudded wildly, and I jumped out of bed. *I have to wake up Sierra and Mitch!* For a second, I forgot where I was and what happened. Then I remembered. Mitch had betrayed me—just like Tomas, just like my mother. I went to grab my bag, but that was gone, too. I was alone and empty-handed, but whatever that alarm was warning about, I was not going to die locked in this room.

I ran to the door to get out. A large, burly soldier blocked my way. He had that mark on his forehead.

"You're not going anywhere," he ordered.

"But the alarm," I protested. I was panicking now.

"That's the call to worship." He looked at me like I was an idiot. "Get back in there."

Confused, I obeyed him without another word, carefully closing the door behind me. There was no lock on the door on my side. I moved over to the window and saw dozens of people in the street below me. As they passed by, I noticed marks on many hands and some on foreheads.

"What is going on?" I said aloud, crouching by the window, not wanting to be noticed by the people passing.

I perched by the window for a few minutes, watching the procession, wondering where the people were going and who were they going to worship. The mood of the crowd was definitely upbeat. Everyone looked well-fed and happy. Children skipped along, some pulling their parents by the hand, urging them to go faster.

This is like a dream. I thought. Outside this town were devastation and monsters, but here, everything was tranquil. *Was it true that allegiance to the Global Union, President Bellomo, and Angelo Cain brought safety? Was it worth it?*

Seeing all those happy parents smiling at their children stung my heart. This was how it was meant to be. Children shouldn't have to face terror after terror without a chance to breathe. I curled up on the bed, clutching the pillow. Tears ran down my face as I thought about my parents. *What kind of mother hates her child? What kind of father would kill Daphne?* I thought of the way Mitch loved Sierra, loved her enough to betray me.

After a while, I rolled onto my back and stared at the ceiling and thought about Tomas. *I should have listened to my instincts,* I thought. *He sold me like an animal to be used.* The memory of smashing him in the face was satisfying. After the Compound, he was the first person I had trusted. I should have known better.

"Why am I always rejected?" I whispered fiercely at the ceiling. The anger brewing in my heart made me feel strong. The only one I could trust was me. I would find a way to get free and I would do it on my own. I just had to do what Daphne always told me, not panic. *Panic only makes a bad situation worse.*

I wrapped my arms around myself, closing my eyes and remembering the last time she hugged me. I felt a sense of peace as I thought about Daphne, the only person who ever truly loved me,—who was for me.

It's not you, child. It's them. Her comforting words came back to me. I breathed in raggedly and got out of bed.

I didn't know what was coming next, so I decided to take a shower while I could. I wasn't gone long, but when I came out of the steamy bathroom, someone had taken my clothes. In their place was a white tunic, embroidered along the collar in white curling flowers, edged with gold. The white pants were soft and form-fitting. Creamy white shoes sat on the floor.

Next to the bed was a cart. There was orange juice in a glass, placed next to a plate of eggs and bread with meat and potatoes, finely cut and steaming. Shoveling the food into my mouth, I hunched over the cart, keeping my eyes on the door handle where the guard stood on the other side.

When I finished, I clicked on the television again, carefully keeping the sound down so the man in the hall wouldn't hear. A woman appeared on the screen. She was young and beautiful. I sat down at the edge of the bed to hear what she was saying.

". . . President Emanuel Bellomo led the coalition army to decisive victory."

Soldiers dressed in sandy-colored uniforms stood attentively in rows before a platform filled with flags. The center flag was larger than the others, colorful like a rainbow, with a strange circular symbol in the left corner. The camera focused in on the president, standing in front of the flag. Dressed in the same uniform as the soldiers, Bellomo smiled winsomely at the crowd and began to speak into a microphone.

"It's been a tough battle, but you were strong and courageous." He stopped speaking as the men cheered loudly and waited laughing, holding his arms out in an embrace as the shouts and applause grew louder.

He approached the microphone again. "This is for you!" he shouted and gestured to his right. Soldiers dragged three men, one by one, out of a shiny black truck. Supported by the soldiers, the men could hardly stand. I felt sick when I saw the state they were in; one of them was unconscious. All of them had been severely beaten. The crowd roared in approval.

President Bellomo motioned for the crowd to be quiet and was instantly obeyed. He spoke quietly and confidently. "Victory is ours, and today vengeance is ours. These Regents betrayed the world's trust and the fragile peace. Each of them was entrusted with one of the ten world regions and each betrayed that trust."

The crowd erupted in angry shouts of condemnation. President Bellomo waited until they quieted.

"Their betrayal brought the increase of natural disasters as our allies in this cosmic war withdrew their protection because these men sowed distrust between the Global Union; their civil war sparked famine and disease. Remember, it's our union and peace that keeps the world safe. As I have told you, I have negotiated peace with the world and with our cosmic allies. These men wanted to destroy our peace and safety!"

The scene shifted to the three men. One of the two men still standing fainted. One of the soldiers guarding him kicked him viciously.

"It's estimated that more than one-third of the world's population died—all due to these traitors. We, the Global Union, trusted these men to rule as three of the ten regents, yet they broke their vows and brought devastation upon our world through their treason, and they must pay!" President Bellomo's voice was full of hateful condemnation. Along with the rest of the watching crowd, I found myself drawn to him, believing him.

Again, the audience cheered riotously as the men were led to a guillotine just like the one I'd seen before when we were looking for Mitch's wife. One by one, they were pushed down on their knees; the lever was pulled, and the blade fell. One by one, their heads rolled to the ground, and the crowd cheered.

The food in my stomach felt heavy. I heaved it all onto the floor. Wiping my mouth, I turned back to the television. The camera panned from the grisly sight back to the president. He was laughing in delight. I was disgusted by his enjoyment. *How could I believe this guy?*

"As you know . . ." he intoned, as the crowd quieted. "As you know, I brokered the peace treaty with Israel. We all know that small nation,

Israel, the center of three major religions, has been the source of many of the world's problems. Since its inception, there has been nothing but conflict and inequality. I achieved the peace for the first time, not only in the Middle East, but also in the world. Those traitors," he nodded to the dead bodies, "betrayed that peace. What they meant for evil, I say, we will use for good!"

The crowd exploded with loud acclamation again. Bellomo waited for them to quiet down, a fatherly smile on his lips.

"We have one final battle to win! Those two in Jerusalem must be dealt with!" His voice was intensely angry. "The ones who call themselves the Witnesses are spreading lies and upsetting the peace I have negotiated with our cosmic allies."

I remembered what I had seen on the TV at Tomas's apartment: the two men in Jerusalem who had cursed the land and stopped the rain. I didn't know what Bellomo meant by "cosmic allies," but the scorpion creatures were proof there was some kind of supernatural battle going on. President Emanuel Bellomo had somehow brought peace; I could see his power in this town, which seemed protected from the chaos. Then I remembered the vomit on the ground and the bodies I had seen the day before.

"Peace at what cost?" I whispered aloud.

I looked back up at the TV again. President Bellomo was still talking about the two Witnesses. "It has not rained in many places for months because of the curses they have brought on us in the name of their *God*. What kind of god curses humanity?

"As His Excellency, Angelo Cain, has told you before, our world is the battlefield for an ancient war between two powerful factions. Our cosmic allies promote and support the peace of the Global Union and our united, global religion. Those Witnesses spread propaganda for our enemies. As you know, they claim to be the representatives of the one true God."

Again, the crowd cried out in rage and anger, calling for the death of the Witnesses.

"Where is their God? I tell you the truth. I have met our cosmic allies! They have guided me along the way. Now, they realize they must make themselves known in the face of the lies spewed by the Witnesses. So, I'd like to introduce you to them: meet our allies!"

President Bellomo gestured grandly to the sky and the crowd gasped as a shining silver disk appeared in the sky above and hovered above the president. Two large, super human-like figures appeared in the window of the craft, raising their arms in greeting then disappeared. The crowd was strangely quiet.

"There is nothing to fear!" Bellomo shouted. "These are not aliens but ambassadors from our true ancestors. I've met with them, and they are going to help me destroy the Witnesses!" As the camera panned over the assembly, I saw hope on many faces as they gazed at the charismatic leader.

I switched the television off and began to hyperventilate in panic. Fear washed over me in a cold sweat. Nothing made any sense. *Super human creatures. Aliens. Witnesses? I was in a town controlled by the maniac in charge of the world. I had to escape.*

There was no way I could get past the guard, so I went to the window and looked out. No one was around, and there was a tree to the left of the window. Pushing the window up, I swung my left leg and then my right over the ledge, so I was sitting up outside the window. I clung to the window frame with my right hand and could just reach a branch with my left. Letting go of the frame, I swung my body onto the tree, wrapped my legs around the narrow trunk, and shimmied down to the ground. I was breathing hard.

Before I could run, two massive arms grabbed me from behind. "No, you don't!" a rough voice ordered and called for help. I struggled as hard as I could, but the man's grip was firm. Two women rushed out of the building toward us.

"We've got a trank," one of them blurted to the man as she held up a syringe. I felt a sharp sting.

FLOOD

Chapter 18

Then he sent out a dove from him, to see if the water was
abated from the face of the land . . .

Genesis 8:8

One night, around the hundredth day in the ark, we sat in the family living quarters around the dinner table. Empty plates were pushed toward the middle to make room for one of our favorite games: a guessing game.

"We should play the women against the men," Taina trilled. Everyone agreed and switched seats, so we could sit with our teams.

"It's so good to have you joining us, Taina!" I smiled at her. It was nice to see her feeling better. Her skin no longer had that pale, sickly look.

"Yes, I'm sure you like having her back," Noah teased. "Your team lost every single game without her." The taunting went on throughout the game, each side boasting in its skill. The rivalry was intense, but Team Woman won.

"This is my favorite time of day," Shem remarked, "even when we lose. This has been a hard time for the family with all that's happened, but I think we are closer than we've ever been before." I agreed and saluted the family with my cup of water. We all raised our glasses and drank.

Portraits I'd painted of the family were slowly covering the warm wooden walls. Noah and Laelah were set on the top, with their three sons spaced evenly below them. I was still working on Nua's picture. It stood on a stand Japheth had made for me, just across from where the family sat.

The evening ended warmly. As the family shared some of Noah's wine in celebration, I couldn't help but feel hopeful. The world had been filled with evil, but this sweet fellowship would be the start of a new world.

After a hundred and fifty days in the ark, many weeks after the rain stopped, the whole ark suddenly shuddered as it struck the crest of what had once been a mountain. I was sitting with the birds, laughing at the tiniest ones because they were snoring as they slept, when the terrific jolt tossed me to the floor. Terrified, I left the birds and ran up the ramp to find Japheth and the rest of the family scrambling up to the bridge.

When I got up there, the hatches were already opened. The ark was still in water, but Japheth told me we were caught at the top of a mountain still unseen below us.

"It's like a rocky cradle holding the ark," Nua remarked to me.

We stood gazing on the scene around us for quite some time; the bright sun sparkled on the waves. For the first time in months, the ark was still. Water lapped against its side. I had been feeling dizzy for a few weeks and hoped the stillness would finally calm my head and my stomach.

"We won't know where anything is," Ham remarked.

"What do you mean, son?" Laelah asked.

"Who knows how far we have traveled? The land has been underwater for so long . . . how has the land been changed? Will we be able to recognize the rivers and hills of home?"

No one answered. No one knew.

It had not occurred to me that all the water surrounding us could have enough power to blot out all that we knew of the world. *Would nothing be familiar?*

"Now, there is really no way for us to ever get back to Eden," Ham complained angrily, punching the side of the ark with his fist.

"No one could get there anyway," Japheth answered, abruptly changing the subject and turning to face Noah. "Father, has the Lord told you how long we will have to wait for the waters to recede?"

Noah shook his head. "No, but it seems to me that since we have been on the water all this time, we should expect it to take a while. Thankfully, we have plenty of provisions."

Japheth and I stayed up on the bridge after everyone left. "That was a strange thing my brother said," he commented.

I agreed, although I knew what Ham meant. I, too, had wanted to go to Eden and walk in its beauty and see the famous Tree of Life. A few times over the past months, I had thought about it, deep under the water. Was it still alive down there? Were the angels still guarding it?

"Methuselah told me that an angel guards the entrance there." I said.

"Yes, an angel with a flaming sword! No one could ever return there, though Ham thinks there is a way."

"How?" I wondered again if it even still existed under all that water. Surely even the Flood could not destroy the Tree of Life?

"The Nephilim whispered lies to anyone who would listen about a way into Eden." We all knew the powers of the Tree of Life: eat one fruit and become immortal. It would be hard to turn away from a whisper of how to get in.

"How did Ham hear these whispers?" I asked.

"Years ago, on one of our supply trips to the city, we ran into the Magistrate. If you recall, Lamech, who called himself the Magistrate's father, was Noah's father. The Magistrate talked to us under the guise of familial bond. While we spoke, he told us his desperate theory."

"Did Noah say anything?"

"Just that no one was more powerful than the angel God sent to guard Eden's entrance. But later, Ham insisted that the Magistrate had told him the way to the Garden."

"What was it?" I wondered briefly why the Magistrate would tell such a tale. Then I remembered his dark, deceitful ways.

"Something about appearing to the angel as one of the First Ones would allow a person to gain entrance to the Garden. It was a silly tale, but it seems that it took root in my brother's heart. I suspect that is why he wants the garments made by the Creator."

Japheth turned from the hatch and said he was going back to work on some repairs below. I stayed up on the bridge. The bright sun sparkled on the waters that splashed softly against the ark; the surface was calm, reflecting the fluffy white clouds above.

I heard a splash and looked down in time to see a fin submerge below the water. Wondering what kind of animal it was, I stood there for some time, hoping for another glimpse, but it did not reappear. Sighing, I returned to work, too.

Day followed day, and the waters continued to recede from the land, taking over two months to withdraw from the mountaintop. It became apparent the ark really was caught up in a kind of "cradle," as Nua described it, so we did not drift away with the water as it faded back to its place.

It was forty days after we saw the top of the mountains that Noah called the family to join him on the bridge. All of the hatches were open to allow fresh air to circulate. As I got to the ladder, I looked up and saw Noah holding one of the bird cages in his hand. Clambering up, I joined the family.

"I have not heard from the Lord about leaving the ark yet, and as you know, we can see nothing from this vantage point except the mountain tops," Noah explained. "I sent out a raven a week ago, and it did not come back. Foolishly, I forgot that it eats carrion, and there must be," he paused, closing his eyes and bowing his head a moment, "quite a lot here near the mountain top. This morning, it occurred to me that a dove would give us more information."

"Oh, yes!" Taina exclaimed. "Doves will return to their homes instinctively! My grandmother kept dovecotes and would use her doves to send messages to her sister, who lived in one of the cities. Her sister also had a dovecote, and the arrangement allowed them to communicate with one another."

I did not follow her meaning. "So, who will communicate with us through the dove?"

"Not who but what," Noah said. "The dove knows instinctively how to find her original home. If she does not return to us, we will know that she has found her home."

"And that means the waters have receded enough for the tree line to be revealed," Taina finished for him, smiling her approval.

Tenderly, Noah scooped the dove out of the cage and tossed it gently into the air. We watched as it stretched its wings and flew up and out of sight. One by one, everyone but Noah and Nua left the bridge. There was much to do to care for the animals below.

It took some time, but the dove returned. Later that night over dinner, Noah shared his plan with us. He would wait another seven days and then try the experiment again.

Seven more days passed, and he took the dove out for another flight. That second time, she reappeared with an olive branch in her beak. It was such a wonder to us, that olive branch. After nothing but rain and flood for months, to see a green thing growing again was remarkable. But because she returned, we knew the time had not yet come to leave the ark, so Noah waited another seven days before repeating his experiment. That time, the dove did not return. We knew she had found her home.

That night, as the family sat after dinner, we discussed leaving the ark.

"While this is an encouraging development, the ground will certainly still be too wet for us to leave," Noah said.

"But we do need to plan how we will get out," Japheth interjected. "The door is sealed shut."

"Why don't we just make a hole on the first level?" Ham asked. "We can just walk out."

"That is a very good idea, brother!" Japheth answered. "If we make an opening in the lower deck, we can easily lead the animals out and cart out supplies to build a home."

Laelah sighed. "I cannot wait to leave this place and have a real home again!"

"But where will we get wood to build a home?" Ham objected. "How many trees could survive a flood like this?"

"We can take planking from the ark to build the house," Japheth suggested.

"I do not know what we will do," Noah responded, "but I am confident the Creator did not bring us through the great Flood safely with all of these animals only to leave us without shelter when it is time to leave the ark."

I stood up to get some more water and was suddenly overcome by dizziness. Swaying, I grabbed my husband's shoulder for support.

"Ariana!" Japheth got up and wrapped an arm around me. I sat down again and put my head on the table. Hoping the dizziness would stop.

I felt a cool hand on the back of my neck. Laelah. "She doesn't feel warm. Here, Japheth, take her to your room."

After he helped me to the bed, Laelah asked Japheth to leave the room. She sat down next to me and took my hand in hers and asked me some questions. As I answered them, I felt the excitement of hope growing.

"Could it be?" I asked her, afraid to say the words.

Her dark eyes twinkled brightly back at me. "I think from your answers it is certain! Let me get Japheth." She left the room, and my husband came back alone.

"Are you all right?" he asked anxiously. "Mother would not answer any of my questions."

"She helped me answer mine, though." I smiled up at him. "I've had some symptoms that have been worrying me, but now I know there is nothing to worry about." I laid his hand on my belly. "We are having a baby!

"Praise the Creator!" Japheth whooped and picked me up, swinging me around. I laughed, wrapping my arms around his neck and kissing him over and over.

After all we had been through in our short time together, this new life was a promise of a better future. Surely our children and their children would learn the lesson of the great Flood and the ark and follow after the ways of the Lord. Surely, the world would be as it ought to in the future! That is what we dreamed of together that day—a bright future full of peace and hope and love between our three families.

FIRE

Chapter 19

You came to my rescue, Lord, and saved my life.
Lamentations 3:58

The sensation of suddenly falling woke me with a start. I was lying on a couch. Dizzily, I tried to sit up, but it was too hard. *Why was it so loud?*

"Don't worry. It's normal to feel groggy." I looked over to my left. An older woman sat in a chair facing me; she looked blurry to me. I blinked trying to see her.

"You've probably never flown before."

With a start, I saw clouds through the window. "What? Are we flying?" I pushed myself up. Just then, the plane shook. I grabbed the arm of the couch and screamed.

"It's just a bit of turbulence, dear. No reason to be afraid. We're fine," the woman told me. The shaking stopped a few moments later. I'd seen planes fly over the Compound occasionally and always wondered what it would be like to fly in one. It was a waking nightmare.

"It'll be a bit before you feel steady. We gave you some sedatives to help you sleep. We're flying to Jerusalem for the ceremony. I'm so excited to go! I'm a true believer."

My mind spun. *Jerusalem?* I tried to escape, and now, I was being dragged right into the lion's den.

She smiled at me reassuringly, leaning over to pat my hand, and my eyes focused. She had the mark on her forehead. "You really should feel honored. Of course, there aren't many young women who are still . . . well, still pure. Every city is sending a virginal offering for the unveiling."

I pushed myself up, groggy and uncomprehending. It was like she was speaking a different language. Closing my eyes, I tried to pull myself together, but my head wasn't cooperating.

"What are you talking about?"

"Here, try some water." She pushed a small bottle of water into my hand, and I drank it. The cool liquid soothed my dry throat. I thanked her, and she smiled with a nod.

I was getting scared. *Virginal offering? What did that mean?* I started breathing hard. On the Compound, Dominic always talked about being "pure" for your husband. I knew what that meant. But how would this woman know? With a sick feeling, I knew. Someone had examined me while I was unconscious.

"You violated me?" I glared up at her.

"Oh, no! Of course not! Our doctor examined you. He's a professional. I was there as a witness. You have no reason to be upset." Then she put her hand on my shoulder and patted me like a dog.

"I was unconscious. I didn't give you permission to examine me!" I screamed at her and raised the water bottle to throw it in her face, but she was faster. She gripped my wrist painfully.

"You need to stop fighting. This is going to happen." Her ghostly white face smiled down at me. Her touch was cold.

I wanted those flat eyes to turn away from me. There was an inhuman quality to them—much like the malignant evil I'd seen in the scorpion monsters' eyes back in Spokane. Incredible fear washed over me. I wasn't sure she was totally human. There was something else behind those eyes.

"I'm fine." I spit the words out.

She abruptly let go of my wrist.

"I'm here to serve you. It's a huge honor to be going to Jerusalem for the unveiling! Everyone's been talking about it, and it's a privilege for me to escort one of the volunteers. I am Sister Charity Rose."

As I sat and ate a sandwich Sister Charity gave me, she droned on and on. My head was spinning, but without realizing it, she was helping me understand what was happening. All I had to do was ask a question, and she'd go off on another diatribe to answer it. She talked for hours, and as she babbled, a picture started to form in my mind. Sorting through the inane comments for nuggets of reality, I was able to grasp some solid information. It was worse than I could have ever imagined.

When the plane started its decent, I thought we were going to crash. Finally, we came down with a big thud. I was thankful to be back on the earth.

"This is the Old City," Sister Charity Rose informed me.

I watched through the dark window as we drove past ancient buildings that looked like castles to me. Like Creston, Jerusalem seemed like a bustling place. There were many other cars and people walking the narrow streets. The streets were so narrow that I wondered if two cars could pass at the same time. Everything here seemed strange and ancient.

The car stopped by a white building. "This is the embassy," the driver told us.

"Let's go," Sister ordered. I opened the door and got out; she followed me. "This way! I want to introduce you to the ambassador."

The next few days were filled with boredom, punctuated by appointments where I joined the other women being kept prisoner in preparing for the ceremony. Our hair was cut and styled, and we were fitted with gowns for the ceremony. We were to stand alongside President Bellomo as he made his speech and follow him into the Temple. The ambassador ran us through our part over and over, determined we would not ruin anything on the great day approaching.

"You know what he has done for the world! He's saved us from the brink of extinction and you get to honor him. Demonstrate your devotion!" Both her hand and her forehead bore the mark, which I now knew was a symbol of allegiance to President Bellomo.

I hated every moment, but there was nothing I could do. None of the other women even spoke to me. *How were we going to demonstrate our devotion?* There were women among us who had the mark. They responded to everything with great eagerness. Maybe they had actually volunteered for this honor.

The morning of the ceremony, we split into two groups. Ours was taken to the cafeteria for breakfast but only given a bit of tea and some toasted bread. The tea tasted strange, but I drank it anyway. As we were led out of the room, I regretted drinking it. My brain felt foggy, lethargic. Looking around at the other women, I realized that none of the women who were marked were in my group.

We followed a guard, and as we walked down the corridor, we passed an open door. I looked in and saw a long table covered in a white cloth and heaped with food. The other group of girls, those with the mark, were sitting at the table, feasting and laughing together.

After we got dressed, we were taken to a large bus. I had to pull the long skirt of my dress up to climb into the bus. We'd been severely warned about getting the white garments dirty. I sat down in the back, blinking my eyes in the bright sunlight, struggling to think clearly.

We sat and waited for some time before the other women joined us. One by one, the women entered the bus and settled themselves in the seats at the front. "Let's sing!" one of them shouted, and they began to sing praises to the Promised One, pledging their allegiance and promising to serve him even to the point of death.

There was a strange disconnect between their joyful mirth and the quiet fearfulness emanating from the rest of the women. I was groggy as the bus drove through the old city. Abruptly, the bus stopped, and I was thrown forward. My face hit the seat in front of me, and I let out a cry of pain. Blood poured from my nose all over my white gown. I held my nose in horror, unsure of what kind of punishment I would receive.

I heard a man's voice shout for the women to leave the bus. Since I was at the rear, I was one of the last ones off. Although I pinched it, blood still poured from my nose.

"Oh, look at her!" An angry woman dressed in a white robe embroidered with the same mark, which she also had on her hand and forehead, stood on the pavement, glowering up at me as I navigated the stairs of the bus. My mind was still foggy and disjointed.

Two women came over to me and tried to wipe away the blood. The angry woman joined us. "This is unacceptable! There is no way she can be cleaned up in time!" she screamed. "Take her away! Take her away! Get the other women ready! The ceremony has already started, and it's almost time."

I was jerked away by a guard and taken up a massive stone stairway into a beautiful building. Tall columns stretched an immense height, and the carved tops were covered in gold that glinted in the hot, bright sun.

"Hurry up! I don't want to miss the ceremony!" the guard muttered darkly. "The Regents have just begun their entrance. You're ruining everything!"

We came to a door, and I was pushed through. "This one needs some help. She's your problem." The guard turned and left, slamming the door.

I was stunned and relieved. *What had I just been delivered from?*

"What did you do to yourself?" a woman snapped. She walked over to a cabinet, pulled it open, and grabbed some items from it.

"Sit there," she ordered, nodding to a tall, black bench covered with white paper. I sat on the crinkly paper, still dazed and confused.

"Looks like they drugged you. They talked about doing that just in case anyone decided to freak out at the last minute."

Roughly she wiped the blood away from my nose and packed one of my nostrils with tissue.

"Got whacked pretty bad, but nothing's broken. You lucked out, but you're not going to make me miss anything. I can't leave you here, so you'd better behave, or I'll make you sorry!" She pulled out a small knife from her pocket and flicked it open. "I'll have no problem cutting you."

Numbly, I nodded and followed her out of the room. We entered a large courtyard filled with people. The woman pushed her way through the crowd, and we ended up under a roof supported by pillars. I realized we were in the great Temple where the ceremony was going to be celebrated.

"I saved you a place here. Who's she?" her friend exclaimed, scowling at me. "What a mess!"

"Yes, that's why she's with me. I'm responsible for her, so just shut up about it. There's nothing I can do."

The woman ordered me to stand behind her. Through the middle of the crowd ran a red carpet, which led up to a beautiful staircase and massive golden doors, tightly shut. To the right of the staircase was tiered seating, filled with well-dressed men and women. I think they must have been the Regents and other important people. I wondered which one was the representative for United North America. Suddenly, horns blew and the enthusiastic crowd was silenced.

I looked up. On either side of the stairs were two towers. That's where a row of men stood, dressed in costumes. They held rams' horns in their hands and blew them.

A movement to my left made me turn, and I gasped as I saw the other women I'd been held with, the volunteers, entering the courtyard, their white dresses trailing behind them. They crossed the courtyard and lined the stairs, standing in two lines as we were taught. The massive golden doors at the top of the stairs swung open, and two men stood in the opening. They were dressed in white garments and began chanting in a language I didn't understand. Smoke billowed out from golden dishes they swung on the golden chains they held in their hands.

The entire assembly erupted in cheers of joy and celebration as the president and a man I assumed was Angelo Cain emerged. They both crossed the red carpet and mounted the stairs. Standing at the top in front of the open doors, they turned and raised their arms in victory as the crowd shouted praises. The hair on the back of my neck stood up. I couldn't take my eyes off them.

Angelo Cain, the religious leader of the Global Union, raised his arms and began to speak. "After his great victory against the rebel forces led by the three traitorous Regents, I received a great blessing. One of our cosmic allies appeared to me," his voice crackled with emotion, "to me, Angelo Cain, and confirmed what I have been telling you all along. President Emmanuel Bellomo is the Promised One!"

Enthusiastic applause and shouts of praise erupted from the crowds, though I noticed the two men by the golden doors looked alarmed.

"As such," Angelo Cain continued, "by the authority vested in me as the leader of the one true, global church, I declare to the world the one promised in every religion, known by many names, the savior of the world, President Emmanuel Bellomo!"

Again, the crowd erupted in shouts praising Bellomo. Angelo Cain raised his right arm and waved at the crowd to quiet down. "In honor of our blessed savior, to commemorate this inauguration, he will now enter the Holy of Holies."

FLOOD

Chapter 20

Behold, children are a gift of the LORD,
the fruit of the womb is a reward.
Psalm 127:3

Finally, the time came to leave the ark. We unloaded the animals first. Getting them off the ark took less time than loading them all into place. It was a sad relief for me to watch them leave. I was grateful for all the sketches of them I'd painted on the wooden panels Japheth had made for me.

It didn't take us long to find a spot where we wanted to eventually build our home, a lovely place at the base of the mountain not too far from where the ark had landed. After surveying the area, we agreed to live in one of the many caves we discovered until we could build a proper house.

But before anything else, the first thing we built was an altar, a place of sacrifice where we could give thanks to God. We searched for stones around the mountain and built a wide, stone circle. On it, Noah made an offering of one of the lambs we'd brought along for just such a purpose.

I'd seen animal sacrifices before the Flood, but I had watched this little one being born, and played with it. Tears filled my eyes as it was sacrificed. *Don't let it suffer.*

As Noah raised his arms in prayer, the Lord spoke to us! We could not see Him, but the glory of His light shone intensely around us, and we all fell to the ground in worship.

A voice spoke out of the light, "I bless each of you and command you to go and repopulate the earth."

I felt my first child move in my womb at the sound of His voice.

Then He gave us instructions: "All of the land animals and the birds, all that lives in the sea, will be fearful of you. I have put them in your power. Just as I gave you fruit, grain, and vegetables, I now give you animals for food.

"Noah," the voice said, "I make a covenant with you and with your descendants. Never again will I destroy the earth with a flood."

I began to weep with relief. We'd made it through the great Flood. Surely, our children would do better than the world before.

Listen. The same voice whispered in my mind, and I shivered as He continued, "Each human being is made in My image, so I will require the blood of anyone who murders one of my image bearers. If a wild animal kills a human being, it must be killed. If anyone takes a human life, human hands will take that person's life."

"Look!" Laelah pointed to the sky above us, and we all gaped in wonder.

"This rainbow is the sign of My covenant with you, and all flesh on the earth; never again shall the water become a flood to destroy all flesh."

When he finished speaking, the glorious light left, but the bright, colorful arc across the sky remained, the sign of the Creator's promise. We stood silently watching the rainbow arching across the sky above us. Japheth pulled me close against him, and I rested my head on his chest. "One, two, three . . . " I spoke out loud, reverently counting, "seven, there are seven colors!"

"We can actually see His promise!" Japheth replied. I looked up and saw the wonder in his face. We watched until it faded away.

We moved into the large, shallow cave, using the furnishings from the ark. But since the ark had been pitched inside and out, we were not able to use much of the wood to build.

"Why did you pitch the inside of the ark, anyway?" I asked Japheth, as we pulled out the iron bars from the animal cages to use for building an entryway to our new cave home.

"Those were the Lord's instructions; He didn't tell us why. We did talk about it amongst ourselves and came to the conclusion it was to preserve the ark for some reason." He picked up another beam of iron as he concluded, "I think we have enough here."

Japheth and I moved the wood and iron rods out of the ark onto a small cart, pulled by one of the donkeys, and trundled the load down the mountain to the cave that was now our new home. The entrance was quite broad, so Japheth and Shem fashioned a wooden wall, complete with a narrow window and barred with the iron rods we'd pried from the animal stalls, so predators could not enter.

"I feel safer now. We're not on the ark anymore, and I don't want to take the chance that one of the bears won't come in here after the food." Shem closed the door and slid a heavy, metal latch across it to hold it shut.

Nua nodded her approval. "I feel much more secure now."

The cave was large enough that each family had its own curtained off area for sleeping and some privacy.

Before the Flood, Laelah, with foresight, had thoughtfully planted vegetables and fruits in pots and stored them in a special room in the upper level of the ark, where slats in the ceiling allowed in sunlight for the plants after the rain had stopped. One daily chore everyone was happy to do was caring for the plants. It was a pleasant room, and the food growing there was essential to the family's wellbeing.

Once things dried out enough, we took the vegetables and fruits from the ark and planted them in a garden. Noah also planted a vineyard on the side of the mountain. I took seeds Laelah had packed away in small cloth bags and planted them around the outside of the house. It did not take long for them to sprout. Once they bloomed, the flowers provided nectar for the bees we kept, as well as some of the smaller birds that lived in the area.

$$\text{♪}$$

Months sped by, and finally, it was time for our child to be born. My labor was mercifully short, and each of the women helped in the delivery. By then, both Nua and Taina were also pregnant.

I heard a cry, and my heart burst with joy. Laelah quickly cut the cord and wrapped my child in a blanket. "You have a son," she told me tenderly, as she placed him in my arms. Tears rolled down her wrinkled cheeks. "I will go and get him."

Japheth must have been right outside the cave because he was by my side in a moment. "Are you all right?" he asked me, sitting down carefully by my side and taking my free hand in his.

"Of course," I answered, carefully handing him the baby. "Our son."

Japheth's face shone and tears filled his eyes. I had never seen him so happy. After bathing the baby and wrapping him in clean linens, the other women left us alone. Japheth and I basked in our joy, gazing in wonder at our newborn son for a long time.

"What will we name him?" Japheth asked. We had discussed the matter seriously several times but still hadn't come to a unified agreement.

I snuggled our tiny boy and kissed his sweet-smelling head. "Isn't he wonderful? We must choose his name carefully. This little one has made us a family."

He thought for a moment.

"What if we call him Gomer?" He smiled at the play on words. Gomer means "complete." I nodded in approval. The birth of our first child was a complete blessing.

As the months progressed, the other women came to their time and also gave birth to sons. Shem and Nua named their first child Elam. He was a strong, healthy boy. Ham and Taina's boy was Cush. His birthing was long and complicated, but he, too, was a healthy baby.

In thanksgiving, Noah declared a day of feasting to celebrate the births of the first children in our new world. The men prepared offerings to the Lord, as well as a fatted calf for our own meal. It took some doing to prepare all the food and care for the babies, but we managed to create quite a feast.

Noah gave thanks to the Lord and made the offering; after which, we all sat down to eat and drink. There was ale, as well as wine, the first we'd had in some time—the first fruits of the vineyards Noah had planted. Between the long day preparing food and caring for our son and a full stomach, I was exhausted and went to bed early.

I woke up to Gomer crying. Japheth was not there, which was odd. When the baby finished nursing, I got dressed.

Scooping up Gomer from our bed, I went out into the family living area to look for Japheth, but he was nowhere in the cave. It occurred to me that he might be with Noah and Laelah. Since the second baby had been born, they had moved out of the cave and were living in a tent far enough from the young children so as not to be disturbed by the crying infants.

In the early morning light, I could see the table, sitting in the yard outside of the house, had been cleared off and wiped clean, with no sign of the feast from the night before. Breathing a sigh of relief that everything had been taken care of, I made my way across the yard to the large tent belonging to Noah and Laelah. Japheth and Shem were stretched across the threshold of the tent, sleeping. Something was off.

Alarm streaked through my body, and I looked around in fear. Surely nothing could have survived the Flood, but what if somehow some of the Nephilim had? Water covered the whole earth, but they had super-human strength and powers. Irrational scenarios raced through my mind, and I was about to wake the men when I heard Taina talking to someone.

Turning around, I saw she and Ham were leaving with their baby. I made my way over to them.

"Ariana," Ham muttered as a greeting.

"Do you know why Shem and Japheth are sleeping by the tent? Are Noah and Laelah all right?"

Taina looked away from me to her baby, stroking his cheek. Ham told her to come, and they walked away.

"Where are you going?" I asked.

"We are moving into the ark," Ham barked in response. I noticed the bundles he was carrying—their possessions.

I watched them walk away. Ham was obviously angry. I wondered what had happened after I went to bed, but there was nothing I could do but watch them walk away.

I moved over to where Japheth slept and shook him. "Wake up! Japheth, wake up!" I whispered. He usually slept lightly, but he was so soundly asleep that it took me some effort to wake him up. I led him over to the garden, so we wouldn't disturb Shem.

As soon as we got to the garden, I turned, with Gomer on my hip. "What happened last night after I went to bed? Ham and Taina just left, saying they were moving into the ark."

Japheth sighed. "Ham went too far." He picked a berry from one of the bushes and ate it. "The other women all went to bed after we cleaned up. The rest of us were enjoying the cool evening and decided to make a fire. As we sat talking and joking, Father decided to pull out some more of the new wine he'd made to share with us. You know how meticulously he tends the vineyards." I nodded. "Father opened the keg, and we all enjoyed a cup of wine together by the fire. Between the feast and the wine, and the warmth of the fire, I fell asleep as they were talking. It must have been several hours later that Ham woke me and Shem up, laughing."

"So, Shem fell asleep outside as well?"

"Yes."

"So why did Ham wake you?" I asked, wrapping my arms around Gomer to pull him out of the sling so I could cradle him.

"He was laughing about Father being passed out naked in the tent. He wanted us to come and see."

"What?" I was shocked.

"Yes, I couldn't believe his arrogance . . . the way he was mocking Father. Shem hit him, knocking him to the ground, but Ham rolled around laughing, with tears pouring down his face."

As he recalled his brother's foolishness and disrespect, anger deepened the color on Japheth's face. "I came back here and took one of the blankets from the trunk, then Shem and I walked backwards into the tent and covered Father."

"That was kind, my love," I whispered, grateful for his respect and honor toward his father. It was so unlike Noah to drink so much that he would be intoxicated. I said as much to Japheth.

"It is. We all drank a lot, but what Ham did was wrong." Japheth then came closer to me and whispered into my ear. My ears grew hot as he described what Ham had done. He had disrespected Noah in a way that was unimaginable, taking advantage of Noah's vulnerable state.

I put my hand over my mouth as he spoke. What Ham had done to Noah was unspeakable. I opened my mouth to say something, but couldn't find the words. Japheth just nodded and pulled me into his arms. Nothing was the same after that.

FIRE

Chapter 21

Yes, rescue those being dragged off to death,
won't you save those about to be killed?
Proverbs 24:11

The music swelled as President Bellomo, the so-called "Promised One," according to Cain, entered the golden doors into the Temple, followed by Cain himself. The two men with the long beards followed them, and then the women entered the darkness, one by one. The golden doors swung shut. I watched them disappear and with every step, was filled with relief to not be among them.

The crowd waited for quite some time. Suddenly, there were screams and shouting. *What was happening in the Holy of Holies?* The crowd grew agitated, unsure of what to do. The golden doors burst open and men with guns raced down the stairs. These men were dressed in a different uniform than the Global Union army.

"They've desecrated the Holy of Holies!" a man with a gun screamed as he started spraying bullets at the crowd. He continued shouting in a language I didn't understand.

The woman guarding me, and her friend, screamed in terror as the wall next to us was riddled with bullets. They left me, rushing out of the

Temple along with the panicked crowd. I was caught in the stampede as people raced to leave the courtyard. Screams and gunfire pierced the air amid the wild and unrestrained chaos.

I managed to wedge myself behind one of the pillars, wrapping my arms around my head as shots were fired. As I crouched, shaking, I felt a hand on my shoulder. A boy around my age was saying something to me, but I didn't understand. Finally, he spoke in lightly accented English. "Are you hurt? You're covered in blood."

I looked up into his dark, worried eyes. "It's not safe here," he said as he surveyed my bloodied white gown, "especially for you. Come with me, and I'll get you to a safe place."

I hesitated. Trusting men who were offering me help had not gone well for me up to this point. Against my better judgment, I stood up and reluctantly took his offered hand.

We navigated the mayhem of the courtyard and through a narrow, nondescript door just across from where I'd been hiding. I could still hear gunshots behind us. The door opened to a brightly lit hallway. We raced down its length, stopping abruptly. He barreled through a door on our right, pulled me through and then slammed it shut, locking it. The Temple complex was large and complicated, but he seemed to know where he was going.

"We don't have much time. The girls, the volunteers, they were all killed," he told me. I gasped. I'd guessed that was our purpose from the beginning but to know the reality was shocking. "I don't know how you escaped, but you're not meant to be alive, and we need to get you out of here."

As he spoke, he opened drawers and cabinets. "Here, this should do!" He handed me some clothes and told me to change into them. With fumbling fingers, I managed to get out of the blood-stained white dress and into a sandy-colored, long-sleeved dress. He changed out of the long white robe he had been wearing.

My mind was starting to feel clearer; the effects of the drugged tea were wearing off. He turned to face me and smiled. "That's better. We won't draw too much attention," he said as he picked up a piece of fabric from the floor. "Wear this scarf."

He tossed the scarf to me. "What am I supposed to do with this?" I asked helplessly.

Sighing, he took it back. "Good thing I have older sisters. They used to make me help them with tying theirs." Deftly, he put the scarf on my head and wrapped my hair up in its folds.

I looked up to thank him and our eyes met. He stared down into my face. "My name is Jannik. What is yours?"

"Dani," I said, staring back at him.

"Dani," he said as put his hand softly on my shoulder, "listen, we're leaving here. The men who were shooting are Jewish nationalists. They've been against the peace treaty since our leaders signed it over three years ago. The Global Union army must be on its way. They'll have this place on lockdown and detain anyone who's suspicious. Since you didn't participate in the ceremony, it might make you a target. I'm assuming you don't have any official papers to be here?"

"No." I shook my head. "Do you know what happened?"

"A terrible thing happened, and somehow, you were spared by God. I was one of the attendants in the Holy of Holies when the President and Angelo Cain entered. It's totally forbidden; but in they came. We were all shocked to hear Cain call Bellomo the Promised One and were even more shocked that they would dare come into the Holy of Holies!

"In the peace treaty between the Global Union and Israel, the GU promised it would not mess with the Temple. We should have known when they demanded their ceremony take place in the courtyard . . ."

Jannik's voice trailed off as we both heard a scream, and he stopped talking for a moment.

His voice cracked as he continued talking. "Before we knew what was going on, they slaughtered the women before the altar. I think they were human sacrifices for President Bellomo!" His hand trembled as he ran his fingers through his hair. He was clearly shaken.

"What?" I gasped. No wonder they drugged us. No one would have fought back.

"One of the Temple priests grabbed a gun from one of the president's guards and shot the president in the head. It was all chaos from there."

Just then, we heard sirens. Jannik took my hand and pulled me along behind him to a door that led outside to the street. I followed him out the door, through cobbled streets filled with scrambling people. I'd never seen so many people in one place before. Jannik took my hand in his and led me like a child. The air was hot and heavy.

The city seemed so ancient, the stone streets and walls, the narrow alleys. Finally, we turned into an empty street; the walls on either side were so close, I thought I could touch both sides, but I didn't want to let go of Jannik's hand.

I desperately needed a hand to hold.

"This apartment belongs to a friend of mine. He's in Tel Aviv visiting his parents. He gave me a key, so I could water his plants, get the mail . . . he won't mind if we stay here." Jannik gave my hand a tug, "It's just up here."

We walked up a flight of stairs to an oval green door. I waited while Jannik fished a key out of one of his pockets and opened the door.

I walked in and was amazed by the coolness of the apartment. Jannik remarked that it had air conditioning. The spacious main room had two couches and in between was a strange piece of furniture. It stood on four legs and had a large, curved box set on top of it. Walking over, I touched one of the black and white rectangular buttons on it and jumped at the sound it made.

"We probably shouldn't play the piano. Don't want to attract any attention from the neighbors," Jannik warned. He led me into the kitchen. I had never seen anything like it. I ran my hand along the sleek, grey countertop. Jannik handed me a glass of water.

"I don't get it," I said to Jannik. "Why did you help me out of that place? Why bring me here?"

He looked down at me and smiled. "I don't know . . . I recognized the robe you were wearing. All of the others who wore those robes were killed, but somehow, you escaped. I couldn't let you die like they did."

"And you're still helping me." I smiled up at him, his dark eyes seemed friendly, but I wondered what he wanted. I knew better than to trust people. Still, he seemed sincere.

There were some stools in front of the counter. "Why don't we sit and talk?" Jannik suggested. "I'm sure you're as freaked out as I am, if not more!"

We sat down. I took a sip of the water. I felt disconnected.

"Where did you come from?" Jannik asked. "Obviously, you're not Israeli!"

There was something about Jannik, something warm, which reminded me of Daphne. Without thinking, I told him the whole story—about the Compound and how I'd run away, about Tomas and his betrayal, and about the creatures.

"Interesting," he remarked when I described how I escaped being stung. "There are many here in Jerusalem who also were not stung, myself included. No one is certain why."

He reached over to a basket full of apples on the counter and offered me one. I bit into the crispy juiciness and wiped my mouth with the back of my hand. As we ate the apples, I told him about Mitch and Sierra and how I ended up in Jerusalem.

"It's obvious God has been protecting you," he commented earnestly.

"Someone is for sure. Do you have family here?" I asked, interested to know more about him.

"No," he shook his head. "They were in Alexandria on business." His dark eyes looked pained.

"What happened in Alexandria?" I asked, almost afraid to hear the answer. By the look on his face, I knew it couldn't be good. I listened in horror as Jannik described the events of the previous week. Demonic monsters, different than the scorpion creatures but equally violent, had attacked many of the largest cities in the world, including Alexandria, where his parents were.

"There were millions and millions of them. My mother actually sent me a video of them approaching their hotel. Look." Jannik pulled a phone out of his back pocket, clicked on it a couple of times, and held it up.

I watched thousands of horse-like black creatures, with heads like those of lions. Unbelievably, fire and yellow smoke poured out of their vicious mouths. They wore red and purple armor. On their backs were other creatures, like men in formbut not men, wearing the same colors as the horses. As I watched, the people fleeing the creatures were overcome by the yellow smoke and fire. Many could be heard screaming in agony and crying out to God for mercy.

"There are other creatures?" I whispered. "Will they come here?"

"I don't know," Jannik replied doubtfully. "There were other videos taken by other people; I watched so many of them looking for any sign of what happened to my parents. I hoped they escaped, but after the attacks were over, neither one answered their phone. I've imagined them suffering over and over." His voice cracked and tears ran down his face.

I didn't know what to do. "I'm so sorry," I told him, hoping my sympathetic presence would give even a small amount of comfort to my new friend.

"My parents were believers, but it didn't save them."

"Believers?" I asked quizzically.

"Yes, in President Bellomo. They believed he was the Promised One, the Messiah. We argued all the time about it. They were in Alexandria to take part in a special service for those who were committing their lives to him."

"You don't believe he's the Promised One?" I wanted to distract him from his grief over his parents' deaths.

"No, I believe the two Witnesses. My parents hated them . . . absolutely despised them. The arguments were tearing us apart. I stayed here with my friend a lot these past few months. It was getting really bad at home."

Jannik got up and threw away our apple cores and washed his hands before sitting back down.

"I only know a little about the Witnesses," I ventured. "I heard they have supernatural power over rain."

He nodded. "To be honest, most people here hate them. They preach every day in various places in Jerusalem. No one can touch them. They claim to speak for God, and they often predict judgments before they happen. They warned about the creatures that killed my parents. I warned them, but they went anyway."

"Oh, that's terrible." I reached my hand out to cover his.

He smiled at me for the first time, deep dimples creasing his cheeks, "Let's get you settled." Jannik led me out of the kitchen and down a short hallway.

"Here is the guest room. You can stay in here. It has a bathroom of its own, so you'll be more comfortable." Jannik opened the door, revealing a small bedroom. The bed was tucked under a small window covered with black bars. *Bars on the windows.* My heart started racing. I stepped back into the hallway and ran for the front door.

"Wait, wait!" Jannik ran after me and got to the door first.

"Let me out," I demanded.

"You have nowhere to go, Dani. I want to help you. What's wrong?"

"There are bars on the window in that room." I glared at him furiously.

"Dani, look around this living room. There are bars on every window."

I glanced over the room and felt like an idiot. "Oh."

Jannik ran his hand through his hair. "Why don't you rest for a bit?" he suggested. "I need to figure out what to do next."

FLOOD

Chapter 22

Now the whole world had one language and a common speech. As the people moved eastward, they found a plain in Shinar and settled there . . . they said, "Come, let us build ourselves a city, with a tower that reaches to heaven, so that we may make a name for ourselves."

Genesis 11:1–2, 4

When he woke up, Noah was furious. He cursed Ham's son so angrily, he frothed at the mouth. Ham and Taina had already packed up all of their belongings and moved into the ark, away from the entire family. The family felt fractured, and I missed Taina. I couldn't imagine her taking care of her son all alone. I don't know if it was shame that kept Ham and his family away, but we rarely saw them as the years passed.

Our family grew and life got busy. Nua and I were blessed with many children. Japheth built a home for our family in the valley, not too far from the original home in the cave. Shem and Nua also built a home near ours. Noah and Laelah built a small home closer to the mountain. All of us worked together, expanding the fields and herds of cattle, sheep, and goats.

The years quickly passed. Our children grew and married—often first or second cousins at first—and had their own children, and the family expanded greatly. Some of our children found husbands and wives among Ham and Taina's descendants. Many times, the family was blessed with twins or even triplets. From the eight of us who walked off the ark, we were creating a new world, and it was expanding faster than we imagined. Decades turned into centuries.

Learning from Laelah, I grew into a skilled midwife. I was present at hundreds of births, often called in the middle of the night to aid in difficult deliveries. Laelah and I developed tinctures, remedies, and tools to soothe mothers and bring babies safely into the world. With each new birth, I was filled with hope. We were fulfilling the mandate of the Creator to fill the earth.

Noah was careful to record each birth, just as his father, Lamech had before him. The family records were kept in the special chest that had been placed securely on the ark, the same chest that held the garments the Creator made for the First Ones.

One night, when I was up late tending to one of my grandchildren while his mother slept, I saw the light on in Noah's house and was surprised he was still awake. Taking the baby with me, I went over. I knocked on the door. Noah invited me in, smiling at the little one.

"Please have a seat," he said. He was sitting at a table, with the family records spread in front of him. Those records were kept on carefully prepared animal skins and meticulously documented.

"Would you like to see the records?" he asked. Eagerly, I sat down and listened as he traced the family lineage all the way back to Adam, the son of God. I was reminded that Noah's father had been born during Adam's lifespan. It was so long ago, but it felt recent, knowing that Noah's father had known Adam. I asked Noah to talk about it.

"Adam lived near our homestead. Of course, by then, many had turned away from following the Creator, as you know. According to my grandfather, Methuselah, it was Adam's influence that kept our family from following the ways of the Nephilim." Noah looked thoughtful. He pushed the parchment toward me. "If you look here at the first names, many were written by Adam himself!"

I was reminded what a privilege it was that I even knew how to read the parchments. In the days before the Flood, under the Magistrate's rule, women had been denied that privilege. Mother had secretly taught me herself, as she had learned from her mother before her. I studied the ancient parchments before me and traced the family line with my finger.

"Methuselah learned much from Adam, and passed it on to me. I have written my own notes." He pulled out some more parchments from a box on the bench next to him then unrolled the scroll he had pulled out. "Adam and Eve both were instrumental in teaching each generation about the Creator. Nine generations of our family lived together west of Eden. We stayed away from the cities and followed the Old Ways."

It frightened me a little that in only a few generations, things could go so terribly wrong. I thought of the little one in my lap and hoped we had created a better world for our descendants. *I wonder if Ham and Taina are teaching their family about the Creator?* I thought to myself.

Noah pushed the scroll he'd pulled out toward me. "You can read what Methuselah told me here. I transcribed his words."

Again, I took the scroll and read it eagerly. There was the story of the creation of the man and woman and the serpent's successful tempting them to violate the one rule the Creator had given them. I felt a twinge when I read how they had strung leaves together to cover up their nakedness. *How naturally we all tried to cover up our misdeeds.* But the Creator had stepped in and truly covered their nakedness by sacrificing an animal and making its skin into clothing for the man and the woman.

I looked up at Noah. "Those are the same skins that are stored in the chest, are they not? Ham thinks the skins have some kind of power. Is that because they were made by the Creator himself?"

Noah laughed scornfully. "They have *value* because they were made by the Creator, but no power in and of themselves. The Nephilim believed they have power because they listened to the lies of the evil one. From the beginning, he has sowed hatred and evil among the sons of Adam. Unfortunately, there have been many who turned from the Creator and allowed those attributes to take root in their souls."

I thought about the impressive cities destroyed in the Flood, all of those people now drowned. "You said that God regretted making men and women, Noah. Why allow us to survive?"

"Remember that the lineage of many humans had been tainted by the Nephilim. I preached to the people for many, many years, but they repeatedly turned to the Nephilim. All of the faithful were going to come onto the ark with us, but they were murdered." I shuddered, remembering the horrible scene on the field that day. "Indeed, it was the incredible violence and evil in humanity which made the Creator condemn it."

Noah and I talked nearly that whole night about our hopes and dreams for the future.

There are many lessons we should have learned from what happened, but we did not.

Our families expanded incredibly in number so that, by the third generation, a great many people filled the land. As humans did before the Flood, they would live out life spans of hundreds of years for the next few generations, although that would eventually change. Our children and grandchildren spread out and moved away. It was happening just as the Lord had commanded: we were repopulating and filling the earth. But we did not live in harmony.

I don't know how it began—squabbles over land here, walls around towns there.

Our descendants began to call us, the original eight, the "Mothers and Fathers." We tried to mediate between them, but it seemed the Flood had not eradicated selfishness and hate from their hearts.

One of Ham's grandsons, Nimrod, rose to prominence. Over the years, he became a ruthless warrior and built up an army of men from all three families who were completely devoted to him. They wanted more than peaceful lives. They wanted more than the mandate to have families and continue to spread across the earth. They wanted to be powerful and rule over the others.

Together, they defied the command to spread out over the earth and instead built a city in the land of Shinar and called it "Babylon." Other cities followed. While I knew it was wrong, I understood why. In cities, you could accumulate wealth. They were full of stability and culture and power for those who ruled over them. Nimrod ruled over Babylon and other cities as well—Erech, Accad, and Calneh—but it was Babylon where he began building his tower.

Noah heard about it and decided that some of us should journey to Babylon to see what was going on. Gathering together with some of our sons and their wives, Japheth and I organized a caravan to travel the long distance. Nua and Shem joined us, along with some of their family. There were seventy of us altogether.

Noah blessed us before we left, reminding us of the great evil that had arisen in the cities of men before the Flood, and charging Shem and Japheth, as the Fathers, to lead us well. All of us had horses, and each of us was armed—men and women. There were aggressive bears in the hill country but also human enemies. There were so many generations roaming the earth that we didn't know everyone, and they didn't all know us. How quickly the world changed from the day we stepped off the ark into an empty world.

It took us almost three months to reach Babylon. One of the blessings of the journey was that we got to visit family along the way. I had delivered many of the people we saw and was asked for remedies and midwifery advice by anxious mothers. I loved seeing my children, grandchildren, and great-grandchildren. There was no better sight than children running excitedly toward us as we approached each farm.

We were still far from the city when we saw it—a large tower, stretching upwards toward heaven. "So, it is true," Japheth said solemnly.

There were walls surrounding the city, so we had to make our way to one of the gates. Guards stood before the entrance, barring the way. Shem and Japheth approached them. The men recognized their forefathers and greeted them with great respect.

I breathed a sigh of relief. As we approached Babylon, I vividly recalled the great city from which the Magistrate ruled and was filled with a dreadful sense of foreboding, but the kindly manner in which Shem and Japheth were treated put me at ease.

Welcoming us into the city, our guides led us to a great field to the west of the gate. It was a pleasant expanse of grass with a small river running through it. At the end of the field was the huge tower. The tower was covered with people working in various capacities. It seemed it was not quite finished.

"You may put up your tents here, Fathers and Mothers. I will go and inform the king that you have arrived." The guard spoke respectfully.

"You knew we were coming?" Shem asked.

"The king's wife has the gift of foresight," he answered.

"Who is his wife?" I asked. None of us knew Nimrod had taken a wife or that he called himself a king.

"She is Semiramis, the Gift of the Sea," was the response. I looked at Japheth warily.

The guard turned and left. We tended to our horses and then began to set up camp. Not long after he left, the guard returned and asked Shem and Japheth to follow him, along with Nua and me.

As we followed the guard along the dusty city streets, I could not help but stare at the women and men I saw. They all had to be my distant relatives, some even my great- and great-great-grandchildren. The women were elaborately dressed, their hair piled up in embellished bundles covered in decorative gold headdresses. They wore sensual dresses draped luxuriously around their bodies. The men wore skirts made from woven fabrics. Brightly patterned, they were split in front and angled up the middle, some up so high that there was nothing left to the imagination. Once again, I was fearfully reminded of the Magistrate's city, Sumeria. The same spirit seemed to walk the streets of Babylon.

We arrived at Nimrod's residence; it was truly a palace fit for a king. I put my hand on my husband's shoulder. He stopped walking, and I whispered to him, "Japheth, this is the first such place since the Flood." He nodded and took my hand in his as we walked up the staircase into the palace.

FIRE

Chapter 23

I saw one of his heads as if it had been slain,
and his fatal wound was healed.
And the whole earth was amazed and
followed after the beast.
Revelation 13:3

When I woke, it was dark outside. Pushing back the blanket, I got up and made my way into the bathroom. I assumed Jannik was still sleeping in the other room. As I washed my hands under the warm running water, I stared at my reflection in the mirror. My blonde hair hung in a disheveled mess over my face. I found a brush and went to work on my hair, brushing out the tangles. There was an elastic band wrapped around the brush handle. I used it to pull my long hair back into a ponytail away from my face. There was nothing I could do about my bruised nose or the dark circles under my eyes, so I left the bathroom and went back to the bedroom.

I switched on the small lamp next to the bed and looked around the room. There was a large closet, its doors painted a cheerful yellow. Getting back up, I opened the doors carefully, determined not to make too much noise and disturb Jannik.

It was empty, except for some books piled on a shelf. One of them had the word "Jerusalem" printed in large, bold letters across the top. It was filled with old black and white pictures, paired with newer color photographs, labeled with the phrase "today." I wondered how old the book was as I looked carefully through its pages. There were many names that were familiar to me—the Tower of David, Absalom's tomb—from the small Bible that belonged to Daphne. I knew who David was. How strange to see his name in this book, and the name of his son, Absalom.

The stories about David were my favorite ones in Daphne's book. All along, I'd thought they were just old stories. But the names and places in them were real. I wondered for the first time if the whole book was real. I must have fallen asleep again because when I woke up it was light, and I could smell Jannik cooking in the kitchen.

Jannik and I stayed in the apartment for a week before we ran out of food. It was the best week of my life. We spent the days eating and talking, secluded from the outside world and all its troubles. I found some cozy clothes in one of the closets, and we lounged on the couches most days, relaxing in each other's company and talking nonstop. We never ran out of things to say.

I felt comfortable around Jannik. Never had anyone paid such thoughtful attention to me. After hearing my story in detail, he insisted on giving me history lessons so I would understand what was going on in the world. We played card games, watched old movies, and ate together. For the first time in my life, I went to sleep unafraid of what the next day would bring.

The morning we ran out of food, he closed the pantry door in the kitchen and came and joined me at the table. There was still tea, so I'd made cups for both of us. We drank in silence for a few minutes. I watched him intently and noted how his dark brown eyes looked worried under furrowed brows. Strangely, I wasn't overly concerned. I knew he would figure something out.

"I was thinking it might be okay if we go out for a walk today," he suggested. We chatted for a few minutes about where we'd go.

"You're going to need some different shoes," Jannik pointed out. The shoes I'd been given to wear for the ceremony were still by the front door where I'd left them when we'd first arrived at the apartment. They were white, small heeled, and too tight.

He left the kitchen and came back a minute later with a pair of shoes in hand. "These will work! The streets of the Old City have many steps and cobblestones."

I put them on and then tied my hair back in a scarf. "Where will we go? I asked.

"For some reason, I really want to try and see those two Witnesses," Jannik answered. "After Bollomo's assassination, I'm sure the streets will be heavily monitored, but I think this beard will throw anyone off!"

I laughed. I'd teased him over breakfast that he looked like a grizzly bear with his bushy beard. "I think you're right!"

We left the apartment, carefully locking the door behind us. Jannik led the way, talking nonstop. "I've felt so cooped up! It's good to be outside, isn't it?"

After nearly ten minutes, we were in front of the Temple in the plaza by the Western Wall. There were many people in the plaza, including Global Union soldiers. They stood between the crowd and the two young men who were sitting on the stairs that led up to the Temple.

Jannik put his arm around me and pulled me close as a couple of men pushed roughly past us. I glimpsed a gun on one of the men as his suit jacket flapped back and whispered my observation to Jannik. He kept his arm around me.

"Look over there," he said, nodding to the street. Three black trucks pulled up to the curb and soldiers dressed in black uniforms and black helmets piled out, forming a pathway from the street to the soldiers and blocking the way to the Temple where the Witnesses sat.

"I think we should go now," I told Jannik, but he insisted we stay. I had been wary before the long black car pulled up, but when I saw Angelo Cain get out, I panicked.

Jannik kept his arm tightly around me. "Look, all of the streets out of here are blocked by soldiers. We can't go anywhere now." He pulled me closer to him and backed up against a wall. I looked back to the street and gasped in horror. President Bellomo!

"I thought you saw him die!"

"It's impossible! He was shot in the head!" Jannik muttered in disbelief as a figure that clearly looked like President Bellomo strode confidently along the pathway lined with soldiers. As he passed, each of the men saluted him before returning to a stance that looked ready for action.

"What's going on here?" Jannik hissed.

People around us started screaming Bellomo's praises. "He died and he lives! He rose from the dead! He's a god and not a man!"

I watched as the two Witnesses stood up. They were too far away for me to see their facial expressions clearly, but someone had put up a giant screen in front of the old wall to our right. "Someone planned this event," I whispered to Jannik. Fear coursed through my whole body, and I began to shake. I was certain no one in the plaza would survive the showdown happening in front of us. Because of the screen, we could see the events in detail as they unfolded.

"So, the beast himself comes!" one of the Witnesses laughed jeeringly. "We watched your fall from heaven!"

Bellomo stopped moving toward the men and stood still. The camera switched to him. His face was bright red with fury.

The other Witness continued, "You know the prophecy, that the time has come, but you're not sure we won't harm you in the process, are you?"

Angelo Cain screamed, "How dare you threaten the Promised One! He died and has risen from the dead. Repent and bow before him, and you will receive mercy!"

The Witnesses turned to the crowd and shouted, "Woe to you who dwell on the earth! Terror has come upon you because the devil has been cast down and walks among you!"

The plaza was eerily silent. Bellomo began moving again. The two men stood still as he approached, hands hanging at their sides. Suddenly, the president grabbed a machine gun from a soldier and blasted the two men until their bullet-riddled bodies fell to the ground.

The crowd around us erupted in shouts of acclamation and praise. Some fell to their knees, praising President Bellomo as the Promised One. Jannik grabbed my hand. "We need to get out of here right now!"

The crowd was going wild in celebration. Jannik backed us away from the crowd, slipping past some soldiers and into an ally. I clutched his hand like a lifeline.

When we got back the apartment, breathing hard, we shut the door and locked it behind us. Jannik had turned his phone off when we first got to the apartment, but as soon as we locked the door, he went to the kitchen and pulled it off the counter and turned it on.

We both stood in the kitchen and watched a live feed from the Temple, where the crowds were still celebrating wildly. The camera pulled in for a close up shot of the two dead Witnesses. Soldiers stood on either side of the corpses, preventing anyone from coming near the bodies.

The scene changed to show Angelo Cain standing behind a podium with the Global Union flag emblazoned on it. After the thunderous applause of the crowd died down, he raised his arms in triumph. His voice boomed over the loudspeakers, "The Promised One lives! Clearly he is God and not a man. Now, he will take his place of destiny. Having eliminated the so-called "Witnesses,' he will continue to rid the world of all opposition to his rightful rule." The crowd erupted again in cheers. Motioning for them to be quiet, he added, "The time has come to anoint him.

He *is* the long-awaited Messiah. We will enter the Holy of Holies and use it for what it is intended—to confirm our new and rightful leader!"

With a mechanical smile stretched across his face, Cain declared a three-day celebration of the Witnesses' defeat, stating the celebration would officially end on the evening of the third day with a redo of the ceremony at the Temple. Again, Angelo Cain would anoint President Bellomo as the Promised One and enter the Holy of Holies.

"They are going to try it again." Jannik sat down heavily on a stool by the counter. I took the stool next to him.

"What does this mean? Why do they need to go into the Holy of Holies?" This was all so confusing to me.

"It is the Abomination of Desolation the prophet Daniel spoke about." Jannik hit the counter with the palm of his hand angrily. "This means President Bellomo is breaking his treaty with Israel. It is a declaration of war instead of the peace he promised over three years ago!"

"What are you talking about?" I asked, still a bit confused.

"Three and a half years ago, President Bellomo ratified a peace treaty with our leaders, guaranteeing Israel's right to the Temple. When they tried to enter it last week, it was pandemonium, as we saw. But he is going to do it again, claiming to be the Jewish Messiah—which he's not. The prophet Daniel warned about this."

I put my hand on his shoulder, and he turned to me. Tenderly, Jannik placed a hand on either side of my face. "I've saved you, but I have no idea about what we should do now."

Staring up into his eyes, I saw concern mixed with fear. I wanted to say something that would help, but I couldn't think of anything. Just then there was a chirp from the phone in his hand.

"It's from Noam. He's one of the other Temple attendants." Quickly Jannik clicked on his phone and began speaking. I could hear Noam, but I didn't understand Hebrew, so I had no idea what they were talking about. They spoke for several minutes before Jannik hung up and turned the power off again.

"We're going to meet my friend and some others. There is a meeting tonight for those who don't believe Bellomo is the Promised One. Maybe they will have a plan for what to do next."

FLOOD

Chapter 24

But the LORD came down to see the city and the tower the people were building ... If as one people speaking the same language they have begun to do this, then nothing will be impossible for them. Come, let us go down and confuse their language.

Genesis 11: 6–7

As we were ushered into Nimrod's throne room, I was speechless. Nimrod sat on a great golden throne perched on a high dais. The room was spacious, with high ceilings and marble floors, and filled with rows of soldiers standing at attention before their king. The walls on all sides glittered with painted images traced in gold, detailing exploits of Nimrod the Great, grandson of Ham, hunter of animals and men. His prowess in ending life was on display to all who entered the hall. Surely, the great Flood had failed to drown out the wickedness of mankind.

Nimrod's wife, Semiramis, sat on a similar throne next to him. Never had I seen such beauty. Nua had heard from a farmer in the marketplace that Semiramis was one of Ham's great-granddaughters. Named Semra at birth, she had run away from home as a young woman to a nearby city where she had sold herself to any man who would pay for the privilege. How she came to find herself married to Nimrod, Nua did not find out.

Of course, Nimrod did not stand in courtesy when the Mothers and Fathers entered the room, as was the custom. Instead, he nodded his head, his golden crown appearing heavy.

Japheth spoke first. "Nimrod, I recall seeing you at a gathering many years ago. You were a child, barely able to walk. Now, it seems you have taken a lofty place for yourself."

Nimrod looked down haughtily at his elder and did not respond. Instead, Semiramis lashed out, "How dare you speak so to Nimrod the Great, builder of cities and the Tower of heaven?"

"We have come to see this self-proclaimed king," replied Shem, wryly. "You have defied the law of God by building these cities and the tower, which can never reach heaven. You both are like children play acting, but your actions have great consequences."

"You are an old man," spat Nimrod. "Yet you dare come here to confront me in my own palace, before my own guards." Nimrod stood up, his neck and face turning red with anger. "I refuse to adhere to the elders' rules. They are inventions of the imagination of a foolish old man. By the power of my own might, I have built Babylon and other cities. My tower will stand against any so-called god who tries to destroy us. No flood can reach its height or drown us out."

"Pride has twisted your mind, Nimrod," Japheth responded. "Only one so utterly foolish would contend with the Creator. Each of us before you saw the great Flood. We have seen what the end is for those who refuse to walk in the paths set by the Creator."

"I have lived long on the earth," Nimrod boasted. "Yet, I have not seen your God. We are a great people, and together we have built this city and the great tower reaching to the heavens. We have made a name for ourselves, and our unity is our strength. There is nothing we cannot do, and there is no one who can oppose us."

Nimrod held out his left hand in the middle of his speech and grasped the hand of Semiramis. Her black hair glinted under a large golden headdress made to look like water lilies floating on a pond. She caught my eye just then and looked at me with studied contempt, from my uncovered head down to the simple sandals on my feet. Although I did not seek admiration for my looks, for the first time, I felt my lack of charm and my great age, in comparison to the youthful, alluring woman before me.

Shem and Japheth tried to reason with Nimrod, but his convictions were clearly unalterable. We left the palace, resigned, and went back to the field where our tents and families waited.

Tables had been set up in the field, and some of the daughters of Shem and Nua had made food over a fire by the riverside. We sat down to share a meal with our family and discuss what to do next. We had seen great evil in the city, but Nimrod, we now saw, was drunk on power and impervious to our warnings. Shem and Japheth decided to cry out to the Creator in prayer, asking Him to help our descendants see wisdom.

Then, we heard a voice breaking through the noise of our prayers, and we turned.

Three men approached us, walking across the field. The one in the middle spoke with the voice of authority. "I have come down to see this city and the tower, which the children of men have built."

It was the same One I'd encountered so long ago in the woods, the One who had brought joy and peace to my heart! He was larger and somehow brighter than any man I'd ever seen. There were two in attendance with him, lesser than he, but still more than human. While the Nephilim had a spirit of darkness around them, these men had a spirit of light. All of us fell to the ground in reverence before him. One of the two with him instructed us to look up and listen to the Word of the Creator.

"They are united in their defiance and have traded in brick and mortar for devotion to the Most High, so we have come down to divide them. No longer will the children of men speak one language but now many."

Shem spoke up, "Lord, we have come here to speak to Nimrod, to make him see the truth."

The first man smiled approvingly at Shem. "You are a man of great renown. Because of your faith, out of you, I will make a nation to demonstrate My truth to the world of men."

He then spoke a blessing over all of us, and raised his hands up toward heaven. Then he and the men with him disappeared.

No one moved or spoke for some time. After a while, people began to slowly get up and move around the camp. We were all silently trying to comprehend the wonder of the visit we had just received.

I was in the tent with Japheth, fast asleep in the early morning hours, when shouts and screams woke me. Japheth was already up and moving out of the tent. "Stay here," he ordered, but of course I followed him out. There were soldiers all over the field, torches in hand. The dragon symbol of Nimrod glittered in embroidered gold on their tunics.

I watched in disbelief as soldiers grabbed Shem and Japheth. One of them struck Nua as she attempted to free her husband, and she fell to the ground. Our families tried to intervene, but Japheth commanded them to cease fighting. I went to Nua's side, and one of the men shouted at us. His words were garbled and strange. I had no idea what he was saying, but Nua and I followed as they took our husbands toward Nimrod's palace.

It began to rain as we trudged barefoot behind them toward the palace, and although it was past dawn, heavy clouds darkened the sky. The grand building was foreboding in the dark, despite the torchlight the men carried. We made our way up the stairs, into the palace and through the maze of corridors to the great throne room. Nimrod stood alone on the dais; a simple white robe wrapped around him. Semiramis was not there.

As soon as we entered the room, Nimrod began screaming at us. My husband answered him calmly, asking what the trouble was.

Nimrod stood on his dais, flustered and angry. He continued to yell, but it was incomprehensible.

"This is the will of the Creator in response to your defiance!" Shem responded angrily, yanking his arm out of the guard's grasp and pulling Nua protectively to his side. I put my hand in Japheth's as I stared at the man before us. Spittle foamed on the sides of his mouth as he continued his tirade of accusations.

Nimrod babbled furiously at us, but not one word made any sense. He came down off the dais and stood face to face with Japheth, who tried to calm him down. Spit flew from Nimrod's mouth onto Japheth's face. Dropping my hand, Japheth tried to grab Nimrod's shoulders, to push him away. Nimrod was uncontrollable; he rushed back at Japheth, who pushed him away harder. Nimrod fell back, hitting the ground hard. I screamed a warning to Japheth, but I was too late. One of the guards rushed toward us, spear raised. Before the scream left my mouth, the spear pierced Japheth, and he fell to the ground in anguish.

The room was suddenly silent. Despite their rough handing of us, no one yet had dared to touch one of the Mothers and Fathers. I rushed to Japheth. I screamed as I fell next to him and pulled him into my arms. "No, God, please, no! Make it not true. Make it not true . . ."

I screamed over and over as Japheth's blood poured onto the floor. I pleaded for God to change what had happened, to turn back what had been done, but Japheth died in my arms.

The world turned silent for a moment. Everything seemed to move slowly as I held my dead husband, my Japheth, in my arms. I saw his spirit leave his body, like smoke. Smiling tenderly at me, he turned away and disappeared. I think Nimrod saw it, too, for the moment Japheth's spirit disappeared, he exploded in maniacal anger, barking orders out in guttural, slurring commands.

At that moment, four guards grabbed Shem and Nua and hauled them out of the throne room. One of the other guards grabbed me up off the floor, tearing me away from Japheth's body. Screaming, I stumbled along, trying to keep up. Each time I tripped, he yelled at me and shook me harshly, speaking in the same strange way Nimrod had. I was pushed into a small room and locked in.

I turned and looked around numbly. A pile of cushions sat against one of the walls; there were no windows in the room. Sinking down on the cushions, I put my head on my knees and cried until I passed out. My Japheth was gone.

FIRE

Chapter 25

*These signs will accompany those who have believed:
In my name they will cast out demons, they will
speak with new tongues.*

Mark 16: 17

We walked through the old streets of Jerusalem for almost an hour. The
streets were filled with people celebrating the deaths of the two Witnesses,
and we had to go around several checkpoints. Global Union soldiers were
roaming the city, looking for dissenters. I was nervous to be outside the
apartment, but Jannik was convinced this meeting would be worthwhile,
and I trusted him.

Never having been in a city as large and ancient as this before, I was
overwhelmed by the number of people, the sounds, and the smells and
clung to Jannik's hand as he led the way. It was nearing sunset when we
met Noam outside of a complex of buildings. He and Jannik greeted one
another enthusiastically, hugging and talking at the same time in Hebrew.
I waited awkwardly to be introduced.

Jannik turned, gesturing to me, "This is my friend, Dani. Dani, this
is, Noam."

Noam greeted me with a quick bow. "Tamas, one of the 144,000, will be here tonight!" I didn't know what this meant, but I smiled at Noam, grateful that he spoke English.

Noam turned, and we followed him up some cobble stone stairs and through an archway. The whole complex reminded me of an ancient palace. There were towers and walls everywhere. We came to an arched door. Over the doorway, there were words in Hebrew and English on a metal plaque that said, "King David's Tomb." I was stunned. The King David from Daphne's book. This really was an ancient palace. *All of those stories in Daphne's book . . . must be real!*

As we entered the building, I noticed two signs: "Men" and "Women." Jannik turned to me, motioned for me to follow him, and walked over to the "Women" sign.

"You must go in there."

"What?"

"Women and men must be separated. The women have this space in the tomb."

I'm not sure why, but that irritated me. I didn't want to be separated from Jannik. "Why?" I whispered, not wanting the women streaming past me to hear me. "Where are you going to be?"

"Really, it's okay, Dani. I'll be on the other side of that partition." He patted my hand and then walked away. I stood still for a moment before reluctantly following the women who were moving into a small, crowded room. We were fenced in by stone walls and gold-paneled partitions. Each of the partitions had a white, rectangular panel centered on it with words written in Hebrew. I assumed it was some information about King David. I found an empty plastic chair and sat down.

As I sat there, I fumed. I was angry and worried. *What if something happens, and I can't find Jannik?* I imagined all kinds of scenarios that ended up with me being alone again. Then I noticed a few women standing in front of something that resembled a small house. It was covered with a black cloth, with patterns embroidered in gold across the top and golden words in Hebrew embroidered on the front.

An older woman made her way through the crowd of women and sat next to me. Smiling, she asked me a question in Hebrew.

"Oh, sorry, I only speak English," I murmured. Jannik had taught me some phrases, but it was so hard to get them right, even though I had been practicing in bed at night.

"I asked if you were here with someone, and if you mind if I sit here?" she replied in perfect English.

I wasn't sure what to say, If Jannik were here, he'd know what to say. "Kind of; he's on the other side." I felt so awkward and irritated. My feelings must have showed because she laughed and patted my shoulder.

"Yes, there are still some places in Israel where the women are segregated like second-class citizens. King David's Tomb is one of them."

Some of the women standing in front of us were rocking back and forth; one of them was touching the tomb, her eyes closed and lips moving silently. I could hear the men next to us. Some were chanting; others were clapping. Then there was silence from the men, and the women all sat down.

I heard a man's voice speaking in Hebrew. He spoke for a few minutes before his speech became emphatic. He repeated a phrase a couple of times, and then I saw hands grasping the partition between the men and the women. Within a few minutes, the golden partitions were moved away.

A thin man dressed in a white shirt and blue jeans strode across the room and addressed the women, who all clapped and smiled at his words. I must have looked confused because he caught my eye and came toward me. Smiling, he placed a hand on my head and raised the other hand up in prayer. Suddenly, I could understand every word he was saying.

As he continued to address the crowd in Hebrew, I was shocked that I could understand what he was saying as easily as English. I fell from the chair to my knees, my eyes riveted on the thin man, my arms wrapped around my body trying to hold it together because I was shaking so hard. I had never felt such power and brightness.

"Lord God, I ask that You give each person here the ability to understand my words, so that they may hear the truth of Your gospel. I know that You hear me when I speak to You. By Your power, and for Your glory, let each one here know by this miracle that what I say is the truth. In the name of Yeshua, amen." He moved back to the front of the newly expanded room and stood quietly for a moment.

"What have you come to see tonight? Miraculous healings? A word of prophecy? I am Tamas, only one voice—one of a hundred and forty-four thousand voices from each of the twelve tribes of Israel, sent out into the world to proclaim the glorious truth that the Promised One, the Messiah, has come and is the way of salvation to everyone who will believe—to the Jew first and also to the Gentiles."

He stopped talking and looked around the room at each person. Many faces were bright and hopeful, while some were confused or even angry. He caught my eyes again in his gaze and smiled. I felt known somehow—and welcomed.

"We stand at a critical time in Israel's history," he continued as he looked around the room, his eyes seeking. "Today, as many of you know, the evil one killed the two Witnesses. As we know from the Scriptures, they will lie in the street for three days; then the Lord God Almighty, Creator of heaven and Earth, will raise them from the dead!"

Many in the room began to shout out praises and cries of thanksgiving.

"Do not rejoice, brethren!" the young man shouted, tears running down his face. "The evil one himself has entered President Bellomo. Cast out of heaven, he knows his time is coming to an end, and he is filled with fury."

One man stood up and yelled, "Blasphemy!" and stormed out. Others around me were talking, obviously upset. The feeling of fear in the room was palpable and strong. Many were crying. *What hope was there when the devil himself was incarnate?* Desperate, I spoke up.

"Is there any reason to hope? I read the Bible a long time ago. I thought it was just stories, but it seems to me now, it was true. There really was a David. And the story of Jesus, who died here in Jerusalem and who rose again from the dead, is that real, too?"

Tamas moved through the crowd and stood in front of me. "What is your name?"

"Dani."

He placed a hand on my shoulder. "Do you believe this, Dani? Do you believe that Yeshua—Jesus—died and rose again to pay the penalty of your sins to save you?"

It all fell into place at that moment. All I had read, all that had happened to bring me to this place, now made sense. It was true!

"Yes," I whispered, then more emphatically, "Yes, I believe!"

Tamas grinned, shouting out, "Praise God!!"

Some men, dressed in black suits, long curls on either sides of their faces and wearing black hats, stood up on the side that had been the men's and began to shout at both Tamas and me. Raising their fists, they began screaming curses at us. I saw Jannik stand up across the room, looking panicked.

Tamas raised his hand, and the men fell to the floor writhing in pain. Shaking his head in disgust, he turned his back to them, addressing the others in the room. "You stubborn people! This is why Gentiles like this young woman find the Messiah, while you continue—now, even now—to reject Him, despite all of the evidence, and then seek to harm those who find Him! Isaiah was right about you! You honor Him with your lips, but your hearts are still far from Him!"

The people grew eerily quiet, I could see many were filled with fear, but incredibly, I was not afraid. Tamas spoke to me briefly and prayed for me before returning to the front of the room. He stood staring at the tomb of King David for a moment before turning back to the people in the room.

"What was David told? That one of his descendants would be the Promised One and reign on the throne of David forever, right?"

The crowd murmured in agreement.

"We missed His coming to us! We rejected Yeshua the Messiah when He came to us over two thousand years ago, just as the prophets foretold! Now the evil one seeks to kill every Jew before we can repent and call for His return. Will you continue to wait, or will you repent and turn to Yeshua in faith, as this young Gentile girl has done?"

The room exploded in a great emotional response as many made the same choice I had just made. Tears ran down my face as I watched Jannik kneel on the floor and raise his hands toward heaven. The power and spirit of God was in that room. The singing and rejoicing went on for hours, as Tamas made his way through the crowd, praying over each person.

It was some time before Tamas addressed the group again. Standing before us, he explained there was no time for us to go back to our homes, no time for us to gather any belongings or warn any of our loved ones. It was time to flee Jerusalem before the evil one, President Bellomo, the Antichrist, set up his troops around the city. Some of the older women began to cry.

"Do not fear," he said tenderly. "A place has been prepared for you. There, the Lord will keep you hidden. Though President Bellomo will seek to destroy you, he will not be able to do so. The Lord will be a shield to you and will shelter and deliver you!"

Tamas prayed for our journey and our safety. As the people got up to leave, I made my way through the crowd to Jannik and his friend, Noam. I was delighted when Jannik gathered me into his arms in an enthusiastic embrace. Noam stood back, with his arms crossed, as Jannik and I spoke excitedly about our experience, our words spilled joyously over one another. *Noam didn't kneel.* The thought flickered across my mind, but I didn't pay much attention to it.

Then we left the tomb of David and followed the small crowd making their way outside to the street where Tamas stood. Lifting his hand up,

Tamas signaled someone in a car across the roadway. It pulled away from the curb and up next to him. Tamas opened the door and gestured for some of the people next to him to get in. The car left, and another pulled up to take its place; a caravan of automobiles had been mobilized to take us out of Jerusalem.

When it was our turn, a minivan pulled up. Jannik, Noam, and I got into it along with a few other people. "I'll see you there!" Tamas promised as he closed the door.

"Where is 'there?'" I asked.

Our driver answered, "There is a place for us in Jordan called Petra."

Noam and Jannik started asking more questions and got into a conversation with the driver about our route. Since I had never heard of Petra and had no idea about where we were headed, I tuned them out and stared out of the window at the passing scenery.

Tamas had told us that only a third of the Jewish nation would survive through the next three and a half years. I wondered about some of the people on the street as we passed by. *Would they survive? What was going to happen next?*

FLOOD

Chapter 26

Put me like a seal over your heart, like a seal on your arm:
for love is as strong as death.

Song of Songs 8:6

Japheth was dead, and I was being held hostage. Nimrod feared retribution for Japheth's death from Noah and the others who were loyal to the Creator, but he also felt proud and powerful to be holding one of the Mothers prisoner.

The days turned to weeks. Weeks turned to months. Months to years. Nimrod had no intention of letting me go.

At first, I was kept in the palace, under lock and key, only let out to walk in the extensive gardens around the palace, chaperoned by an armed guard. For a long time, I didn't care. My heart was dead within me, and I mourned deeply for Japheth.

Nimrod assigned one of the daughters of his chief bodyguard to serve me, Amalthai. She was a descendant of Shem, a kindly, young woman. Her long, blonde hair reminded me of Nua and her sister, Eritza, who had been murdered by the Magistrate's men before the Flood.

Gradually over the first year, I learned the language spoken by Nimrod and his people. It was not something I tried to do. In my misery over Japheth, all I wanted to do was relive every moment with him, but Amalthai established a routine for my days that kept me from completely turning myself over to grief.

She woke me in the morning with a gentle greeting and made sure I ate something before getting a bath ready for me. Throughout the day, she would prattle on, lifting or pointing to objects and naming them for me, much like a mother with a young child learning to speak.

After breakfast, it became my practice to sit in the garden beside a fountain. There I would sit in the shade of large fig tree and trace over my life with Japheth. Amalthai made sure I had water and a cloth to dry my tears and drawing materials.

Instead of drawing animals, as I had in years past, I drew scenes from my life with Japheth. The bower he made for our wedding night. The room in the ark where we shared so many happy, loving moments. Our first child, Gomer, held in Japheth's arms.

Amalthai always wanted to see them. "Ariana, I feel like I'm right there on the ark with you and Japheth! I feel like I know him through these pictures!"

Despite her kindness, I felt alone and isolated. Not only had my husband been murdered in front of me, I was kept from my children and grandchildren. I worried about all of them and wondered how they were . . . and where they were.

When the Creator confused the language of men, many panicked, and there were misunderstandings that had led to violence. When I could understand her language, Amalthai told me what had happened that day in the city.

"The city woke up with hundreds of new languages. Once they figured out what had happened, Nimrod sent a whole group of his soldiers who spoke our new language to divide the people according to the language they spoke. Many resisted leaving their homes, and the soldiers simply ran them through with their swords."

"How many died?" I asked, shocked at such an extreme act.

"Almost five thousand. At least that is the official account. There are rumors it was much more. The next morning, Nimrod ordered everyone who didn't share our language to leave, except those who were already close to him."

"So they learned the language like me, only not as prisoners."

One morning, Amalthai urged me to come along with her to the market.

"But I'm not allowed out of the garden," I reminded her.

"I got permission from the king!" She smiled at me with pleasure, dancing around me laughing

I shook my head at the lively beauty dancing in front of me and smiled.

"I don't know how to thank you, Amalthai. I'm so sick of being cooped up in here." I ran to the bedroom and got dressed.

When we left the palace, guards followed to make certain I would not escape, I walked close behind Amalthai. Her hair, cascading down her back, swung back and forth as she strode ahead of me, a great basket balanced on her head.

I was surprised by how much the city had grown since I'd been imprisoned in Nimrod's palace. New buildings stood just outside the palace grounds, two or three levels in height. I saw groups of men, miserably chained together, herded through the streets by Nimrod's soldiers. Sorrowfully, I realized where he got his workforce. I recognized some of the men from my travels visiting family. One of them caught my eye—a tall, emaciated man. He bowed his head in respect before his elder, as had been the custom long before the languages were confused.

Tears filled my eyes, and I moved toward him.

One of the guards pushed me roughly as another barked a command. "Don't talk to anyone else!" I fell to the ground.

"What are you doing?" Amalthai screamed at the guards. She pulled me to my feet and wrapped me in her arms protectively. "This is one of the Mothers! You must show her respect, or I will personally tell the king of your vicious attack against his guest."

The guard laughed. "She's a prisoner, not a guest, and I don't care who she is," he sneered.

"Let me remind you that I am a favorite of Queen Semiramis. How do you think I got permission to take Ariana out of her chambers? Shall I turn around and tell her what you did?" She stared the guard down. He muttered and fell in behind us as we continued to the market.

The marketplace was like nothing I had ever seen. We entered through a dark, arched passageway between two tall buildings and came to a gate. Amalthai greeted the guard there, and we were allowed to enter the large square into the market.

Vendors displayed incredible varieties of items for sale: fruits and vegetables, cloths, pottery, jewelry, furniture—anything desirable was there. Although it was quite hot, the black and white striped cloths draped ingeniously across wooden frames throughout the square offered welcome shade.

Overwhelmed by the crowds pushing past us, the babble of so many voices, and the thick, humid air, I grabbed Amalthai's shoulder, feeling faint. She called for help as I began to collapse.

A tall man rushed toward us and caught me in his arms.

"Mother Ariana, sit here." Gently, he helped me to my feet, speaking in my native tongue. He gestured to a man standing behind the table of fine linen where I had collapsed. "Find some cool water for her," he ordered, switching back to Babylon's language, obviously fluent in more than one language.

My head was spinning, and darkness edged my line of sight as I looked up at him. He was a mirror image of Shem! Blinking my eyes, I realized this man was much younger than Shem and must be one of his great-grandsons. With difficulty, I asked him his name.

"I am Terah, son of Nahor, of the lineage of Shem," he answered in the language of Nimrod's people so that Amalthai could be included in our conversation.

So he was one of the descendants of Arpachshad, son of Shem. I wondered what he was doing in the city of Babylon.

Amalthai put an arm around my shoulder and offered me some water the vendor had brought. After I drank, she passed the cup back to the man and, turning to Terah, offered her thanks for helping me.

"It is only right to show respect to the Mothers and Fathers," he humbly responded. "I knew who you were because I asked someone who the beautiful young woman was, and I was told she served the Mother staying in Nimrod's palace."

I noticed Amalthai's pink cheeks grow darker.

"Would you come visit us in the palace one day soon?" she offered. "I must take Mother Ariana back, but I am certain she would like to speak more with you. This has been a very difficult experience for her." She finished her statement in a whisper, thinking I could not hear her, but neither my grief nor my age had affected my hearing. Amalthai meant well, so I was not offended.

"I would be honored," Terah said. "I have come here to be of service to the great king, Nimrod."

"Well, you must join us then! I, too, am from the house of Shem, of Joktan's line. There are a few of our family here. My father is the king's personal bodyguard."

They talked for a few minutes before we made our way back to the palace. Terah thoughtfully called for a litter, a chair attached to two wooden poles carried on the shoulders of two men. Servants would carry illustrious persons throughout the city on gilded plush chairs, while ordinary citizens could hire more simple conveyances for a modest fee. As soon as I was bundled into the wooden chair, we left the market and returned to the palace.

I fell asleep for the remainder of the day, worn out by the heat and the crowd. I was overwhelmed by the strong resemblance it bore to the Magistrate's city. There was the same spirit among the people. I had felt it in the palace, but in my solitude, I had not realized how pervasive evil was throughout Babylon. It made me sick.

Later in the day, Amalthai patted my shoulder gently and woke me. "Mother, we are invited to dine with the king tonight. You must wake and get ready." Reluctantly, I dragged myself from the haven of sleep and sat up in my bed. Light from the courtyard danced across the room. After bathing, Amalthai brushed and braided my hair.

"Why am I suddenly allowed to go out? Suddenly invited to a banquet? Nimrod has had me locked up here as a prisoner for years, and now all of the sudden, I'm being treated like an honored guest?"

Even though I couldn't see her because she was standing behind me, I could feel her hesitation. "There have been rumors going around the city that you were being beaten and mistreated. The common people are already angry because the king has doubled their taxes, while giving the nobles a much more favorable rate."

"So instead of returning to the poor what's rightfully theirs, he's placating them by showing me off in public?" I was indignant.

Amalthai tried to distract me. "Look at this, Mother." She held out an elaborate golden headdress. "It's a gift sent to you by the king himself."

"No, I won't wear that," I put the headdress back in her hands. "A simple braid is good enough."

Without a word, she simply braided my hair, wrapping the braids together in a loose coil at the back of my neck.

"Queen Semiramis sent this gown for you, Mother Ariana." Amalthai held up a deep red sheath. Diagonal rows of glittery multicolored beads were embroidered in layers across the front. I could see the asymmetrical dress would leave one arm bare while the other would be draped in a stately manner with more red fabric. I stared at its blood red color, unable to speak, and just shook my head.

Amalthai stood before me, a confused expression on her face. She was dressed in a sheer brown asymmetrical sheath; the intricately laced cream colored shawl looped over it reminded me of a fisherman's net. As was the style in the city, one arm and breast were bare. "Mother, this is a great honor," she whispered.

"Let Semiramis keep her honors. I will not wear that. The white gown you purchased for me in the marketplace a while back will do just fine."

Bowing her head respectfully, Amalthai took the red sheath out of my sight and came back a few moments later with the white gown.

I put on the simple white gown and then picked up the yellow belt embroidered with wildflowers that Amalthai had purchased with it, weaving it around my waist from front to back before tying it together in the front with a simple knot.

"Allow me to finish my hair, Mother, and we will leave for the banquet hall." Amalthai crossed the room and moved through the doorway to her quarters, which joined mine. She returned shortly wearing a cap covering her head, formed with leaves of gold hanging down in layers from the top. Her blonde braids looked like vines growing from an exotic plant. By the standards of the court, her headdress was quite simple.

"Shall we go?" she inquired, and we made our way to Nimrod's banqueting hall.

FIRE

Chapter 27

Then the woman fled into the wilderness, where she had a
place prepared by God, so that there she would be nour-
ished for one thousand two hundred sixty days.

Revelation 12:6

When I awoke, we were still driving and dawn was breaking. Streaks of pink and gold stretched across the sky, revealing desert on either side of us. I wiped my eyes with the inside of my shirt collar and noticed Jannik and Noam were asleep in front of me in the van. Noam snored softly.

I stared at the back of Jannik's head resting against the van window. Dark curls feathered around his neck. I was filled with a rush of tenderness. Besides Daphne, he was the only person who had ever shown me true kindness.

I closed my eyes and let the years I passed on the Compound play in my mind. My earliest memory involved being beaten with one of Jack's old shoes. I think I was four years old. My crime was not having opened a door quickly enough to let my mother in from the cold, Montana winter. It was the first memory I could recall but not the last. Not by far.

The van swerved suddenly. Opening my eyes, I saw devastation all around us. Abandoned cars lined the roadway. The hillsides on either side bore the charred remains of bombed out homes. Some large buildings on my right were completely demolished.

"What happened here?" I called out to the driver without thinking. He smiled at me in the mirror and patted the empty seat next to him. Carefully, so as not to disturb the others sleeping, I made my way along the narrow aisle to the front and sat in the passenger seat next to him.

"We are in Jordan now, getting close to our destination. There were quite a few hotels and resorts here before. That's what remains of them. The King of Jordan resisted the Global Union, and this destruction was part of the consequences. He still resists and continues to be inexplicably successful. He's a thorn in President Bellomo's side."

The driver was an older man, maybe in his sixties, white-haired and bearded. He glanced sideways at me for a moment and smiled. "My name is Asher. What is yours?"

I hesitated. After what had happened the night before, I hesitated to lie. Asher leaned over and whispered, "What do you call yourself?"

"Dani," I whispered. "I call myself Dani."

Asher put his hand back on the steering wheel and looked forward. "Sometimes the most honest name is the one we call ourselves. My name just happened to be the most descriptive of me. So, I kept it."

"What does Asher mean?" I asked.

"Lucky. Asher means lucky. I am a fortunate man, indeed!"

He paused, slowing the van down. There were many cars ahead of us in the caravan. I saw red lights flashing ahead of us. "There must be something blocking the road," Asher remarked as the van came to a stop.

Panic rushed through me, and I looked around wildly, wondering where the attack would come from.

"No worries, it's just a broken-down truck. The road is narrow here, and the driver must not have been able to pull over. Those men will move it. No one comes out here anymore. It's safe. Really." He patted my hands again. I gripped his hand.

"Are you sure?" I whispered, staring up at him. His blue eyes were bright and calm.

"This whole area has been marked off limits to the Global Union by the Jordanian government. It is set apart for us, those who believe in God!"

"How?"

"After the Vanishing, but way before Israel signed on to join the Global Union in a seven-year peace treaty, several countries began to attack Israel: Russia, Turkey, and Iran. But God Himself destroyed all the armies. It was an incredible thing that made the whole world pay attention. Israel did not so much as fire a weapon. Instead, the invading armies turned on each other. It was like something in the Tanakh. In fact, it was something the prophet Ezekiel predicted exactly, many thousands of years ago."

"What's that?" I asked, turning in my seat so I could see Asher better.

"The Tanakh is what Jews call the Old Testament," he answered. One of the uniformed men on the road motioned us to move forward, and Asher skillfully navigated around the disabled truck.

"That event—when Israel won the war without so much as firing a single shot—made many people all around the world believe in God. The King of Jordan was one of them. And when he studied more of the prophecies in the Bible, he learned that it had also been predicted that Israel would find refuge here in Jordan, in Petra. He's fought ever since to keep this land from the control of the Global Union."

Asher was a natural storyteller. His deep voice and accent were gripping.

"What about the "judgments," and the creatures and natural disasters?" I asked, thinking about all the devastation I'd seen since I left the Compound. "Is this place protected like the Global Union cities?" I thought of Jerusalem, Creston, and the other cities controlled by the Global Union.

"We are protected by God. Those places are under President Bellomo's protection for now, but his power is failing, and soon, even those places will experience God's wrath. Except in the place God has prepared for us."

"So, we will be safe from the creatures? What if not everyone is a believer?" I wanted to have hope in this place of safety, but I was still scared. Asher glanced over at me before turning his eyes back on the road.

"We'll be safe. It's complicated. The way I understand it is that we're like ancient Israel when God delivered them from slavery in Egypt. God protected the Israelites supernaturally, even though they weren't all believers yet."

"So, He knew we would believe and protected us all along?" That made sense to me. Even if a baby doesn't know its father, a good father knows his child and would do everything to protect the baby.

"There it is!" Asher gestured ahead to where other vans were parked or in the process of parking.

"Everyone, get up!" he ordered, "We're almost there."

I turned back to smile at Jannik, who was on the bench seat directly behind us, stretching and yawning. "Did you know you drool when you sleep?" I teased, chuckling as he quickly wiped his mouth. Noam pulled his dark black glasses off, wiped them with his shirt, and glared at me. His expression unnerved me, and I turned back around in my seat. As we pulled into a parking lot, I mentally reviewed my interactions with Noam. It was a short list, and I had no clue what caused his negative response toward me.

Asher directed the van into a parking lot, and we got out. I glanced back down the road and was astonished by the billows of dust thrown up into the air by dozens and dozens of vehicles making their way toward us.

"There will be more." Tamas came up to me and greeted me, Jannik, and Noam.

"Where are they all coming from?" I asked him.

"Jerusalem. Last night they moved a statue of President Bellomo into the Temple. Tomorrow is the day that false prophet, Angelo Cain, will declare him the Promised One in the Holy of Holies. Many Jews and believers are heeding the warnings of the Witnesses and fleeing the city. My brothers are busy throughout the world, but especially here in Israel. The remnant will be saved, but there is much to do."

Tamas smiled reassuringly and told us he would see us later before he moved on to welcome other people who had just arrived.

"Follow me," Asher boomed. He turned and began walking to the hillside across from us. Noam jogged to catch up with him, but Jannik fell in step next to me.

"Have you been here before?" I asked, looking up at him.

"Yes, but I was a young child. I . . . " His voice trailed off and he stopped walking, so I stopped, too.

We stood there staring at each other, other people streaming around us to an opening in the canyon wall just ahead.

"Is everything okay?" I whispered. His eyes darkened as he bent his head toward me and gently kissed my lips. It was a brief kiss, sweet and full of promise. Without a word, Jannik took my hand in his, and we moved toward the opening to the canyon.

As we walked into the gorge, the height of the immense walls on either side of our path amazed me, stretching hundreds of feet upward. There were people waiting on either side of the path with bottles of water, which we eagerly accepted. Donkeys and horses waited, as well—some saddled, others tethered to small carts. Their handlers approached the young and elderly with offers to ride into the city. Apparently, it was a long walk.

I pulled Jannik's hand and moved over to the side so I could slide my free hand along the rocky surface of the wall. My hand brushed the rough surface.

The variations of colors in the canyon walls were stunning. At one point, the rocky walls met together over the path, forming an incredible archway. As we rounded the last curve, we had a glimpse of an incredible building carved out of the rosy red rock.

"Oh!" I gasped as we moved into a large open area filled with people. I turned my head up to view the vast masterpiece in front of us and observed a long line of people winding its way into the edifice. We were told to wait in line to receive housing and a work assignment.

"This is an ancient city, long empty except for a Bedouin tribe that once lived in its cave homes," said Jannik as we got in line. Over the years, archaeologists have uncovered the city. "I've been told we can house millions of people here."

"Millions?" Noam asked. "But we're in the desert. What about water?"

Asher laughed. "Do you think the Almighty is able to snatch you away from the evil one's grasp only to let you die of thirst in the place He's prepared for you, Noam! There is a vast system of cisterns and dams the Jordanian government thoughtfully renovated for us years ago!"

A sandy-colored kitten rubbed itself around my ankles. "Oh, how precious!" I picked up the purring fur ball and rubbed its small head with my chin. "There are so many animals here!" I exclaimed, as a small herd of goats was driven past us.

It was a long time waiting in the heat. Noam finished his water and threw the bottle on the ground, complaining. He quickly snatched it back again after a tall woman with a gun holstered at her side approached us and instructed him to pick it up and keep it. After giving us a quick lecture on community resources and responsibilities, she moved on to address some rowdy kids standing in line ahead of us.

"Good going, Noam!" Jannik joked. "Now, we're marked as trouble-makers." They insulted one another good naturedly as the line moved. Well, Jannik was good-natured, anyway. At this point, I wasn't so sure about Noam.

Finally, we entered the dark recesses of the building I'd seen carved into the red rock. The first thing I felt was relief, as it was much cooler than outside in the sunlight. Although the ceiling was high, the room wasn't very large. People stood along the walls waiting to approach a bank of tables on one end of the room. There were four people seated, tablets in hand, taking information and giving assignments to the newcomers. Above them was a handwritten sign in Hebrew. Jannik read it out loud, translating it into English for me. "Welcome to Petra. You will be given a place to stay and assignments for work details. There will be an orientation meeting tonight after the evening meal."

Once we were inside the building, it was only a short wait until we were given our housing and work assignments. After I received my slip of paper, a young woman came forward and greeted me. "Hello! I'm Zivah. If you will come with me, I'll show you where you will sleep."

I was reluctant to leave Jannik, but Zivah assured me that we would see each other at dinner. "We know it is difficult to come to a place where everything is unknown. We keep families and friends in the same area. Your friends' home assignment is close to yours."

Jannik and Noam were asked to wait for their advisor to return from helping someone else, so I said goodbye and followed Zivah out into the sunlight.

FLOOD

Chapter 28

There are three things that are too amazing for me, four
that I do not understand: the way of an eagle in the sky, the
way of a snake on a rock, the way of a ship on the high seas,
and the way of a man with a young woman.
Proverbs 30:18-19

Everyone in the great hall stood in respect as Nimrod and Semiramis entered. When the queen came into view, there was a great gasp from the assembled crowd. Semiramis was stunningly dressed in an elaborate golden headdress, her silken black hair wound about in great loops. She glided across the room barefoot. A great gold and blue collar hung about her neck and shoulders and her breasts were bare.

Nimrod was no less splendid in his golden crown and silken, deep-red robes painted with gold palm trees. Regally, they moved through the crowds and took their seat on the royal dais. Semiramis caught my eye and looked at me disdainfully.

The banquet was unlike anything I had ever seen. Elaborate platters of wild boar, shellfish, roasted pheasants, fruits, and vegetables were brought out, followed by elaborate confections for dessert. Vast amounts of wine and beer sat ready on tables along the walls to be delivered to guests by waiting slaves.

The feast was held in honor of the dragon-snake god, Marduk, who was worshiped by Semiramis. Directly opposite from the royal dais, on the other side of the great room, stood a great golden altar, where a deep alcove housed a solid gold image of the dragon-snake himself. Before each course, priests poured out wine as an offering before Marduk.

The high priest, Akkadab, officiated the banquet. A strong, well-built man, Akkadab had once been a mighty warrior in Nimrod's army but had suffered a fatal wound in battle.

"It was said that Semiramis herself tended to his needs and miraculously raised him from the dead," whispered Amalthai.

I looked over at Semiramis. "There are only two sources of power that could raise the dead."

"Yes, she is so powerful! Some say she is actually one of the gods. Only a god could heal a fatal wound and raise the dead. After Akkadab recovered, he devoted himself to serving the dragon-snake god she worshipped."

As the feast came to an end, Semiramis stood up and, to my surprise, addressed me in front of the guests. "Tonight is a special occasion, Mother," Semiramis spoke. "You have finally agreed to join us! We rejoice in your presence!" She held up her wine goblet, and everyone in the room stood.

"To Ariana," she intoned.

"To Ariana," they responded.

"This is the day we celebrate the beginning of a new year. After we feast, we offer a special sacrifice to Marduk."

She nodded toward the entrance to the great hall, where I saw four of Semiramis' priests carrying a lamb strapped to a pole. Akkadab, the high priest, tore the poor creature apart without killing it first; the screams of the animal were drowned out by the rapturous shouts of the guests. When he finished, the high priest cut a bloody chunk of flesh and offered it to the idol in a great show of piety before eating it himself.

The crowd became silent at the blasting sound of trumpets. Akkadab held up a bloody hand, and proclaimed, ". . . in the same manner, the god Marduk slew his great enemy long ago, before the so-called Flood." Marking himself on the forehead with blood, Akkadab began chanting and the crowd joined in with him.

I turned to look at the royal pair and was stunned to see, standing just behind their golden chairs in the shadows, the winged creature I had met in the forest long ago. Fear struck my heart. Once again, I watched as he took the form of the Magistrate, his black eyes staring back at me and smirking victoriously.

Once more, the crowd erupted in cheers, this time rising to their feet and raising their hands in salute. The commotion afforded me the opportunity to hide myself among the throng and slip out, hopefully unnoticed. No one stopped or followed me, but I was sure I heard Semiramis laugh as I left the room.

Not long after the feast, Terah came to visit me. I was sitting in the garden under the fig tree when Amalthai led him out.

"Mother, Terah has come to visit with you!"

Her cheeks were flushed, and her eyelashes fluttered as she directed Terah to the chair next to mine in the shade, promising to return with some cool wine. I watched Terah's response with interest.

"She's very beautiful, isn't she?" I commented.

Terah turned his eyes back to me. "Yes, she is. I'd like to get to know her better."

Amalthai returned with the wine, a smile on her face. As she poured a glass for each of us, she glanced quickly at Terah and then away when he tried to catch her gaze in his.

"Amalthai, I hope that you will excuse me." I stood up. "I think I'll go in and lie down for a while. The heat is tiring. Why don't you sit and keep our guest company?" I made my way into my rooms, smiling to myself.

From that day on, Terah became a regular visitor. With her father's permission, they married a few months later. The wedding was a joyous occasion. Thankfully, the king and queen were not in attendance. They were in the city of Nippur dedicating a new temple to their god, Marduk. I certainly did not miss them, and it didn't seem anyone else did. Terah and Amalthai's happiness was contagious, and the feasting and dancing lasted for many hours.

Amalthai's family, like most in Babylon, worshipped Marduk. At the end of the ceremony, Terah and Amalthai kneeled before Akkadab, the priest, as he spoke incantations over them and recounted Marduk's history.

Although I had been a prisoner in Babylon for quite a while, that was the first time I had heard the twisted history of the idol. Indignation rose in my heart as Akkadab spoke of an evil one who tried to destroy Marduk and the other gods with a flood. In a deep voice, he uttered this treachery, making the Creator the evil one in his tale. I tried to cry out against the lies, but I couldn't speak. I was being restrained in some way, and I didn't know how to fight against it. To my horror, I watched Terah and Amalthai vow their loyalty to Marduk. Akkadab pulled a knife from the belt on his waist and made a small cut on each of their wrists. Placing their bloody wrists together, he bound them with a strip of white cloth.

Under the auspices of Akkadab, Terah quickly grew in influence in Nimrod's court, eventually becoming the king's chief advisor. Whenever Nimrod would go out to war, Terah would go with him. Every battle was victorious, and Nimrod's fame grew great. Whether by chance or design, stories spread about Nimrod and Semiramis and the great dragon-snake god who brought them victory.

A few years passed and Amalthai failed to become pregnant. This became a bitter burden for her. I tried to pray with her, but she insisted that only Marduk could help her, so I prayed for her alone and watched with sadness as she tried remedy after remedy the priests gave her.

When Nimrod returned from war against Calneh, one of the many kings in the land of Shinar, he held a great feast to celebrate his victory. Everyone at court was required to attend, so I went. As one of the Mothers, I was given a place of honor at the king's table. Nimrod and Semiramis used my presence to validate their false religion. All sorts of rumors were spread that I came to court because I recognized Nimrod and Semiramis as the faithful servants of Marduk. No one seemed to remember the truth, that I was a captive of the wicked man who murdered my husband. Truth was a rare commodity in Babylon.

I sat at the table next to Terah and Amalthai. As we waited for the royal couple to make their appearance, Terah shared some troubling news.

"While we were fighting against Calneh's army, there was a great blazing light that soared over us one night as the armies rested from battle. Nimrod was troubled and sent for his wise men and soothsayers."

"Because of a falling star?" I asked wryly.

"Mother." Terah looked around to make sure no one else heard me. "Please only share your opinions when we're in private. The king takes this seriously. They told him it was an ominous sign."

"What did it mean?" Amalthai asked.

"The astrologers told the king that there would be a child born who would outshine his glory and take the place of preeminence in the land. So Nimrod ordered every male baby born to be sacrificed to Marduk."

I noticed Amalthai grow pale but had no chance to ask if she was well because the trumpets sounded at that moment. Nimrod and Semiramis entered the banqueting hall to shouts of acclamation and praise. With shock, I saw that the queen was quite far along in pregnancy. She had not been seen in public for months, keeping to her chambers—due, it was said, to ill health. I glanced at Terah and Amalthai, but they did not seem surprised.

Terah had been with Nimrod for the last year fighting for the cities of Accad and Calneh.

"You and Nimrod just returned two months ago. This is shameful!"

"No, it is a miracle, Mother! Do you recall the prophecy spoken to the First Ones when they were cast out of the Garden? This is the promised son!" Terah's eyes shone with joy as he spoke.

Shaking my head in dismay, I turned back to watch the spectacle before me. Men and women were on their knees, weeping and shouting praise to the two heading toward the dais. With a shock, I realized that Nimrod and Semiramis were wearing the garments I had seen long ago in the ark—the garments Ham had tried to take, the garments made by the Creator for the First Ones. Semiramis had cut the center out of her garment, her stomach proudly put on display.

"Where did they get those skins?" I demanded of Terah.

"Mother, of course you must remember that they were given to Ham," he replied.

"That is a lie!" I retorted, sick of the distortion of history. "Ham stole them. Those two are not emissaries of the gods; they are vessels for the evil one to manipulate and use. There is no miracle pregnancy, but an immoral woman who has committed adultery!

"How can you not see the truth?" I implored both Terah and Amalthai to see the truth, but they only shook their heads, looking around fearfully to see if anyone heard my outburst. Before I could say another word, guards grabbed me by the arms, dragged me out of the feasting chamber, and took me to my room.

Almost seven long months passed before I saw Terah or Amalthai again. Although I was treated well, I was kept a prisoner in my room. A slave who was deaf and dumb would bring me food, but I had no company. I was allowed to go out onto a patio outside of my bedroom, where I would sit and look at the gardens below. One morning, as I sat in the shade under a canopy on the patio, I heard footsteps from inside my chambers. I entered my rooms to find Amalthai.

"Mother! I am so sorry, truly, I am! This is the first time I have been allowed to see you!"

We embraced, both of us crying. She had become very dear to me in the years of my captivity. As we hugged, I realized Amalthai was with child. She slipped her cloak off and proudly rubbed her round belly as she informed me her time of confinement was near. I could tell she was troubled, and I asked her why.

She began to weep. Pulling her down to sit next to me on a bench, I pulled a clean cloth from a basket next to the bench and handed it to her. Amalthai shared with me how her heart had been turned against the king and queen and their god, Marduk. Hundreds of infant boys had been sacrificed to the evil god in the Temple over the last months. Amalthai feared the death of her child. Only the infant son born to Semiramis was allowed to live, Tammuz.

"I honestly believe he is the son of the priest, Akkadab," Amalthai whispered, wiping her eyes while looking around to make sure that we were still alone. "You should see the way he looks at the baby. Terah said that Nimrod is doubtful as to the child's origin, but he cannot refute Semiramis without losing honor."

"There is to be a special feast to honor Tammuz in a few days," she went on. "Semiramis commands you to attend the feast and publicly worship the boy." She began to weep. "That is why I have been allowed to see you."

"I will never do such a thing!" I stood up. "She must know I will never worship anyone but the Creator."

As we stood there together, I was afraid for a moment. The spirit of the Magistrate was strong in Babylon. I wondered if the blood of all those children made the evil spirits stronger. *Surely, they were not stronger than the Creator?*

Shivering, I led Amalthai out to the patio so that I could feel the warmth of the sun. "Amalthai, I worship the true God, the Creator, the one who made the sun and the moon and all of the earth. He is the only God! He brought eight of us through the Flood. Surely, He will hear us call to him now! Surely He will save us!"

I sank to my knees and began to pray fervently. Amalthai knelt next to me and confessed her unbelief and turned to the Creator. Then she asked me to intercede for her and Terah. He was blinded in his devotion to Nimrod, and she feared what he would do if their child was a boy. I do not know how long I prayed before a loud clap of thunder and a torrential downpour of rain interrupted my prayers.

Both of us ran inside. As we watched the deluge, I felt my cries to the Creator were heard.

FIRE

Chapter 29

I will surely assemble all of you, Jacob, I will surely gather the
remnant of Israel. I will put them together like sheep in the fold;
like a flock in the midst of its pasture they will be noisy with men.

Micah 2:12

Although I was far from all that was familiar, Petra quickly became my home. For the first time in my life, I felt safe and cared for by people I trusted.

I was assigned to the same multi-level cave home as Zivah and a few other young women. Inside it, stone stairs led from the exterior to the main living level, with several doorways along the way opening to individual rooms. I shared a small room with Zivah. We slept on pads on the floor, but we had sleeping bags and candles to light up the room at night. I was afraid there might be mice, but there were many semi-feral cats living around us, and thankfully, I never saw any rodents.

From the moment I met her, Zivah took me under her wing like a mother hen. She came from a town not far from Jerusalem, Ma'aleh Adumim, which had been settled by her grandparents and about twenty other families many years ago. Just after President Bellomo negotiated the peace treaty between Israel and the Global Union, her family all turned to faith in Yeshua.

Zivah told me how, when President Bellomo rose to power in that first year, severe persecution against those who followed Yeshua began. Zivah's entire family was murdered in one night by neighbors who turned against them; only she escaped.

Everyone who could work was assigned something to do. Zivah and I were responsible for a herd of goats. I didn't see much of Jannik or Noam during the daytime. They were part of the team that cleared out old caves and tombs to make room for the new arrivals. Every day, people made their way through the gorge into Petra, although as time went on, the number dwindled.

The night Jannik and I met Tamas was the last day people could get in and out of Jerusalem freely. We were lucky; many who followed Yeshua were slaughtered in the days following our escape. President Bellomo—now claiming to be the Promised One—was anxious to destroy every Jew in Israel but especially those who followed the true Promised One, Yeshua.

"How is it we're not discovered or attacked by President Bellomo?" I asked Jannik one day as we strolled to our favorite spot to watch the sunset.

"I don't know how, but God is keeping us from being found. The 144,000 are specially sealed, safe from the Antichrist." Jannik no longer called the President by his name, preferring to call him what he was—the name the Bible gave to the one who would rise up in the last days.

According to Tamas, Jannik went on to tell me, there were 144,000 others like him, Israeli men, 12,000 from each of the original, biblical twelve tribes, set apart by Yeshua to take the message of salvation to people throughout the world. Some of these men led many to faith in Israel, but once the Antichrist set up his image in the Temple, they heeded Yeshua's warning to flee and took many refugees with them to Petra, in Jordan. Tamas, and three others, stayed in Petra to oversee the refugees there. They made up the Council.

The Council was able to keep up with world events through an encrypted system the King of Jordan had set up for the refugees. It was through this that we discovered that, three days after we saw the Witnesses killed, they came back to life and rose up to heaven in front of the whole world! I was dumbfounded.

Jannik continued, "Just like the Witnesses had power, so do the 144,000. No one can harm them. I was talking to a man who'd escaped from Russia with one of them. He said they literally walked unseen right out of a prison!"

I pressed in closer to Jannik. He was warm, and the desert air was cooling quickly. "I know I've been protected in ways that couldn't just have happened."

He wrapped his arm around me. "For which I am so grateful."

About a month after we escaped to Petra, Zivah and I took our small goatherd from their pen to graze. The early morning air was cool, so I shrugged on a sweater from my backpack.

"Where are we going today?" I asked her.

Zivah smiled. "Up toward the monastery. I have a surprise for you." No matter how I tried to wheedle it out of her, she refused to tell me any more about the surprise as we trudged along the dusty path with the goats.

As we neared a stairway winding up through a narrow opening, I saw Jannik sitting on a rock. He stood and smiled, with his arms outstretched, and I ran to him, delighted.

Zivah laughed behind us. "Okay, here's your surprise, Dani. Jannik is going to tend the goats with you today. I'm going to take a turn clearing out caves in his place."

I thanked her before turning back to Jannik. The expression on his face was tender and made my stomach jump. Our eyes locked together.

"It's so hard not having a chance to see you alone," he grinned down at me. He glanced up the stairway and back at me. "Have you been up here before?"

Chatting eagerly together, we clambered up the sandstone stairway, the bleating of the goats adding background noises to our conversation. After a while, the growing heat of the day combined with the steepness of the climb was too much, and we paused to rest in a sheltering alcove carved out of the stone. The goats didn't seem to mind as they foraged for succulent bits of the hardy plants growing in the desert. I took my sweater from my waist, where I'd tied it, and shoved it into my pack.

We sat on the dusty ground and talked for almost an hour, draining much of our water. Jannik leaned into me with his shoulder. "I really have missed you, Dani. I miss the time we spent at the apartment when we could talk for hours."

"That was good. You're the first person in my life, besides Daphne, that I've felt completely safe with, you know?"

Wrapping his arm around me, Jannik kissed my lips softly. It was our second kiss, and it only lasted a moment. I sighed.

"I've never felt like this about anyone before," he whispered.

It seemed even hotter when we got back on the trail, a mixture of stairs and dusty pathways, but finally, we made it to the top where the majestic monastery stood. Its massive, rosy walls soared high above us. There were a few people sitting around its opening.

Jannik told me more about the monastery and how he'd visited it—and Petra—as a child with his parents. Inside the facade was only one room, which was now the communication center for the leadership of Petra.

"Who do they communicate with?" I asked.

"I think some of the 144,000, mainly some of the others in Israel. They get news about what is happening."

I didn't want to think about the horrors going on in the world as I looked around me. Although there were quite a few people here, the desert around us seemed quiet and serene. I hoped that Petra would prove to be a sanctuary, but I had seen President Bellomo kill the Witnesses. Shuddering despite the heat, I suggested we take a break to eat.

Long ago, there'd been a restaurant overlooking the Monastery. The Council decided to utilize the space where it had sat as a dining hall for the people who lived near the monastery. There were people sitting outside at café tables, as well as inside a tented area in the shade. After driving the goats into a small pen, complete with a water trough, Jannik and I went into the tent for some lunch. Just as we had tasks assigned to us, there were people responsible for providing meals for Petra's citizens. There was nothing fancy, and it wasn't much, but we didn't go hungry.

Because of the goats, we couldn't take too long to eat, but every moment was wonderful. When we finished eating, Jannik asked, "Can we leave the goats alone for a little while longer? I want to show you something incredible."

I followed him back toward the monastery. We walked in front of the building to a staircase hidden on the side and made our way up. The staircase came out next to the round lid of the circular urn perched on top of the monastery. Carefully following Jannik's lead, I made my way onto the lid and sat on the edge, overlooking Petra. The view below my feet was incredible! I saw the tent where we'd had lunch, a few cave homes, and the red sandstone mountains in the distance.

"Wow."

We sat holding hands for a few minutes in silence. I could hear the bleating of the goats below us.

"Jannik," I whispered, staring off in the distance.

"Yes?"

"Why does President Bellomo want to kill the Jewish people? Zivah told me that is why we had to flee Jerusalem. She said he hates the Jewish people and was behind the attack on her family."

I turned to look at him. He shook his head. "There is an old prophecy that says the Messiah will come to our people, the Jews, when we mourn for him. President Bellomo, the Antichrist, wants to prevent Yeshua's coming and keep up his façade as the Promised One. If we are all dead, the prophecy can't come true."

I thought about that for a few minutes. *Could he do that? Could he prevent Jesus from coming back?* Although I tried, I couldn't remember much from the end of the Bible that Daphne had given me so long ago.

"Tamas is planning on speaking to the people tomorrow," Jannik said, "Something amazing has been found in one of the caves. We found it a few days ago."

"What did you find?"

Jannik grinned, and one dimple flashed as he teased that maybe he shouldn't tell me.

"Oh, come on!" I begged. "Don't make me wait until tomorrow!"

"Do you promise not to tell Zivah? I'm supposed to keep it to myself."

I smiled back at him and promised.

"Noam and I were cleaning out one of the caves," Jannik began. Something twisted inside me when he said Noam's name. I had no real reason for the way I felt about Noam, so I said nothing and gestured for him to continue.

"There was a lot of stuff piled up from many, many years ago: old furniture, rugs, that kind of stuff. We pulled it all out into the open to see what could still be used. After moving much of it out, we discovered a stash of boxes at the back of the cave." His eyes shone with excitement.

"What was in them?"

"Well, at the top of every box was a letter, written in Hebrew, all saying the same thing, that the books in each box were a gift from an American who followed Yeshua, William Eugene Blackstone. Apparently, he spent eight thousand dollars to purchase and send the books to the person who wrote the letter, who in turn brought them here to Petra."

"What? How strange! What kind of books are they?"

"All of them New Testaments in Hebrew! I was allowed to keep one for myself. Look." Jannik pulled his knapsack open and pulled out an old book. Its pages were yellowed with age. Opening it, I saw this inscription pasted on the inside, written in English and Hebrew:

Dear one, if you will read this, you will find out how to escape the destruction of your soul. The Lord has made a way of salvation for His people! He has given the most precious thing to Him—His only Son—so that you will not perish. Please read this book and find eternal life!

Yours truly,

W.E. Blackstone, servant of Yeshua and friend of the Jewish people

1931, Pasadena, California, USA

I thumbed through the pages, the symbols meaningless to me. When Tamas had laid his hands on me back in Jerusalem, I'd been given the ability to understand Hebrew, but I couldn't read it.

"Someone did this over a hundred years ago?"

"Yes, before Israel was even made a nation again!"

"I don't understand why he would do this. And why send these here to Petra? How could he know that there would be so many Jewish people here?"

Jannik answered, "I don't know, but I think Tamas will have an explanation for us tomorrow."

Handing him back the book, I shook my head in wonder. It was time to return to the goats, so we carefully navigated our way back to the stairs and down to the front of the monastery.

FLOOD

Chapter 30

The Nephilim were on the earth in those days,
and also afterward."
Genesis 6:4

On the day of the feast, where I was supposed to worship the son of Semiramis and her dragon-snake god, Marduk, I waited nervously in my room. Suddenly, someone banged loudly on my door. I opened it with trepidation. Akkadab, the high priest, stood before me, his dark eyes glinting with hatred. Three soldiers stood behind him at attention.

I stared back, trying to stop the quivering fear in my heart from betraying me to my enemy, for I could clearly see in Akkadab's eyes the presence of the same spirit which had possessed the Magistrate.

"Motherrrrrr." He hissed out the title with contempt. "King Nimrod and Queen Semiramis command you attend them immediately." Without waiting for a response, he grabbed my arm and pulled me down the corridor. The guards followed menacingly, swords drawn.

"There is no need for such treatment," I protested, trying to pull away from the evil priest. His only response was to grip my arm even more tightly.

Praying silently as Akkadab dragged me through the palace, I suddenly felt the peace of the Creator fill me with warm encouragement and strength. I knew He had brought me to this place with a purpose. I trained my anxious thoughts onto that truth.

At the end of a long, brightly lit corridor lined with ominous guards were two immense bronze doors, each carved with the symbol of drag-on-snake. Two guards pushed the doors open, and we entered Nimrod and Semiramis' private chambers.

The gold-painted walls were draped with tapestries embroidered with scenes from Nimrod's many victorious battles, as well as images of him and Semiramis portrayed as gods. I was hauled behind Akkadab as he strode quickly to an alcove to the left.

There in a white, sun-filled atrium, was a pool filled with water lilies glinting in the sunlight. Semiramis stood naked in the water, holding her son, Tammuz, in her arms. As Akkadab pushed me forward, I noted with alarm the size of the child. He was not even a year old, yet he looked twice that size. Nimrod reclined on a plush red couch, draining a goblet of wine.

"Here she is, your majesty," Akkadab intoned. I noticed his eyes raking Semiramis possessively.

"Well," Nimrod spoke, wiping his mouth with the back of his hand. "Mother Ariana, how gracious of you to visit our small family." His tone was mocking.

"Mother, do you see this most glorious son of mine?" Semiramis trilled. "I saw you noting his great size."

Just then the child himself turned his dark eyes to gaze at me. Without any expression, he spoke. "Hello, Mother."

I trembled. This was one of the Nephilim. He was not the son of Ak-kadab or any human man. My skin crawled with revulsion as he prattled some strange, childish rhyme. His melodious voice was eerily charming, his lips curled into a winsome smile.

Semiramis laughed. "Do you see how clever he is! Truly a child of the gods!"

She handed the child over to a servant on the side of the pool before exiting herself. Although I didn't turn to look, I could feel the heat of pas-sion roiling off of Akkadab by my side as his body tensed. Only then did I notice Terah, Amalthai's husband sitting behind Nimrod. The expression on his face was dismal.

"Terah, it is good to see you. How is Amalthai?" I asked.

Terah looked at Nimrod, who nodded consent for him to speak. No one spoke without permission in the presence of Nimrod or Semiramis.

"She is in intense labor, Mother. It's gone on now for three days, and she's growing very weak, yet still the child has not come."

"May I help?" I asked Nimrod.

"That is why you are here. Terah is of great importance to me and to the plans for my kingdom. He has been distracted for the last few days, and I need him by my side, fully in service to me. You will go and aid his wife in her delivery. We know you have an extraordinary reputation as a midwife." Nimrod said.

Semiramis wrapped a robe about herself and took a seat on the couch by Nimrod's side. "I would not have to remind the midwives of Babylon, but you would do well to remember this, Ariana. Any male child is to be disposed of at once. There is a fire burning before Marduk in his temple just outside of the Palace gates."

Bile rose up in my throat. There was no way I would participate in their treacherous murder of those most vulnerable, but I kept my mouth shut. I would do what I could to help my friend.

Terah rose and walked across the room toward me. "Follow me," he said in a subdued tone. Without a word to the others, I turned and followed Terah.

We left the palace and climbed onto a waiting chariot. We left the city, racing through the gates to Terah's home in the countryside. I gripped onto the handles of the chariot as we lurched to the right, following a fork in the road.

"How bad is it?" I shouted to Terah.

He turned his head to look over his shoulder at me. "She is very weak. I'm afraid."

We spoke no more as we sped to help Amalthai. When we pulled up to the small estate, servants opened the gates for their master. We drove down the lane lined with cypress trees toward a stately home. There were men waiting by the door to take care of the horses. As soon as we stopped, Terah threw the reigns to one of the men and helped me down.

"Come, Mother; we must hurry."

Terah and I raced into the house. I followed him down a bright corridor to the right and into Amalthai's room. I had to stifle a cry of dismay. It was dark and dank; the distinct odor of blood permeated the room. Some priest of Marduk waved a metal censer, smoky incense billowing out of it. The perfumed incense made the smell of the blood more noxious. Quickly, I went and opened the shutters to the windows and ushered the priest out of the room.

In the light, I could see Amalthai was covered in bloody sheets. I ordered the servants to bring me clean linens, towels, and water. Then I turned to my young friend.

"Amalthai?" Her eyes were clenched in pain, but she opened them at the sound of my voice.

"Mother Ariana," she choked. I notice her lips were chapped and dry, and I ordered a servant to fetch me some wine. Amalthai managed a few sips before falling back onto the bed.

"What do you think, Mother?" Terah was clearly frightened.

"I need to examine her," I said quietly, bending down beside my friend.

I sent everyone out and had the servants help me change the linens. We helped Amalthai into a clean, linen shift before getting her back onto the bed. Then I examined her.

I finished my examination and washed my hands before turning to speak with her.

"I already know, Mother," she whispered. "I can feel my life slipping away." She began to weep and beg, "Please save the child." Of course, I quickly assured her, I would do what I could.

I knew what needed to be done, but I also knew the servants, not understanding, would try and stop me. I sent them to bring Terah to me. While we waited, I told Amalthai what I needed to do in order to save the child. I had a drug that would cause her to fall into a deep sleep so that she would feel no pain. But it was a sleep from which she would likely not wake.

As soon as Terah came back, I told him Amalthai needed to speak to him. Leaving the room, I ordered the servants to leave with me. After a few minutes Terah came out and found me.

"Why must you do this? I have never heard of such a thing!"

I took his hand in mine and looked up into his tear-filled eyes. "I have done this many times. Usually, the mother survives, but Amalthai is so weak. I cannot promise she will."

"She wants our child to be saved, no matter the cost to her." He was clearly pained to speak the words, and he began to weep.

"Terah, she will not live if I do not try."

Wordlessly, he nodded and led the way back to Amalthai. I looked at the servants in the room and chose two of the women who seemed most competent before sending the others away. I ordered water to be boiled and a sharp knife, along with clean linens to swaddle the baby.

While those were being prepared, I asked Terah where Amalthai kept her herbs and tinctures. Over her years of service to me, I had taught her all that I had learned from my mother-in-law. Even in those early days after the Flood, much knowledge about medicines had been lost. It had been my hope that Amalthai would carry on after me; now I only wished for her to live.

Following Terah's directions, I moved quickly to find the small room where she kept her medicines. Neatly marked clay pots filled the shelves. Finding the few roots and herbs I needed, I quickly ground them together and hurried back to my friend. She was screaming in pain when I entered the room again. With horror, I watched as she sat up in bed, blood gushing from between her legs. I ran to her side, pushing Terah out of the way.

"Bring me some water," I ordered one of the female servants, who quickly retrieved a cup of water, pushing it into my hands. I poured the ground roots and herbs into the water and mixed it together quickly with my forefinger before turning again to Amalthai.

Hardly conscious, she moaned. I slipped my left hand under her head and, with my right hand, put the cup to her lips.

"Please, please drink this," I begged. She turned her head away from the cup. Terah sat down on the other side of the bed and pulled her up by her shoulders, begging her to drink. With great difficulty, she managed to get down half of the cup before passing out completely.

Terah ordered everyone out of the room. It would have been useless to convince the others of the need for what we were about to do, so just the two of us worked together to save Amalthai's child.

I do not know how Terah managed through it all, but in the end, we saved the child. I prayed to the Creator as I stitched up Amalthai's belly. Perhaps I was wrong, and she would somehow survive. As I worked, Terah tended to the baby.

Finishing, I covered my friend with a few blankets. Her body was trembling as if she were very cold. I clung to hope.

Terah told me he needed to take the newborn to the kitchens for some clean water to bathe the baby. I nodded, half-listening, more concerned now for the mother than the child. He was gone less than half an hour, returning with a squalling infant, swaddled properly in clean clothing.

Amalthai stirred at the sound and opened her eyes. "Terah?" She saw him with the baby and managed to smile. Terah moved to her side and showed her their child.

Tenderly, she stroked the baby's cheek. "What is it? A girl?" Tears filled my eyes, hearing the hope in her voice.

"It is a son, Amalthai," Terah said through his own tears. "But I will not let him die. I promise you. I will save him. You must trust me." Her eyes stared up into his, tears falling soundlessly down her cheeks. I watched helplessly as the light of life left them and all that was left was a soulless stare. She was gone.

FIRE

Chapter 31

Alas! That day is so great there is none like it; it is a time of distress for Jacob; yet he shall be saved out of it.
Jeremiah 30:7

The day after Jannik and I spent together, Tamas called for a meeting in the amphitheater. Thankfully, Jannik had anticipated how hard it would be to find each other in the crowd, and we made plans to meet by the pillars at the base of the ancient amphitheater thirty minutes before the meeting.

Zivah and I were in our cave room, washing up after a hot day of goat tending. I was excited to see Jannik two days in a row. I pestered Zivah to leave with me early.

"Come on! I don't want to be late!"

She laughed at me. "What's it like to be so in love! So impatient, you're annoying!"

I looked out of the window, noticing people passing by, heading out to the amphitheater. I felt the excitement of seeing Jannik bubble up inside me.

"Zivah, please! You look fine. Can we please go now?" I implored.

She sighed and smiled at me. "I give up, Dani. Let's go."

Eagerly, I grabbed her hand, pulling her along beside me. Once again, I described to her how wonderful the day with Jannik had been and thanked her for organizing it.

"He is very nice," she admitted. "I can see why you like him, but isn't this a crazy time to fall in love? We don't know how bad things are going to get."

My pace slowed, and I dropped her hand. "Of course, I've thought of that . . . but my heart wants him, and I can't talk myself out of it. I'm not sure, but I think he feels the same way. Maybe it's better to have someone to go through this together?"

"Oh, Dani, I don't know! Who can say? Are we safe here? What will keep airplanes from just dropping bombs on us? Or demon creatures from attacking us? How long do we have? Hopefully Tamas will have something to tell us."

We walked together in silence. Her questions had dispelled my eagerness. Maybe it was foolish to think there was a place where I would be safe or that there was anyone who would be mine, that anyone would love me.

After walking for twenty minutes, we came to the amphitheater. I spotted Jannik right away. As his eyes caught mine, he smiled, and every fear vanished, replaced by a hopeful certainty. I might not be safe, but I was loved.

"Dani!" Jannik embraced me and then more formally greeted Zivah.

"Where is Noam?" Zivah asked.

Noam spoke from behind me. "I'm here."

The hairs on the back of my neck stood up, and I moved a bit closer to Jannik as I watched Noam greet Zivah with a warm embrace. His eyes caught mine as he hugged her. It was unnerving.

Someone blew a ram's horn. That was the signal for us to take our seats. Thankfully, Jannik and Zivah were between Noam and me. As we waited for Tamas and the other Council members to appear, I tried to figure out what it was about him that made me afraid. I had trusted people before and been betrayed; if I had learned anything, it was to trust as few people as possible. I decided that I would go with my gut instinct and stay as far from Noam as I could.

The Council meeting began. One of the Council members gave an update on what was happening in Petra. When he finished, Tamas stepped up to the podium and spoke about something exciting that had been found in some of the caves. I noticed piles of boxes on the stage.

"Some of you have been here for a year or so now, while many of you fled Jerusalem that terrible day when the evil one stepped into the Holy of Holies and declared himself the Promised One."

The crowed hissed and booed; many stamped their feet and the sound filled the amphitheater. Although I knew we were supposed to be safe from President Bellomo and his troops, protected by God Himself according to Tamas and the other Council members, I was nervous at this direct rebellion. Zivah had told me the Global Union had satellites that could see our faces from high in the sky. Surely, they were searching for all of these people. *Can God really keep them from finding us?*

Glancing to my right, I saw Noam smirking.

Tamas continued, "We are in the day of Jacob's Trouble, as predicted by the prophet Jeremiah. As many of you know, all of this was predicted. We are in the Tribulation. It was predicted that the Temple would be rebuilt and then desecrated, which President Bellomo has done! Yeshua himself warned about that in the gospels. He said when we saw that abomination of desecration in the holy place, we were to flee to the mountains. So here we are!"

One of the other Council members went to one of the boxes, took a book out, and handed it to Tamas. He spoke out loudly, saying, "The prophet Amos spoke of a day when there would be a famine in the land for hearing the Word of the Lord. Truly, we came back to the land in 1948, but how many have come to Israel as secularists, as atheists? How many of you were raised in religious homes?"

Very few raised their hands and the crowd murmured their agreement. "Until the day Yeshua appeared to me, I had no knowledge of the true

Promised One, although he was spoken of in the Tanakh. Many in Israel had not heard the good news until the two Witnesses began to testify about him, just after the leaders of Israel signed the peace treaty with Bellomo. They witnessed to the entire world with signs and wonders and great power."

An outburst of heartfelt applause caused Tamas to fall silent and wait before speaking again. "Their witness to the world and their deaths at the hands of the Antichrist, President Bellomo, were foretold, as was their resurrection on the third day before a watching world."

The crowd applauded wildly, Jannik and I turned to each other and smiled.

Tamas held the book in his right hand as he paced back and forth. "But none of this is new," he called out as he held up the book. "This is a New Testament in Hebrew! There are many prophecies in the Tanakh, what the Gentiles call the Old Testament, but there are also prophecies in this, the New Testament, the Testament of Yeshua! It is an inspired book of God, about the Promised One and His followers. It is filled with prophecy regarding the Jewish people and the Gentile nations. The rise of President Bellomo is foretold within its pages!" His voice grew in enthusiasm as he went on, ". . . and his ultimate demise at the hands of Yeshua himself!"

The crowd rose to its feet with a spontaneous roar of praise. Ecstatic dancing and singing broke out among the crowd. I couldn't help but join in with the throng. Jannik was singing next to me, his eyes closed, tears streaming down his cheeks. I have no idea how long the crowd carried on in praise for Yeshua's deliverance, but eventually, we all sat down, wanting to hear more from Tamas.

"Over a hundred years ago, the Holy Spirit moved a Gentile believer, living far away in North America, to send thousands of New Testaments written in Hebrew here to Petra. Not only did the Lord prepare a place for us here in the wilderness, but He gave us His Word! We have enough New Testaments for all of you to read! We have almost ten thousand souls here in Petra now. We have enough that each of you may take one of these Hebrew New Testaments. As you leave tonight, take a book. Begin to read it!"

"The Council has prepared a schedule for evening meetings here over the next few weeks. Two of my brothers from the company of the 144,000 will open this Word to us and teach us about the times we are in. God will give us insight and understanding."

Jannik put his arm around me and pulled me close. Wrapping both of my arms around him, I pressed even closer. I felt reenergized by the prospect of reading the Bible again and by being so close to Jannik.

At the end of the meeting, Tamas called for people to help pass out the Hebrew Bibles. Jannik and Zivah both ran up to the stage, leaving me alone with Noam.

He slid over toward me on the bench. It was all I could do not to pull away in fear.

"So what do you think of what Tamas just said?" He lifted up his hand and boldly traced my cheek with his finger, slowly. "I've decided that it's a bunch of rubbish."

His finger ran down my neck. I grabbed his finger and twisted it backward. "You can keep your hands to yourself, Noam."

Noam laughed. I looked around and realized with a start that we were alone on the stone bench in this part of the arena. People were waiting in line for their books or leaving to go to dinner.

He leaned in and tried to graze my neck with his lips, but I pushed him away. "There's no one here to stop me," he whispered. I pushed him away and stood up. "I'm going to find Jannik."

Before I could get away, he grabbed me and pulled me down in his lap. "You ruined my life. Jannik was my friend, but now, all he thinks about is you. Since you're all he can think about, you're all I can think about."

Frantically, I looked around for help, but no one was near.

"Let me go now or I'll scream, Noam," I ordered. He dropped his hands and held them up over his head.

"No need to get so mean. I'm only playing, Dani. It's just a joke. Do you honestly think you're so beautiful no one can resist you?" He scoffed in my face.

He stood up and laughed again. "This is all garbage. I don't buy any of it. Everyone here is deluded—including Jannik. I'm going back to Jerusalem. President Bellomo isn't a monster; he's trying to bring peace to the world. Peace and safety."

Weirdly, Noam got down on his knees in front of me. "Listen, Dani, listen. I've had the most amazing dreams. President Bellomo appeared to me and said he is the true savior of the world. You can go back to Jerusalem with me! Leave with me tomorrow, and I will give you everything you could ever want. He told me that every single person I bring back will receive great riches and protection!"

"You're crazy! Get away from me!" I shouted. Jannik must have seen what was happening because he came running. When he reached us, he shoved Noam away from me—hard. Noam fell on the stone bench and rolled around, suddenly laughing hysterically.

"You . . . think . . . you're safe?" he squeezed out the words, laughing up at both of us, pointing a finger at us. "He's coming for you. He's coming for all of you."

Jannik pulled me closer to him and shouted at Noam, "Have you lost your freaking mind? Look, Noam, I don't know what's going on, but you stay away from Dani. I don't know if you have heat stroke or what's wrong, but you need to leave. Now."

Noam stood up, still laughing mockingly. He saluted Jannik and tried to take my hand. I yanked it away from him.

"Okay, okay. I'm leaving. But I'll see you soon," he promised before turning and walking away.

Jannik watched him go. "I've known him for years. I've never seen him act that way. There has to be something wrong."

I agreed. There was definitely something wrong. But even though I knew there was something off about Noam, I didn't tell Jannik what

Noam had said. Noam's words made me feel insecure. *Who was I to think someone would fall in love with me? What if Jannik didn't feel the same way about me that I felt about him?* The questions rolled over and over in my mind and I felt anxiety rise.

Jannik turned to face me and cupped his hands on either side of my face. "Dani, I'm here, and I will never let anyone hurt you."

FLOOD

Chapter 32

For He will conceal me in his shelter in the day of adversity . . .
Psalm 27:5

Terah clutched Amalthai's lifeless body, weeping uncontrollably. I took the newborn in my arms and left the room to give him privacy.

The hallway outside of their bedroom was empty. I found the kitchen and began to boil some water to clean myself up and make tea. The child was a boy, destined to die under the orders of the king. We had to plan what to do next, how to save the boy. But Terah needed a moment with the body of his wife, and I was exhausted and still covered in blood. And I had not yet had time to process my own grief at the loss of my friend.

I had just finished wiping myself off, the baby still sleeping in my arms, when the banging began. I heard a loud crack of wood breaking and the shouts of men coming closer. I looked around, terrified. There was nowhere to hide.

"Where is Terah?" a loud voice demanded. "The king demands his presence at the feast." I recognized the captain of the guard standing in the doorframe. He smirked when he saw the baby in my arms.

"Terah is with his wife in the bedroom, grieving. You will find him there." I tried to keep my voice from quivering. I thought if I was calm, he would just leave me there, and I could somehow hide the child.

"What sex is that child?" The captain of the guards strode across the room as he spoke and pulled the baby away from me. Ignoring my pleas, he uncovered the baby. The boy screamed.

"Well, this will be a pleasant addition to the plans Semiramis has for tonight's festivities," he laughed cruelly. "What better way for Terah to pledge himself completely to Marduk's son, Tammuz?"

Clutching the child, the captain ordered one of the soldiers to escort me back to the palace and left the room. I was marched out of Terah's home, away from my dead friend and away from her child I had failed to save. All I could do was pray. So I did. I prayed the entire ride back to the palace, tears flowing silently down my face.

When we pulled up in front of the palace, I was dragged to my room.

"Change your clothes quickly. The banquet has already started," one of the men ordered.

Numb with fear and grief, I went in and changed my clothes, rejoining the soldiers waiting outside my room. We walked through the palace, passing room after room. I paused as we came to the banqueting hall.

"Keep moving," the man on my right ordered. "A special pavilion has been prepared for this auspicious celebration."

I stumbled along as they led me through corridors and then outside the palace through the gardens. Finally, we came to a noisy field. There were tables spread out upon the grounds, which were already filled with celebrants feasting and drinking. All faced a large platform, tented with purple and gold cloth. It was near sunset and torches had already been lit. The royal family was seated on the dais. As I was hauled before them, I saw they were again wearing the skins made by the Creator for the First Ones.

"How dare you!" I spat out my bitter accusation at the bold couple. Semiramis stood up. The creamy leather dress clung to her voluptuous figure. It was still open in front, revealing her flat abdomen. Her long, dark hair curled down to her narrow waist. Scarlet painted lips sneered back at me, as she held her giant child on her hip.

"Silence!" Nimrod ordered. I turned to face him. My friend was dead, and this was all so, so wrong. No longer was I afraid. I was angry.

"How *dare* you put those skins on! You bring judgment upon yourselves wearing them and honoring that evil idol." I pointed to the huge golden statue of Marduk that stood right to the royal platform. The dragon-snake figure was outstretched over a blazing fire. Smoky incense rose all around the idol, obscuring its evil visage.

Nimrod nodded to the guard, and I was made to sit at the end of the table by myself. It was meant to be a humiliation before the crowd, but I was grateful. A slave poured some wine into my goblet, and I was given a plate of food, but I touched neither.

The celebratory meal went on for some time before trumpets were blown and a procession of temple priests entered the field, led by Akkadab. They were naked, except for loincloths and ceremonial swords at their sides. All were clean-shaven and their bodies oiled. Akkadab strode up the stairs of the platform, his dark eyes focused on Semiramis.

Without bowing before the king and queen, Akkadab turned and addressed the crowd, now quiet in anticipation.

"Tonight, we honor the son of Marduk, Tammuz." The high priest announced. The crowd exploded in enthusiastic praise. Akkadab turned and took the child in his arms before turning back to the people. Raising his free arm, he indicated that the crowd should quiet. "As you know, the oracle predicted the miraculous birth of this child. Tammuz is not the son of man but of the gods!"

Again, the crowd clapped with enthusiasm and shouts of praise. Akkadab turned his face my way. With horror, I watched the image of the Magistrate appear just behind the priest. He lifted his right fist in victory smirking at me, and Akkadab mirrored his movements like a puppet.

The Magistrate laughed, but the laughter came out of the wicked priest's mouth.

I stood up, afraid but also angry. The Flood, all that death, Japheth dead, and this evil creature still walked the earth. He had stuck his claws back into the world and the world had grabbed his hand. Anger coursed within me, and I rose to my feet, shaking. I began praying out loud, but one of the guards pushed me to my seat and slapped my face with the back of his hand. Tasting blood, I glared up at him and tried to stand again.

"Do it, and I'll tie you down and muzzle you myself," he threatened.

I looked back to Akkadab. The Magistrate smirked at me as he mouthed the words the priest spoke, "The oracle also warned us there would rise up, from the servants of the king, a son who would betray Tammuz. Because of this, the king has ordered each of his servants to offer up their sons to Marduk as a sign of their allegiance to the royal family. Join with me now, in reverent silence, as these faithful ones bring their offerings to the god."

A solo flute played, eerie and terrifying, as a line of men entered the field and approached the glowing idol. With horror, I saw Terah—his face ashen, his eyes deadened with grief. In his arms was Amalthai's newborn son. No one was forcing him to walk toward the flames or to place the screaming child in the metal arms of the idol. *How could he do this?*

"No! Stop! No!" I screamed as Terah approached the idol and placed the child in the flames. I couldn't think. A piercing scream left my mouth, mingled with the screams of the innocent baby. I was undone by the horror of it all.

I tried to get up from my chair and stop it, but unseen hands held me down as, one by one, innocent children were consigned to the fire, and their fathers knelt in homage before Nimrod and Semiramis. All I could do was wail, begging the Creator over and over to help the innocent children being burned alive as an offering to evil.

As the last victim fell into the flames, the crowd erupted in celebration. Unbelievably, I saw others like the Magistrate walking among the throng with their fists pumping the air in victory. The Fallen Ones were daring once again to walk the earth. They were darkly beautiful, like men—but not men. Sculpted muscles rippled as they moved about the crowd. I saw them whispering to women, gliding through the crowd.

I turned back to look at the royal family and saw one of the larger ones standing behind Semiramis, whispering into her ear as he caressed her arm. Her child, a Nephilim, half fallen angel, half human, sat at her feet playing with a toy, unaware.

Semiramis called to Akkadab, "It is time now for the offering to be made for the New Year."

Nimrod looked about the field. "But there is no lamb here." He obviously did not know about this part of the celebration.

Semiramis stood up and offered her hand to Nimrod, pulling him up before her. Leaning in, she kissed him seductively, distracting him as Akkadab crept behind with a dagger lifted up. She pulled away from the embrace as the blade plunged into his back. I gasped, but the crowd erupted, relishing their bloodthirsty queen.

"You, my love, are the sacrifice."

While Nimrod lay dying on the platform, the crowd cheering, Akkadab cut out a piece of his flesh and fed it to the evil queen and declared her a living goddess, wife of Marduk, and the queen of heaven.

The crowd fell on their faces, worshipping Semiramis, calling her Mother, and begging her favor, asking her to intercede for them with her son, Tammuz, the son of the gods. The evil creatures rejoiced mightily as the people groveled before Semiramis and Tammuz.

I screamed as Terah made his way up with the others to the priest and queen, "No! Terah! Don't!"

He took the piece of Nimrod's flesh on his tongue and raised his arms in a show of praise, tears flowing down his face.

There was nothing in my stomach, but I vomited, sobbing between dry heaves. There was nothing I could do but beg the Creator for help.

In the midst of the chaos, the unseen hands holding me back let me go and, somehow, I made it out of that place, weaving in and out of the crowd, back to my apartment.

Away from the presence of great evil, I collapsed. I sobbed and cried out to the Lord. As I cried, I felt a hand lovingly stroke my forehead. Warmth enveloped me, and the wracking sobs slowed down. I wiped my eyes and sat up. Before me was a man, dressed in shimmering white garments.

"Who . . . who are you?" I asked in wonder.

"Do not fear. I was sent the moment you first started praying, but the fallen angel of Babylon intercepted me. I am here now. Follow me, child; you are safe."

I felt like I was in a dream, but I got up and followed him. We left the palace and made our way through the dark streets of Babylon to a small hut on the edge of the city. The man entered, and I followed him. Sitting there by the fire was a young woman nursing a baby.

"This is the son of Amalthai and Terah," the man said. "Take the child and his nurse and return to your people. Shem is waiting for you just outside the city gates."

I grabbed the infant from the young woman, so eager in my relief. I pulled the swaddling clothes off, I turned him over and saw the pink mark on his thigh. This *was* Amalthai's baby. I turned to thank the man, but he was gone. I looked back at the child and wondered whose baby had died in the fire to save this child. But I didn't have time to think about that.

"We need to leave now," I told the young woman. Wrapping the child tightly in my arms, we left the hut and the city.

FIRE

Chapter 33

Keep me, O LORD, from the hands of the wicked; preserve
me from violent men...

Psalm 140:4

"Dani, wake up!" A voice pierced through my dreams. Groggily, I sat up, my eyes still closed against the bright sunlight. I couldn't remember my dream, but it had been lovely.

"What?" I was exhausted. I had stayed up late into the night talking with Jannik. It had been wonderful, better than any dream. No wonder I was so tired.

"Where is Zivah? Neither one of you showed up to tend the goats this morning! I had to pull someone else away from his work to do yours. Get up. At least you can go out and relieve the poor guy."

Blinking my eyes open, I blearily made out our work supervisor, Maya, standing in the opening to the cave, hands on her hips. Maya was well intentioned but had a short fuse.

"I'm sorry," I said quickly, jumping up, wanting to appease her before she erupted. "I stayed up late talking to Jannik. I don't know where Zivah is. She was sleeping when I came back."

Maya snorted, told me where to find the goats, and left, muttering under her breath. I quickly poured some water into the basin across from our sleeping bags and splashed water on my face. A small mirror hung over the basin, and I laughed at my image. I was exhausted but happier than I'd ever been in my life. During our late-night talk, Jannik had told me he loved me.

It only took me a few minutes to brush my teeth and get dressed. I pulled on a pink cap, pulling my ponytail out of the back, the way Zivah had taught me, and left our room.

Near our cave was one of the commissaries that dotted the Petra community. I grabbed a bagged lunch from the counter and a bottle of water, thanking the man who worked there before heading off to find the goats. As I walked in the blistering heat, I wondered where Zivah was. It wasn't like her to let me sleep in, and it sure wasn't like her to miss work. Zivah was very responsible.

Get Jannik and look for her. A voice, unlike my own, spoke clearly in my mind. I was startled. I stopped walking and looked around. There was no one else there. I was alone in the rosy red canyon.

I looked back toward our cave. Jannik stayed in a cave about ten minutes away. A goat bleated in the distance, and I thought of how annoyed Maya had been, so I ignored the prompting voice and continued on my way to relieve the person who was doing my job. Perhaps Zivah was ill and had gone to the clinic. She sometimes suffered from fierce migraines.

I made my way along the dusty trail and climbed the rocks over the hill to the place where Maya instructed me to go. As I got to the top of the hill, I could see the flock in the distance. Once again, I heard the voice telling me to go back. I turned around. *Was someone else here?* I had already slept in and slacked off my job this morning, I didn't have time go back. Whatever these thoughts were, I didn't have the time to go find Jannik, however nice that sounded. I went on down the hillside, determined to do my job.

As I neared the goats, I could see someone sitting among them on a rock. I couldn't make out who it was, but I could hear a man's voice singing in Hebrew.

"I worship you, O Great One, for who is like you? You have authority over all the earth, even here where the foolish think they're safe! Those destined for the sword have been stabbed. Blood covers her now like a deep scarlet shroud."

I stopped abruptly, fear rushing through my body. It was Noam's voice. I turned to run away, but I was so close to him now; he saw me and started running toward me. He was fast and caught me before I could get to the ridge.

I struggled in his grip, but he held me against him tightly and laughed. "Do you like my song? The next line is for you. Would you like to hear it?"

His voice was strangely high-pitched. I stopped struggling, remembering Daphne's warning to me when I lived at the Compound. *Panic only made things worse.* Noam slowly licked my face. I was revolted but stayed perfectly still, hoping his grip would loosen.

"Those destined for captivity," he whispered the next line of his strange song into my ear, "to captivity must go!"

Noam roughly pulled my arms behind my back and viciously bit my ear. I cried out in pain, and he laughed again. Warm blood trickled down my neck. I don't know where the rope came from, but he twisted my wrists together and roughly tied them up.

"Why are you doing this?" I screamed at him.

"Because you ruined everything. It's all your fault. You came along and seduced Jannik with your beauty!" He spat in my face.

"I did no such thing!" I protested, but he ignored me and went on a tirade as he pulled me away from Petra along a thin, dusty goat trail. "He would have been mine! That was the promise!" Noam finished with a screech.

"Who promised you that?" I asked and was slapped hard for asking.

"Shut up! You're the price I have to pay to get my friend back. You and all of the others in this rosy city."

There was a jeep ahead of us. I knew then that this whole thing had been planned ahead of time. "Where is Zivah?" I demanded.

Noam stopped pulling me and turned to face me. His watery blue eyes were bloodshot. He smirked. "Power requires sacrifice, you know. The great one is strengthened by sacrifice, and so he strengthens us in turn."

I could hardly believe what I was hearing. "You killed her?"

"Well, I'm not sure she's dead, yet," he chortled wickedly, in the same strange high-pitched tone. " I bent over and vomited, gasping between dry heaves. Noam caressed me as I threw up. Then he hauled me up and shoved me in the back seat of a jeep. His red hair glinted in the sunlight, and I could see blood smeared on the back of his neck as he started to drive away.

I should have listened to the voice warning me to turn back. I should have listened and gone for Jannik, I thought over and over as we bounced along the desert track. All I could do was pray desperately for Zivah, wherever the maniac had left her, and try to think of a way to escape.

We drove for hours. I wish it were in silence, but Noam talked nonstop. Insane banter back and forth between himself and an invisible someone else. I don't know how to explain it, but Noam's part of the conversation was completely deranged. The other one spoke intelligently and with authority. Both used Noam's mouth to talk.

I'd heard the other one before—it sounded exactly like Dominic, the psychotic leader back at the Compound, who would make long speeches all the time. The one using Noam's voice was eerily similar.

As I listened with horror, I realized he was giving Noam instructions about me. Back and forth they argued. Noam wanted to kill me in the desert, stake me in the sand, and watch me die.

Bile rose in my throat, and I struggled against the rope that tied my hands behind my back. *If I can get free, I can open the door.* I glanced up and realized he could see me in the mirror. I had to be careful.

Noam said a lot of other disgusting things, but the other one kept insisting that Noam take me to the city. He promised Noam would be richly rewarded and that it was the master's will. It took a long time for the other one to convince Noam, but he finally agreed, pounding the steering wheel with his fists, screaming in frustrated defiance while obeying the other voice.

I tried to push my body as close to the door as I could, making it harder for Noam to see me. I wanted to hide. I wanted to escape. Frantically, I tried to think of a plan, but I began to panic. Fear took over, and I started screaming for help.

The car slammed to a stop, and I was thrown against the front seat. Dazed, I was too slow when Noam yanked the door open and grabbed me by my hair.

"Shut up! Shut up!" he screamed in my face, covering it with spit. He made me sit up and then took a towel off of the floor next to my feet. Ripping it into a strip, he tied it around my mouth.

"Now stop causing trouble!" he ordered. Slamming the door shut, he got back in the front seat and kept driving.

For hours I'd seen nothing but sand on either side of the deserted highway, but just a short time after Noam's screaming fit, I glimpsed a vast city ahead, filling the entire horizon.

How would Jannik ever find me?

"There, there," came the voice out of Noah's mouth, "Do not fear! We won't let this worm touch you. No, we have better plans for you! The master needs your services."

Disgust pushed the panic back and righteous indignation filled me.

"I will never serve your master!"

He laughed. "Yes, you will. Not willingly, but you will."

I was about to shout in defiance, but the voice that had warned me earlier in the day spoke again in my mind. It was like my own thoughts but different in tone.

Do not answer.

Realizing with dismay how different my situation would be if I'd only obeyed the voice earlier, I clamped my mouth shut. We were close to the great city now. Blossoming out of the sands of the desert were huge, glittering skyscrapers, many topped with images of a half moon. Bordering the city were gigantic, craggy mountains, standing like sentinels. Some were so high I could see snow covering the tops.

We slowed down, and I could see barriers ahead . . . and armed soldiers. After a few minutes, we pulled up to the guards. Noam handed a small red book to the soldier.

"Welcome to New Babylon. What's the purpose of your visit?"

"I have a delivery for the Propagation Institute," Noam answered.

I had no idea what the word propagation meant. If I had known, maybe I would have fought harder to get away.

FLOOD

Chapter 34

*I know that you can do all things, and that no purpose of
yours can be thwarted.*
Job 42:2

The sun was just rising when we found Shem, of all people, outside the gates, waiting with a horse and a cart. The baby was asleep in my arms and had stayed miraculously quiet as we snuck through the city toward the city gate. Oddly, there were no guards at the gate, so we went through unchallenged.

I couldn't believe it was really him. After years of imprisonment in this city of nightmares, I began sobbing when I saw his familiar face and ran into his arms. The last time I'd seen Shem was the day Japheth was killed.

"We must leave quickly," he said after hugging me tightly and kissing my cheek. I bundled the nurse and child into the cart before climbing in. We raced away, leaving the city shrinking behind us.

After a while, we slowed our pace to spare the horse. So far, no one had come after us. The baby slept securely in the nurse's arms behind us, but I kept looking back to make sure he was safe.

"Ariana, I can't imagine what you've been through," Shem said tenderly.

I closed my eyes for a moment. They felt hot and dry and tired. The past years in captivity had crept by slowly, but the last few days, each horrible second, had felt like a lifetime.

"All of it was hard, but yesterday was the worst," my voice cracked. "They murdered infants last night. They put them on the metal arms of their idol and the babies fell into the fire."

My heart began to pound at the memory. Bile rose in my throat, and I could smell the horrific stench of burning human flesh again. Brokenly, I described all of the abominations that had happened in Babylon the night before, beginning with the death of my friend.

Shem sat next to me, too stunned to speak, tears pouring down his face. He stopped the cart, stumbled out, and vomited on the ground. Then he fell to his knees.

I got out and knelt next to him. We cried out to the Creator. We'd thought the evil of the old world had been drowned in the great Flood. We'd hoped that our children, our grandchildren, all of our family would live in a better world than the one we'd left behind. Our hearts were broken.

"We are the problem," Shem cried out, lifting his hands to the sky. "This evil is in the heart of all of us! What can we do? Who will save us from ourselves?"

Heavy with grief, we gradually got up and returned to the wagon. The nursemaid stared at us with a troubled expression as she nursed the infant.

"Is something wrong?" I asked anxiously.

She shook her head no and ran a finger from her eye down her cheek and pointed to us, then put her hand on her heart. I suddenly realized that she must be mute. Shem must have realized, as well, because he asked her. She nodded, opening her mouth.

My heart felt fiery with rage. "Nimrod cuts his servants' tongues out so that they can't gossip about him and Semiramis." I spat the words out bitterly

Shem and I climbed back onto the cart and rode on in silence.

We followed the dusty road that ran parallel to the Tigris River. Only a few travelers had passed us, heading toward Babylon, and we kept our heads down and the baby out of sight.

"I think we should stop soon and find a place to camp." Shem turned back to look behind us. "I think we are far enough ahead if anyone is following us."

I felt uneasy. *What if the people we met along the way tell others about seeing us here?* We decided to veer off the road and camp in a grove of dense trees. It was out of sight but still close enough to get water easily.

I got down from the cart and took the baby from the nursemaid. I watched as Shem unhitched the horse from the cart's shaft and carefully pushed the cart into the trees. I felt uneasy but knew we all needed rest.

Shem and the nursemaid left to fetch water for the horse and for us, and I sat with the baby, my back against a tree. He was so small, just two days old.

"Your mother wanted you so much," I whispered. He made the precious tiny noises and grunts all newborns make.

"They waited too long to call me," I moaned. My heart felt like a heavy stone. Amalthai had been my one beacon of light during my captivity. I still could not comprehend how someone with so much liveliness could be dead. I was exhausted.

The baby began to cry. Placing him against my shoulder, I walked in the shade under the trees, comforted by the little one in my arms. His cries slowed down, and I kissed the top of his head. "What a sweet boy you are!" I told him quietly.

As hot as the desert was in the day, it was cold at night. Shem made a fire, and we slept next to it, the nursemaid and I on either side of the baby so he could stay warm in the heat from our bodies.

I woke from a deep sleep the next morning, stretching slowly before opening my eyes. No longer a young woman, my body was stiff from sleeping on the hard ground. For a few moments, I kept my eyes closed, recalling a trip into the wilderness I had taken with Japheth after the floodwaters receded. We spent a few months exploring together with our baby, grateful for some time alone after being in the ark with the others. Even so many years later, I vividly recalled his tender kisses waking me in the dawn's soft light as we lay together.

The baby started crying. I opened my eyes and sat up, startled. The nursemaid was gone. I gathered the babe into my arms and looked around, my heart sinking. Though I hoped she was just nearby, I knew in my heart that was likely not the case.

"Shem, Shem! Wake up," I called frantically.

He sat up, rubbing his eyes. "What's wrong?"

"The nursemaid is gone! I heard her crying during the night. I think she's gone back to the city. What are we going to do?"

"Maybe she just went to get more water," Shem said reassuringly as he patted my shoulder. "I'll go look."

I walked quickly after him, desperate to find the girl. But when we got to the river, as I feared, there was no sign of her.

It was early afternoon when we climbed into the cart. Shem handed the baby to me, and I cradled him in my lap. We traveled in silence. I prayed to the Creator for the child, who would starve if we could not find another wet nurse. *After all of this, surely you wouldn't let him die. He's all that's left of Amalthai.*

As we rode on, I shared my fears with Shem. "How far are we from your village?"

"We still have another few days journey. You can see the foothills just now ahead. We should reach those tomorrow. It will be much cooler and fresh water will be easily accessible."

"If he were a little older, that might work, but he will not survive without milk."

We fell silent again and traveled on until it was time to stop for the night. We shared water and some dried fruit and nuts Shem had brought with him. Cradling the baby in my arms close to my breast, I dipped my finger in the water, and he eagerly sucked. My heart ached, despairing for Amalthai's son.

"He cannot die unnamed," I whispered.

Shem nodded in agreement. "I think that you should name him."

In the dusky firelight, my eyes traced over the child's face. I wanted to make his name a prayer.

Just then a silvery streak shot across the starry sky, leaving a shimmering trail of dusty light behind it. I took it as a sign from the Creator that he heard my request.

"Surely this child was saved for a reason! It is my prayer that the Creator will be his father, and that one day this little one will grow old enough to be a father himself! Yes, Shem! That is the prayer! I name him Abram." Then I gasped, "Look at the sky!"

We stared in wonder at the sight before us. Showers of stars were falling in a dazzling display. I thought of the evil I had seen back in Babylon, the terrible child sacrifices and the spirits of the wicked Fallen Ones. Evil was growing in Babylon. I had first encountered it in the Magistrate, long ago, before the great Flood, and now, it was growing in Babylon and sought to destroy this one child. *Maybe the evil one wants to destroy this child because the Lord has a special plan for his life?*

This child had been spared for a reason. I had fought for his life the night he was born, and silently, I vowed to continue.

FIRE

Chapter 35

*Some of our daughters have already been enslaved,
but it is not in our power to help it, for other men
have our fields and our vineyards.*

Nehemiah 5:5

Noam was instructed to pull his vehicle into an area to the left of the large city gates, where an armed guard approached the vehicle. "Step out, please."

Noam got out, opened the back door, reached in, and pulled me out. "I have brought this woman here for the Propagation Institute. I was told I would get a finder's fee."

The soldier laughed. "Lucky you! The Institute is very generous! Not many like her left, you know." He went on to make nasty comments while insisting he had to make sure I didn't have any hidden weapons. I tried to pull away as his rough hands ran over my body, but Noam held me in a vice-like grip.

Finally, the guard finished his search and instructed us to follow him. We went into a small building. Immediately, cool air enveloped me. Despite my circumstances, I was amazed at how much the change in temperature revived me.

The soldier went up to a counter and typed something into a computer then returned to us. "A car from the Institute will be here in about thirty minutes. You can wait over there." He gestured to a space filled with chairs and low tables. There was a large plastic jar filled with water. My throat was dry, but there was no way I would ask Noam for a drink of water.

"And I suggest you untie her," the soldier told Noam. "The Institute insists on treating their producers well. If they think you've damaged her in any way, they'll dock the finder's fee."

He moved off, and Noam untied my hands, muttering wildly to himself. As soon as my hands were free, I hauled off and punched him in the nose. Blood spurted, and he fell back with a look of great surprise.

"You little—" he screamed, coming at me. The soldier came rushing back and pushed him against the wall, ordering him to calm down.

"You," he barked, looking at me. "Go sit over there!"

Instead, I sauntered over to the water jug, took one of the white plastic cups hanging from a dispenser, and poured water into it. I stood there staring at both men and slowly drank its contents before filling it again and taking a seat.

Noam was ordered by the guard to sit on the other side of the room. "I can see I need to stay here," the soldier complained.

I crossed my legs and sipped the water, inwardly seething and keeping my eyes on a fuming Noam, who sat across from me, Zivah's dried blood still on his shirt. If I'd had a weapon, I would have killed Noam right then and there.

It wasn't long before the automatic doors to my right opened. A tall man, well-dressed in a suit and tie, strode into the waiting room. Even larger men, also well dressed, flanked him on either side. I could see holsters bulging just inside their jackets.

Noam stood up and went toward them. One of the larger men pulled his gun out and ordered him to stop his approach. Noam complied and stood with his hands raised as the other man patted him down.

"I brought her here for the reward," Noam stated arrogantly, nodding his chin at the man in charge. "I expect the full amount."

Without a word, the tall man walked past him and stood before me. Although he had dark, swarthy skin, his eyes were the palest blue I'd ever seen.

"Stand up," he ordered. I quickly obeyed.

He took my arm in his hand and pulled a silver object from his jacket pocket. I stifled a gasp as he put the object against my skin. There was a sharp sting like a wasp. He pulled it back, and I put my hand over the bloody spot left on my arm, rubbing it. He shook the silver cylinder and watched a display on the side of it for a few seconds.

"She's clear of the primary diseases. Once we get her to the Institute and verify she's clear of the others, and intact, you will be paid," he stated, before turning to one of the guards. "Take her out to the vehicle."

"I want to be paid now," Noam complained loudly. "You can't just take her. She's my property."

I didn't get to see what the tall man's response was because I was taken back out into the dazzling heat and pushed into a sleek, black vehicle. I stared out the windows as the vehicle drove by itself through the towering city gates, leaving Noam far behind me—and everything else I had ever known, for that matter.

The city was certainly like nothing I had ever seen before. I was stunned as we drove for almost an hour through the futuristic, silver shine of the city that appeared to be made entirely of metal and glass. The sidewalks were meticulously clean. It didn't feel like the desert anymore.

A shiver ran through me as I saw huge men, like the ones I'd seen on the screen when President Bellomo introduced his "supernatural partners" back in Jerusalem. We passed two walking together, much taller than any men I'd ever seen. *Those super humans again.* One turned, and his eyes caught mine. They glittered with evil.

Terror gripped me.

"Who—what—are those men?" I breathed slowly as I inquired of the guard sitting across from me.

He laughed. "How do you not know that? Those are two of the Progenitors. They're from another dimension. Have you not heard President Bellomo telling us about them? Their race has watched over the world since they seeded it with life long ago. Some say they are the biblical Nephilim returning.

"But you won't see them where you're going. They only interact with the world leaders. They're here in New Babylon in great numbers, of course."

"Of course." I wanted nothing to do with those creatures.

I had more questions. "New Babylon—is it the world's capital?" He looked at me like I was an idiot, then patted me on the head without answering what, to him, was clearly obvious. Changing the topic abruptly, he commented drily, "At least you're pretty."

If my knuckles didn't hurt from punching Noam, I might have hit him, too. I glared at him instead.

We drove for quite some time before I saw the ocean glittering turquoise in the distance. The guard, obviously taking pity on my ignorance and filled with pride for his city, droned on next to me.

Finally, the vehicle slowed as we approached a massive steel and glass building formed like two gently rolling hills. Between them was a large cube, also formed out of steel and glass. The turquoise color of the nearby ocean sparkled off the glass. We came to a stop, and I was ushered into the building. The words "Propagation Institute" were above the doors.

The space was immense. In the center was a well-appointed reception area. Men and women stood behind a desk, speaking to richly dressed people on the other side.

The guard hustled me along. I tried to keep track of where we were going, in case I was able to escape. We entered an elevator, made purely of glass, with glowing buttons, and I noted he pushed the number 33. The doors opened, and the guard led us down a brightly lit corridor and through glass doors marked "Intake."

Another desk stood just inside the door; an older woman dressed in white sat behind it. She stood quickly and bowed to the tall man. A tag on her shirt read "Intake Specialist."

"Ah, Dr. Winston," she greeted the tall man in a servile way. Obviously, he was someone of importance. I listened as he instructed her to have me showered and ordered a workup done. He wanted the results on his desk by the end of the day. Without another word, he turned and left.

The intake specialist led me to a bathroom. "You will shower in here and dress in the clothes set there by the sink. Just leave your things on the floor. One of the staff will see to disposing of them." She turned and left. I was alone.

I stared at my reflection in the mirror, noting the desperation in my eyes. *How would Jannik ever find me here? Even if he found Noam, how could he ever enter the city gates or find me?* This building seemed inescapable.

Stripping off my clothes, I got into the shower, which flowed from the ceiling like rain from a large, round head in the ceiling. I sat on the tiled bench built into the wall and let the warm water pour over me as I gave in to despair. I had no idea how I could escape, no hope that the man who had just told me he loved me would ever be able to find me.

Why does this keep happening to me? Does God even care about me? I finally find another human being who really loves me, whom I really love . . I felt so hopeless. There was no way out.

Sudden pounding on the bathroom door interrupted my grief. "Hey, you in there! Hurry up!" It was the guard's voice.

Fear shot through me. I worried that he would burst into the room. "Sorry!" I shouted. "I'm coming right out!"

Quickly turning the water off, I got out and dried myself off. On a small metal bench, neatly folded, were the clothes I'd been told to put on. I noticed a hairbrush and other necessities next to them. It only took me a few minutes to get ready.

The guard was standing right outside the door, glowering at me. "You're to go through that door there." He nodded his head toward a door on the opposite side of the room.

"Well, it's about time!" the intake specialist said as I entered. The room was windowless but brightly lit. There was a desk with a computer on it and a strange bed draped in white sheets.

"Sit down there," she ordered pointing to the bed, taking a seat herself at the desk. She asked me dozens of questions. Many, I just didn't understand, but she explained them to me, skeptical of my ignorance.

"Seriously, you don't know what I'm talking about?"

I shook my head, "No."

Clicking on her computer, she pointed to some pictures and gave me a quick lesson on human fertility. I knew the basics of course but not the specifics.

"Why am I here?" I asked when she finished.

"Really, where have you been kept? In a cave somewhere?"

"Something like that," I answered.

She softened momentarily. I could see she believed me. She scratched her forehead with her right hand. I couldn't help noticing the tattoo it bore. It was the same mark I'd seen on Mitch's hand when he betrayed me.

"Since the Vanishing, years ago, fertility rates throughout the world have plummeted—mostly, we think, due to sexually transmitted diseases. Many of them have become resistant to any treatments we've developed so far. That's what they tested you for when you first arrived."

She smiled broadly with pride. "Of course, His Excellency has healed many of the faithful. He healed me two years ago when I made the choice to serve the Promised One." She picked up a photo frame on her desk and showed me a picture of two babies held by a grinning man. "They're mine! A reward for my allegiance to President Bellomo!"

I felt sorry for the woman in front of me. She thought she'd really found the Promised One, but instead, the one she was following was clearly an imposter. The Antichrist! She talked on and on about her children and her plans for a future she wouldn't have. I knew the time was short. What I didn't know was if I would make it to the end myself.

She finally finished and asked me another question. "So what was the first day of your last cycle?"

I'm not usually that slow. But it was then I finally realized why I was there.

FLOOD

Chapter 36

"For I know the plans I have for you," declares the LORD,
"Plans to prosper you and not to harm you, plans to give you
a future and a hope."
Jeremiah 29:11

As Shem and I traveled into the mountains the next day, I prayed for the child's life. Abram did not make a sound. He had been in a deep, unnatural sleep for many hours, and I fretted over him. Shem worried as well.

"Have you ever seen this before?" he asked. Shem held the reigns, guiding the horse and pulling the cart up the narrow trail while I cradled the babe in my arms.

"No." I had raised dozens of children and helped countless others more be born. I had never seen a child so silent for so long. Placing my hand on the infant's chest, I felt it rise and fall. I listened to his heart beating sturdily. "He does not seem to be in any distress."

We rode on in silent concern. As the hill grew steeper and the trail even narrower, Shem clambered off the cart and led the horse up the path. The air was much cooler, so I wrapped the baby in my shawl close to my body to keep him warm and climbed down, as well. I prayed for the child in my arms, and I prayed for his father, Terah. I prayed against the evil of Babylon, and Nimrod, and Semiramis.

"We still have a few more days until we make it to the settlement," Shem stated again, his eyebrows creased in worry.

I looked at him, my eyes widened. "What!" I was alarmed that we still had that far to go. We were almost to the crest of the steep hill. My legs were sore from the unaccustomed exercise, but I ignored the pain as I thought about the baby.

"The nurse was feeding him just before I fell asleep," I thought out loud. "That means his last meal was yesterday. He has been wetting himself, so the water I have been able to give him is helping."

At the top of the hill, I got back into the cart. Nothing seemed to disturb the baby's deep sleep. *He doesn't seem to be suffering.* I put my finger below his tiny nose and felt his breath on my skin.

"I've never seen anything like this before," I marveled, repeating myself to Shem.

We continued on in silence for a while. The desert was behind us, and the mountain trail wound on ahead. The ground was still a bit arid, but there was grass. The mountains towering around us were capped with snow. The last time I'd seen snow was with Japheth, so long ago. It was on one of our last trips, or "adventures," as he liked to call them.

"This is very different from Babylon," I said, trying to take my mind off my anxious litany.

"Yes, wait until we arrive at the settlement. It is lush and green. Also, much cooler than it is here. I do have a few skins I brought with me. We can wrap him in those when it gets colder."

I noticed the horse's ears prick up and motioned to Shem. He pulled the horse to a stop, listening. Horses are prey animals, with much better hearing than we have. Shem tightened his hand on the reigns. If the horse felt threatened, it would bolt for safety.

The horse neighed, greeting someone unseen ahead of us. The horse did not seem sense danger, but it meant someone was approaching.

"Best to be safe," he said, handing me the reigns. Moving between whoever was coming down the mountain and the cart, Shem pulled his sword out of the scabbard, holding it in a defensive position.

A group of young people appeared on the trail ahead of us. Right away, I noticed my youngest granddaughter, Raisa. I shrieked with tremendous joy. It had been years since I had last seen her. Eagerly, I clambered off of the cart and ran toward her, still holding the child. Seeing me, she dug her heels into her horse's side and hurried toward me.

"Mother!" she squealed in delight. As she got closer, I noticed she had a baby strapped to her chest in a sling.

She came to a stop in front of me. She dismounted and we embraced.

"Who is this?" I asked, tenderly touching the head of one of my grandchildren. The young woman's blonde curls reminded me of Japheth. Tears of joy and sorrow mingled, threatening to fall. I blinked them back and smiled at my sweet granddaughter and the baby securely strapped to her back.

Unwrapping him from his sling, she held him out to me. "This is Ebe, Grandmother." Shem took Terah's son from me so I could hold my grandson.

"Oh, my," I whispered, mesmerized by Ebe's dark eyes and smile. He pulled at my hair and laughed.

"Raisa married one of my grandsons," Shem informed me. "Kal. They wed almost two years ago. Ebe is their first born."

At that very moment, the newborn in Shem's arms woke and began to cry vigorously. Surprised, we all turned to him; Raisa quickly took the child from Shem. I explained his hunger.

"The poor thing, let me feed him," she gasped and began to nurse him while I held my grandson. Relief flooded my mind and my body.

Shem introduced the others in the group. I knew most of them, but they had changed over the years, so I was grateful for the reminder. Raisa's husband Kal embraced me, calling me Mother.

When Raisa finished feeding Terah's son, we climbed into the wagon together, her horse tethered behind. Raisa had many stories to tell me about her brothers and sisters. Two of my other daughters had also married into Shem's family.

"How did you know we were coming?" I finally asked her, after she caught me up on my family.

"A man came to our village two days ago and said you had escaped Babylon and were on your way. Kal immediately got some of his cousins to join us, and we hurried to find you." Raisa answered.

I silently wondered if it had been the same messenger who had led me out of Babylon.

"Now, Mother, tell me about this baby. Whose is he?"

So I told her about the child's parents, Amalthai and Terah. When I described his difficult birth, Raisa's eyes filled with empathetic tears, but when I got to the part about the ceremony and the child sacrifice, she cried out in horror.

"Abominable and wicked!" She gazed down at the baby she had just nursed, now sleeping securely in her arms.

"Even where we live so high in the mountains, rumors of Babylon's wickedness have reached us, but I have not heard anything like this! Terah must never know where this child is!"

"Raisa, I think he did it to protect the boy."

She shook her head indignantly. "No, Mother! He sacrificed someone else's child instead. He is a murderer and a liar."

I sighed. Raisa was right. Terah had done evil. *Was his grief over Amalthai's death an excuse?* I didn't know. But as a mother, I could not imagine the choice he'd had to make.

As we drove on, I thought about Terah.

"You know, Raisa," I said gently, "Terah's grandfather, Serug, one of Shem's sons, left the family and went to Ur long ago. He rejected the Creator and worshipped idols, along with his wife. Terah and Amalthai had some of them in their home in Babylon."

"I do not care, Mother. His family life may explain his actions, but it does not excuse them."

I had come to love Terah and Amalthai. I wanted to somehow excuse his behavior, but I had to agree with Raisa. How someone treats the most vulnerable tells a great deal about who they are.

◆

The rest of our journey passed uneventfully. Finally, we arrived at the village. Shem shouted a greeting and people came pouring out of their homes to meet us. I was grateful to see my other daughters and their families and to embrace dear Nua again. It was a joyous reunion!

Tables were set up in the field by Shem and Nua's home and covered with food. Bread and cheeses, grapes and figs, and a cup of cooled wine started the celebratory meal while the meat was prepared. I was delighted when Noah and Laelah joined us. They had just returned from visiting some of their other grandchildren in a village on the other side of the mountain. We embraced warmly.

"Ariana!" Laelah cried holding me. "When Shem and Nua returned without you I never thought I would see you again—just like Japheth."

Noah looked pained at the mention of his son. He just gave me a hug and squeezed me tightly. I started to cry then. Seeing all of them together made Japheth's absence more pronounced. I pulled away and wiped my tears. "It looks like you found a wonderful new home here! Japheth would have loved to see it."

"He would have. He always liked the mountains." Noah suddenly grew serious. "Ariana, I want you to know we did tried to rescue you," he explained, his eyes tender and shiny with tears. "But Nimrod's army was too large for us to attack."

I smiled, looking up at Noah. He had aged quite a lot since the last time I saw him. Surely losing Japheth had caused both of his parents' great grief.

I moved to reassure him. "I know, I know. Shem told me what you tried to do to rescue me. God had a purpose. Truly. Wait until you see!" Turning to Raisa, I motioned for her to bring me the child.

"This is Serug's great-grandson," I said, as he took the baby from Raisa. Everyone around us stopped talking and turned to watch the patriarch of the family gazing down with delight at the babe in his arms.

"He has the look of Serug," Laelah said, tracing the baby's cheek gently with the back of her finger.

"Let us pray that is all of Serug he resembles," Noah barked gruffly. "What is his name?"

"He is named Abram because it is my prayer that he grow old enough to become a father. In his short life, he has been spared certain death several times: at birth and at the hands of his own father."

"So many attempts to end his life," said Noah wonderingly. "That has all the marks of the evil one! This young man must have a special future marked out for him by the Creator. 'Abram,' exalted father. That is a fitting name.'" Noah nodded in approval.

Noah offered a prayer for the child and handed him over to Laelah, who received him eagerly. We sat down to the table and ate, talking and catching up and laughing for hours.

When we finished the meal, some of the younger people took out musical instruments and began to play. The sun set, and torches were lit.

One of my younger granddaughters approached the group of musicians and asked to sing a song especially for me. She began sweetly singing, her voice clear and lilting. It was a song Japheth had written and taught to our children, who passed it on to their children.

Japheth had a strong faith in the Creator, a faith that he had passed on to our children through his stories and music. As I heard my husband's words again from the lips of our granddaughter, I marveled that love was stronger than death. Babylon had not defeated me, but its evil had taken a great toll on my heart. I had lost Japheth, Amalthai, and years with my family. Tears escaped unchecked, running down my cheeks as she sang.

I was grateful to be with family once again, but there was a hole in my heart that would never be filled. "It's so hard to be here without Japheth," I said to Nua, who was sitting beside me. She took my hand in hers.

"I miss him, too. It's strange to see you without him. You two were together every chance you had. I've watched your sons grow into men just like their father." She nodded toward the other table next to us. "Look at Gomer. He treats his wife exactly as Japheth treated you!"

I looked at our son, now in his seventies, with his wife. She was laughing at something someone else had said. Gomer's eyes were intent on her. I felt the grief subside as I watched them.

Turning back, I saw young Abram sleeping soundly in Raisa's arms.

Nua wrapped an arm around me and squeezed me close to her. "You are safe here, Ariana. You and the child are safe here."

FIRE

Chapter 37

*They have also cast lots for my people, traded a boy for a
harlot and sold a girl for wine that they may drink.*

Joel 3:3

"Get moving!" The guard yanked my arm, pulling me down a long,
polished hallway. I glimpsed the shimmering surface of water out of a floor-
to-ceiling window. Crowds of people walked freely along the waterside.

I was photographed in one room then taken to another. A man sat
waiting next to an empty chair attached to a table. There was a strap on
the table. I recoiled and tried to run.

"Sit!" the guard commanded. He pushed me into the chair and
strapped my right hand to the table, keeping a hand on my shoulder to
hold me in place. The man next to me pulled on black gloves and picked
up a weird sort of tool with a sharp end.

"I'm not going to lie; this will hurt." He turned on the machine and
began piercing the skin on the back of my hand. I tried to keep a stoic face
as the needle entered my skin. I felt numb and defeated and cried as my
hand was poked over and over again.

The mark wasn't like the ones President Bellomo's followers had. Instead, it was a grouping of thick and thin lines the guard said would be

used to keep track of my records. As soon as the mark was finished, I was hustled into a glass elevator.

As I watched the building fall away beneath my feet, my stomach lurched, but my fear was mixed with awe at the pristine glass structure in which I found myself. We emerged into a garden lounge, lined with more floor-to-ceiling windows. Outside, far below, was the water stretching out as far as I could see—clearly the water I had seen earlier. Turning, I could see the magnificent city of beautiful glass and steel buildings.

The lounge was filled with trees and flowering plants and dotted with benches throughout. I could hear a fountain from somewhere within this floating greenhouse. Women sat in groups on benches and chairs placed around the room. When I looked closer, I realized that not all of them were "women." A shocking number were girls much younger than me. Some reminded me of my little sisters back at the Compound. Everyone was dressed in the same white garments. *Like prisoners,* I thought.

"One of the staff will show you to your room and schedule your first appointment with Doctor Winston," the guard informed me. Then he left.

I stood alone awkwardly for a few moments, feeling eyes on me. To my left was a large water tank filled with colorful fish and strange plants swaying with the water's movement. I meandered over, pretending to survey the fish but really looking at the women reflected in the glass.

A tap on my shoulder caused me to start in surprise. I turned around to find a freckled-faced, red-head girl about my age. "Sorry! I didn't mean to scare you! I'm Nikki," she said in a friendly British voice, holding out her hand. I shook it.

"I'm Dani," I said without hesitation. There was something trustworthy about her, even familiar. I couldn't help staring at her huge belly.

Her smile faded. "Twins," she said so softly I had to strain to hear her. "This is my third time." I must have looked horrified because she continued quickly, "I won't actually have to birth them. It'll be a C-section. They don't want to risk childbirth and harming the babies."

She mistook my horror for fear of the birthing process, but I was finally putting all the pieces together.

"That's what I'm here for? To breed babies?" My voice was rising in my hysteria.

"Shhh! Don't be so loud," Nikki whispered, looking around. "When I first arrived, I didn't know either—." She took a deep, shaky breath looking down at her belly. "Many of the girls have chosen to be here. They basically sold themselves to the Institute to serve President Bellomo and enjoy the standard of living here." She spat out Bellomo's name like filth. "But there are a few of us here . . ." She pulled me over to a couch in the corner away from any of the other groups in the large room.

"A few of us?" I asked.

" . . . are believers in Jesus," she spoke softly. "Do you know Him?"

I was shocked at her boldness. Nikki saw my surprise at her confession and reassured me, "Oh, don't worry about that. They don't care what we believe here. It's our bodies they're after."

It was good to know that Nikki was a believer, and I nodded that I was too. Back in Petra, Tamas had told me that everyone who followed Yeshua, Jesus, was part of God's family. I wondered if that was why she seemed familiar. *So do we recognize each other? Was this a trap, or could I trust her?* I felt overwhelmed and scared. But I needed more information, and Nikki was my only option.

Carefully, I looked around. Many of the women had marks on their hands or forehead. Cold sweat broke out under my armpits. I looked down at my hand, still bloody and wrapped in plastic. "This thing isn't some kind of mark that says I follow President Bellomo, is it?"

Shaking her head, Nikki took my hand. "No, this is called a bar code. Whenever you see one of the doctors or have a test, they will scan that code. The information goes right to a file on a computer to keep track of your medical care here."

I let out a breath I did not know I had been holding. I had a mark, but it wasn't the mark of Bellomo. I looked at the other women and girls in the room. Most of them had a mark on their hands or foreheads in addition to the barcode on their wrist. Nikki did not have one.

I remember how the leaders in Petra had shown us from the book of Revelation in the Bible that anyone who took the mark of the false Promised One could never be redeemed. They would be lost forever. "I'll never take it," I muttered as I clenched my teeth together. "They can kill me, but I won't do it. I will never say President Bellomo is the Promised One, and I'll never worship him. He's the Antichrist." As I said this, I watched Nikki. She smiled and held my left hand tightly.

"Me neither, Dani. I am glad the Lord brought you to me."

Nikki stood up and stretched, rubbing the right side of her belly. "It must be tight in there because I can't sit for long without one of them kicking me. Listen, you don't have to be afraid in here. No one cares what we believe. They won't make you take the mark. All the Institute cares about is that you produce children for their customers."

Someone called my name. "That's one of the nurses. She'll set you up with some appointments and show you to your room. I'll come and find you. You'd better go. They expect immediate obedience."

An old, grey-faced woman stood by the elevator, tapping her foot. "You'll need to come much faster the next time I call for you," she snapped. "I've got ten girls I'm responsible for overseeing. I don't have time to wait on you."

"I'm sorry," I blurted out over her last few words. I watched her face grow intensely red but wasn't expecting the backhand that smashed my left cheek, and I reeled from the pain, falling into the closed elevator door.

She muttered a curse before grabbing me and shaking me fiercely. "How dare you interrupt me?" The elevator door opened up, and she shoved me in. I lost my balance and fell.

"Stop!" I yelled as she started kicking me viciously. I tried to roll into a ball and protect my head.

"Don't you talk to me, except to say, 'Yes!'" she screamed, kicking me after each word.

When the elevator finally stopped, I heard men cursing. The kicking stopped, and I rolled into a corner of the elevator and squatted there looking out. Two men held the struggling woman between them.

"Stop right now, Paniz! You've been warned about losing it with these girls! Doctor Winston is going to have a fit if he examines her and sees bruises."

One of the guards hauled me up off of the floor, and I gasped in pain.

"She's a defiant one!" the nurse protested. "I just needed to make sure she knows who's in charge here. You know how it gets if we don't keep them all in line."

The man telling her off shook his head. "Don't give me that load of crap. She's half your size, and you'll be fired if you damage one of the producing females." He looked at me.

"You okay?" I nodded. I'd had worse at Jack's hands.

"Doctor Winston wants to see her." He turned back to Nurse Paniz. "Now."

My abuser shoved her thick brown hair back from her face. Her forehead wasn't branded with President Bellomo's mark; instead, it was tattooed in silver and gold colors that glittered in the light.

As we walked down the hallway, she muttered obscenities, holding my arm in a tight grip. Finally, we entered a room with a mural of a tree on one wall and the same floor-to-ceiling windows I'd seen elsewhere, showcasing the sparkling turquoise water of the ocean outside. White, geometrically-shaped chairs were scattered in appealing groups throughout the bright room. I sat where I was told, on a white chair in front of a desk. The woman on the other side of the desk asked me some questions before scanning the mark on my hand.

"You can take a seat in the waiting room over there," she said, "You won't have a long wait."

As I moved over to take a seat on a chair by the mural, another nurse entered the room in a doorway to my right and called my name. She led me to a small room, where she instructed me to undress and put on the robe she gave me. I complied and waited for about twenty minutes before the door opened again.

It was Doctor Winston. "Well, let's see what we have here," he said in a clipped tone that made the hair on the back of my neck stand on end.

When the appointment was over, I was taken to my room. I collapsed on the bed, too stunned by what I'd been subjected to even to cry. I didn't hear Nikki knock or come into the room, but I jumped when she sat on the bed.

"Don't worry, it's just me," she said, putting a hand on my shoulder. "I'm so sorry that Paniz is your supervisor. She's the worst of them."

I rolled over and threw myself into her arms. "I can handle her, but the doctor . . ." I sobbed out all of the ways he had hurt and humiliated me. Nikki ran her hand through my hair and held me.

"Dani, they were just examining you, to prepare you for getting you pregnant. It's called *in vitro* fertilization. Doctor Winston has the best success rate in the world, but he's a mean man. He enjoys inflicting pain when he can. Once you're pregnant, he won't touch you again. None of them will. They can't take the chance."

I pushed myself up on the bed, groaning from the humiliation of the exam and the pain of the beating I'd received earlier. Nikki stroked my hair comfortingly.

"This is an evil city, Dani. Only the most faithful of President Bellomo's followers get to live here. It's got every technology known to mankind and technology that has never been known to mankind, until now—thanks to Bellomo's cosmic allies."

I was stunned and disgusted. I didn't know what to think. Pulling the pillow from the bed, I hugged it close to my chest.

"So is that what happened to you?" I asked. "They impregnated you artificially?"

She nodded her head yes.

"Why did God let this happen? I mean, He could've kept us safe."

Nikki shifted on the bed. "I don't know the answer to that, Dani. I've had so many questions and doubts myself. I literally feel like dying when I think about them taking my children. I don't even get to see them. They take them away before I even hold them. I didn't get to see or hold my first . . ." Her voice broke, and she curved her arms around her abdomen. "I'm afraid that I'm going crazy sometimes."

I tried breathing in and out slowly. Closing my eyes, I pictured Jannik and Zivah. *Oh God, why can't I still be safe in Petra with them?*

Nikki stood up, rubbing the same spot on her belly as before as she walked over to the large window overlooking the city.

"This place was originally a dream of a young Saudi prince. He envisioned a utopia built right next to the Red Sea, filled with the best and brightest humanity had to offer. Instead, it's a cesspool of evil."

"Is this where you're from?" I asked her.

"No, I'm from the UK. My family were all believers in Jesus. Mum and Dad put their faith in Him right after the Vanishing. We managed to stay off the radar for quite a while. We lived in a shantytown of sorts, made up of tents and caravans in a forest in Northumberland."

"How did you end up here?"

"Soldiers found us. They rounded us up and took us to a camp. I was separated from the others and tested to see if I qualified for the Institute. Then I was sent here." She turned away from the city scene and leaned on the windowsill.

"What makes us qualified?" I asked her.

"You have to never have had sex. There are sexually transmitted diseases people catch from having sex that make them unable to get pregnant. It's so bad out there that almost no children are being born. That's why the Institute was started."

"So they make us get pregnant for other people to take our babies?" My whole body ached, and my head felt like it was going to explode. *How much more could I take?*

FLOOD

Chapter 38

The Lord your God will restore you from captivity,
and have compassion on you . . .
Deuteronomy 30:3

Shem, Nua, Noah, and Laelah, along with others who wanted to stay close to family and continue worshiping the Creator, had moved to the mountains while I was in captivity in Babylon. When I arrived, the settlement was still fairly new and there was lots of work to do.

Abram and I settled in with my granddaughter, Raisa, and her family. I helped her with chores and cooking, while she fed her son, Ebe, and Abram. After years alone in captivity, I loved living with my granddaughter, but I yearned for my own space.

When it came time for Abram to be weaned, Shem insisted it was time for a home to be built for me and Abram. I picked a site overlooking the narrow river flowing just below our settlement. Some of the younger men erected a sturdy, little hut for us. They formed mud bricks and topped the small building with a flat wooden roof, which we could sleep on in the summer.

Once the men finished building, I decided I wanted to paint the small place after the old style of my childhood home. It had been so long since I had been able to mix paints and take on a large project. I was finally back home.

∾

One warm afternoon, soon after we moved into our own home, when Abram was around five, Nua and I went up into the mountain caverns in search of minerals to make some blue paint.

It was a long trek to the caverns but pleasant. Nua and I had always been close, but in the time since I had returned from Babylon, we had grown even closer. We chatted away the hours as we leisurely hiked up the mountain, easily following the directions given by her son.

"It should be just up ahead," Nua announced, stopping to pull a goat-skin flask from her rucksack. She tried to drink from it.

"Empty . . . but there is a stream just there. I'll be right back." Dropping her bag on the ground, she made her way to the stream through a thicket of trees. I sat down on a rock to wait for her, rubbing my ankle where it was chafed by my boot.

Despite the light of the midday sun, it suddenly grew dark. My heart froze in fear and dread seized me. Something malevolent was present. The hair on the back of my neck stood up, and goose bumps rose on my arms and legs.

He appeared out of the air, ghostly, but glorious in all of his foul beauty. Despite the difference in appearance, I recognized the same spirit that had once inhabited the Magistrate's body and had also whispered to Semiramis.

I stood up, shouting, "How dare you show up here! Don't come any closer!"

The creature snickered but obeyed my command. Just then, I heard Nua scream. Immediately, I ran toward the direction of her cries. "You're too late! She's mine now!" The creature taunted, but didn't follow me.

Rushing through the trees, I didn't feel the branches whipping about my face and arms, scratching my flesh. As I neared the stream, I scanned the area ahead but saw nothing. I turned in a circle.

"No, no, no!" I cried out, breathless. I felt fear twist inside my chest. There was no sign of Nua, but the goatskin, filled with water, was lying on the ground.

I picked it up. It was sealed. She must have been heading back when something happened. Carefully, I looked at the ground around me but could see no obvious signs of distress. No footprints, nothing. I put the bottle back down as a point of reference. I had to get help.

Running as fast as I could, I raced down the mountain. I saw one of the young men tending the goats and waved at him, "Help, help! I need help!! Quick, get the others!"

He turned and raced ahead. By the time I arrived in the center of our settlement, many people were streaming from every direction, some shouting questions.

"What's happened!?"

Shem pushed past the people around me, as I struggled to catch my breath enough to speak.

"Give her some water," he ordered, and a wooden ladle filled with water was pushed gently into my hands. I gulped it and sank to the ground as my legs gave way under me.

"Where is Nua?" Shem gasped.

I blurted out the terrible answer. "She's been taken!"

Within minutes Shem had a group of men arming themselves and getting their horses prepared to go after Nua. Another one of the Mothers gone.

"I want to go with you," I told Shem.

"No, you stay here. I think this is a diversion to make an attack on the settlement. I've got to go after my wife and rescue her. I'm going to take these men, but you stay here with the others and help get everyone ready in case we're attacked."

As the men raced off, I ordered the other people gathered around me to grab whatever weapons they had and meet at Shem's home. His house was large enough to accommodate all of us and had the advantage of being two levels, so we could see anyone trying to attack us. There also was a cellar in his house with a small well in it, so we would have water.

"I need to get Raisa and the children," Raisa's husband, Kal, told me. "They are napping."

"I'll help you." We rushed to their home, Kal calling out for Raisa as we entered it. She was sound asleep in bed with Ebe and Abram cuddled next to her. Kal shook her awake, picking up Ebe. I scooped up Abram, still asleep. By the time we returned to Shem's house, Noah was there with Laelah. He took charge and arranged men at the shuttered windows and barred the doors.

While we sat waiting, I explained to Noah and Laelah what had happened.

"It was the same spirit who controlled the Magistrate. He boasted he had her."

Laelah's face turned white and her face crumpled, "Oh no, oh no!"

Noah pulled her into his arms and comforted Laelah as she wept, his head pressed against hers. I turned away; the closeness between them was bittersweet. I went outside and looked down the path for any sign of Shem returning with Nua.

"Oh, Creator, please, please bring her back. Please."

It was quiet for many hours. Some of the women put together a simple dinner of cheese and fruit, along with some bread. We drank water from the well. It was a somber meal; even the children were quiet, sensing the worry and concern of their elders.

Sitting on the rough wooden floor by the well, an untouched plate of food in my lap, I watched Abram eat, worrying about what was to come next.

"You are like a mother to him," Laelah observed, sliding down on the floor next to me, holding a small platter of food. She ate slowly.

"But I'm not his mother. I wonder when he will mind that?"

"Maybe he won't mind that you are not his mother, but what about his father? Have you decided what you will tell him?" she asked.

Just then Abram turned to me and smiled. My heart was warm with concern, but my answer was ready. "I will tell him the truth."

"The truth about Terah is harsh," Laelah said.

I thought about the evil spirit I'd seen just before Nua was snatched. *Who took her? Was it Semiramis?* I didn't want to scare Laelah, so I didn't share my fears with her.

"I wish the great Flood had rid us of evil, but it didn't. It's still with us."

We fell silent then, each of us lost in our own thoughts. When we finished eating, Laelah and I gathered the dishes and cleaned up. The children were taken into the small yard in the back of the home by some of the young mothers to run off some energy. After sunset, we settled down as best we could to try to sleep. The men divided into a watch schedule to keep vigil through the night. I cuddled with Abram in a corner of the main room and fell into an exhausted, uneasy sleep.

Just before dawn the war screams startled me awake. Springing to my feet half asleep, I stood ready to defend my boy. I saw him still sleeping, undisturbed by the alarming noise, so I crept over to an oval opening in the wall to peer out.

The dusky sky was barely illuminated, but I could clearly see the green field in front of the house filled with fierce-looking men stamping their feet and howling their war chant. They held torches in one fist and vicious clubs made of wood, studded with sharp metal points, in the other. Their faces contorted in aggression as they chanted menacingly.

There had to be over a hundred of them. If all of the men had been there, we might have stood a chance, but I feared few of us would survive the night.

The rabble finished their war cries and silently parted into two groups, making way for two men on horseback.

"Serug!" I gasped. One of Shem's early sons, Serug was Terah's grandfather, Abram's great-grandfather. I feared he had somehow found out about Terah's child and come for his great- grandson. *But how could that be possible?*

Noah stepped out of the shadows and addressed him. "What do you want?"

"I know you have my grandson. Give him to me, and we will leave you in peace."

"I know nothing of your grandson," Noah stated calmly, folding his arms in front of his chest.

"The oracle told me about him, so I came to find out for myself. I know all about his parents in Babylon and how he was brought here." Nodding his head to one of his men, Serug commanded, "Bring her out."

Nua was carried out like a sack of grain by one of the men in the group and tossed to the ground. My heart dropped in my chest. She cried out, and I was grateful to hear it, though it was obvious she was in pain. Her clothes were streaked with blood, and gashes in her flesh were evident, even from where I stood inside watching.

Noah cried out and ran out of the house to her. Two of the muscular, tattooed men grabbed him and pulled him away from his injured daughter-in-law. Serug, seated haughtily on his dark horse, smirked down at him.

"Terah's son lives here," he stated loudly. "Give him to me, and I will leave. You will not be harmed, nor any of the others with you."

"Why do you want him?" Noah demanded, trying to pull away from the warriors who held him in place.

"According to the oracle, he will defeat the powerful one in Babylon. The one called Tammuz. The oracle told me to take Terah's son and raise him as a warrior. One day, he will face Tammuz and defeat him."

No sooner had Serug finished speaking than the whole army before us began howling. With a start, I caught sight of young Abram running toward them in the yard.

I screamed, turning from the window to run down the stairs and out of the house. As I ran toward him, Serug dug his heels into his horse's flanks and raced to the boy, scooping him up.

I screamed his name, but my voice was drowned out by the army's victorious shrieks. The two men on horseback turned and galloped away. The warriors let Noah go, and the army followed their leader.

When I reached Nua's side, Noah was already with her.

"Has she woken?" Laelah asked me. I sat in a chair next to my friend, my wounded sister. I shook my head.

"I brought you some stew. You need to eat, Ariana." She handed me the steaming bowl. I tried to eat a few bites.

"I'm sorry, I'm just not hungry." I put it down on the small table next to me. "Has anyone come back? Is there any news about Abram?"

Laelah's face said it all. No.

Why didn't I watch him? I should have been paying attention to him.

I turned and looked at Nua. Her face was nearly unrecognizable. They'd beaten her so badly her nose was broken, and her eyes black and blue and swollen shut. I watched over her until I fell into a deep sleep.

As I slept, I dreamed a dream unlike any other. It was not hazy, but crisp—like an important memory told in advance. I saw the event as if it were happening in real time before my eyes.

In my dream, I stood in the doorway of my hut. Before me, was a strong young warrior, a stunning dark-haired beauty at his side. The handsome warrior smiled down at me. "Mother, it's me, Abram!"

The joy that filled my heart washed over all my grief. Abram caught me in an embrace, and we cried with happiness. Then, he pulled away and introduced me to the young woman. "This is my wife, Sarai."

I woke still feeling his embrace.

I turned my head, but I already knew. Nua was gone. The joy of my dream felt far off, fading into the nightmare of reality. *My dear friend. My boy, Abram. Gone, they're both gone.*

Somehow, in my grief, I found a sliver of hope in the memory of the all-too-real dream. I held on to the memory of that dream, like a talisman, for years.

FIRE

Chapter 39

Though I am surrounded by troubles, you will protect me
from the anger of my enemies, you reach out your hand,
and the power of your right hand saves me.

Psalm 138:7

Nikki was right. As soon as they did their procedure, no one mistreated me, not Paniz or Dr. Winston. But I was still a prisoner.

The Institute had routines set up for all of the women and girls. I followed their rules. Each morning, soft chiming bells would wake us. Everyone had her own small suite, complete with private bath. We had an hour to shower, or bathe, and prepare for the day in clean, white garments set out by our nurse supervisors the night before. Then we were expected in the dining hall on the second floor for breakfast.

After breakfast one morning, I walked into the lounge to join Nikki and invited her to go on a walk with me.

"I'm sorry, Dani," she responded apologetically. "My ankles are so swollen I can't walk. Can we just sit here?" We made our way to a table. I pulled another chair up for Nikki to rest her feet on. "Do you want anything to drink?" I offered.

"No thanks, I'm fine for now." She looked around the room disgustedly. "In a few days these babies will be born, Dani," she said. "I don't think I can take it again."

I didn't know what to say. I felt the same way. Most of the other women and girls there seemed to like living at the Institute; it was beautiful, and there was plenty to eat. But all that didn't matter to us. We were prisoners kept for breeding.

"I wish we could escape," I said for the millionth time.

Nikki and I sat quietly for a long time. She closed her eyes. I looked past her out of the window.

"My life is ruined," I told Nikki. "I don't care that I'm safe here from all the terror of the world. I'd rather face the monsters out there than face having my own flesh and blood sold and taken away from me." *How had Nikki already done this twice?*

We had access to all kinds of things to pass the time: tablets, computers, books, and movies. Nikki showed me how to find maps on the Internet, and I'd been studying them. *Maybe the yacht I get on will go to the Gulf of Aqaba and stop in Haql? Then I'd wait until dark and sneak off of the boat.* I imagined myself going all the way back to Petra, back to Jannik.

Whenever I imagined my reunion with Jannik, my stomach lurched. *What would he think, if I were pregnant? Maybe he wouldn't want me.*

Nikki whimpered and gripped her belly. "Oh no," she moaned. She stood up and for a second, I thought she had wet herself. Her water had broken.

"No, no, no . . ." Nikki started crying, clutching her stomach.

I knew what would happen next. Her nurse supervisor would hustle her to the infirmary to prep her for surgery. Nikki would be unconscious while her babies were taken from her. She would hear no cry, have no memory to carry with her—only the feel of them moving inside her and a ghostly image she'd managed to see on a screen.

"I can't do this again," she whispered to me as I wrapped her in my arms. "The emptiness after . . . to not know where they are, how they are. It haunts me, Dani."

I didn't know what to say. I gripped her hand in mine and kissed it tenderly. Paniz, trolling the room, noticed the movement and immediately scurried over.

"What's going on here?" she demanded. The tattoo on her forehead seemed lit from within. Involuntarily, we shrunk back from her.

Her sharp eyes saw the wet floor. "Let's get you going, then." She pulled Nikki up and led her out of the room.

Nikki didn't come back the next day. Or the next. I grew frantic waiting for her return. Finally, five days later, I was sitting in the library reading when Nikki's nurse supervisor, Cressa, came to find me.

"She's back in her room now. She wants to see you."

Setting my book aside, I rushed to the elevator and pushed the button. As soon as the doors opened, I ran down the hallway to Nikki's room and pushed open the door. Nikki sat in the dark, huddled in a chair.

I moved over and knelt beside her, placing my hand on her shoulder. There was nothing I could say, so I kept my mouth shut. After a while, great gulping sobs began silently racking her body. Pulling her into my arms, I held her, as the silent cries became guttural groans. She began to scream.

"My babies, where are my babies?" She grew frantic and panicked, her voice growing horse with the screaming. There was nothing I could do but hold her and pray. *Dear God, please rescue us.*

I was surprised as another week passed, and the blood tests the doctors ordered were negative. I wasn't pregnant! Daily, I prayed that God would protect me from this horror. I felt comfort knowing that somewhere, Jannik and my friends back in Petra were praying for me. Though I was physically alone, I was not spiritually alone. I believed Jesus' promise that I had read in the Bible, that He would be with me, "even to the end of the age." *Surely, this must be the end of the age!* I thought. *How much worse can it get?* I felt a strange peace, a peace I couldn't even understand.

One day, not long after Nikki's babies were born, I was summoned to Doctor Winston's office. The doctor was nowhere in sight. An unfamiliar nurse motioned for me to have a seat at her desk, where she was looking at a medical report on her computer screen. I could make out my name at the top of the screen.

"Well," she said in a businesslike fashion, "It appears you are not a good candidate for in vitro fertilization, after all. The condition of your uterus shows evidence of endometriosis, and the risk of miscarriage is too great. The doctor will have to find a new form of treatment for you."

Two days later, I was getting dressed in my room when there was a tap on the door. It opened, without any invitation from me. It was Dr. Winston. My heart tightened and began to burn and my hands curled into fists, ready to fight. I wasn't going to be subjected again to his violations.

He stood by the door with a smirk stretched across his handsome, evil face.

"You can relax. I'm only here to talk to you."

Winston took a step toward me, and I raised my fists up and snarled at him. I would defend myself, even if they killed me for it. This time I wasn't defenselessly tied down on his examining table.

He stopped, raising his hands up in mock surrender, chuckling. "Seriously, I'm not going to touch you. Come with me; I have someone I want you to meet."

He led me to his office where a woman was seated on the couch. My mouth fell open in stunned silence as I stared at what appeared to be an older, richly dressed version of myself. Strawberry-blonde hair, streaked with darker and lighter tones, tumbled over her shoulders. Her green eyes glittered into mine.

"You were right, Dr. Winston; it is an uncanny resemblance!" Turning from me, she sat back down, smoothing her yellow linen skirt as she perched on the edge of the seat.

"Now, can you explain to me how the process works?"

Dr. Winston droned on for about five minutes about the Institute's proprietary process and *in vitro* fertilization. The woman was leaning forward, listening intently.

Winston continued, "Now, I know you particularly want this girl as a surrogate, due to her close resemblance to you physically and her excellent health. But there will be a delay as she receives treatment for her condition. It is curable, but it may be a few months before she is ready to be impregnated."

"She must come home with me, then," the woman insisted. "I will see to it that she receives every comfort in order to expedite the process."

"Of course, it is our pleasure to serve you, Ms. Figoli. As the sister of his Excellency, Angelo Cain, we offer you carte blanche."

The woman nodded, sitting back in the chair, her arms resting on its arms as if it were an imperial throne.

"It's essential to me that I oversee every aspect of my child's development. I want to be there for every exam, ensure the best care is given to the host."

I wanted to scream. They were going to use me after all. And my child would go to the sister of Angelo Cain, the one who served the Antichrist.

Dr. Winston preened. "Of course, Ms. Figoli!"

"You may call me Gabriella." I could see the curve of her cheek rise as she smiled across at Winston. "I want to watch *every* moment of my child's development and my dear brother insists I stay near him in Jerusalem."

Winston sputtered, "Oh no, madam, we keep our producers here to ensure their safety."

Gabriella stood and announced, "You will be well compensated. I insist you take advantage of my patience. As you know, many of the Jews are rebelling against the Promised One. President Bellomo is furious and has ordered my brother to punish them for their rebellion. Angelo wants me by his side; he depends on me in so many ways."

Winston reluctantly submitted, a simpering smile stretched across his face. He moved from behind the desk and took the woman's hand and kissed it. "Of course, we are honored to serve a member of the Promised One's inner circle!"

They left the room, walking past me as if I were invisible. A nurse told me to stand up and follow. I never got a chance to say good-bye to Nikki.

FLOOD

Chapter 40

So I will restore to you the years the locust has eaten.
Joel 2:5

After Serug took Abram and Nua passed away, life went on. Children grew and married and had children of their own. And although I missed my child and my friend, life was blessed by the Creator, and I was grateful to be back with my family.

The Creator protected us on our mountain, but we heard stories about Tammuz from people who had fled Babylon—about how he was now the ruler of the city and about his ruthless armies. The land was filled with constant war as Nephilim kings sought to gain power.

I lived alone in my small hut, now painted blue, and spent a great deal of my time gardening. My dwelling was small, but it had a large table by the fire. I kept a pot filled with flowers from my garden on it, and it was often graced by guests: Noah and Laelah, Shem, and some of my own children, along with their children and grandchildren.

Over the mantle of the fireplace hung one of the pictures I had drawn long ago when we lived on the ark, in the days of the great Flood. Raisa brought my things to the settlement in the mountains for me. All the time I was in imprisoned in Babylon, she had believed I would return. The sketch of young creatures sleeping in their pens on the ark was one of my favorites. A sketch of Abram perched on the mantle beneath it.

Often, when I was alone in the hut, my eyes strayed to the sketch of Abram, and I would feel a stab of pain. *Where are you?*

I knew he was alive. I was sure of that in my heart. Twenty years passed, and every single day, I hoped for his return.

One evening in late spring, I was alone in my little home, making dinner. I bent over the fireplace and stirred a stew, scooping up a succulent piece of lamb. As I straightened to taste it, I heard a knock on my door. Since Raisa's son Ebe often popped in around dinnertime, I thought it might be him. *He knew I was making lamb stew! Trust him to show up just in time for dinner.*

I opened the door, ready to tease Ebe, but it wasn't him.

Standing on the doorstep was the young warrior from the long-ago dream, and by his side, the stunning dark-haired woman. I gasped in amazed delight, already knowing what he would say.

"Mother Ariana, it's me—Abram!"

Smiling down at me, a now-grown Abram pulled me into his arms and enveloped me tightly. Tears of joy poured down my cheeks as I took his face between my hands.

"Thank God, oh thank God! I can't believe it! It's really you!" I said, looking up into his dark eyes, the same dark eyes as the child I had lost so long ago. "It's been over twenty years, and now my dream has come true!"

Abram drew back and put his arm around the young woman.

"This is my wife, Sarai."

She looked exactly like the woman in the dream.

"Sarai, oh, my goodness!" I hugged her, kissing her on each cheek. Her dark eyes shimmered. "Abram told me all about you, Mother Ariana. I'm so happy to finally meet you."

I shook with joy.

"Noah! Laelah! Shem! We have to go and find them!" We raced to Noah's home, the three of us chattering excitedly.

When we got to the house, I burst through the door. Noah and Laelah were sitting by the fire.

"He has returned! My Abram has returned!"

Abram knelt down between Noah and Laelah, embracing each one in turn, respectful of their old age and fragility. Noah clung to him, weeping and praising the Creator.

That night, we had a huge family feast, celebrating Abram's return. Noah and Laelah, Shem, and most of the community gathered together in the field by the communal well. Tables were set up and torches lit against the darkness. We talked and asked questions far into the night.

Incredibly, Abram remembered quite a lot about living with us on the mountain. He spoke lovingly of his memories of me, Raisa, and Ebe. When he mentioned the night he was taken, I felt the familiar pang of guilt for not watching him closer.

"No, Mother, the night Serug came, I was woken up by the Creator. A holy one led me out of the house and told me not to be afraid."

"A holy one?" Noah asked, his aged face wrinkled in wonder. "The Creator must certainly have a plan for your life!"

"Indeed. I was taken by my grandfather, Serug, to the city of Ur. When I was old enough, I trained with Serug's men in the arts of war. Serug is a man easily offended, so there were many opportunities to hone my skills on the battlefield." Abram stopped to take a sip of wine.

"One day, a messenger arrived from Terah—my father! He warned us that the powerful Tammuz of Babylon and his mother Semiramis had heard from their god that Terah's son lived in Ur and that I was a dire threat. Tammuz planned to attack Ur and kill me."

"How is Terah?" I asked with great concern. Despite his atrocious action sacrificing an infant to save his son, I still cared about him. *Sweet Amalthai loved him so dearly.*

"For his betrayal in warning the enemy of the attack, Tammuz imprisoned Terah and his entire family," Abram responded.

"So he remarried?" Shem asked.

"Yes, he remarried, and they have three children, one of them Sarai, my wife."

I turned to Sarai. "Where did they keep you?"

"We were held in the palace dungeons for weeks. It was so terrible." Tears shimmered in her eyes. She was a natural storyteller, and her voice was captivating. We listened attentively as she described the wretched conditions they lived in: little food and filthy water.

Abram continued, "When Serug heard that his grandson had been imprisoned, he planned a daring rescue. As soon as we could make preparations, we left for Babylon with Serug's army."

Sarai piped in, "The first man who entered our cell was Abram," she said gratefully as turned to smile at her young husband. "He was covered with the blood of our captors, but I never saw a more handsome man. More of Serug's soldiers came in, and they escorted us out of the city, and we escaped to Ur."

"Yes, and we married just a few months later!" Abram said.

"We are grateful you have returned here," Noah remarked warmly. "You have never been far from our thoughts since Serug took you away from us."

"Serug took much from us," Shem added stiffly. He had never forgiven Serug for Nua's death. Everyone seated grew still. Shem's bitterness was shared by many of his family. Abram broke the stilted silence, quietly asking what else Serug had taken.

I answered, "His men kidnapped Shem's wife, Nua, up in the mountains. When Shem and some other men went to search for her, Serug came with his soldiers demanding you in return. They carried Nua out from their ranks and threw her battered body on the ground. She was alive but died later from her wounds."

"I am sure you knew nothing of this," Laelah inserted quickly, laying a hand on Abram's shoulder.

"Serug is a brutal man. There is no charge against him I would doubt," Abram said. "He serves a vicious, powerful god, Nergal, the moon god. Serug called upon him to help defeat the dragon-snake god, Marduk, and his servant, Tammuz."

Again, the family grew quiet and ill at ease.

"And what is your opinion of these gods, Abram?" Noah asked.

"They are not gods but evil creatures," He bowed his head reverently. "Recently, the Creator spoke to me. He told me to come here with Sarai and learn from Noah and Shem so that one day I may pass on the history of the family to my own children."

"We are grateful for your return, Abram," Shem reassured him kindly, easing the tension. "And grateful that you serve the Creator."

Abraham and Sarai lived among us in the mountain settlement for a few years. Abram helped tend the flocks, and Sarai helped me with my ever-expanding garden. I grew to love her like one of my own daughters. Her beauty was enhanced by a sweet nature and keen intellect. She quickly learned all I could teach her about midwifery and utilizing various plants and herbs to create healing medicines.

"So I can just harvest some from the branch?" Sarai asked. We were in the woods foraging willow bark.

"Yes, you don't want to take bark from the trunk because it will affect the tree's health. Just snip a few branches. We'll take some from different trees."

"Once we get enough bark, what will we do with it? Make a tincture?"

I nodded. "Yes, with some; the rest we'll dry and store away. It's the only thing that helps Laelah's knee pain."

We chatted all the way back to the settlement. "Let's make the tincture at Noah and Laelah's house," I suggested. "I think Abram is there today."

"Of course!" Sarai agreed; then she hesitated. "Before we return, can I ask you a question about a remedy?"

"A while ago you were talking about mandrakes and, umm, how they can help a woman have a baby," her voice cracked. "It has been years since Abram and I married and . . ." She stopped walking and bowed her head.

"I didn't want to ask you, dear, but I did wonder." I put a hand on her shoulder.

"It's so embarrassing. The other women in the settlement whisper about it. I overheard one of them at the well saying that Abram should divorce me and take another wife."

"They should mind their own business!" I snapped. "Abram adores you, Sarai. I hope you don't doubt his love."

"No, I know he loves me. He says he doesn't care. But I don't believe him. You've seen him playing with the children." She lifted her head up and looked at me wistfully.

I pulled her into my arms and hugged her.

"Everyone else gets pregnant so easily, usually in the first year of marriage. Do you think the mandrake remedy will work?" Sarai looked at me earnestly.

"Some say it does," I spoke carefully. "I am sure you and Abram have prayed about this."

"Oh, so many times—every day. Sometimes, I look for signs, you know? Every time I see a pregnant woman, or a baby, I feel so jealous. Why is this happening to us?" I just hugged her tighter.

When we got to the house, Abram was helping Laelah make bread. Noah sat at the table where they worked.

"Finally!" Abram's face lit up when Sarai and I entered the room. He greeted me warmly but pulled his wife into his arms and kissed her heartily on the mouth, getting flour all over her back.

Noah teased them both, making Sarai's face turn red. Abram laughed and moved back to the mixing bowl.

I set my basket down and sat down at the table next to Noah.

"Now that you're back, Mother," Abram said, "I have something to tell you. Noah and I were talking about my father."

I did not like the way this conversation was going. "And?" I responded warily.

Abram took a breath. "You know, Mother, that he worships Marduk, the dragon-snake idol. After living here for the last few years, I feel like I've learned so much about the Creator from Noah, Shem, and you, Mother. Well, from all of you. I want to win my father's heart to the Creator."

I was stunned. *I just got you back. Terah doesn't deserve you.* I couldn't speak my worthless words out loud, so I said nothing.

Abram came and knelt in front of me, taking my hands in his.

"Mother, you said that my mother believed. I know that one day, I will see her again. I want to have that same hope about my father." I sat there looking into his dark eyes, which were pleading for me to give my blessing. So, I did.

"I want you to have that hope, Abram. But," I smiled down at him, "I'm going with you and Sarai."

FIRE

Chapter 41

. . . the kindest acts of the wicked are cruel.

Proverbs 12:10

Gabriella's estate was just outside Jerusalem. As one of the inner circle, being Angelo Cain's sister, she was shielded by her immense personal wealth from the deprivation faced by many in the world and the great power granted to those who personally served Emanuel Bellomo.

At Gabriella's, I lived in a proverbial gilded cage, actually a guesthouse set in a lavish garden. Perimeter walls kept me from running away. If I could manage to scale the walls, electrically charged razor-sharp wires stretched on top would keep me from going over.

I had the guesthouse all to myself. Each room had high, wood-beamed ceilings and a uniquely-styled fireplace I was never permitted to use. The kitchen was kept stocked with food for me, and I was free to take what I wanted, though there was no stove. Gabriella had it removed. She had everything removed from the guesthouse that I could potentially use to harm myself.

Luckily for me, Gabriella despised anything that was unattractive and refused to take Paniz with her to Jerusalem. Instead, she chose a young nurse, Taarini Patel. Taarini was a gentle soul. Originally from India, Taarini had worked at the Institute for just over a year. She was kind to me but absolutely devoted to Gabriella and obeyed her completely.

Day after day passed. Taarini monitored my meals and my health and my medications. Most days I sat, staring at the garden, alone and praying. I still thought of Jannik, although now it was hard to remember his face. That was a lifetime ago.

After three months, I was taken to a clinic in Jerusalem and artificially inseminated. The doctor there was much kinder and more talkative than the ones at the Institute.

"Just lie back and relax," the doctor ordered. "This won't take long—all the hard work's been done already!" he joked. The nurse standing behind him rolled her eyes and smiled at me from behind her mask.

No, I will do all of the hard work, I yelled in my mind. *I'm the one who will get pregnant. Give birth. Give up my child.* I closed my eyes, not wanting to look at the doctor.

"Actually, this is a very old technique." I wasn't interested, but he kept talking. "Decades ago, a Dutch guy—actually a Jew named Jacques Cohen—came up with the technique of taking cytoplasm from one donor's egg and transferring it to another, along with sperm, in the late 1990s. It was a promising treatment for infertility but was shut down. About twenty years later, another fertility specialist in the UK perfected the process."

"Is this my baby, then?" I asked.

"No, not really. You're just the host for the gestation." As hard as I tried to remain expressionless, tears rolled down my face. The doctor didn't notice. He finished the procedure, whistling off-key, and left me in the room with the nurse. She pulled the mask down.

"I'm sorry," she spoke softly, helping me sit up. "He is good at what he does, but he's thoughtless."

"Could you tell me something?" I put my hand out and touched her arm. "Whose baby is this? How can a child have three biological parents?"

She glanced toward the closed door and spoke softly and quickly. "Everything is done in a lab. The hosts are anonymous. That's all I know.

You'd better get dressed. The doctor has probably finished giving Mrs. Figoli an update. You won't want to make her wait."

She left and I quickly dressed. There were cabinets and drawers in the room, and I rummaged through them looking for something that might be useful—anything sharp—but there was nothing. I opened the door and followed the waiting nurse to the doctor's office, where Gabriella was waiting.

"Well, so that's done," Gabriella smiled at me. "The doctor said we come back in twelve days to see what your hormone levels are like." She turned back to the doctor and thanked him, and we left. Twelve days later, I was tested. It was negative.

The next day, feeling sick to my stomach and suffering from a blistering headache, I sat in the garden on a cushioned lounge chair. All the hormones they had injected into me to make the pregnancy "take" affected me terribly, as did the isolation. At least at the Institute, I'd had Nikki. Here, there was no one. I was treated well but in the way a favored pet is treated.

"Here," Taarini said as she came into the garden. "Take this water, and let's try this for your headache. Put it on the back of your neck." She handed me a damp, cool cloth and set the water down next to me.

"Gabriella and her husband want to make sure you're eating well. They want you to join them for dinner tonight. Dinner's in an hour."

"Great," I said sarcastically. Not only was I their baby machine; now, I had to eat in front of them to make sure I was taking care of the "equipment."

Taarini left. I threw the wet cloth after her. My head pounded like thunder, so I got up and went inside where it was cooler and darker.

"I can't even think!" I complained aloud to God. "Why do I have to go through this?" I broke down weeping from the pain in my head and my heart.

🔥

Gabriella's husband, Matteo, was one of the most attractive human beings I'd ever seen. He was also completely creepy.

"So how are you feeling?" he asked me. His eyes were not focused on my face.

I muttered an answer. Thin-lipped, Gabriella snapped. "You will answer politely, young lady. Remember you're living in luxury here as our . . . *guest.*" The way she said "guest" made it clear I was anything but.

"Fine," I lied. Picking up my fork, I stabbed some green beans and put them in my mouth.

"Please do me the courtesy of looking me in the eyes when you answer me," Matteo scolded with a laugh.

I raised my eyes to meet his, trying to remain expressionless. I could see he was trouble. He laughed again. "That's better!"

"We should talk about names, Matteo!" Gabriella lifted her wine glass. A servant rushed to refill it. She sipped her drink while they discussed baby names.

I didn't exist to them outside of a vehicle for the child they hoped I would produce for them. I felt miserable. Taarini tapped me on my shoulder and nodded toward my plate. It was still mostly covered with food. Reluctantly, I nibbled at it. None of it tasted good.

"Oh, Matteo! I want to show you the fabrics I have for the nursery! Taarini, would you go up and get them for me?" Taarini nodded and left the dining room.

"I'll be right back, darling." Gabriella stood up, grabbing the table to steady herself. "I've got to use the facilities."

As soon as she tottered off, Matteo turned to me.

"You know the resemblance you have to my wife is quite remarkable," Matteo observed. "Although you're much younger than she is, and I think much more biddable." He blew a kiss at me.

I must have looked shocked because he snickered again. "Oh, we have an open marriage. Gabriella and I have an understanding about such things. We each take pleasure where we want."

Somehow, I doubted that. Gabriella seemed the kind of woman who would mind that very much. I breathed a sigh of relief when she came back in the room then.

"What are you talking about, Matteo?" she asked him suspiciously, her voice raised.

He stood up and approached her, arms stretched out. "Oh, nothing dear, I was just joking with her," he snickered.

Her cheeks turned blood red, and she screamed, "Liar!" and slapped him across the face, ordering me out. I raced out of the room, the sound of broken glass following me.

I was not invited back into the house, for which I was grateful.

Once again, it was time for a fertilization attempt, and I was taken to the doctor's office. This time, I stayed in the hospital for a week to make sure it "took." I was alone, except for nurse and doctor visits.

Toward the end of the week, I tried to plot an escape. I was in the city of Jerusalem and out of my guesthouse prison. If I were going to escape, it had to be now. But as much as I tried, I never found an opportunity.

So I was returned to the guesthouse. I determined to be as compliant and helpful as I could, anything to give me a chance to escape.

I kept thinking of Jannik. What if I did become pregnant? *How could he want me after this?*

FLOOD

Chapter 42

... where you go, I will go; and where you stay, I will stay.

Ruth 1:16

And so I packed up my home to follow Abram and Sarai to Ur. I would not be separated from Abram again. I had love for them not only as a mother but also as brother and sister of the Creator. Abram and Sarai both had a unique quality of faith in the Creator, and I sensed that theirs was an important destiny. I prayed for all of my family, but for some reason, my heart was weighed with intense concern for them.

I also went for Amalthai. She had cried her repentance to the Creator, the true God. I never had the chance to share that truth with Terah. I felt that if I didn't tell him, I would bear some guilt for his continued rebellion against the Creator.

We gathered the provisions we needed for the ten-day journey. Ur was not so far, but Shem and Noah insisted on giving Abram many sheep and goats to take back with him.

"But I came with nothing," Abram protested, insisting they were too generous.

"Nonsense," Noah responded. "Certainly, you are responsible for the great increase in our flocks since you arrived. The hand of the Creator is on you, my son. I am pleased to bless you, Abram." Then Noah placed his right hand on Abram's shoulder and blessed him.

"May the great Creator of heaven and earth richly bless you, Abram. He has told me you will be a great man of faith. I truly will miss you. You are like a son to me. I'm so glad you've spent the last few years here with us."

Noah pulled Abram into an embrace, kissing him on both cheeks. Turning to Sarai, Noah blessed her as well, asking the Creator to favor her with many children.

I said my good-byes to my loved ones and climbed onto the cart next to Sarai, who held the reins. Abram leaped onto his fine black stallion and wheeled the prancing creature in a circle.

"Come along, Ebe," Abram called out. Ebe had decided to join us and help Abram tend the flocks. He hugged Raisa before mounting a strong mountain pony. Ebe waved the shepherd's crook and yelled at the flocks, urging them toward the trail down the mountainside from the back of the pony. We followed the herd slowly. A lump formed in my throat as I looked at all the dear faces smiling at me. *Who knew how long we would be apart?*

The journey to Ur was uneventful and pleasant. The summer heat had not yet arrived. When we made camp each night, Sarai and I would prepare supper over an open fire while the men tended to the needs of the horses and the flocks. After dinner, we would tell each other stories. Sarai especially loved to hear about life before the Flood. Both Abram and Sarai would tell stories about their family and friends in Ur.

"Ur is a lush, rich city surrounded by canals and farmland, Mother," Abram told me one evening. "Much greater even than Babylon. Many years ago, my grandfather, Nahor, went with his father, Serug, to find a place they could build a city. They decided to follow the Euphrates River and came to a place where the Euphrates and Tigris River run into the sea. Knowing this would be ideal for trade, they decided to build a city dedicated to their god, Nergal."

"That was wise to build by those waterways," I commented.

"Yes. They then searched out men of understanding and abilities to design the great city. Everything, where the houses are built, the grand canal that brings water through the middle of the city, and the great temple to Nergal that rises into the sky was planned in advance."

"Is that where they worship their idol?" I asked.

"The moon god, Nergal, is the main god worshipped by the people of Ur. The temple can be seen for miles; the courtyard itself can fit thousands of people. Many come and bring their offerings and sacrifices."

Ebe poked the campfire with a stick. "I find myself wishing I'd stayed in the settlement in the mountains," he remarked.

"You will get used to it," Sarai reassured him. "The temple is large, but no one forces anyone to worship Ur's god. Serug insists on religious freedom."

"Good for Serug," I said dryly.

None of their stories prepared me for the city as it appeared before us on the horizon. It was enormous. Encircled by walls to keep out invaders, Ur spread along the plain between the great Euphrates and Tigris Rivers. A massive ziggurat rose on the western side of the sprawling city. As we drew near, I could see tiny figures moving up and down the expansive stairs leading from the ground to its dizzying height where the large temple to Nergal stood, its blue bricks gleaming in the sunlight.

When we reached the nearest wooden gates, bound with strong, iron bands, Abram was immediately hailed by the guards. By their greetings, I gathered Abram was well-known and respected in Ur. Abram instructed Ebe to take the flocks to a great field to the right of the gate, within the city walls. Apparently, it belonged to Serug.

"Tell the men there whose flocks these are, and they will get you settled. Once I get the women home, I will come to you." Abram nodded toward the direction of the field, and we wound our way through the cobbled streets.

I looked at everything around me, astonished. *Abram wasn't exaggerating!*

Even Babylon did not measure the richness of Ur. Although there must have been a lower class, I saw no evidence of poverty. In fact, the wealth of Ur was evident in the splendid homes we passed after entering the city gates. Immense two- and three-storied homes lined both sides of the broad streets through which we drove. Each home was walled and gated. I glimpsed lush gardens and sparkling fountains through gates wrought of copper and fine woods. We passed parks and markets, driving for quite some time before we came to Abram's home.

We turned onto a long drive, lined with palm trees on either side. I sat in stunned silence, for I had not seen this level of sophistication since before the Flood. I gasped at the splendid home. Their home would have housed the entire settlement we had just left in the mountains.

As Sarai pulled our cart up to the house on the curved drive, servants raced out to take the horses, unpack the cart, and help us dismount. There were glad shouts of acclamation for both Abram and Sarai from their servants as we entered into the cool of the house. It was two-storied and centered around a vast courtyard garden filled with flowering plants growing on either side of a long, rectangular pool. Blue water sparkled invitingly as I moved through the front entrance, passing under intricately carved wooden arches. I stopped at the sight of the great Euphrates River. I could make out many papyrus boats sailing along the water.

"I have not seen anything like this since before the Flood," I gasped to Abram.

He grinned down at me. "Serug has gathered many gifted craftsmen here in Ur. Men and women of talent are encouraged to develop their skills. There are many guilds here; often you will note they wear amulets particular to their work. Potters, jewelers, carpenters, and stonemasons have their own gods, but as I told you before, almost all here in Ur revere the moon god, Nergal, as well."

How quickly the world turns to idols, I thought.

"I know what you're thinking, Mother," Abram said. "Remember that my grandfather, Nahor, was an idol maker. He made them in that room over there. One day, I was playing in his workshop, and I accidentally knocked a large image of Nergal to the ground. Nahor had worked on it for almost two weeks. I panicked and took a hammer from one of the shelves and put it in the hand of another idol, the sun god Utu."

"So you were putting the blame on another idol?" I laughed.

"Yes, I was terribly afraid of how angry Nahor would be, so when he questioned me about what happened, I scrabbled out the story I'd made up."

I shook my head, "Did he believe you?"

"Not the whole story, but yes," said Abram seriously. "Finally, Sarai and I became so weary of the idolatry in our family that we decided to set out to find you and the others."

A servant appeared and led me through the fragrant gardens and up the winding stairway to a beautiful, three-roomed chamber overlooking the Euphrates River. *I wonder what it will be like to see Terah again.* Ever since Abram had rescued him, he had lived here in Ur with his family in Serug's palace.

I walked into the bedchamber. Opposite the bed, covered in colorful woven blankets, was an intriguing mural—a picture of the First Ones by a tree in a garden, a large serpent twisting in the branches of the tree. Through the opened doorway, I could see into another room. I moved into it and was startled to see large bathtub. Copper pipes led into the tub, and I was sure if I turned them on I would discover hot water.

The floor of the bathroom was made of small, stone cubes, forming a mosaic. The artistic quality amazed me; I had truly not seen anything like it. The design depicted leopards, bears, elephants, and other small animals leaving a large boat. With a start, I realized there were eight people worked into the mosaic, standing on the deck of the boat.

I stood there, mesmerized. How incredible that a boy, taken from his home as a toddler and immersed in an idolatrous culture, would reject the idolatry and recall all that he had learned at a young age.

"This is your work, God," I whispered, tears forming in my eyes as my heart rejoiced.

FIRE

Chapter 43

My God, my God, why have You forsaken me?
Psalm 22:1

When I returned from the hospital, I suffered agonizing headaches and stomach aches. But this time, they wouldn't go away. No matter how hard Taarini and Gabriella tried to get me to eat, I couldn't keep much down. I lost weight instead of gained.

After a couple of weeks, they took me to a private hospital for treatment. The doctors did some testing and then admitted me. I was lying in bed, an IV dripping nutrients into my arm, when one of the doctors came in, firmly closing the door behind him.

"I am Doctor Amir Herson," said the dark-haired, middle-aged man looking down at me over the top of his glasses. "We have a problem."

"What is it?" I asked, sick and tired of it all. "Am I dying?" Half of me hoped he would say yes.

"No, you're not dying. But you're not pregnant either."

Relief washed over me.

"But frankly, Gabriella Figoli is not a woman you want to disappoint. And I'm not sure how long we can continue trying. This is two failed attempts already."

What is going to happen to me? I became alarmed. Clearly, he believed there was much at stake here, and that I could be in danger if the procedure didn't "work."

I know my fear was probably obvious. I also sensed he was sympathetic. I asked tremulously, "Can you help me?"

"There's not much I can do," he replied soberly. "I can't go against whatever Ms. Figoli decides. No one crosses President Bellomo's inner circle, especially Gabriella. She and His Excellency have a very special friendship." His tone was sarcastic. There was clearly more to that story.

"You don't like President Bellomo?" I asked, hesitantly, hoping to find some ground to connect with this doctor who might be the only person to help me.

He scoffed. "Many of us did six years ago when we signed the peace deal with him. What a deal! We got the Palestinians out of Gaza. We got real peace for the first time since we became a nation again, and best of all, we were able to build the Temple. It was all great, until Bellomo's prophet set up that foul image of him in the inner sanctuary. It's an abomination to every God-fearing Jew."

Abruptly, he stood up and walked over to the window.

"Now every one of us is fearful for our lives. Israel's no longer a safe place for us. President Bellomo has been systematically killing Jews for the last year or so. People just disappear. Those who have special skills, doctors like me, are allowed to live without taking the mark of allegiance, but it's only a matter of time. Jerusalem has become just like the ghettos of the Holocaust."

My thoughts raced. "I know a safe place! There are many who have found refuge there. I could take you!"

He didn't move from the window for a few minutes. I started to panic, but then he turned to me. "I've heard rumors of that place. They say President Bellomo can't get in there with his troops, and there's some weird magnetic frequency preventing satellites or drones from flying over. It's not something you should be so quick to tell someone about."

"We could escape," I spoke softly, tentatively. A small sliver of hope rose in me. *Did I finally have an ally? Could this be a way to actually escape and go back to Petra . . . and to Jannik!*

"I have no family to save." He sat down on the bed next to me. "There are many rumors about this safe haven. I don't know if they're true."

I sat up in the bed and put my hand over his. "Oh, they are true! I've been there. I was kidnapped and sold to the Institute, but I lived in Petra for over six months."

We spoke for quite some time, planning our escape. He planned to recommend a third fertilization attempt. When I returned for a checkup, we would make solid plans.

I was in the hospital for one more day. Taarini came to escort me back to the Figoli estate.

"I brought you some things to wear home." She held out a small duffel bag. "Madam Figoli wants you to join her for lunch before we go there. We're to meet her at the Rooftop; you know it's her favorite place!"

As she talked, she hurried me out of bed and fussed with my clothes and hair. "You're so lucky to be invited. I've never been before, but I've read about it. Madam Figoli is so elegant, isn't she?"

Taarini chattered on and on while I dressed in the clothes she had brought me. My mind felt heavy and blank as I went through the motions. I didn't care about Gabriella. I didn't care about anything except making my escape.

We left the hospital in a long, dark sedan. The windows were tinted, dimming the blinding sunlight. I leaned back in the seat as the car made its way through the streets of the city. Oddly, the streets were empty. There was no traffic, no crowds.

"Where are all the people?" I asked Taarini.

"The Jews," she spat, "keep rebelling against the Promised One, President Bellomo. The Israeli Defense Forces have been fighting guerilla warfare against the Global Union Army ever since the Promised One declared himself God and built the Global Church on the Temple mount. There was a big battle while you were in hospital, and now remnants of Jews are blockaded into several neighborhoods."

"What happened?" I was shocked.

"A group of them blew up the Global Church. They said only their Temple could stand on the Temple Mount. They killed hundreds of worshippers. So the President declared them terrorists and that's when the battle started."

My head hurt. *What else could go wrong?*

"But where are the other people?"

"The President declared martial law in Jerusalem. Only those with official passes are allowed to leave their homes. The Global Union army is clearing the city of Jews street by street. But don't worry; they've cleared the Old City where we're going to meet the mistress. The only Jews there are those useful in service."

The sedan pulled up to the Hotel Mamilla, one of Gabriella's favorite places in Jerusalem. A young man ran up to open the back door. Taarini slid out before me. As I was getting out, I heard the sound of a slap and Taarini's harsh voice, "You filthy Jew! Don't you dare look me in the eye!"

I stood up shakily from the car. Taarini had stormed off toward the hotel door. The man, the Jew Taarini must have slapped, still held the door open for me. I lifted my eyes, wanting to give him some sort of apology. When I saw his face, my heart stopped. I froze. *Jannik.*

I hardly recognized him. His hair was shaved off, and he was so painfully thin the sight of him wrenched my heart. He was dressed in grey clothing, a blue star embroidered on the left side of his shirt. A red mark highlighted his cheek, but other dark bruises on his face told me he was being roughly treated.

"Jannik," I whispered. His eyes met mine for only a second before Taarini's voice barked at me to join her. I had no choice but to break eye contact and follow her.

My mind reeled as we entered the cool darkness of the hotel, and I followed Taarini to the bank of elevators. *Jannik! How did he get here? How can I help him?* And then, *What must he think of me, being with the sister of Angelo Cain? Does he think I've gone over to their side?* I worried about what he might have assumed and wondered how in the world he had come to be here. My thoughts raced.

We exited the elevator and made our way out to the rooftop restaurant. Breathtaking, expansive views of the Old City showed little signs of the violence and devastation its population was facing in its streets. An old phrase Daphne used to say came to mind as I looked out at the city. *The calm before the storm.*

I saw Gabriella before she saw me. She was seated with her brother and was speaking intently to him. Officially, he was known as His Excellency. Besides President Bellomo, he was the most powerful man in the world. I'd seen him long ago at the Temple. That was the day I'd met Jannik. *How weird that he and Jannik are both here now. What is going on, God?* I felt lightheaded walking in the blaringly hot sun.

I desperately needed to sit down and have some water. I swayed and Taarini slipped an arm around me. Gabriella noticed the movement and motioned for us to join them. Taarini led me forward.

"She can sit there," Gabriella said, indicating the opposite side of the table. I was grateful to slip under the cool shade of the oyster-colored canopy. Using the armrests of the wicker chair to steady myself, I sank into its soft cushions. Taarini poured a glass of water and set it before me.

"Do you need me any longer, Madam?" she respectfully asked Gabriella.

"No, thank you, Taarini. You may wait downstairs to escort Dani back to the villa after lunch." Taarini bowed and left us.

Although I was thirsty, I kept my hands tightly gripped on the arms of the chair. Gabriella noted my fear and laughed, leaning over to her brother to whisper in his ear. I couldn't hear what she said, but the tone was mocking.

"I'll leave you now, dear one," Angelo Cain said to his sister. Their lips brushed together too long. Cain ambled off, leaving me alone with Gabriella. She sipped her icy drink for a few moments, eyeing me over the edge.

"I've decided to completely forgive you," she announced, with a fake smile, ". . . for being unable to get pregnant, I mean. My brother and I have discovered what an impediment Matteo has been. I no longer want to have a child with him, and he and I are divorcing."

She gazed at her brother as he got onto the elevator, smiling, "You have done us a favor, actually, Angelo and me." We've decided to cast aside the restraints to our love, and we have you to thank for it. If this surrogate pregnancy disaster had never happened, I might never have known the consolation and joy Angelo has brought me."

I was revolted, but I kept my face emotionless. My childhood had prepared me well to know the best way to survive among ruthless, evil people.

Smiling brightly, she held her hand out to me. Cautiously, I placed my left hand in hers. She squeezed it gently but didn't let go. "I have a gift for you," she confided, pulling my hand up and sliding on a silver bracelet. Ornate letters were etched on its surface in a language I didn't recognize. I traced the words with my other hand.

"It means, 'Blessed be the fruit.' Angelo and I have decided to start our own family. Of course, we want you to carry our baby. We need a third partner to avoid any genetic mutations. He said you look so much like me that we should use your genetic material."

No. I thought. *No, no, no.* Gabriella kept talking. She and Angelo wanted a large family to carry out their dynastic plans. I was going to continue to be used and imprisoned. With all of the trauma I had experienced, I was numb to the news.

My mind should have been horrified, but all I could think of was Jannik. With that one look, I had gained a will to live. *He's here! I know he's here for me.* I thought about the look on his face for that one moment. *Please, God, make that true and help us escape,* I prayed over and over.

Gabriella and Angelo Cain could make their plans, but Jannik was alive, and I would make mine.

FLOOD

Chapter 44

You are the LORD God, who chose Abram and brought him out
from Ur of the Chaldees and gave him the name Abraham.
Nehemiah 9:7

Soon after our arrival, we were invited to the palace for a celebratory feast. I was quite surprised I had been invited, given the past history, but I reluctantly went along to Serug's palace. He was responsible for Nua's death and kidnapping Abram all those years ago, but Terah would be at the feast, along with the children of his second wife—Sarai's brothers, Nahor and Haran—and their families.

The sprawling palace was perched alongside the Euphrates River, far enough back from its banks to be safe from flooding. As we drew nearer, I observed a few snowy-breasted eagles lazily flying in circles near the water's edge.

I didn't want to say anything critical about Abram's family, but as we got closer to the palace, I felt waves of foreboding wash over me. My spirit recoiled as we passed through the gateway, and I felt the too familiar evil of the Magistrate simmering about us. The evil of the Nephilim, those half-human, fallen angel spirits, inhabited any god or idol the devil could fool people into believing. I'd seen it happen throughout my long life, called by so many names. I knew the familiar foreboding when I felt it.

"We shall be fine, Mother." Sarai took my hand in hers and squeezed it, smiling reassuringly at me.

"It's imposing, isn't it?" Sarai misunderstood the reason for my obvious discomfort, but I was not afraid of the large palace walls or guards that stood above us.

Why doesn't she feel the evil presence? I asked the Lord. I kept my hand in hers and prayed silently for protection.

The massive walls surrounding the palace were wide enough for a chariot to race on the top. Guard towers roosted on top of the walls in evenly spaced intervals while armed men stood in their shade, watchmen on the wall. Serug kept himself well-protected, even within the walls of his own city.

Servants greeted us with flowery wreaths at the palace entrance, bowing respectfully before placing them around our necks. One of them, an older man, escorted us through the great garden. We passed many sparkling fountains and great statues depicting Serug's god, Nergal, vanquishing his enemies in battle. Never had I seen such workmanship. The faces of the dying men inspired pity and dread.

"Serug means this collection to be a warning to any who might aspire to take what is his," Abram remarked to me.

As we neared the great hall, guards opened the substantial bronze doors for us, bowing with deference as we passed them. Stunned, I stopped in the doorway. Before us, beautiful columns and arches framed the turquoise blue sky and sparkling water of the river outside. Long tables were filled with hundreds of guests who stood and shouted enthusiastically, welcoming Abram, Serug's highly valued warrior, and his beautiful wife, Sarai.

On the right was a broad dais where Serug sat on a golden chair at a table with a few other people. Following the servant, we made our way through the crowd to his table. Terah sat to the right of Serug. Although I smiled at him in welcome, he quickly averted his eyes.

Serug belted out a welcome to Abram, rising from his chair and enveloping the younger man in a hearty embrace before kissing him on both cheeks. Turning, he bowed gallantly before Sarai. "Once again the fair moon shines on Ur!" Then Serug turned to me.

"So, Mother Ariana has returned with you," Serug stated, somewhat flatly. There was no warm embrace or kindly compliment for me. I was not surprised to see a shift in his countenance and a shadowy look in his eyes.

"The Creator instructed me to come," I replied loudly. At the mention of the Creator, I felt the mood of the crowd around us shift. For a city that proclaimed religious freedom, it was obvious that while it was allowed, those who wished to attend such an event were expected to pledge allegiance to Serug's own god, Nergal.

Serug made no response. I could hear people murmuring, but I was not afraid. I would not keep quiet—not in a palace, not for any royalty. Serug knew Abram, Sarai, and I followed the Creator when he invited us to this banquet. He should not have been surprised.

We were led to our table and sat down. Piles of food and drink were before us. We began eating as friends and merchants stood up to make speeches and welcome Abram home.

A young man sitting next to Terah stood up to make a speech. It was Haran, Sarai's older brother. I felt the crowd grow tense.

Haran shouted loudly at the crowd, "For all the generations since the great Flood, you have resisted the Creator and followed after gods made in images you carved. In Babylon, the Creator came down and confused the languages to keep you from greater evil. Although you were scattered, you quickly made fortified cities and went to war with one another."

Some in the crowd looked down guiltily—but only a few. The majority glared as Haran went on in his indictment of their guilt. As Haran spoke, the tension at the feast grew. There was agitation; this was obviously not what the crowd had come to hear.

"Haran told me that in the years we've been gone, there's been trouble brewing in Ur between the small group of believers he leads and those who worship Serug's god," Abram whispered to Sarai and me.

"He's hated living here from the beginning. The idolatry outrages him," Sarai breathed.

Abram continued, "He said they think it's a matter of allegiance to Serug to bow down to his god."

"That explains the crowd's anger," I commented as looked around the room. Men pounded the tables and shouted out vile names at Haran. People were standing, agitated.

Sarai's face grew pale as she gripped the table and stared at her brother. Abram stood up.

"At the first sign of trouble, get out of here. Sarai knows the way. Some of my men are still out in the courtyard. Have them escort you home."

Abram turned to make his way to Haran's side, but a small group of men were already making their way toward the dais, knives drawn. I watched in horror as they fell on the young man, stabbing him mercilessly. The whole room erupted in pandemonium.

"Go!" Abram shouted back at us, drawing out his sword and racing toward the murderous men. Sarai grabbed my arm, and we ran through the kitchens to the outer courtyard. Two of Abram's men were sitting there on the edge of a stone fountain. Sarai called to them and told them what happened, her eyes scanning the area around us for any sign of danger. One of the men ran to get reinforcements for Abram while the other took us back to Abram's estate.

Sarai and I sat in the inner courtyard garden, watching as guards were set up along the perimeter of their home, and waited for Abram. It was not long before he returned home with Terah and an older boy.

Sarai rushed to greet them. "Father! Abram! What happened to Haran? Did he survive?"

Terah sat down heavily in a chair next to me. "They killed him," he moaned. "They killed my son, Haran." He wept inconsolably.

The boy sunk to the floor next to Terah and wrapped his arms around him in an embrace. "Grandfather," he sobbed. "This can't be happening."

Terah wiped the boy's face with the edge of his robe gently. "My poor Lot. Your mother and now your father . . . gone. Who will care for you after I am gone?"

Abram moved to his father's side. "We will, Father. Sarai and I will care for him. You have my word on it."

We all went to bed, but Abram kept guards around the house, not knowing what would happen next. Late in the evening, I went out of my room and sat on the terrace, looking at the garden below. Although it was night, the moon was full. Its silvery light illuminated as brightly as early dawn. The scent of lilies growing below drifted up to me. The cloying scent revolted me.

They smell like death, I thought.

Just then I heard shouting coming closer to the house. I rushed down the stairs just as the door to Abram and Sarai's room opened across on the other side of the courtyard. Abram raced out and ran down the stairs, sword in hand. He returned, looking worried.

"Mother Ariana!" He barked my name. "Terah went to the palace with some men and killed many of Serug's family. They're coming here to retaliate. Go quickly upstairs with Sarai and bolt the door." Turning on his heel, he dashed out of the courtyard.

I went back upstairs with Sarai and barred the door with a thick wooden beam. Sarai looked worried. Her eyes were dark from weeping for her brother, Haran.

We sat in anxious silence, listening to the sounds of the mob nearing the estate. There was a window in the room looking out over the Euphrates River, and I could see the water sparkling in the moonlight. *I wonder how this night is going to end,* I thought. The water looked so peaceful. The screaming mob came closer.

"He hated living here." Sarai broke the silence, putting down her goblet on the floor.

"Your brother?" I asked.

"Yes. He hated Babylon, too. From the time he was a young boy, he loved the Creator and hated idolatry."

"I wonder in Babylon where he would have learned about the Creator?" I asked. Terah was dedicated to his god. Surely, he would not have told his son about the Creator.

"Even in Babylon, they tell stories of the great Flood and the First Ones, of you Mother. But they are twisted tales. They have only a vague idea of what really happened because their worship of idols has tainted their thinking." The screams grew even closer, and we both sat still listening to the sounds of battle. Sarai bit her lip.

"First they kill Haran. Now, they will kill all of us."

We heard screams from the rioting hoards who had reached the house. It seemed like the whole house shook with the sound of their fighting. Then I realized the house was truly shaking.

"The earth is shifting!" Sarai cried out. We both stood up and rushed out of the room and into the courtyard where we gathered with the servants, uncertain whether it was safer to brave the earthquake inside or the mob outside.

Finally, after what seemed like hours, the earth stopped trembling. Abram and Terah came back into the house. Sarai threw herself in Abram's arms, sobbing in relief.

"It is over," Terah announced. "The moment the mob began to attack, the earth shook. A great wall of dust was kicked up by a sudden wind between them and us. The intensity of it drove the mob away."

"We can no longer stay here in Ur," Abram said solemnly, looking around at his household. "The great God of glory appeared to me when the earth shook. He told me to leave this place and go to a land He will show me."

Everyone grew still. I saw Terah open his mouth to speak, only to close it without saying a word. Of course, he had seen manifestations of power from his idol worship but not anything like the divine protection that had saved the family from the mob.

"Let's gather together our goods and flocks and travel upstream along the Euphrates until we find the place where he wants us to settle," Abram ordered. "We leave tomorrow."

"What about the servants?" Sarai asked. Unlike many others, she and Abram refused to own slaves.

"If they want to come with us, they are welcome," Abram answered. With that announcement, we got to work. Every one of the servants chose to stay with the family and move away from Ur.

FIRE

Chapter 45

And there were flashes of lightning and sounds and peals of thunder; and there was a great earthquake, such as there had not been since man came to be upon the earth, so great an earthquake was it, and so mighty."
Revelation 16:18

As Gabriella droned on, all I could think of was Jannik. We sat on the hotel rooftop restaurant looking over the city. Not only was Jannik in Jerusalem, he was here, downstairs. Or at least he had been an hour ago. I tried not to appear eager to leave, but all I could think about was going back down the elevator and seeing him again. *Please Lord, let him still be there. Let me see him again. Let him know I did not betray him. Let him know I still love him.*

Finally, Gabriella dismissed me. I got up from the table without a word. Gabriella nodded to the waiter standing by, and he led me to the elevator. I entered quickly, wanting to get as far away from her as I could. The waiter pushed the button for the lobby and left me alone. I watched the numbers on the display each floor until it stopped on the main floor. Taarini stood waiting.

"Let's go," she ordered. "Madame wants you to get home and rest. She told you the good news? Carrying Angelo Cain's children . . . such an honor for you! Surely, you are highly favored to bear the son of His Excellency!"

I wanted to push her down and run and look for Jannik. But I was weak, and she dragged me quickly through the lobby. I scanned around frantically looking for Jannik, but he wasn't there.

Outside the limousine was waiting. As the door shut, I wanted to cry. I had found Jannik and lost him again.

The driver's window between the front and back seat was closed, which blocked my view to the city through the windshield. That was odd; often the driver and Taarini would gossip together when we went out. But I was thankful for the lack of chatter. All I wanted to do was block out the world anyway. I told Taarini I wasn't feeling well and closed my eyes to avoid hearing any more of her gushing babble.

As we drove, I thought of one desperate plan after another to find Jannik and escape with him. I held back the tears as I remembered his face, so thin. *What had he been through?*

Finally, we got back to the estate, and Taarini escorted me to the guest-house and left me alone. I wandered out to the garden and sat in a chair under the shade of my favorite tree.

After a month in the hospital, I thought I would be grateful to be back, but after all that had happened, all I could think about was escape. But how would I find Jannik? *Lord, why do you keep allowing slivers of hope when it all feels so impossible?*

I sat outside until dusk turned to night. Suddenly, out of the darkness I heard a soft whisper, "Dani."

It was Jannik. I knew it immediately.

Turning, I saw him standing in the shadows behind me. I couldn't believe my eyes, but when he stepped into the light, I knew it was really him. Without thinking, I rushed into his arms and we kissed each other in joy, laughing, and crying softly.

Suddenly, I remembered where I was. We weren't safe out here. Usually, Taarini would check on me before I went to sleep, and I wanted to make sure Jannik was safely hidden before she came. I pulled him into the house.

The closet in my bedroom was actually a small room with a long, high window that ran along the wall near the ceiling. No one could see in the window, and I would have time to get to my bedroom when she came in the front door.

"In here. We should be safe." I clicked the light on as we entered the closet. There was a bench along one wall, and I sat on it. Pulling his cap from his head, he sat down beside me and turned to face me.

"How did you find me?" I asked him, my eyes searching his. Dark shadows underscored his brown eyes.

"Noam returned after he sold you to the clinic in Jerusalem. He boasted about it. Not knowing that Zivah had survived his attack, he walked boldly into Petra without any fear." I breathed a sigh of relief when I heard about Zivah. Jannik went on, "Zivah might have died if Tamas hadn't been told by the Lord to go out and find her. Her wounds were terrible when we found her."

My heart constricted with fear, recalling Noam's vicious words. I breathed in a deep, ragged breath. "How is she?"

"Tamas laid his hands on her and asked the Lord to heal her. It was miraculous! She was completely restored." Jannik smiled grimly. "That monster thought he was free, but Zivah saw him walking boldly down the main street and called for help. Then, Tamas began asking Noam questions about you." Jannik's eyes darkened angrily at the memory. "Noam stared at me with a smirk on his face as he boasted about how he'd raped you, killed you, and left you dead in the desert. I rushed at him, but others held me back."

I gasped, drawing my hand over my mouth. "Did you know he was lying?"

"No, but Tamas knew. I don't know how, but he knew and ordered Noam in the name of Messiah to tell the truth. He started foaming at the mouth and then fell to the ground, screaming to stop saying that name. He said horrible things, made dreadful pronouncements about the end of the Jewish people. But then Tamas commanded the spirit controlling him to be silent and Noam finally answered his questions."

I could see how pained he was. Jannik had considered Noam a friend. My heart went out to him. I could see that he, like me, had suffered greatly.

Jannik took my hands in his. "As soon as I heard where you were, I left Petra. I was determined to find you, Dani. I got some food and water and left right away."

Jannik had been searching for me all this time. I began to cry. Jannik pulled me in his arms and held me.

"But how did you get here if you were going to New Babylon to find me?" I asked. He described how the Global Union Army had found him only a few hours away from Petra.

"The soldiers beat me badly then tossed me into the back of one of their transport vehicles. It was filled with other people, mostly other Jews. Strangers pulled me up from the floor of the truck and told me that President Bellomo was killing all the Jews he could find."

"Where did they take you?" I held his hand in mine, marveling that he was actually with me.

"To a camp just outside Jerusalem. They made us wear the clothes with the blue star you saw me wearing earlier. We were brought to Jerusalem to work in the hotel."

I sat back and realized he was now wearing the same uniform the driver had worn. "So that's how you got here! What happened to the driver?"

"One of my friends helped me grab him when we saw him head into the alley. We managed to knock him out, tie him up, and take his clothes. He was roughly the same size as me; I put on his uniform and got into the car." His eyes flashed, and I knew he was doing the mental calculations about how much time he might have before the driver came after him.

"How did you know where to go?" I asked.

Jannik grinned then. "Easy, the car has a GPS system with a button marked 'Home.'" I wanted to grin, too, but I was scared.

"Jannik, that driver surely went for help after he came to. He's going to lead them right here."

"You're right," he agreed grimly.

Just then I heard Taarini call out. I motioned to Jannik to be quiet and left the small room, closing the door behind me. Rushing to the bathroom, I closed the door quickly and flushed the toilet. Then I ran water on the tap before leaving the bathroom.

Taarini stood in the doorway. "I'm just checking on you before I go off to bed. Are you feeling better?" I nodded and thanked her. Saying goodnight, I closed the door behind her softly. There was no lock, so I took a chair and wedged the back of it under the doorknob, so I'd have some warning if someone tried to come in.

We sat on my bed and talked in whispers all night. Even the things I was afraid of telling him poured out of my heart and past my lips in gasping sobs and were met with a comforting embrace and whispers of love.

"I can't believe you're here and that you still love me," I said quietly, wrapped in his arms. Jannik nuzzled me, gently kissing my face.

"Dani, I will always love you. I can't believe God actually brought us back together."

"I can't believe it either. It has been so hard. But Jannik, we've got to get out of here!" I pushed myself up and got out of bed and began pacing. We needed to come up with a plan.

We fell asleep, both exhausted. When we awoke, just before dawn, I crept into the kitchen of the cottage, careful to keep the lights off. I took some fruit and cheese from the refrigerator and quietly poured two glasses of water then went back to my room. I'd already pulled down the shade so no one could see us. We sat on the bed, the bowl of fruit between us, and continued plotting our escape. As the sun rose, we heard a loud humming sound outside.

I pulled the shade to the side and looked out into the garden. An intense light flooded my eyes. The humming noise grew so intense, my ears hurt. I gasped as I felt the earth tremor below my feet. Jannik ran to my side just as the light vanished. The world went pitch black.

Emergency lighting flickered on, and I heard people shouting from inside the main house. As I stood looking out of the window, I saw a man run out of the big house and look up at the sky, pointing.

Huge rocks began falling out of the sky. Terrified, Jannik and I dropped to our knees, and he began to pray out loud, "Yeshua, help! Keep us safe!"

I crawled to the front door and wrenched it open. Jannik followed me, and we sat in the doorway. It didn't seem to matter now if we were seen—and watched the unbelievable devastation outside. We clung to each other as great flashes of lightning bolted toward the earth, landing in explosions all around the small house. I cried out as a huge gap in the earth appeared between the main house and the garden. Loud screams filled the dark air.

My own screams joined in the shared terror as I watched the main house fall away out of sight. I lunged forward, wanting to get away—to where, I didn't know—but Jannik stopped me and held me firmly in place.

"We can't go out there right now."

I screamed as the earth rose up in great waves, and we fell to the ground.

"God help us!"

Jannik and I tried to get on our feet, but we only stumbled back to the ground. He put his body over mine protectively.

I screamed again as part of the guesthouse collapsed right next to us. The devastation went on and on as we clung together in terror.

Finally, it was over. We could see nothing but complete darkness.

FLOOD

Chapter 46

By faith Abraham, when called to go to a place he would later receive as his inheritance, obeyed and went, even though he did not know where he was going. By faith he made his home in the promised land, like a stranger in a foreign country.

Hebrews 11:8

We left Ur the next morning. Surprisingly, the crowd in the street just stood by as our carts and horses, cattle, and herds of sheep and goats passed through the city to the gates. Abram rode before the caravan, dressed in armor, his face stern. Sarai rode beside him, dressed in a simple white dress, a stunning bride. All of the servants were armed and vigilantly watched the crowd. Abram believed all his male servants should know how to defend their valuable flocks, so they were trained in combat skills. Together, they were a formidable small army.

I rode in a cart with Terah, Lot, and Ebe. Haran's body followed in a cart behind ours, at least his bones did. The vicious crowd had set fire to his body after they killed him. Late in the night, Abram had gone to the palace and gathered Haran's charred bones and brought them back to his grieving father.

I prayed silently as our cart barreled through the city gates, looking behind us for any sign of the mobs from the night before. I was anxious to be gone from the city.

We traveled many weeks, always keeping the Euphrates River on our left. When we came to villages, we stopped a few days to rest and resupply as best we could. Even as we met people far upriver from Ur, Abram and Sarai were known by name. His prowess as a warrior was widely celebrated, or feared, while Sarai's beauty was legendary. Wherever we went, people stared at her.

One day, as we traveled near the river, I looked back at Terah and noticed he was looking ill. *Terah looks grey,* I thought worriedly. Abram saw me looking at his father, pursed his lips together, and nodded at me silently. *He's worried, too.*

The next day, we came to a small city built on the banks of the Euphrates River. Its arched houses were made of mud and looked like beehives rising out of the ground. It was quaint. We would stay. Our family settled in a long house made from several connected beehive structures near the edge of the town.

The whole family was gathered in Terah's room, by his bedside.

"I am grateful you never gave up on me," Terah managed to tell his son breathlessly. His skin was grey, and his lips had a blue tinge. He was stretched out; Abram sat on the bed next to him. Sarai stood behind him, her eyes red from crying. I rested in a chair across from them.

"I would never give up on you, Father," Abram assured him. "Mother Ariana told me how much my mother loved you and prayed for you to know God."

Tenderly, Terah took Abram's hand in his. "I lived my life to please myself all of these years." He paused and drew in a deep breath. "I regret I resisted the Creator's goodness until now, but I have peace, knowing that soon, I will see Amalthai and your mother, too, Sarai. Please bury me next to Haran, your brother."

Lot and his wife stood at the end of the bed, their arms intertwined. Lot wept quietly.

"I promise, Grandfather. I will bury you next to Haran."

Sarai spoke, the rich timbre of her voice muted with grief.

"Father, we have talked to the leaders of the city. You know, thanks to the blessings of the Creator, our presence here has brought wealth and protection to this place. I have asked the leaders if we may name this part of the city Haran in honor of my brother, and they have graciously agreed. So, Haran's memory will live on."

Terah managed a weak smile and closed his eyes. "Thank you, my daughter. I know Abram will take good care of you and of Lot, my grandson."

Terah closed his eyes. His breathing grew more and more shallow. "Oh, Father," cried Abram, as he bowed over Terah and wept.

I clasped my hand to my heart and prayed silently. *Thank You, Lord, that he believed before it was too late.*

One evening, Abram came home from the fields where the shepherds tended his flocks. His cheeks were ruddy from the sun, and his eyes were flashing with excitement as he described to Sarai and me and incredible experience he's just had.

"I was walking along the river when all of a sudden a great light appeared all around me, and I heard the voice of the Creator."

"What did he say?" Sarai asked excitedly. I wondered myself. The Creator had spoken to Abram years before in Ur, telling him to leave the city and go to the land he would show Abram. Instead, when Terah grew weak, we had settled here.

"I'm to leave and go to a land the Lord will show me. We are to live as pilgrims, not in the cities of men, but in the place where the Creator will lead us."

"Did he say anything else?" I asked him. Abram turned to look at me, his eyes glittering with excitement from his encounter.

"He said that he would bless those who bless me and curse those who curse me," Abram told us. His face shone with an intense glow. We sat together at the table eating a platter of dates and nuts as we listened.

"Where are we to go?" Sarai asked. She enjoyed living in Haran in our quaint beehive home and had made many friends in the city She must have been somewhat dismayed, though she would not show it. Sarai, above all else, was supportive of her husband.

"I do not know. He said he would show me. We leave tomorrow. Please have the household servants pack what is necessary. I will have Ebe go to the marketplace and purchase tents."

Abram stood up from the table, grinning. "I must go and tell Lot!"

We left Haran with all of the possessions we brought and all that the family had acquired in our years in that city, along with Lot and his wife and the many servants that Abram employed. We headed to the land the Creator directed Abram to go, a land called Canaan.

After many weeks, we came to the hill country near a place the locals called Bethel. One night, Abram, Sarai, and I sat around the fire watching the stars and talking. Suddenly a great light appeared over Abram. He stood and raised his hands in prayer.

Sarai scuttled over to sit close to me as loud, thunderous noise reverberated the air around us.

"What is happening?" she yelled into my ear.

"I think it's the Creator!" I called loudly back. I watched in astonishment as Abram's face reflected the glory around him.

Then, as suddenly as it appeared, the light was gone. Abram ran over to us and pulled Sarai to her feet.

"Sarai, Sarai! We're going to have a child! We're going to have a child!" He spun her around and around, repeating the promise and yelling for the servants to wake up.

"What? What! How?" Sarai asked.

"The Creator said this land around us will be for our descendants!"

Some of the servants appeared in the firelight.

"Quick!" Abram ordered. "Bring stones so we can make an altar to the Creator. We will worship him right here."

Abram tucked Sarai close to him and his arm wrapped around her. "God is giving Sarai and me a child! He's giving this land to our descendants!"

Sarai was delighted. She flitted between Abram, the men building the altar, and me, literally dancing with excitement.

She grabbed my hands. "Mother, dance with me! The Lord told Abram we will have a child! Our descendants will live in this land! It's going to be theirs!"

I danced with her as she laughed and sang. Once the altar was built, Abram called for a sacrifice, and we all worshipped the Creator.

"Thank God for his great might!" Abram called. I raised my hands and praised the Creator for his goodness to Abram and to my dear Sarai. *You are giving them their heart's desire! Thank you.*

After years in the place the Creator promised Abram, a famine fell across the land. We traveled across the land from Beersheba in the north to Kadesh Barnea. After several weeks of trying to find food to feed our people and animals, Abram called for a family meeting. Lot and Ebe came in from tending the sheep, and we joined Abram and Sarai.

"We can't go on like this." Abram sat on the ground in the tent he and Sarai shared. "Soon our need will be so great that we will be too weak to travel. Lot told me there is food in the land of Egypt in the south."

"How do you know that?" I asked. I hadn't seen any strangers in weeks.

"We met some travelers as we went north looking for land to graze the animals," Ebe answered. As he talked about the men and what they told him and Lot, I noticed how thin my grandson had grown.

"Yes," Lot spoke, "They told us about the capital, the city of On, where a pharaoh lives with hundreds of wives and concubines. However, they warned us that the king's men are always looking for beautiful women to bring to him."

We all looked at Sarai. Wherever we traveled, everyone marveled at her beauty. Her dark eyes flashed with intelligent humor, and she was quick to smile, revealing deep dimples on either side of her red lips.

"Without a doubt, Sarai is the most beautiful woman I've ever seen," I worried aloud.

"But we need food," Abram pondered. "This pharaoh is a problem. Sarai, you are so lovely that I'm afraid if he knows you're my wife, he will kill me to get you."

Lot and Ebe murmured their agreement.

"What can we do?" Sarai raised her hands. "If we stay here, we all will die!"

Abram nodded in agreement. "We can try and keep you hidden among our people, but if they see you, what if you say you're my sister? They won't kill me then, and as your brother, I can refuse to let them take you. Our men can protect you."

Sarai nodded her head in agreement. We left for Egypt the next morning.

We stayed outside the city gates of On with our people, flocks and herds. Lot and Abram would take some of the men with them into the city to buy food while I stayed with Sarai and the other women in the tents.

After weeks of this, Sarai grew restless.

"I am tired of having to stay in this tent," Sarai complained. "I think we're far enough away from the city that we don't have to worry, what do you think, Ariana?"

"I do feel bad for you," I conceded. "Abram is very protective but with good reason! Ebe told me yesterday the pharaoh has over three hundred wives and concubines! I was shocked by such a horrible thing. Can you imagine all of those poor women?"

"It is shocking, but I have to get out of this tent, Ariana. Please, can we just go out for a short walk?"

"Maybe just a short one, away from the city," I reluctantly agreed. Sarai threw her arms around me and hugged me.

"Let's go!"

FIRE

Chapter 47

*But immediately after the tribulation of those days, the sun
will be darkened, and the moon will not give its light, and the
stars will fall from the sky, and the powers of heaven will be
shaken ... and they will see the Son of Man."*

Matthew 24:29–30

I was frantic.

"Do you have a flashlight in the house?" Jannik asked. Although it was morning, the sky was black.

I told him there was one in the nightstand by the bed, and he made his way through the debris and found it. Stumbling, we left the house. Amazingly, most of the guesthouse had remained intact. The garden was a ruin. Huge boulders had smashed into the earth all around us, and we had to carefully make our way around them.

"This has to weigh almost a hundred pounds," Jannik whispered, flashing the light over a tremendous rock. I gasped and grabbed his arm as another tremor shook the ground beneath our feet. Thankfully, it was less intense.

"I'm sure, as bad as that was, there'll be a lot of aftershocks," Jannik remarked. We scrambled through the devastation to the edge of the great rift in the ground and looked over the edge to see if there were any survivors. The main house was somewhere in the darkness below us.

"We'll have to wait for more light," Jannik said, his voice flat.

We stumbled back to what was left of the guesthouse to wait. We sat outside it in dazed silence. There were more aftershocks. Every time the ground shook, I was terrified. Finally, the blackness gave way to a dim grey light. Grit bit at our eyes, but we made our way back to the cliff's edge.

We could just make out the shape of part of the mansion below us. It had fallen into the hole and was about fifteen feet below where it had once proudly stood. There was only silence.

Suddenly, there was another aftershock and the ground beneath us began to crumble. I jumped back as the ground gave way. Jannik also jumped back, in the opposite direction, and I watched in horror as a chasm opened up between us. The rest of the cliff and the house fell away, and Jannik with them. Smoky dust poured up from the hole below, obscuring everything.

"No!" I screamed. "Jannik!"

"Jannik! Jannik!" I called frantically over and over into the dark crevice before me. I fell to my knees sobbing uncontrollably.

"God, what can I do? Please help me. Please help me!" I moaned. *Could I find a rope to reach him? Was he even alive?* Desperate thoughts raced through my mind. I thought of one plan after another, but none of them would work.

"Jannik! Jannik!" I screamed again over the edge. "I can't lose you again!"

I held the flashlight, but it was useless. Its flickering light hardly penetrated the darkness.

Ask me.

My thoughts grew still. It was the same voice that had warned me not to go out in the desert. The voice I'd ignored.

I looked up and saw a streak of blue sky through the dusty grey light.

"God, I need you to rescue Jannik," I whispered, as tears streamed down my dirty face. *Where would I go, what would I do?* I went back toward the guesthouse, the only safe haven I knew. I had barely reached it when a loud sound pierced the air and the ground shook again.

"God, what now?" I cried out. "Please, please help us!" I'd never heard anything so loud. Thankfully, it only lasted a few minutes.

"Please, God, please help me," I prayed again, out loud. "I know Jesus is supposed to come back again at the end of all this. Please, won't you send Him back now? Jesus, we need You more than ever! Please help us!"

Suddenly the dark room filled with a great warm light.

Awestruck, I looked around me and felt a trembling hope for the first time in a long, long time. The light was intense, but it didn't hurt my eyes. It spilled into the guesthouse in a glorious display that glittered with hinted shades of color. It seemed to joyously chase away the smoky darkness from the room, like a sunrise after weeks of rain.

I went outside, hoping for a miracle. Tears streamed down my face as I took in the scene before me. The entire sky was filled with fiery rainbow clouds that arched down across the sky toward the Mount of Olives, on the east side of Jerusalem. I knew from the teaching I'd received at Petra that this was where the Bible prophecies said Jesus would return some day—when He came back. Hope filled my heart. *Was it true? Was it now?*

Where the fiery rainbow clouds met the mountain, there was a glorious light that I can only describe as otherworldly in its beauty. *It must be Him! He's here! He's really come back!* My heart beat wildly, and I looked around me, hoping.

The devastation remained, but everything was bathed in the glorious light. My mouth dropped open as I noticed the people around me. All of them wore white, shimmering clothing. *Am I dreaming?* They were gloriously beautiful.

Some of them carried injured people on stretchers, taking them away from the ravages of the destruction. Still others were working together to descend into the crevice in the earth where the house once stood. I rushed over to see what they were doing. I was startled when an arm wrapped around my shoulders and squeezed me.

"We're here to help you."

The voice seemed familiar. I turned and looked into the face of a radiant young woman. She was beyond beautiful, glowing with the same light the others had about them. There was something about the way her eyes crinkled as she smiled.

"I know you, don't I?"

Her smile grew warmer and her eyes glittered. She laughed and my heart filled with joy at the sound. "I should hope so! I spent many days and nights taking care of you back at the Compound."

"Daphne?" I asked in amazement. She nodded, and I embraced her. I cried as she held me. I cried for all of my sisters and brothers, for my cold parents, and for all of the terror and loss I'd been through.

Daphne pulled back. She could tell my distress was more than just the awe of what was going on around me. "Yet, you are troubled still," she said earnestly. "Tell me."

"I explained to her what had happened. "Can you help me?" I begged her.

"Some of the others are already down there looking for anyone they can help," Daphne said, wrapping an arm around my waist and pulling me close to her as she nodded toward the deep hole.

I turned to look below. Others, dressed like Daphne in various kinds of white clothing, were scrambling over the devastated mansion. I trembled with grief. Surely no one could have survived in the heap of rubble.

I gasped when I saw Gabriella's body pulled out of a hole. Two men gently placed her body on a stretcher. I couldn't help but silently rejoice that she was dead. *She can't hurt me anymore.*

"Look, over there! Is that Jannik?" Daphne asked, pointing down below to our right.

I saw him, his limp body slung over another man's shoulder. I watched, holding my breath, as the rescuers clipped him into a long basket and others at the top pulled him up.

I ran over as they pulled him over the top and saw that his face was grey. He was dead.

"No, no, no!" I screamed, falling to the ground, weeping. Daphne knelt by me and wrapped me in her arms. It took quite a few minutes for her quiet words to penetrate my grief.

"Stop, Dani. Stop. Watch and see the power of God manifested in His people." Her voice was filled with joy.

I took a ragged breath and opened my eyes. Two of the men dressed in white and shimmering with the same light as Daphne were touching Jannik and speaking. Daphne stood and pulled me up with her. As I watched in astonished wonder as healthy color flushed Jannik's cheeks, and I saw his eyelashes flutter open.

"Dani," he whispered, smiling up at me, his brown eyes filled with wonder and love. Before I could bend down to embrace him, he clambered out of the basket like nothing had happened to him. He grabbed me in his arms and kissed me. The crowd around us exclaimed joyously.

"Dani, my sweet love!" Jannik's lips traveled over my face, as he planted light kisses everywhere before enveloping me in his arms.

"Thank you, God," I said over and over, my heart overflowing with gratitude and love.

"Jannik, look at that, look!" I pointed upward. The fiery rainbow clouds still glowed across the sky.

"What's that light over on the mountain?" he asked.

"That is the glory of the Son," Daphne said. We both turned to her.

"Daphne, this is Jannik."

She greeted him warmly with a hug.

I asked Daphne to explain what was happening. "I know more now than the day I left the Compound, the day you were murdered. I know from Tamas, back in Petra, that the rule of Emmanuel Bellomo and Angelo Cain is limited. He said that God would send His Son back to the world to destroy them."

"Yes, God did send Him. We came from heaven, following the Son on white horses." She smiled at my incredulous look. "I know, it sounds impossible. But we did! Those rainbow clouds were the path we rode on. First, we went to Petra, where the evil one's armies were coming to attack the Jews there. The Lord killed the army with a simple word."

"Did everyone there come back?" Jannik asked her.

"The angels are bringing them back," Daphne said. "You'll see your friends soon."

"So what happened next?" I asked. "What about Bellomo and Cain?"

"They were leading a huge army in the Valley of Meggido. The Antichrist and false prophet were the first to die. The Lord simply breathed, and they both were gone, straight to the pit, just the way the Apostle John described in his writings in the Bible." Daphne's voice was solemn. "I can't tell you how incredible it was to me to live out the last bit of the Good Book. When I lived on the Compound all those years, it was my great comfort and hope, but I never really thought about being a part of what I read."

"I took your Bible with me when I left," I told her. "I didn't really understand any of it until I met Jannik."

He put his arm around my shoulders and kissed my forehead again. "I didn't understand until we met Tamas, but I'll be honest. I'd given up hope of making it to the end when the house collapsed. I don't remember anything after that, until I was . . ."

I leaned into him. "Raised from the dead!"

I laughed, looking at him. Jannik was completely restored. All of the bruises and scars on his face and arms were gone.

"You're here with me, and all of the terror and suffering is over, Jannik. Do you realize that? It's all over. We'll never be separated again!" My voice cracked, and I stopped talking, turning my face toward his.

"I'm so grateful, too," he whispered. "There were so many times I asked God to keep you safe, to help me find you. And He did, Dani. He did."

My heart nearly beating out of my chest with elation, I chimed in, "I was so terrified when the ground gave way and you disappeared. It was the worst moment of my life . . . I felt so helpless and hopeless. But now this!"

Tenderly, he kissed my forehead. I continued, "Then, there was this voice in my head telling me to ask, so I asked God over and over again to bring you back to me and send Jesus back."

"Help was sent as soon as you called," a voice interrupted.

Looking up, I saw Him, and knew Him right away. My eyes filled again, and delighted tears ran down my face as I beamed up at Him. Both Jannik and I sank to our knees in worship, as did the others around us.

Glimpses of my life at the Compound, my life on the run, my time with Jannik—and away from him—flickered in my thoughts, tumbling one after the other. Every tangled, frayed, fearful, terrible moment flashed across the screen of my mind, along with the moments of joy, love, and friendship. As I watched, I saw the chaos of my life from His perspective. In each moment shown to me, a common theme appeared. In awe, I realized that even the evil meant for me had been turned for my good. What seemed jumbled and random and hard to me had purpose because all of it was sifted through the hands of the One who now stood before me.

Peace flooded my whole being as I realized that He loved me, the unwanted child of a murderous man and a selfish woman. Me, the terrified girl, desperate for sanctuary. Me, the young woman who was nearly forced to bear other people's babies, only to have them snatched away. Every horrific moment, every lonely, desperate thing I'd been through melted away in His love.

Kneeling beside the one I loved, I looked up and realized that love in all of its forms could be traced to its true source in the One who stood before me, tenderly calling me Home.

FLOOD

Chapter 48

If a man dies, will he live again? All the days of my struggle I will wait until my change comes.

Job 14:14

When Sarai left for our walk, it was early in the day, but the sun was already beating down. Our encampment was busy. The women were tending children or cooking. Most of the men were away tending to the flocks or buying food in the city.

"See, we are safe," said Sarai as we strolled past an ancient sycamore tree. "Abram has soldiers guarding the camp, and we won't go far." One of the soldiers was sitting under the tree's shade on a pale grey horse. He bowed his head to us as we walked by but not before I saw the nervous look on his face.

"I think he's worried that you are out of the tent," I whispered to Sarai.

"I don't care. He won't dare say a word to me." She sounded confident, but she quickened her pace.

"It is so good to be outside, even if it's as hot as an oven. I know Abram is worried, but I cannot stay cooped up in the tent day in and day out."

I let Sarai talk but remained silent. When we got to the edge of our encampment, I stopped walking.

318

"I don't think we should go any further," I said, laying a hand on her shoulder.

Sarai looked annoyed but agreed, and we turned back to make our way to her tent. As we meandered around the other tents, Sarai stopped to talk to a group of children. They gathered around her, pulling on her robe, vying for attention. I smiled as she picked up a chubby toddler. *Please give her the child soon,* I prayed. Every month when her time came, she would cry for hours.

Just then, I heard the sound of horses and turned toward the road where the guard sat. He rode out to a group of riders coming from the city. I could see him shake his head at them and hear him shouting.

"Sarai, I think there's trouble! Get back to the tent quickly!" I yelled, racing over and taking the child off her lap. We were still far from their tent.

The riders entered the encampment; there was no way we could out-run them. Other women quickly gathered around us, forming a human shield around Sarai. I wished I had a sword or some way to defend her.

The riders pulled up their horses. Each had shaved his head but wore a single lock of hair on the side, braided and clasped with gold. They were bare-chested but wore rich, gold necklaces around their necks. They looked like men of importance.

"We are the pharaoh's brothers," one of them announced in our language with a thick, clipped accent. "We came to invite Abram to have dinner with the pharaoh tonight."

"Abram isn't here," one of the women said, staring up at him in awe. I glared at her.

That was when he noticed Sarai. His eyes locked on her, and his mouth slid into a licentious grin.

"I must admit my brothers and I were curious about your women. This one is the most desirable woman I have ever seen. Who is she?"

Before I could say a word, Sarai spoke, "I am Abram's sister."

The man who spoke our language whispered to his brothers then turned back to Sarai, "Tell your brother the king invites him to dinner tonight." Then they turned their horses and rode back toward the city.

That night, while Abram dined with the pharaoh, a small army of guards led by one of the pharaoh's brothers came into our encampment and took Sarai.

"Please!" I cried. "At least let me go with her!" I had my arms clamped around her.

"Let her come," shouted the pharaoh's brother. "Let's get out of here." Abram's men had put up a gallant fight, but they were no match for the pharaoh's guards.

They bundled us onto horses, and we rode back to the city. Sarai looked grim. I was terrified. Even in the dark, I could tell the city was magnificent. Gleaming pillared buildings were everywhere, all dwarfed by a giant black obelisk taller than any I'd ever seen. It seemed to be the center point of the city of On.

The air was pungent with the smell of garbage and urine, mingled with velvety plumes from incense burning in front of the many idols we passed. Although it was night, people still filled the streets. Most men, like the king's brothers, were bare-chested. The women dressed in sheer white garments that left little to the imagination.

Finally, we stopped. Strange statues of half men, half animals stood guard at what looked like a temple. "What is this place?" I demanded.

"This is the great house of Ra, our god." The pharaoh's brother dragged Sarai behind him up the stairs. Quickly, I ran up the stairs after them.

The temple walls ahead of us were white, reflecting the torchlight. I passed huge black stone statues with the bodies of men, and the heads of birds. Crouching black stone lions perched on either side of the walkway, their heads like men. I felt their eyes follow us into the temple.

Inside the cool darkness of the temple, the pharaoh's brother called for the priests. Just as I reached Sarai's side, other men, dressed in long white robes, all bald and clean-shaven, came into the room and bowed on their knees to the pharaoh's brother. He laughed, "Since my brother is a god, they think I am, too." He turned to Sarai and stared at her longingly. "I have never been jealous of my brother until now. Most women he's willing to share, but I know he will want you for himself. You will be treated well. What is your name, Abram's sister?"

"Sarai."

"And who is the old woman?" he jeered at me.

"She is Mother Ariana, and you will treat her with the respect she deserves," Sarai spat at him.

He only laughed and looked at me with some interest, bowing his head sardonically. "So you're one of the eight who lived through the great Flood. I'm surprised any of you still live. We are descendants of Ham."

"Of course you are," I snapped. "What's your name?"

"I am Seti, Pharaoh's second brother. These men will take you to your chambers. Please do not worry about your brother, Sarai. By now, my brother has told him of his intention to marry you and given him a generous bride price."

His eyes lingered on her face and swept down slowly over her body before he sighed and left us in the temple with the priests.

We were kept in the temple for two weeks. Finally, Seti came to take Sarai and me to the palace.

"The wedding ceremony will take place tomorrow," he informed us as we entered a large room. "You will stay here tonight. After tomorrow, you will both live in the harem with the other women."

Sarai looked frantic. "Where is my brother? Where is Abram? I want to see him now."

Seti moved over to a table and poured a glass of wine and sipped it, staring at Sarai. "Your brother is very protective of you. He's been here every day demanding that the pharaoh let him see you. He will be at the ceremony tomorrow. You will see him then and be able to say your good-byes before you move to the harem. Now, I must leave you both here. There are guards at the door," he warned. "Let them know if you need anything."

He left us alone.

"Ariana, what are we going to do?"

I hugged her. "The same thing I've told you every time you ask me that question. We're going to pray."

2

Early the next morning, we were shaken awake and rushed to the throne room. Something was wrong. I saw guards in front of golden doors ahead of us. We heard shouting as we got closer.

"You said she is your sister!" a man screamed. As the doors opened, we could see Abram, Lot, and some of Abram's fighting men standing in front of the screaming man, wearing a strange crown on his head.

"Why did you do this to me? Why didn't you tell me she is your wife?"

Sarai ran to Abram sobbing and threw her arms around him. I stared at the pharaoh and his brothers who stood next to him. They were all covered in leprous sores.

"Everyone in the palace was struck with this plague in the night!" the pharaoh screamed at Abram. "My high priest made an offering to Ra this morning, and the oracle told him about your great deception. Leave now and take everyone with you. Go! Out of my sight."

Abram wrapped an arm around Sarai, and we all rushed out of the room. Horses stood outside the palace. Lot helped me mount one of the horses. Sarai sat in front of Abram.

Dust rose behind us like a trailing cloud as we galloped back to our encampment.

"Sarai," I heard Abram say. "I tried everything I could to get you back. I am so ashamed that I lied and didn't tell Pharaoh that you are my wife. I was afraid. I am so sorry."

We arrived at the encampment, and Abram called his people to assemble.

"We leave today for the Negev," he ordered, still sitting on the horse with Sarai. The people quickly began to pack up their goods and tents and gather their flocks.

"We're going ahead," Abram told his people.

We galloped north along the road for a while before Abram slowed the pace. The horses walked along the dusty road. We were going back to the land the Creator had promised Abram.

As we made our way back to Bethel, I became very ill. Fever and chills racked my body with pain. I could barely keep water down, let alone food. Sarai tended to me as faithfully as any of my own daughters, but nothing helped. I do not remember much of the journey at all, only tortured moments of consciousness when the cart I lay in rattled my weary body awake.

I saw Japheth in my fevered dreams. He would appear just out of my reach, and I would rush toward him, desperately trying to reach him. Sometimes, I was with our children, tending the gardens or the flocks, and he would join us for a few joyful moments.

I woke up in a small room. A cloth covered my face, but I no longer felt ill. I removed the cloth, sitting up and looking about me in wonder. The room was filled with glorious light that shimmered in the way rainbows do after the rain. Standing there in radiance was Methuselah, but he appeared as a young man.

"How are you here?" I asked, somehow already knowing the answer. Strangely, I felt like a young woman again; strength and vitality coursed through my body like fire and I stood up.

Miraculously, the walls of the room dissipated like morning mist, and we stood together in a lush green valley surrounded by great mountains.

The air was fresh and cool and somehow charged with shimmering colors unlike anything on earth.

I looked back to the bed, oddly still there behind us, and saw my body still lying there.

He laughed. "Do you feel dead?"

I laughed, too, because he knew my thoughts. "No, I have never felt more alive. Where is my family? Where are Abram and Sarai?"

He took my hand, and we began walking.

"They are left behind in time, for they still have paths to walk there. But your path in time has finished, and now you will walk with me and all the others who are here with me. Look up ahead. Someone has been waiting for you to arrive."

I turned from Methuselah and looked where he pointed. Japheth stood just ahead of us, smiling at me with great joy. We ran to meet each other and embraced.

"It's been so long!" I cried, looking up into his face, touching it, marveling that he looked just as he did the day we met.

"It hasn't been long here, Ariana. Time doesn't exist here the same way. Look, here come the others!"

I turned and saw Nua, Amalthai, Terah, and my mother! I hugged them one by one, and then turned to my mother, who stood waiting patiently.

"Oh, Mother!" I wept with joy as I held her again. "You look just like you did when I was a little girl!" I marveled at all of them.

Then I heard His voice behind me, and I turned to see the man who had appeared to me in the forest so long ago. In that moment, I also realized he was the same man who had led me out of Babylon to rescue Abram.

I quickly moved toward Him, bowing on my knees in the soft green grass. I heard the voices of the others calling out praises and thanksgiving to Him. I joined the chorus, raising my arms in praise.

As I gazed at His face, moments from my long life on earth ran through my mind, and I saw in each scene He was there with me, not just in the forest with the Magistrate, but in the field where my new friends had been slaughtered, and in the city where my dear friend, Methuselah, died. It was He who had closed the big door of the ark and who had been with us through the great Flood. When my heart broke as I held my dying husband in my arms, He was there. When Amalthai died, and I watched the babies being burned, He was there.

As I watched the moments of my life play out before me, I saw that He was always with me, always close. Tears of joy ran down my face, as I looked up at Him in wondrous love.

My life was over.

But really, it was only beginning.

About the Author

Dawn Morris is an author and speaker who has done extensive research on biblical prophecy for over thirty years and has led numerous studies on what the Bible has to say about the Last Days. She has a Bachelor of Science in Education from the University of Houston and has written numerous articles, Bible studies, and devotionals. Dawn is the author of two other novels, *One Will Be Taken* and *One Will*  *Be Left*. She and her husband Dennis are the parents of five grown children and make their home in Gig Harbor, Washington.

A free ebook edition is available with the purchase of this book.

To claim your free ebook edition:

1. Visit MorganJamesBOGO.com
2. Sign your name CLEARLY in the space
3. Complete the form and submit a photo of the entire copyright page
4. You or your friend can download the ebook to your preferred device

Morgan James
BOGO™

A **FREE** ebook edition is available for you or a friend with the purchase of this print book.

CLEARLY SIGN YOUR NAME ABOVE

Instructions to claim your free ebook edition:
1. Visit MorganJamesBOGO.com
2. Sign your name CLEARLY in the space above
3. Complete the form and submit a photo of this entire page
4. You or your friend can download the ebook to your preferred device

Print & Digital Together Forever.

Snap a photo

Free ebook

Read anywhere